P9-CRH-602

continued . . .

TWISTED CREEK

"*Twisted Creek* will weave its way around the reader's heart. Compelling and beautifully written, it is exactly the kind of heart-wrenching, emotional story one has come to expect from Jodi Thomas."

—Debbie Macomber, #1 *New York Times* best-selling author

"Jodi Thomas is a masterful storyteller. She grabs your attention on the first page, captures your heart, and then makes you sad when it is time to bid her wonderful characters farewell. You can count on Jodi Thomas to give you a satisfying and memorable read. *Twisted Creek* is absolutely delightful."

—Catherine Anderson, *New York Times* best-selling author

"Thomas sketches a slow, sweet surrender, keeping the tension building to a rewarding resolution in this unsentimental, homespun romance."   —*Publishers Weekly*

"*Twisted Creek* is a wonderful, character-driven tale that tells just what a family can be, even if it's made up of a bunch of lonely friends. . . . Romance blooms slowly, but for two nearly lost souls, it's rewarding when it does. . . . As usual, Jodi Thomas kept me up way later than normal! *Twisted Creek* could be anywhere, but Ms. Thomas makes it uniquely Texan with her wonderful characters and great dialogue. This is another thought-provoking novel to add to your Jodi Thomas collection."   —*Romance Reviews Today*

"Romantic suspense and sweet women's fiction are an unlikely combination, but in *Twisted Creek*, veteran storyteller Jodi Thomas makes the pairing work quite well. Allie's love for her aging grandmother is sensitively portrayed, while her blossoming relationship with Luke simmers unforgettably in the background. This is a moving story about overcoming hardship and bitterness and about being brave enough to make a happy ending—no matter what it takes."

—*Romance Junkies*

Just Down the Road

JODI THOMAS

BERKLEY BOOKS, NEW YORK

THE BERKLEY PUBLISHING GROUP
Published by the Penguin Group
Penguin Group (USA) Inc.
375 Hudson Street, New York, New York 10014, USA

Penguin Group (Canada), 90 Eglinton Avenue East, Suite 700, Toronto, Ontario M4P 2Y3, Canada (a division of Pearson Penguin Canada Inc.) • Penguin Books Ltd., 80 Strand, London WC2R 0RL, England • Penguin Group Ireland, 25 St. Stephen's Green, Dublin 2, Ireland (a division of Penguin Books Ltd.) • Penguin Group (Australia), 250 Camberwell Road, Camberwell, Victoria 3124, Australia (a division of Pearson Australia Group Pty. Ltd.) • Penguin Books India Pvt. Ltd., 11 Community Centre, Panchsheel Park, New Delhi—110 017, India • Penguin Group (NZ), 67 Apollo Drive, Rosedale, Auckland 0632, New Zealand (a division of Pearson New Zealand Ltd.) • Penguin Books (South Africa) (Pty.) Ltd., 24 Sturdee Avenue, Rosebank, Johannesburg 2196, South Africa

Penguin Books Ltd., Registered Offices: 80 Strand, London WC2R 0RL, England

This is a work of fiction. Names, characters, places, and incidents either are the product of the author's imagination or are used fictitiously, and any resemblance to actual persons, living or dead, business establishments, events, or locales is entirely coincidental. The publisher does not have any control over and does not assume any responsibility for author or third-party websites or their content.

JUST DOWN THE ROAD

A Berkley Book / published by arrangement with the author

PUBLISHING HISTORY
Berkley mass-market edition / April 2012

Copyright © 2012 by Jodi Koumalats.
Excerpt from *Welcome to Harmony* by Jodi Thomas copyright © 2010 by Jodi Koumalats.
Cover art by Jim Griffin. Hand lettering by Ron Zinn. Cover design by George Long.
Interior text design by Kristin del Rosario.

ISBN: 978-0-425-24692-4

BERKLEY®
Berkley Books are published by The Berkley Publishing Group,
a division of Penguin Group (USA) Inc.,
375 Hudson Street, New York, New York 10014.
BERKLEY® is a registered trademark of Penguin Group (USA) Inc.
The "B" design is a trademark of Penguin Group (USA) Inc.

PRINTED IN THE UNITED STATES OF AMERICA

10 9 8 7 6 5 4 3 2 1

ALWAYS LEARNING   **PEARSON**

Chapter 1

DR. ADDISON SPENCER STOOD BETWEEN THE EMERGENCY room doors of Harmony's only hospital and waited for the next wave of trouble to storm the entrance. The reflection of her tall, slim body dressed in white appeared more ghost than human in the smoky glass. For a blink, Addison feared she might be fading away like an old photograph facing the sun. When she'd been a child with light blond hair, her father had called her his sunshine; now there seemed little sunshine left. If it weren't for her work, she'd have no anchor to hang on to in life.

Saturday night always promised a full house in the ER, yet the howling wind just beyond the glass whispered change. She'd already been up since four A.M. delivering twins to a teen mother who yelled all the way through the birthing, but Addison's shift wouldn't be over tonight until the bars closed. If a fight didn't break out in the parking lot of the Buffalo Bar and Grill, maybe, just maybe, she could be in bed by two.

She thought of the silence at the little place she'd rented ten miles from town. An old four-room house with hand-me-down furniture from decades past. Nothing special. Nothing grand. Only the porch wrapped all the way around, and in every direction she saw peace. A single neighbor's place spotted the landscape to the south. Cornfields were to the east and rocky untamed land to the north and west. Closing her eyes, she wished she were already there.

"Dr. Spencer?" Nurse Georgia Veasey's voice echoed behind her.

"Yes?" Addison turned, trying hard not to show any hint of the exhaustion she felt. One of her med school professors had drummed into everyone he taught that a professional gives her best until she drops and can give nothing at all. He often ranted that a career in medicine left little room for life beyond the hospital walls, and for Addison that seemed perfect. One bad marriage had taught her all she wanted to know of the world outside.

"Harley phoned in from the bar." Georgia moved closer, as though looking through the night for trouble. "Appears we got a pickup load of roughnecks coming in all bleeding and cussing."

A year ago she wouldn't have known what the nurse was talking about. She'd learned that roughnecks were oil field workers. "Who'd they fight?" Addison asked without any real interest. Half the time the drunks couldn't answer that question themselves.

"One man apparently, but the caller said it was Tinch Turner. From what I hear, he never joins in a fight unless the odds are five to one."

Addison understood. "Get six rooms ready." She'd be stitching up the load of roughnecks and probably operating on the fool who took them all on. "I'll go scrub up. You know what to do."

The head nurse nodded. She'd start the staff cleaning up blood and giving shots while their drunken patients turned from fighters to babies. The nurses and aides would comfort the boys in grown men's bodies as they sewed them up and called someone to come get them.

Addison knew Georgia would send the one who was most seriously hurt to the first room. She would be waiting there, ready to do her best one more time.

As she moved inside, Addison stopped long enough to pour a strong cup of black coffee. She hated coffee and yet seemed to live on it lately. Going into her twentieth hour on her feet, she needed something to keep her awake. Odds were good that in a few minutes she'd be going into surgery trying to save the life of some jerk who should have gone home to his wife and family after work.

Some doctors loved the emergency room and practiced there for their entire career, but Addison knew only that she wanted to be a doctor. Her father had spent years pushing her toward what he called a more promising career, meaning more money, more praise, but no matter how hard she tried, she never measured up to his standards. If she'd told him she simply wanted to practice medicine, he would have screamed his disappointment. But these past few months in Harmony had allowed her to love her career again and to think about what *she* wanted.

The latest problem between her father and her, the one that had driven her here, might be over by the time she returned home and she could finally tell him of her plans. If she was lucky, the career path he'd planned for her would no longer be an option.

Chapter 2

TINCH TURNER WAITED IN HIS PICKUP FOR ALL THE OIL field workers to pile out and go into the ER. They'd have a few black eyes, a few stitches, but he knew from experience that none of them was hurt bad enough to be admitted. Tinch just had to break up the fight as fast as he could, and sometimes the easiest way to get trouble's attention is to hit it between the eyes.

Next week he'd buy the boys a drink and explain to them that if they were in Harmony they needed to behave. Howard Smithers shouldn't have started calling them oil field trash, but every one of the roughnecks had been flirting with Howard's wife. She was barroom beautiful and tended to forget she was married when she drank. Tinch had seen her flirt before, and he couldn't help but wonder if she wanted Howard to be jealous or dead.

Closing his eyes, Tinch told himself he should have stayed out of it. Several others in the bar could have stepped in to help Howard. But Tinch had tossed caution out the

window about the time he gave up on caring whether he
lived or died. Somehow, taking a few blows reminded him
that he could still feel, even if it was only pain.

Not that he wanted to feel again. He wanted to die and
lie next to his wife in the cemetery. He just wasn't able to
kill himself. It bothered him that he was just one breath
away from her. All he needed to do was not breathe and
he'd be with his Lori Anne. Only God had played a trick on
them. He'd made Lori Anne fragile and Tinch strong as
a bull. She couldn't make it to her thirtieth birthday and,
with his bad luck, he'd probably live to be a hundred.
Maybe, if he kept drinking and fighting, one night he'd get
lucky and someone would put him out of his misery.

The blood dripping off his forehead bothered him enough
to make him climb out of his pickup and head for the emergency room door. He didn't much care about the pain, but
he hated bleeding all over everything. He'd get a doc to
stitch up the cut, and then he'd go back to his farm and
drink until he washed the memories away and finally slept.

Through the blood, he saw Nurse Veasey. She was frowning at him. Hell, he thought, she was always frowning at
him. "Evenin', Georgia," he said, thinking she had that
same look when she first saw him sitting next to her in the
third grade more than twenty years ago.

"Shut up, Tinch. I don't even want to talk to you." She
grabbed his shirt and pulled him toward the first little
examining room. "Didn't I tell you I'd beat you up myself
if you came in here after a fight again? I swear if there were
two like you in this town we'd have to build another wing
onto the hospital."

Despite a headache the size of a mustang bucking in his
brain, Tinch smiled. "You did threaten me last time, Georgia, and the fear of it kept me away for weeks, I swear."

She slapped him on the arm, and he thought of suggesting that might not be protocol for nurses, but Tinch decided
to wait until he could see to run before he upset her more.
He'd gone to school with her and her two sisters. All three
were good girls determined to make the world a better

place, or at least improve Harmony. Maryland taught school, Virginia married a preacher, and Georgia became a nurse. They were women on missions. The type Tinch had spent his life avoiding.

"Sit down on the table and keep quiet," Georgia said as she shoved his chin back and poked around the wound running half the length of his forehead. "It doesn't look all that bad. If you had any brains, they would have dribbled out a long time ago. I'll send in the doctor."

"Aren't you going to give me something for the pain?"

She shook her head. "Judging from your breath, you've already had enough." She tossed him a towel. "Try not to bleed on anything."

Tinch grinned. "Thanks, darlin'."

"Don't you dare *darlin'* me, Tinch Turner. You're a walking one-man demolition derby. Stay here; I've got people who care about themselves so try and mend."

She was gone before he could bother her more. Tinch shrugged. He liked "the states," as everyone called her and her sisters, but he had a feeling they were passing around a petition to have him banned from town. Maryland had told him the last time she saw him that the way he drove was a bad influence on her high school students, and Virginia had been praying for him for so long, her knees were probably callused.

Tinch lay back on the examining table, wishing he'd brought the rest of the bottle of whiskey with him. When the door opened, he didn't even look up. He was just about beyond caring for anything or anyone in his life.

"Mr. Turner, I'm Dr. Spencer," someone said as she moved close to the table.

Tinch opened one eye, but he couldn't see much through all the blood.

"Lie still and I'll take a look at that cut."

He didn't move as she cleaned the blood away with a warm towel. "Any chance it's fatal?" he mumbled.

The all-business voice answered, "Afraid not. You allergic to anything?"

He closed his eyes. "Work. Women. Hospitals." He felt a shot poke into his arm. "Silence. Snakes. And Wednesdays. I hate Wednesdays. And kids. Strange little things, always running around screaming in stores." He thought of more things he was allergic to, but he couldn't seem to get the words out.

For a few moments he knew the doctor was still there. He felt her pushing his hair away from his forehead like Lori Anne used to do. He could almost see Lori Anne smiling at him, saying she wanted to see his beautiful blue eyes better. She'd claimed she could measure his love for her in his eyes, and he'd never doubted she could.

Lori Anne's face faded and he dropped away into blackness.

Chapter 3

REAGAN TRUMAN WATCHED THE CONSTANT COMING AND going from the emergency room below her uncle's window on the third floor. Her world had become one hospital room, and even watching the drunks stumble out seemed interesting tonight. Part of her wished she were out on a date with Noah McAllen, parked somewhere along a back road where they could talk and cuddle, but tonight, this was where she belonged.

She glanced over at her uncle's bed. The room was lined with machines that moved and beeped and marked time, but for the old man resting, time seemed to have stood still. He drifted between life and death, swinging like a rusty pendulum from one to the other.

If Reagan could see death coming for him, she'd fight with every ounce of her energy to stop it from taking Jeremiah Truman. After five years of living in Harmony, she felt like she had a wide circle of friends, but when she'd arrived, a runaway with little hope of finding anywhere to belong, Jeremiah had taken her in as his family.

Reagan remembered how she told him once that all she ever did was reverse wishing. She was afraid of even hoping for something. It seemed easier to just wish bad things wouldn't happen. Now, at twenty-one, she wished for a world of things, but the top of the list was that he'd never leave her.

"Reagan?" Brandon Biggs poked his head in the door. "You still awake?"

She stepped from the window into the milky light surrounding her uncle's bed. "I'm here, Big." Sometime over the summer she'd begun calling him what all his construction friends called him. She had no idea if the nickname was simply a short version of his last name or an adjective of description. Both fit, and the name seemed to stick. Brandon Biggs was simply Big to all who met him now.

"Did you eat any supper?" He tried to slip his big frame into the room, as if opening the door wider might set off some alarm. The muscular thug who'd bullied her when she'd first tried to fit in at Harmony High was gone, replaced by a mountain of a friend.

"I don't think I've eaten anything today except a doughnut the nurse gave me," she answered, knowing that he'd probably already guessed, for he held a bag in each hand.

At six-feet-seven and almost three hundred pounds, Big never slipped anywhere, but he tried his best to tiptoe in his work boots toward her. He set the bags down in the big windowsill designed to hold flowers and cards. Then, without a word, he circled her waist with his hands and lifted her up onto the ledge.

They would have made an odd couple if they dated, him so big and her so small. He was a construction foreman and she ran her uncle's tiny apple orchard business while finishing her degree from an online college, but somehow they worked as friends. Maybe because they'd both been knocked around as kids, but they believed in each other. She saw the good in him, and he saw the strength in her.

Reagan crossed her legs and smiled as he handed her a cheeseburger. "You got these from Buffalo's bar, I'm guessing. What would you have done if I'd already had dinner?"

"I'd eat them both. And of course I got them at Buffalo's. It's the only place open this late that makes a burger worth eating, but right after I turned my order in, you wouldn't believe the fight that broke out."

Reagan unwrapped her food and asked, "You get involved?" Big was made of muscle. Someone in a fight might get hurt just running into him by accident.

He shook his head. "I was just there to look after Beau and Border. They were playing tonight. Damn, if they're not getting as good as any of those singers on *American Idol*." After taking a quarter of the burger for his first bite, he added, "I might have been tempted to step in, but I knew you'd give me hell if I did, so I just moved over by the band cage and made sure Border could keep playing. One guy came flying from the fight and hit the chicken wire so hard it reminded me of a bug hitting the windshield. I thought about hitting him a few times for scaring the boys trying to play, but I just tossed him back into the fight."

He might be more than double her size, but part of Reagan had always felt like she was his mother. He seemed to live his life by what she'd think of him. She was proud of the way he watched over his little brother, Border, and how he checked in on his grandmother every weekend even when he was volunteering as a fireman.

The big guy leaned against the window frame and told her the details of the bar fight. With her on the ledge, they were eye to eye as they talked and ate. He asked about her uncle, interested in the details of his condition. She liked talking to Big. It wasn't as good as talking to Noah McAllen, but it was close.

Finally, he stuffed his trash in one of the bags and said, "I got to go, Reagan. I promised I'd circle by and pick up the boys' equipment after the bar closes. I'm not sure how, but the boys both managed to get a date tonight. Two giggly girls wanted to take them out to eat breakfast at the truck stop when they finished the last set."

"If the girls were in the bar, they're older women." Reagan laughed, knowing that Beau Yates couldn't be more than eighteen or nineteen and Border Biggs maybe a year older. The sheriff told her once that the only way she'd let them play at Buffalo's was if they stayed in the cage and out of the bar. "Beau Yates stutters when he talks to me or any girl near his age. Two bar babes will probably scare him to death."

Big shrugged. "I don't know, maybe older women will teach those two something. All Beau thinks about is playing that guitar, and Border doesn't bother to shower until I yell at him. I'm no more than a mother hen with two homely chicks. Beau Yates never goes home, and half the time I'm not sure he can see through all that hair. His folks should probably pay me child support for all the meals I feed him."

"You like him around," Reagan cut in. "He's a good influence on Border."

"Yeah, but he might as well be living with us. His old man hates the idea of his only son playing in a band and gives him hell. Beau's always telling me no one knows how to give out hell like a preacher. Beau says Border's got it easy living with me."

Reagan touched Big's rough cheek. "You're a good big brother, Brandon Biggs."

He smiled. "I'd better be. I'm all he's got. We fight from time to time, but we both know what we got now is far better than what we had at home with our mom always high and some boyfriend of hers around reminding us to disappear."

Big Biggs lifted her from the window.

She walked him out the door to the elevator. "Thanks for bringing me supper. I hate to leave Uncle Jeremiah for more than a few minutes."

He looked like he wanted to hug her, but she crossed her

arms and he seemed to understand. "I'll come by tomorrow. Call me if you need anything."

"I will. Thanks."

He stepped on the elevator and she waved, already backing down the hall toward her uncle. When she stepped into the shadowy room, Reagan moved to her computer and checked her e-mail.

Nothing from Noah. He'd ridden in a rodeo in Kansas tonight for big money. If he'd won, he would have called or e-mailed. Noah McAllen had made pro, just like his dad. The whole town was proud of him. Everyone in Harmony wanted him to go all the way. Everyone except Reagan. She just wanted him home in one piece. She felt she was in a love triangle. She loved Noah and Noah loved the rodeo.

Closing her laptop, she reached for a blanket and snuggled into the recliner. She fell asleep as the sound of the machines blended with the beat of the howling wind tapping against the window.

Chapter 4

TRUCK STOP

BEAU YATES COULDN'T BELIEVE HE WAS SITTING IN A TRUCK stop after midnight with a woman who wasn't wearing a bra. He grinned at Border, his best friend. Beau had no trouble reading Border Biggs's mind.

In all the months they'd been playing at the Buffalo Bar and Grill, no one had tried to pick them up. Now, he was sitting right here with two groupies and they couldn't stop chattering about how wonderfully he played and how they loved his songs. Border's girl even kept patting on him and holding his arm like she was afraid he might get away. Every time she leaned close to him, her big bust brushed his arm and Border looked like a pup having his tummy rubbed.

Beau's date seemed more interested in adding another coat of makeup. She talked nonstop, but he wasn't sure her ears worked. She also had the hiccups. Every time she hiccupped, both women laughed. After a dozen times, Beau had trouble seeing the humor and couldn't even manage to smile.

The women were probably four or five years older than them, not as pretty as they'd been in bar light, and maybe a little drunker than they were when they'd asked if the band would like to go to breakfast. But, all in all, this wasn't bad.

This was like a date. No better, the girls were paying. Between school and practice Beau and Border didn't have enough time or money to date, even though they'd spent hours talking about it.

"How did you boys get together and form the band?" the woman whose name sounded like some kind of fancy candy asked.

Border shrugged. "He was the only person who talked to me when I transferred here from Bailee. My big brother got a job in construction and asked me to come live with him a few years ago. I took about a second to think it over and pack."

The hiccupping girl sounded off again and her friend chimed in with a laugh.

"I-I taught him to play," Beau added to the answer before Border told his life story. The girls didn't look like they were into details or even long sentences.

"I love the way you play," the one next to Border said, rubbing against his arm. "Do you have tattoos just on your hands, or all over?"

Both women giggled.

Border nodded like a bobblehead. He wasn't used to girls talking to him. He was a younger model of his big brother, Brandon "Big" Biggs, but Border shaved his head and had been collecting tattoos as a hobby since he was sixteen and could pass for eighteen.

"What did you say the name of the band is?" his girl asked between hiccups.

"T-the P-partners." Beau answered, fighting down his stutter. As an only child, he blamed his parents for his not being able to talk to girls. If he'd had a sister, maybe they wouldn't seem so frightening, or if his father hadn't given him weekly sermons on the evils of females, or if he'd had time to date at fifteen like most guys he knew, maybe he could at least talk.

"I think that's cute that you two are partners," Border's date said, then began repeating "The Partners, the Partners" over and over, as if her brain had gotten stuck.

The waitress, a girl who'd been in Beau's senior class, slung four midnight breakfast specials down on the table and frowned at Beau. He dove into the food, irritated that he cared one way or the other what Willow Renalls thought of him.

The girls picked at their food and complained about the truck stop not serving alcohol. Border's date seemed to be fascinated with the condiment basket that came with breakfast. She put butter and honey on her toast, syrup on her sausage, ketchup and hot sauce on her eggs, and grape jelly all over one pancake while going on and on about how she loved breakfast.

Beau broke into their rant as he moved the basket of little packets away from her. "W-we also play over in C-Clinton once a month and by C-Christmas we p-plan to have a few nights lined up in Amarillo."

The girls giggled, and Beau guessed either he'd gone too deep into conversation or they'd noticed he was afraid of them. The one next to him began circling smiley faces across her pancake, and the one beside Border started patting Border on the head. Her hands were so sticky, they stuck every few pats.

Border tried to push her away as he ate. Her breasts bumping against his arm seemed to no longer hold his interest now that food was on the table, or maybe Border had finally looked up to his date's face and didn't like what he saw. She had that kind of puffy round face that's pretty in the spring of a girl's life, and for her it seemed a very short spring. The dark circles painted around her eyes and the bloodred lipstick didn't help.

Beau ate his free meal and tried to think of something shallow enough to say.

The girls found it first. They both decided they had to go pee. Beau's date stumbled getting out of the booth and drew everyone's attention, even the waitress. Then she asked everyone she passed where the potty was while her friend urged, "Hurry," as they moved along.

Once they were gone, Beau looked at his best friend . . . his only friend. "You want to get out of here?"

"Hell, yes." Border shoved half his scrambled eggs into his mouth. "Even if we got lucky with those two, I have a feeling we'd be waking up itching in the morning."

Beau laughed. "Go outside and call your brother's cell and ask him to come out and pick us up. It's two miles back to town." Beau didn't like the idea of walking back in the dark, but it seemed better than staying here. "Don't come back in. I'll tell them you're sick. After I think your brother should have had time to get here, I'll say I'm going to check on you."

"What if they don't believe you, or worse, want to see how I'm doing? It'll take my brother several minutes to drive out."

"Then we run." Beau tried to smile. "And pray your brother reaches us before the two run us down. I have a feeling they won't be happy when we disappear."

While Border vanished out the front door, Beau pulled out a ten he kept hidden in the back of his wallet and put it under his plate. The women would probably pay before they left, but he doubted they'd leave a tip and he didn't like the thought that Willow would have to clean up this mess.

Ten minutes later, Beau stepped outside. Border was already in his brother's truck, but Beau stood in the dark and glanced back into the window. The two dates were still giggling as they slung scrambled eggs at each other. "I'll never do that again," he swore to himself.

The only thing he'd done right tonight was leave the tip. The rest of the evening, even the kiss in the car on the way out, he wished he could forget.

Chapter 5

TINCH TURNER WOKE SLOWLY. HE WAS STILL ON THE examining table, but someone had pulled up the sides as if fearing he'd fall off. They'd also dimmed the lights and covered him with a white blanket. He wouldn't be surprised if Georgia hadn't taken care of him while he was out. She was sneaky like that. Women with hearts were hard to stay mad at.

Touching his head, he felt the stitches running just below his hairline as he sat up. Most of his aches felt warmed over, as if he'd been in so many fights they all just started hurting again when some new wound came along.

"You feeling better?" the doctor in white asked as she stepped into the room. Blood, probably his, now stained her lab coat.

Without the blood in his eyes, he could see her clearly. Tall, very tall for a woman, with high cheekbones and light hair. "I'm fine. Thanks for stitching me up, Doc." With her starched coat and fair skin he decided she could pass for an angel.

"No problem. You're free to go. I'm guessing from what Nurse Veasey said, you have a charge card on file."

Tinch watched her, not knowing if she was trying to be funny. She didn't look like the type. She was all business and proper. The kind of woman who'd never even talk to him unless she had to.

He stood slowly, feeling his body ache with each movement. When he finally faced her, he found himself looking into pale gray eyes. "I'll be . . ."

The room began to spin and he leaned forward.

The doc caught him and pushed him back against the table. "I don't think you'd better drive, Mr. Turner. I'll have the nurse call whoever you want to come get you, or I could check you in for the night. We've got a few rooms open in maternity."

Georgia stepped in the room and helped him lie back down. He closed his eyes and willed the world to settle. "Thanks, Doc," he managed to say calmly, "but I'm not spending the night. Not in this place."

"Who should I call, Tinch?" Georgia sounded concerned.

"No one. I'll be all right in a minute. I can drive. Give me a minute and I'll walk out of here."

"I don't think so. If Dr. Spencer says you need someone to drive you, we're not letting you go until her orders are filled." Georgia had that general stance about her that hinted she would fight if need be.

Tinch would have laughed if he could have. Two women wouldn't stop him. No one ever stopped him from doing whatever he wanted to do. "I got to go home." He decided to try reason first. Too bad it must have dripped out with his blood.

Georgia patted his arm, but her words were for the doctor. "You rented that place way out on Timber Line Road, didn't you, Doctor?"

She waited for the doctor to nod, then added, "Tinch lives in the only other house out that direction."

When the doctor didn't comment, Georgia set her plan. "You could give him a lift. He's just down the road."

Tinch opened one eye enough to see the doc shake her head.

"I'm not sure it would be the safe thing to do," she said.

Georgia laughed. "He's not dangerous to anyone but himself. You'd be safer driving him than being in a car with him on the road."

"I don't need a ride," he said, wondering if he could manage to stand and make it to his truck before he passed out. He'd slept there before; he could do it again. "I'm not sure I'd be safe with the doc."

"Don't be ridiculous, Tinch." Georgia was in no mood to listen. "If you're not going to take a room for the night, someone has got to drive you home."

Dr. Spencer looked like she'd been asked to pick up a stray dog on a busy highway. "All right," she frowned. "I'll pull my car up if you'll wheel him out. You're right, he'd be a danger on the road."

She was gone before he could argue, so he turned on Georgia. "I don't need or want any help. I'm fine."

Georgia pulled a wheelchair from the corner and helped him into it. "I'm not taking responsibility for you passing out and running off in a ditch. Let someone help you, Tinch, before it's too late."

Tinch fought down nausea. "That Dr. Spencer didn't look too excited about playing Good Samaritan, Georgia."

"The doc doesn't like men, any men from what I can see, so you be polite to her. If she snubs the rich ones who come by to flirt with her, you can imagine what she must think of the bottom-of-a-barrel ones like you."

"Thanks for the compliment." He frowned. He'd never considered himself in any barrel, much less at the bottom of one. He'd loved Lori Anne since they were in middle school and never really cared one way or the other what any other girl thought of him.

"You smell like whiskey and look like something the cat wouldn't drag in." Georgia was on a roll. "I bet you didn't even clean up before you came to town. You got dirt under your fingernails and horse shit still on your boots." She pushed him toward the doors. "I swear, Tinch, germs wouldn't even live on you."

"You finished?" he asked, figuring he probably deserved anything she said. She'd guessed right about him not cleaning up. He'd worked with the horses until dark, then climbed in his truck and headed to town for a few drinks.

"No, I'm not finished," she answered as she shoved him outside. "Lori Anne died three years ago, and nothing is going to bring her back. It's time you got on with your life."

Tinch didn't hate Georgia. He hated the whole world. No one seemed to understand. He didn't have a life to go on with without Lori Anne. She'd been his best friend through school, his lover as soon as they both turned sixteen, and his wife the winter after they'd both graduated from high school. With his parents dead, Lori Anne had been his friend, his lover, his wife, his family, his world. When she'd died of cancer, she'd left him hollow and alone. She left him with nothing inside or out.

He stood as a tiny BMW pulled up to the curb. "How am I supposed to get in that thing? It looks like she drove it off a bumper car ride." He leaned down to see the doctor at the wheel glaring at him. "I've seen toys in kids' meals bigger than this thing."

Georgia opened the door and helped him in. "You're going, so stop complaining unless you want to sleep in the maternity ward."

"No thanks." He swore as he folded into a pretzel and Georgia shoved.

As he leaned back in the seat, the nurse patted his arm again. "I'm sorry, Tinch, but it's time someone said something to you. All your friends are worried about you."

She closed the door without hearing him say, "Tell all my friends to go to hell."

Thank goodness, the doctor didn't say a word as she drove away from the hospital. He caught a glance of her in the fading light. A statue of starch and ice, he decided. Strange that such a cold woman would pick a profession like doctor, or maybe it was just him she was so cold toward.

She didn't ask which house was his. She just drove through the night as he leaned back and wished everything and everyone would go away.

When she pulled up in front of his place, she stopped and said, "You need any help getting in?"

"No," he snapped as he fumbled for the door.

It took every ounce of his concentration to make it out of the car and up the steps. He heard her drive away as he opened the door and moved inside.

Tinch made it two more feet before he crumbled to his knees. He didn't cry or scream or cuss. He just leaned forward, his head in his hands, and wished for the thousandth time that he could stop breathing.

A mile away Addison pulled her BMW into the dilapidated garage and walked across the darkened yard to the house she'd rented. As always, she'd forgotten to leave the porch light on. Her only excuse was she'd never lived anywhere but the city. She'd never known such blackness on moonless nights before.

Her body felt numb, she was so tired. When she stepped on the porch, she looked back south toward Tinch Turner's house. She could barely make out the outline of his place against the sky. He hadn't turned on a light either. Maybe, like her, he liked the shadows now and then. Stepping inside, she walked across the living room and into her bedroom, stripping off clothes as she moved. By the time she bumped into her bed, she wore only a T-shirt and panties as she tumbled into the unmade bed she'd left almost twenty-four hours before.

"Sleep," she whispered, knowing that tonight, finally, she would.

Hours later, a knock on her door woke her. For a minute, Addison couldn't figure out where she was, and then she told herself she was safe. She was in control of her own life. No one was pushing her. Her family didn't even know where she lived.

When the knock came again, she wrapped a blanket around her shoulders and went to find the noise.

A tall man wearing a western shirt, well-worn and well-fitting jeans, and a cowboy hat stood on her porch. Without the blood and dirt, she almost didn't recognize Tinch Turner, the bothersome neighbor she'd treated last night. The thought crossed her mind not to answer, but since she hadn't even latched the screen door last night, and the wooden door stood wide open, it would have been hard to act like she wasn't home. All he had to do was turn around and he'd see her standing on the other side of the screen.

While she thought about what to do, he shifted and she couldn't help but think that he was a man built in balance. He was tall, but not lanky, slim, but not thin, with shoulders that looked strong from work and not from pumping iron. He might spend his nights drinking and getting into fights, but he spent his days outside.

Before she could move, he turned and faced her.

She froze, unsure what to do.

His piercing blue eyes drank her in with a slow movement from her toes to her hair.

"What are you doing here?" Addison pulled the blanket closer, as if it offered her some protection.

"I came to say I'm sorry for not thanking you for bringing me home last night." He smiled, showing straight white teeth, which surprised her. If he'd really been in as many fights as Nurse Veasey claimed, he should have been toothless by now.

"Forget it." She expected him to turn away, but he didn't move. Maybe her one neighbor was one too many, Addison thought.

He finally shifted. "I was wondering if I could ride into

town with you next time you go. I need to pick up my truck. Ten miles is a little far to walk."

"Why don't you call someone?" She didn't want to get to know Tinch Turner. They had nothing in common, nothing to talk about. With her work schedule she didn't have time to make friends, and the last thing she wanted was a man in her life. Between a demanding father still trying to direct her life and the memory of a husband from her teens who'd used her as a punching bag, she'd had enough.

"I don't have a phone," he said. "Never needed one until today."

The idea that someone might not have a phone, even a cell phone, was out of her realm of reasoning. She'd gotten her first phone when she was in grade school and carried a cell since high school. "How'd you get to my porch?"

"I walked. I don't think it's a mile between my house and yours. If you skip the road and head across the field, it's not even that far. When the Rogerses lived here, they'd always ring that bell if they needed me and I'd run over." He pointed to the corner of the porch as if she might not have noticed the huge bell mounted on the railing. "Course, they were both hard of hearing, so I always said I'd fire off a shot and hit the bell if I needed them."

Addison thought of slamming the door. She didn't have time for small talk. "Look." She decided to be direct. "You woke me up. I worked a twenty-hour shift and I'm not due back till noon." She felt for her watch, trying to remember where she'd left it. "What time is it, anyway?"

"Noon," he said. "I figured you'd be awake."

"Oh no!" She looked past him at the cloudy day. If she'd been guessing, she would have thought it was closer to dawn.

Running toward the bedroom, she yelled over her shoulder. "I'll be ready in ten minutes. You can ride along, but I've got to get to the hospital fast. I'm already on duty."

Addison showered, pulled on clean clothes, and walked out of her bedroom with her hair still wet.

If she'd thought about it, she might have guessed she'd find Tinch Turner waiting on the porch for her.

Though all the shutters were open, she saw no sign of him outside, or on the porch. Shrugging, she decided he wasn't her problem.

One step more and she halted. The cowboy was standing in her kitchen, a tea towel tucked into his jeans like an apron and his hat pushed back.

"What do you think you're doing?" Anger and panic warred inside her. He was in her house! She knew he was wild, probably violent and possibly crazy.

"Well, Doc, I couldn't find much in the way of real food, but I made you an egg sandwich."

"You're cooking?" It seemed a strange thing to do before he killed her, but Addison had slept through the few psych classes she'd taken.

"I figured you'd want to eat something before you go." He raised an eyebrow. "You planning on leaving with a wet head?"

"Look, Mr. Turner. I'm not your problem and I'm leaving." Addison rushed toward her purse. "If you want a ride, you'd better be in the car when I back out of the garage."

She knew she was probably overreacting, but she'd had all she wanted of him or any controlling man, and if he was insane, she had pepper spray in her purse. *Somewhere!*

"I don't need someone worrying about my hair or if I'm eating," she said as she kept looking and tried not to sound panicky. "I am none of your concern. I can take care of myself, and I moved here with the nearest neighbor a mile away for a reason."

She wouldn't have been surprised if he'd yelled at her and stormed out, and she wouldn't care. He'd stepped over the line when he'd stepped into her house.

Gripping the spray can in a death grip, she hurried for the door.

He met her there, the egg sandwich in his hand.

She raised the pepper spray and widened her stance, then looked up into laughing eyes.

"Sorry, Doc." He held the door for her as he wrapped the sandwich in a paper towel, unaware she'd been ready for an attack.

With a huff, she stormed past him.

"I'm guessing you're not a morning person," he said, matching her long strides to the garage.

When she glared at him across the hood and opened her mouth, he added, "I know, none of my concern."

She didn't look at him as she started the car and drove toward town. He had the good sense not to say a word. He just sat, his shoulder almost touching hers in the small car, and ate the egg sandwich.

When she pulled into the parking lot, he climbed out and yelled, "Thanks for the ride," as she rushed away.

An hour later, when she told Georgia Veasey about how he'd walked right into her house and made himself at home in the kitchen, Georgia laughed.

"Tinch grew up on that land. I'm guessing he's been walking into the Rogers house all his life."

"It's my place now," Addison said. "And from now on I'm keeping the doors locked. If I never see Tinch Turner again, it'll be too soon."

Georgia shrugged. "When he comes in to get the stitches removed, I'll take care of him. He's a good man on bad times. You might want to get to know him."

"Thanks, but I'm not looking for a man, period." Addison had never said anything to anyone in Harmony about being married in her teens or how her father's determination to direct her life had driven her to Harmony, but Nurse Veasey must have sensed something was broken inside her, and she'd been kind enough not to rush in and try to fix it.

Georgia had offered her friendship without strings. She'd probably noticed that Addison lived at the hospital and slept at a rented house she had leased fully furnished. She had no social life except dinner after work with Georgia and her husband now and then.

When Addison got home that night, she found a loaf of bread and a dozen eggs on her porch. No note. He knew she'd know who they were from. It wasn't a peace offering, it was simply replacing what he'd taken.

She looked to the south and saw a single light shining in the barn beside his house. Somehow the light made her feel even more alone than she already was, but alone was a great deal better than the hell of her marriage or living closer to her father.

Chapter 6

TINCH WORKED WITH THE MATHESONS' HORSE UNTIL LONG after dark. All day he'd felt lousy. Not only did he have a headache and a hangover, but he'd made a fool of himself yesterday. Any nitwit would know not to walk into a strange woman's house and start cooking breakfast. She probably thought he was a product of too much inbreeding in this town. What had he figured, that she'd be happy he'd cooked her eggs? That it would be a peace offering so she wouldn't look at him as if she'd seen his picture on a *Wanted* poster?

Hell no.

The lady had big city written all over her, and he'd just proven to her that she was living next door to a hick. He wouldn't have been surprised if she'd stopped halfway to town and made him get out so she could run over him.

Probably the only reason she hadn't was because she was on duty and would have to be the one to patch him up.

"Crazy thing is," he said to the horse, "from the way I acted, speed bumps are about my equal in brain cells."

The animal tried to nip at the brand on his jeans pocket, and Tinch decided even the horse didn't want to visit with him.

He'd heard of women who hate men, but he could never remember being so close to one. He felt sorry for the first guy who accidentally touched her. She'd probably slice his fingers off with a scalpel. She was pretty, in a plain kind of way, if you liked washed-out women with no hairstyle or makeup. And she was jumpy too, like a newborn colt in a lightning storm.

Tossing the brush in the tub, Tinch led the horse into the first stall. Another few days and the animal would be gentle enough to take back to the Matheson place for their little girl to ride. He'd worked with the palomino for three months, and she was ready to join the family. The wounds where the animal had been mistreated by her first owner had healed, but the scars were still there beneath the hair.

He had no doubt that little Saralynn Matheson would show the horse only kindness and her uncle Hank would keep a close eye on them both.

Tinch checked on the other horses, each damaged in some way the vet couldn't fix, and others about to go through a hard birthing that would need someone close to help. When he walked out the barn door, he noticed the lights were on at the Rogerses place. The angry doctor was home. If she could call it home? Except for a few clothes scattered around, the place looked exactly like it had the night the Rogerses were killed. They'd been in a bad car accident last winter. As far as he knew, the daughter didn't take anything but a few pictures out of the house after the funeral. She wanted to sell the place as is. When that didn't work, she had a leasing company rent it out. No one had ever driven out to look at it until the doctor moved in.

Tinch had always thought some farmer would buy the

property. He would have bought it if he'd been able to scrape up the money. The land was good and water ran through it all year round. There were even a few fishing holes on the spread that he used to love going to as a kid. The house was small, but it would make a good starter place.

If all Addison Spencer wanted was somewhere to crash between shifts, why hadn't she rented an apartment in town? Why come all the way out here?

He answered his own question. "She is someone who wants to be alone."

All the anger toward her left him in one exhale as it occurred to him that maybe the blond lady had something in common with the palomino. Her scars didn't show either, but he'd bet they were there. She reminded him of an animal who'd been mistreated. She hadn't come out here to work. She'd come to Harmony to hide. That might explain why the mail truck never stopped at her box by the road. If the woman was hiding, she'd have a box in town so no one would bother her. That could be the reason why his showing up at her door had riled her so much.

He didn't see her for three days, but she was on his mind. When he went in to have the stitches checked, Georgia took care of him and didn't say a word about the doctor.

Tinch went into town a few days later for supplies and found himself parking in the hospital parking lot.

He wasn't interested in her as a woman, or a doctor for that matter.

So why was he parked watching people come and go in the rain? If she noticed him, she'd think he was stalking her. It wasn't that at all. If he had to come up with a reason, Tinch would have to say it was because he thought she was hurt. For as long as he could remember, he'd never been able to stand to see an animal frightened or in pain. Maybe that was why it was so hard to watch Lori Anne as the cancer took her piece by piece. The last few years before she died, no matter what he did, no matter what the doctors did, she was always in pain.

Climbing out of his pickup, he walked into the hospital.

Someone told him an old friend of his father's had suffered
another heart attack. The least Tinch could do while he
was here was pay his respects.

Fifteen minutes later, he cut through the waiting area of
the emergency room on his way out. He'd about decided
something was wrong with the air in hospitals because he
couldn't seem to draw a deep breath. Lost in thought, he
was almost out the door when Dr. Addison Spencer crossed
his path.

He stepped sideways. "Excuse me," he said, and would
have continued on, but she stopped in front of him and
raised her chin slightly.

"Tinch, isn't it?" she said, as if she barely remembered him.

He smiled. "Yeah, your closest neighbor."

"How's your head?"

"Healing." He realized what she must think. "I'm not
checking in. I just dropped by to see a friend, Jeremiah
Truman." He figured he'd better give details or she might
not believe him. "He's not doing so well. I fear he's counting out what's left by the clock and not the calendar."

"Your diagnosis may be right." She relaxed a bit. "I
check in on him several times a day. So does half the town,
it seems."

Georgia Veasey moved up next to Addison, and Tinch
noticed that both women had on their raincoats.

"How are you doing, Tinch?" Georgia asked in a sweet
voice, as if she hadn't been threatening him a few days ago
with death if he didn't stop fighting.

Tinch recounted his testimony but added, "I was just
leaving."

With Georgia boundaries were between countries, not
people. "Where you going on this drab rainy night?"

Tinch was used to her, so he didn't take offense. "I thought
I'd get something to eat and head home. I'm not planning
on drinking, if that's what you're worried about."

Georgia grinned. She'd finally gotten an answer she
liked. "Why don't you come along with the doc and me?

We're meeting my Greg at Buffalo's. If you promise to behave yourself, you can join us for wings and a beer."

Tinch followed them out trying to think of an excuse, but Georgia could spot a lie.

He walked them to the doc's car. "I might come in and order takeout, Georgia, but I don't think I can stay. I'll say hello to Greg while I wait for my order."

Georgia looked disappointed. Addison appeared relieved.

He got to the muddy parking lot of the Buffalo Bar and Grill first and waited for them. The doc didn't have much luck finding a parking place that wasn't muddy and, from the size of her little car, she could submerge in a few of the holes. She finally parked in the street and walked around to the entrance. Both women looked soaked by the time they got inside.

Tinch held the door, then followed them in, stopping to visit with a third cousin for a minute before finding Greg and Georgia's table. The only seat left was next to Dr. Spencer. She pulled a few inches away when he sat down.

Greg and Georgia didn't seem to notice they were the only ones keeping the conversation going. When the waitress set the beer down, Greg said he'd already ordered for everyone. With only one thing on the menu board every night, it wasn't hard to guess what everyone wanted.

Tinch had a feeling Greg hadn't ordered his to go. He shrugged. It didn't really matter. Living alone meant there was never any hurry to get home, and people like Greg and Georgia knew better than to expect much in the way of conversation.

He and Georgia's husband had been good friends in high school more than a dozen years ago, but Greg went off to the University of Texas and Tinch stayed home to get married and farm. When Greg came back and started teaching, he was dating and Tinch had a sick wife, so there was little time for friendship. Then Lori Anne died a few months before Greg and Georgia married. Tinch didn't even attend their wedding. Over the years, on the few occasions they saw each other, they only talked about old times in high school. Good times, Tinch thought, in memory at least.

Straightening, he realized he hadn't been paying attention. Not that it mattered. Everyone in town probably knew he wasn't any good at small talk on a good day, and this wasn't even a good year.

Greg and Georgia got up to dance, both promising to be right back.

After five minutes, Tinch felt he had to say something to the doctor. He couldn't just sit beside her ignoring her. "You dance, Doc?"

She took a breath, as if relieved she didn't have to start the conversation. "No. I don't know how to do this kind of dancing. When I was in high school, my mother made me take dancing at the club one summer. After three lessons the instructor let me move over to tennis."

He took a long drink of his beer, glad he didn't have to offer to lead her around the floor. "You play tennis?"

"No. I wasn't any good at that either."

He stared at his drink, hoping that if he didn't look at her she wouldn't seem so nervous.

"Do you dance?" she surprised him by asking.

"I used to love dancing. I was pretty good too." He stopped before she thought he was bragging. She probably wouldn't be impressed that years ago he'd won a contest right here in Buffalo's.

"Why'd you stop?" she asked after a few moments.

He was glad she wasn't looking at him when he answered, "My partner died." He said no more. He never wanted to spread even an ounce of his sorrow on anyone else.

"Oh," was all she said.

They watched couples moving around the floor. It was far too early for the place to be crowded. He knew he should say something, but he couldn't think of anything to talk about. What he had said probably depressed her. It had him.

For the tenth time he looked over at the bar and wished his wings were out. All he wanted to do was eat and go home. It occurred to him that the doctor probably wanted the same thing. "Look, Dr. Spencer, I don't want to cause you any trouble, and I'm not some kind of burglar who breaks into people's homes to cook breakfast. I live alone and like it that way. I'm guessing you do too, so why don't we just try to stay out of each other's way. I had nothing to do with this setup tonight."

"I know." She finally looked at him. "Georgia's been trying to set me up since I arrived. I guess you were just the next man she caught to put on my line. She seems to find it hard to believe that I don't want, or need, a man in my life."

He tried to smile, but he was too out of practice to make it seem real. "I know how you feel. She left me alone for a year after my wife died, but since then I've been avoiding her like the plague. This is the first time she caught me off guard."

"You're lucky. I've been tricked into an almost-date three times. Always a meal. Always a surprise extra single male shows up. The only way she got me to say yes to dinners out was if she swore she'd never try to set me up with anyone."

Tinch almost felt sorry for the doc. "How about we pretend this wasn't a setup? In truth, for once, I don't think it was. So you don't owe me any polite rejection and I'll let you buy your own dinner. You're not in my league anyway."

For a second, he thought she looked offended. He rushed on. "Beautiful, smart women cross the street to avoid me, Doc."

She smiled for a moment, then looked away, watching the dancers again. "Stop calling me Doc. My name is Addison."

"You ever shorten it to Addy?"

"No. What's Tinch short for?"

"Nothing," he said.

"You're not bad looking, Tinch. I doubt women cross the street to avoid you."

"You would, Addison"—he tried out her name—"if you got the chance."

"Probably," she agreed, and they both laughed.

The return of Georgia and Greg and the arrival of the food put an end to their conversation. Tinch figured he'd just had the longest conversation with anyone in months without someone throwing a punch.

While he ate, he listened to Greg's stories about the kids he taught. A few more couples pulled up tables and joined them, and Tinch thought about leaving, but he decided to stick around as long as the doc did. He could tell she was getting antsy to leave, so for once he decided not to be the first to disappear.

After they ate, everyone but he and Addison stood up to dance.

"Would you like to try it?" he asked politely.

"The answer is still no," she said.

Tinch stood. "Then I'll say good night. It's time I—"

"Tinch!" a woman screamed from ten feet away. "Well if it isn't Tinch Turner."

He faced Addison as he fought down a groan. Howard Smithers's wife, Donna Lee, who'd caused the fight the last time he'd been in Buffalo's, was heading toward him in full sail. For a blink, his eyes met Addison's and he wondered if he looked as desperate as he felt. All made up and perfumed, Donna Lee was a force of nature. Like tornadoes and fire ants, she left a trail of destruction.

"You're not getting away from me tonight, Tinch. You owe me a dance, and don't go acting like you can't. I remember a time when you made every girl's heart in this place beat faster just watching you two-step." The woman was just drunk enough to be dangerous. She rubbed up against him like she was a paint roller and he was the wall.

"I'm sorry, Donna Lee." Tinch held up his hands. "I can't . . ."

"I'm not taking no for an answer. You gotta dance with me, tonight. Howard won't be here for another half hour, and you can't expect me to just sit around and wait for him, not when a fine hunk of beef like you is in the room."

Tinch shook his head and fought past swear words to think of something to say.

Addison slowly stood by his side. "I'm sorry," she said to the drunk woman a head shorter than her. "Tinch just promised he'd teach me to dance, and I'm afraid if I don't do it now, I'll never have the nerve again."

Tinch breathed. "Maybe another time, Donna Lee." *Like the day after the rapture*, he thought. "The doc's right. I may never get her in here again to learn."

Donna Lee looked disappointed as Tinch followed Addison toward the dance floor.

"Thanks," he said when they were out of hearing distance. "You didn't have to do that, but I appreciate it."

Addison faced him. "It took me a few seconds to figure out that was the woman who started the fight that filled my emergency room last week." She laughed. "You looked so trapped, I had to do something."

He bowed slightly. "I owe you a dance lesson."

She glanced at the other couples molded together. "Can you do it without being plastered against me?"

He raised one eyebrow as if she'd just told him a secret about herself. "Of course, Doc. How about I put my hands here?" He lightly placed his hands at her waist. "And I promise not to get any closer."

She didn't look comfortable, but she nodded.

He looked down at her shoes. "You got socks on?"

"Yes."

"Then kick off those strange shoes. I don't know anyone who dances in rubber clogs."

She slipped out of her clogs and moved them to the edge of the dance floor. "What if someone steals them while you're teaching me to dance?"

He laughed. "You'd never be that lucky, Doc."

His hand nudged her to an open place on the wooden floor. In the same low voice he used when working with his horses, Tinch told her how to move, when to step, when to slide. After a few songs, she moved with the music easily and stopped watching her feet.

"You've danced before. Maybe not country, but you've danced." It was a statement, not a question.

She didn't answer. All her concentration was on her efforts to follow him.

"Rest your wrists on my shoulders," he said. "And relax, pretty lady. Nothing about this is going to be painful. Just move with the music." He could never remember dancing with a woman almost his height, but he found her slim body moved easily with his as if they were swaying to music blowing in the wind.

She touched his shoulders, but she didn't completely relax. He fought the urge to pull her closer so she could follow him more smoothly, but he had a feeling she'd bolt just like a wild mustang.

The fourth dance turned fast and all the other couples began to circle the floor with a stomping promenade.

"Want to try this one?" he asked.

"No." She dropped her hands off his shoulders and he released her waist. "I really need to be going. Will you . . ."

Before she could ask him to excuse her, he said, "I'm leaving too. Dancing with you was safe, but if Donna Lee catches me, I could end up fighting Howard, and I don't want to do that." He reached down and picked up her shoes. "Thanks for the dance, Addison. I may be wrong, but I don't think it was as painful as either of us thought it might be."

She nodded. "It wasn't so bad."

They crossed to the table, grabbed their coats, and walked out, waving at Georgia.

"Smile," he whispered, "and she'll think she was successful at hooking us up for once."

"Good idea. Maybe she'll stop trying and give up on me, at least."

Tinch looped his arm around her shoulder and added, "I love a good conspiracy. When it dawns on her what she's done, she'll be going full out to break us up so we won't blame her for getting us together." He felt Addison stiffen, but she didn't pull away until they were out the door, then she whirled and faced him.

"Don't touch me," she said. "I thought I made that clear. I'm not a woman who likes being handled."

Tinch studied her a moment. Her voice had been angry, demanding.

"You got it, lady." He felt burned. "You want me to walk you to your car?"

"No," she answered as she pulled up her hood and darted down the steps of the bar.

He watched her run through the rain. He'd just danced with a woman for the first time in more than three years, and it hadn't hurt like he thought it might. He hadn't enjoyed holding her, and somehow that made dancing with Addison okay. The entire time he felt a strange kind of satisfaction he often experienced working with a horse. He felt like he was doing some good.

Chapter 7

DEEP IN THE NIGHT, REAGAN TRUMAN SHIFTED ON THE chair that served as her bed in her uncle's hospital room. She'd been drifting between sleep and worry. Dr. Spencer came in just before sunset and talked to Jeremiah as if he still heard anyone, but she shook her head slightly at Reagan. Her uncle was no longer responding.

Logic told Reagan the time was near. No one lived forever, but she wasn't sure she could handle being alone again. As she wiggled in her chair, she heard her uncle Jeremiah whisper, "Sun's coming up, girl. We better get to the eastern chairs or we'll miss it."

Reagan moved to her uncle's side, but he looked the same as he had for days. His breathing was so shallow she couldn't be sure it was there. She took his hand. "I wish the sun were coming up and we were home." He loved watching the sun rise and set. She'd watched it with him most nights, even when it was cold or stormy.

She stared at him awhile, thinking of the hundred times he'd told her what to do to take care of the apple trees and how when she didn't know something he'd always tell her to figure it out and do it. He'd taught her how to live an honest life when no one else had taken the time, and almost from the beginning he'd talked to her about what to do once he was gone.

She curled back into her blanket, smiling at all the times he'd fixed visitors' cars or trucks just because he didn't want his make-believe niece riding in something that wasn't running right. She'd even noticed him rattling off in his old truck when he'd heard someone needed work done around their place and couldn't afford to hire it out. When he'd return he'd never tell her much about what he'd done. It wasn't his way.

Just as she slipped back to sleep, she heard him whisper, "Sun's coming up. I don't want to miss it."

Reagan opened one eye and focused on the clock. Two fifteen. The sun wouldn't be up for hours.

It never crossed her mind that sometimes a sun rises on one world as it sets on another.

Chapter 8

TYLER WRIGHT'S FAMILY HAD BEEN IN THE FUNERAL BUSI-
ness for four generations and, though he cared very deeply
about people, he rarely cried. All his life, dying had simply
been the last step of living. Whether a person marched in
head on into the next life or fought for every last breath
didn't matter; the end was the same.

Only when he'd been called to the hospital in the middle
of the night, Tyler got up and dressed in his best to go pick
up Jeremiah Truman. He couldn't say he liked the man. In
truth, he didn't even know him that well, though he'd known
of him all his life. Truman hadn't been a man who looked
for friends. He attended no town meetings, church, or social
gatherings. He liked his life simple.

Yet when Tyler sat at the rear door of the hospital with
Jeremiah Truman's body in the back of the funeral home
van, he took a few minutes to let tears fall. He couldn't help
but remember the time he'd caught Jeremiah delivering
apples in bushel baskets to families on hard times. Tyler

had been in his early twenties. He'd parked his car, jumped in the back of Jeremiah's loaded truck, and helped him finish the deliveries without ever saying a word to the old man. Jeremiah had brought him back to his car when the truck was empty. Tyler had offered to help again, and the old man had simply said he'd come by and honk if he ever needed any help.

Ten years passed before Tyler heard a honk one night about ten. He looked out and saw the old man's truck loaded down with apple baskets. Tyler climbed into the bed of the truck and they begin passing out apples. He had no idea how the old man knew which houses to go to. He never asked. For nine years, every fall, they delivered apples without ever exchanging more than a dozen words. The old man had to be nearing eighty. In 2006, he didn't honk and Tyler knew the girl, Reagan, must have taken over his job when he noticed apples on a few porches one Sunday morning.

"What say we drive by your orchard one last time," Tyler said to the body resting in the back. He thought Jeremiah might like that. "And don't worry, there will be no extra charge for the service."

Tyler talked to Jeremiah more on the trip out on Lone Oak Road than he'd ever talked to the man while he was alive. "Now don't you worry about Reagan, we'll watch over her. She's a good girl, must have a lot of you in her. Good blood, I guess."

The conversation wasn't much different than the few he'd had with Jeremiah Truman when the old man was alive; Tyler still did most of the talking. "I know you told me you want nothing but a simple graveside service. Since it's almost sunup today, I'll plan the burial for tomorrow or the next day if it looks like rain. If it's all right with Reagan, of course, her being your only kin. Even a graveside takes time to do right."

The old man would fill the last space in the Truman family plot. "You got a nice spot in the cemetery. Up on the hill."

Tyler had no idea how many people would come to the

service at sunrise for Truman, but his crew would spend the day getting ready and hoping it didn't rain.

He pulled the van up beside the orchard. In the night, the trees were only black shadows spreading over the Truman land. He thought he saw a blink of a flashlight moving among the trees and wondered if Reagan had also ventured out among the apple trees to be close one last time to her uncle.

"We better be getting back to town," Tyler said to no one. "It'll be light soon and people will be on the roads."

He drove slowly back to town, circling the old town square. In a strange way, even though Tyler rarely saw Truman, he was going to miss the old man.

An hour later, when his work with Jeremiah was done, Tyler let himself in through the main door of the funeral home and took the time to put Truman's paperwork on his desk. The office and kitchen were still silent. It was even too early for the smell of coffee to greet him.

He tugged off his coat and hung it on the hook in his office and slowly moved up the stairs to his living quarters. Passing through the rooms where his grandparents and parents had lived, he smiled. Tyler didn't believe in ghosts, but he felt people left a tiny part of themselves in places they loved and his home had always been filled with peace. And now, since his future bride, Kate, had almost retired from her army job and moved in, Tyler thought it was truly filled with love. She'd closed her apartment and stored all her belongings here. All she had was one more assignment, one more month, and she'd be the newest resident of Harmony, Texas.

Though they'd both crossed the hall many times, Kate insisted on claiming the guest room in his place as hers, and would until they married. Despite being a major and in her forties, his Kate was very proper, and, he thought, very loved. Not only he, but his staff and everyone she'd met in town had welcomed her to Harmony with open arms.

Tyler tapped on the frame of her open bedroom door. "Sorry to wake you, dear," he whispered, "but may I come in?"

She made a sleepy little noise that sounded something like a yes.

Tyler pulled off his tie and shoes as he walked to her bed. He had only a few minutes, but he wanted to finish the night with her in his arms. He lifted the covers and slipped in beside her, loving the warmth of her as she cuddled into him.

Kissing the top of her head, he whispered, "I love having you here, dear Kate."

Until he'd found her, he'd spent all his adult life alone. No woman had ever set foot in his quarters above the funeral home, except for the housekeeper.

Thinking of his new housekeeper, Autumn Smith, Tyler smiled. He'd found her sleeping in the cemetery with nowhere to go and pregnant. When he'd offered her the rooms next to the kitchen, and a job as cook and housekeeper, she'd been suspicious. Now, she was part of the family and the staff was getting fat on her cooking.

In a few weeks she'd have a baby and everyone, including old Calvin, who worked in the basement, was so excited. Kate had organized everything, and they'd even run drills for when the time came. The cars were never to be less than half full of gas. The suitcase was always at the kitchen door, already packed. Calvin had even installed a buzzer that, when pushed from the kitchen, went off in all the private areas of the house.

For the first time since Tyler had been born forty-five years ago, there would be a baby at the Wright Funeral Home. "Life goes on," he whispered as he rested his cheek against Kate's head and fell asleep.

Chapter 9

BUFFALO BAR AND GRILL

BEAU YATES FINISHED THE LAST SET OF SONGS, SET HIS guitar down, and told Border Biggs that he wasn't feeling well.

Border agreed he should go on home. "I'll get my brother to help load up and take the equipment back to the duplex. Ronny's trying out a few new desserts on us tonight. She says if we live she might cook for a boyfriend someday."

Beau shook his head as the image of Ronny Logan blinked in his mind. It seemed unlikely that Ronny, who lived on the other side of the Biggs brothers' duplex, would ever be brave enough to go out on a date.

"She's way into the 'never get married' zone," Beau said. "Some women miss their window of opportunity, and I'm afraid your neighbor is one of them. What is she, twenty-seven or twenty-eight?" She was a nice lady who worked at the post office, but she had that never-had-a-date look about her. Beau liked her, though, because she never complained when they practiced late, and she sometimes brought them leftovers. The first few months she'd lived next to the Biggs boys, nothing she made was fit to eat, but she was getting better. Now, when he ate her cooking, Beau figured he had better than a fifty-fifty chance of keeping it down.

"I don't know how old she is." Border packed up their guitars. "Maybe when she found out both of us Biggs boys were too young for her, she just gave up and started cooking."

Beau walked toward the door. "That would be a switch." He laughed. "But I can see how you two could turn a woman in that direction." Border didn't just frighten small children, he frightened just about everyone who didn't know him, and his older brother, even without the tattoos, was just about as threatening. Big was the kind of man who could clear his throat in a room and everyone would start running for the door.

Beau smiled at his friend. "I'll come over tomorrow before noon so we can work on a new song."

"Sounds good. We should practice. I got the feeling tonight that a few of the drunks were actually listening."

Beau agreed as he stepped outside and ran for his old car. He'd been thinking about what he needed to do all week long. He had one stop to make before he could sleep.

Border hadn't suspected anything. As far as Border knew, Beau was just going back to his dad and stepmother's house.

Though Beau usually slept on the couch in the Biggs boys' duplex, he often went back to his folks' place late Saturday night. He could slip into his old room and sleep until noon, then pick up clean clothes as he left. As long as he was gone before his parents got home from church, he didn't have to face his dad.

Beau always left a note for his mom in his room thanking her for washing his clothes and for leaving plenty of leftovers in the fridge. She'd been kind to him, but not loving. She seemed more like a shadow in his life, completely dwarfed by her husband's strong personality. She'd been the only woman he'd ever called Mom, but she'd never taken to the role.

Beau had never thought to mind, or even try to change her. It was just the way things were at his house, always had been, probably always would be. When his father preached of women being silent, his mother took the lesson home with her.

Only tonight, before he went home, Beau had something he had to do. He drove out to the truck stop and sat in the same booth Border and the girls had helped fill last week.

The place was deserted except for a few truckers who liked to drive the roads at night when there was less traffic. One man, several booths away, talked low on his cell while he ate. The other was reading a western and never bothered to look up when Beau walked past him.

Beau didn't have to wait long. Five minutes after he sat down, a water glass slid across the table toward him.

"Your friends showing up tonight?" Willow asked.

Beau looked up. "N-no. T-they weren't my friends. N-not that it's any of your b-business."

She shrugged and, to his surprise, smiled. "I really didn't think they were. You and Border looked near panic when I brought out the food. I guess I would have ducked out too if I'd been you."

"S-sorry about that. I-I hope they didn't make a scene."

"They did from the moment they walked in. I don't know why you'd think they wouldn't as they left. I never heard a woman swear so much and hiccup at the same time. Your date said she wasn't going to pay, but my boss stepped out from the back and threatened to call the cops."

"S-she wasn't my date." There, he thought. He'd said what he came to say. "They were just two women who offered to buy us breakfast when we finished playing at Buffalo's."

"I heard you were doing that." Willow put her pad and pencil back in her uniform pocket. "So you joined the bar scene after graduation?"

"Y-yeah, and you joined the truck stop crowd."

Willow shook her head. "We're not exactly climbing the ladder of success, are we, Beau?"

"N-not yet, but I got plans and o-one of them is to stay away from women like those two. I-I could feel my brain cells dying just being so close to their dim light." He fought to keep from stuttering.

Willow didn't disagree with his evaluation of the dates. "I should tell you about some of the folks who come in here."

"I'm listening, but I doubt you can trump my pair." Beau forced each word out slowly.

She backed away a step. "I'm due for a break. Mind if I sit with you for a while? It'll be nice to talk to someone who isn't just passing through on a long haul. I'll buy the Cokes."

"S-sounds grand." Beau watched her disappear through the swinging doors of the kitchen. He leaned back and smiled. He didn't want a wild bar girl with too much makeup and her breasts hanging out. All he wanted was a friend to talk to. He could never remember a time when he didn't know Willow Renalls, though they rarely said much to each other. He thought he remembered asking her to dance at a seventh-grade dance once, and she was his lab partner in biology one semester.

She appeared with the Cokes and a basket of hot rolls. They laughed about his last week's date using all the condiments as they put butter and jelly on the rolls. Then they talked about all they'd done and hadn't done since they graduated. Willow wanted to start junior college, but she hadn't had the money, and Beau told her about his plans to make it big. Now and then he tripped over a word, but she didn't seem to notice.

Thirty minutes flew by, and Willow finally stood to leave.

"I'll pay for the d-drinks," Beau said, feeling awkward for the first time since she'd sat down.

"No, they're on me tonight. You can get them next time."

Beau grinned. "N-next time. I-I like the sound of that." He wanted to thank her for the normal conversation and for not judging him by the company he'd kept last week.

As he walked out he thought about how much easier it was to dream when they were in high school. Just saying you wanted to be something made everyone around you think it was a possibility, but now dreams seemed slippery and distant, layered between days until they were almost invisible.

He glanced back into the truck stop. Willow looked up from cleaning the table where they'd sat. She probably couldn't see him standing outside in the dark, but he could see her clearly, her brown hair pulled in a ponytail and a slight smile on her lips like she was listening to her favorite song in her head.

Most folks wouldn't notice, but she was pretty in her own way.

His kind of pretty, Beau thought as he walked to his car.

Chapter 10

❧

TINCH TURNER SPENT AN HOUR CALMING DOWN A DEVIL
of a mare who'd been in an accident one stormy night a
month ago. The truck she was being hauled in jackknifed
on a slick road, causing a pileup.

The trucker transporting the horse had bloodied the
gray's neck trying to pull her from the wreck with a chain,
and the patrolman on the scene suggested putting her down
because the mare was obviously in a great deal of pain.

Lucky for the gray mare, a farmer who knew horses
stopped to help. He climbed into the wreckage and blind-
folded the horse with his jacket. Unable to see all the flashing lights and lightning, the animal calmed.

The farmer sat beside her stroking the trapped horse's

neck as she gave birth to a stillborn colt. In the chaos
around them, no one noticed. No one cared.

Tinch had heard that it was almost dawn before they
freed the mare. She had several deep cuts. For the next week
Tinch wasn't sure where the horse went or how the gray
was treated. The vet who finally took care of her said
the owner didn't want to pay and told him to keep the animal. He claimed she wasn't worth the cost of putting her
down.

The vet in Clifton Creek called the vet in Harmony, who
e-mailed Tinch and described the problem. Both men knew
that Tinch would go get her and bring the mare home. They
had a hell of a time getting her into a trailer, but they cared
enough to make the effort. The doctor who'd worked on the
mare started calling her Stormy, and Tinch barely noticed
what her name had been when the vet handed over her
papers to him.

Half the horses Tinch kept in his barn belonged to no
one, or more accurately to him by default. Tinch wasn't
sure what the gray had been through between the wreck
and the day he picked her up, but it must have been horrible
because she hated anyone, man or animal, who got near her.

He finally got her in a clean stall, swearing and sweat-
ing as much as the horse. "I don't know if I got enough
lifetime left to gentle you, darlin'," Tinch shouted over her
stomping and snorting.

He grabbed the bucket and headed for the wash stand.
Popping the snaps on his shirt, he splashed water on his
face and chest while the bucket filled.

When the horse kept kicking the sides of the stall, Tinch
yelled, "Stop that, darlin'. Nobody's listening to your rant."
Then in a normal voice, he added, "I know you were
expecting the horse whisperer, but I'm the horse yeller." He
raised his voice again. "Stop trying to kick your way out of
my barn."

To his surprise the horse stopped, proving his theory
that even horses recognized insanity in humans.

Tinch reached for a towel, but the shelf was empty.

Laundry was never at the top of his to-do list. He shoved his wet black hair back and crammed his hat on, thinking he'd just drip dry. He didn't have time to go back to the house for a towel.

He looked out the open barn door at what promised to be a warm sunshiny day. As much as he talked to himself and the animals, it was lucky he lived in the country.

The sound of a bell clanging shattered the silence of the morning.

Tinch turned north to the house no more than a shadow hidden behind the dried cornfield.

The clanging came again from the Rogerses' bell. He'd heard it several times over the years and knew there had to be trouble.

Tinch dropped the bucket and ran for his truck, his mind already full of what-ifs.

Addison could have hurt herself. The house could be on fire. Someone could be robbing the place.

A woman living this far out should own a gun and know how to use it and have a dog, a big one that would bite. Hell, after meeting the doc it might just be easier to tell her to move back to town.

He swung into her driveway and braked, sending mud and rocks flying in every direction. As he jumped out of the cab, he saw her standing on the front porch, dressed in her white lab coat and white slacks. She looked as out of place as a street sign.

"What is it?" he yelled, relieved that she seemed to be in one piece.

"A . . . a . . ."

He ran toward her. Whatever had happened must be terrible. She looked like she'd been frightened. Her face was almost as pale as her coat. "What?" he yelled as he reached her.

"A . . . snake. By my car. I almost stepped on it."

Tinch slowed, took a breath. Just a snake. "Did he strike? Was it a rattler?" If she'd been bitten by a rattlesnake, they needed to be on their way to the hospital.

"I wasn't bitten, and I didn't pick it up to see if it rattled." Suddenly, she looked angry, as if it were his fault.

Tinch held up one hand. "You stay here on the porch and I'll check it out."

"What if it comes this way?"

"You're safe right there. Snakes hate climbing steps." He doubted that was true, but it seemed to calm her some. How could a woman who cut people open daily be afraid of a snake? She'd probably scared the rattler far more than it had her.

Tinch walked around her car parked inside the old garage. The place was cluttered with years of junk. Listening, he watched for any sign of a snake.

Nothing.

He picked up a rake and moved it under her little car. A four-foot-long bull snake wiggled out.

Tinch hooked him with the rake and walked out of her garage. He didn't look her direction, but he swore he could feel her watching him. He made a wide circle so she wouldn't think he was getting closer to her with the reptile. When he reached his truck, he pulled out a grain sack and lowered the snake inside, then knotted the top and set it down in the bed of his truck.

"Are you going to kill it?" she asked.

"No. It's a bull snake just looking for his dinner in your garage. I'm guessing he's not welcome, so I'll take him down the road and let him go."

"Far down the road." She was slowly calming, turning back to ice. "When I rented the place, I didn't know there were subleasers on the property."

Tinch reached her, but she stood two feet above him on the porch. "He's not going to hurt you, Addison. Don't worry about it."

"I'm sorry to have bothered you." She nodded slowly as if trying to allow his words to sink in. "It's just that I've never lived in the country, and the only snakes I've known wore suits and ties."

He smiled as if she were joking, but he had a feeling she

wasn't. "If you see another snake or hear a rattling that sounds kind of like the buzz of a cicada, back away slowly."

She held her chin up. "I'll try to remember that."

"If it's any comfort, that's the first snake I've seen around here in months." Even while he tried to reassure her he wondered why she held herself so tightly in place.

"That is no comfort," she answered.

"Besides for dancing, wearing boots comes in handy out here. You might want to buy a pair."

She shook her head as she stared at the garage.

"You got any liquor around here?"

That pulled her out of her nightmare thoughts. "It's ten o'clock in the morning, Mr. Turner, surely you don't need a drink?"

He shoved his hat low and wondered why this woman was so irritating. "I was thinking *you* might need a shot to steady your nerves."

"I'm fine. Thank you for coming." She turned as if to go inside.

"You're welcome." He propped his foot on the first step and stared at his boots. "Look, Doc, don't take it so personal. We all get scared from time to time. Nobody, even you, has to be perfect."

She opened her mouth, then closed it as if by saying anything she might reveal too much of herself.

He took the chance to change the subject. "You want to see something else I found in the garage? I promise this won't frighten you."

When she didn't answer, he walked into the dark garage and came back out with something cupped within his hands. "This might have been what brought the snake calling. I saw the Rogerses' old barn cat moving her kittens a few days ago. She's probably been living fat on field mice down by the old barn, but decided to move her family into the garage for winter."

He opened his hands and a tiny kitten lifted its black-and-brown striped head. With great care he set it in the basket strapped to the back of an old bike near the porch.

"There's another one still in the barn. They look big enough to survive, so the momma cat may have moved on."

When he returned with the tabby kitten, he saw Addison smile, and for the first time Tinch thought she could be pretty if she tried. She was still too tall, not rounded enough in the right places and far too controlled to be someone he'd be interested in, even if he was looking.

"I can take them home with me, if you don't want them. I got a few other strays around my place."

She walked down the steps and held her hands out slowly until her fingers brushed fur. "I'll take them both. At least until I leave."

He watched her carefully as she brushed one finger over the tiny kitten's head.

"I wanted a cat when I was a kid," she said more to the cat than him. "But my parents wouldn't hear of it. They said an animal in the house would be chaos."

Tinch relaxed a little as he studied her. "Why don't you take Chaos and his brother inside and give them a little milk?"

She smiled at Tinch. "I'll do that, and thanks for coming. I guess I should spend some time looking up the difference between bull snakes and rattlesnakes."

"You do that, Doc." He started to walk away, then turned back. "Friends?" he offered.

"Friends," she agreed.

He went back to his truck fighting down a laugh. Who would have guessed the doc would turn human over a stray cat or two? He'd thought for a minute she was going to kiss him for handing over the kittens.

Maybe he should bring over a horse. Maybe she'd be so tickled she'd sleep with him. It had been so long since he'd been with a woman, even a tall, thin, washed-out one was starting to look good.

The thought of Addison tangled in the sheets almost buckled him to his knees. He hadn't thought of a woman like that since Lori Anne died. Sure, he had dreams of women, but they were only fiction in his mind, not real flesh-and-blood neighbors.

Tinch expected to feel guilt for somehow betraying Lori Anne, but he didn't. Maybe time had washed a little of the married feeling away, or more likely he'd just grown insensitive to the pain. Thinking of Addison was so far away from something that would happen, she might as well have been a fantasy. Even if he wanted to know her better, the doc would never allow that to happen.

Chapter 11

REAGAN SWORE SHE COULD FEEL HER HEART CRACKING as she walked through the rooms of her uncle's house . . . her house. She'd tried to sleep most of Sunday after she'd made it home from the hospital, but today she had far too many things to do.

Only, the house seemed to call to her as the shadows grew long. Memories lined the walls of the old place that had been in the Truman family for more than a hundred years. Lifetimes of living mixed with her short time among them.

She thought of her first days here when she'd counted the hours until Jeremiah kicked her out. She'd shown up with nothing in her backpack but a few changes of underwear, a jacket, and a couple of old T-shirts.

Reagan remembered the day he'd given her a roll of money and trusted her to do what was right. Old Jeremiah had been the first person ever to trust her or believe in her. He'd set up a charge account for her at stores in town and told her to spend what she needed and never questioned her on a dime she spent.

She thought of the party when he'd handed her the deed to this place for her eighteenth birthday. He'd said he did it so she'd never have to worry about having a home.

As she picked up the newspaper he'd been reading when he'd had his last heart attack, she gulped down a sob. Reagan had been in the kitchen, but Foster Garrison, the live-in nurse, had been with her uncle when he dropped in pain. They'd rushed Jeremiah to the hospital. Everyone had done all they could to save him, but Reagan knew it was his time to go.

Funny thing was, Jeremiah knew it too. He spent his last days telling her not to overreact and to make sure she got the apple trees ready for winter.

Standing up straight, she realized she'd miss this old man who would always be her uncle even though they were not blood kin. She'd cried every night in the hospital waiting for death to finally come, but she wouldn't cry anymore. He would think it foolish with all the work to do.

The knowledge of what she had to do, of who she was, settled in around her. She now owned an orchard, and if she didn't take charge, all the apples wouldn't be picked, packed, and delivered. Each year for the past four years she'd increased production. Now she had to meet demand or her business would suffer, not to mention all the pies and jelly in the state that wouldn't get made. Her uncle had loved the trees, but she loved the business of it.

Though she'd come to Harmony as a runaway, Jeremiah not only had taken her in as his niece, but he'd made it legal. As far as everyone in town knew, she was the last Truman. And Trumans, like the Mathesons and the Mc-Allens, founded this town and somehow were responsible for it. And now, unbelievably, she was a part of the history also. She not only had the farm and the business, she also had the town to care for.

Reagan walked out onto the porch and was surprised to see her next-door neighbor, Pat Matheson, sitting in the rocker Jeremiah always sat in.

"Evening, Reagan," the old woman said. "I thought I'd drive over and watch the sunset with you tonight." Her hands were almost as wrinkled as Uncle Jeremiah's had been as she patted the rocker arm with each sway of the chair.

Reagan couldn't get any words out as she took her chair that faced the west.

The old woman stilled and her fingers covered Reagan's as they watched the sun go down in silence. In the shadowy light before darkness fell, Pat whispered, "I believe that was about the prettiest one I've ever seen. Jeremiah would have liked it."

"Did you love him?" Reagan wouldn't have been able to ask if it hadn't been dark, but somehow, today, on the day after his death, it was important to know.

"All my life, child." Pat Matheson gave a sharp laugh. "I never remember a day that I didn't love him. But loving and living with a man are two different things."

Reagan thought of asking why they never married, but maybe they had what they wanted. Maybe looking over the fence and seeing the light of his place just down the road and knowing that he loved her just as much as she loved him was enough for them both. "He loved you too," Reagan said, "but he hated that you called him Dimples."

"I know he loved me, dear, and I called him Dimples because I knew it bothered him. There was always a part of me that got a real tickle out of needling that man."

Reagan rocked back in her chair. Jeremiah wasn't an easy man to care for. His own sister had moved to Oklahoma rather than have to live with him. He had his way of doing everything—the right way, he claimed—and he never listened any more than necessary to anyone.

"Will you sit beside me at the service tomorrow?"

Pat nodded. "I will if you want me to."

A huge black pickup turned off Lone Oak Road and headed toward them.

"That'll be Hank coming to get me. I told him I could walk home, but my sister never believes a thing I say I can do. I think secretly she likes calling our nephew and enlisting his help." She smiled as if enjoying complaining about a sister she'd lived and worked beside all her life. "Will you be all right here by yourself again tonight?"

"Sure. This is my home." Reagan almost smiled. "I can't think of anywhere else I'd want to be."

Hank Matheson got out of the truck and walked around to open the door for his aunt. "Reagan," he said as he helped Aunt Pat in, "you call us if you need anything. We're here if you need us."

"Thanks. I'll remember that," Reagan answered, and waved. She walked into the house and up the stairs to her room.

Just before she fell asleep she tried Noah's number one more time. No answer. Her best friend was several states away at some rodeo and didn't know her uncle had died.

She remembered when she'd been in high school and Noah had told her once, *Everyone wants to hug you when someone in your family dies. They don't know what to say and there really ain't nothing they could say that helps, so about all you can do is stand there and let them hug you.*

Tonight she'd give all she owned for one hug from Noah McAllen. Months had passed since he'd been home, and Reagan felt like he grew less real and more the legend every day. Folks around here talked of Noah as if he were a movie star. Like his father, he'd done the town proud on the rodeo circuit.

She tried to sleep but couldn't seem to empty her head. An hour before dawn, Tyler Wright drove up in front of her house and waited. He didn't knock, or honk. In the country everyone knows when someone comes to the house.

When she walked out dressed in a black pantsuit, Tyler stood by the car waiting.

She tried to smile at him. "Can I ride up front with you,

Mr. Wright?" She couldn't stand the thought of being in the back alone.

"Of course," he said, and opened the door.

They drove to the cemetery and waited in the car while the hearse arrived. The pale glow of first light came as six men, all dressed in suits, carried the casket up a small hill to an open grave.

Reagan watched without really seeing them. She saw the flowers being brought up and put across the simple wooden box. Wildflowers of spring somehow didn't fit with the cool fall morning.

"Did my uncle order flowers when he made his plans?" she asked, realizing she hadn't even checked with Tyler about the details of the funeral.

"No," Tyler said honestly, "but I thought he'd like them."

"He wouldn't," she answered, knowing he'd say they were a waste of money. "But I do. Thank you for thinking of them."

Tyler smiled. "It will be sunrise in a few minutes. I have chairs next to the grave."

He walked around and opened her car door while Reagan tried as hard as she could to convince herself that she could get through this. When the door opened, it was not Mr. Wright, but Brandon Biggs who offered his help. Big stuck out his huge hand and waited for her.

Reagan looked behind her and saw people all around emerging from their cars in the gray dawn. Then she looked at Big. He always seemed to know when she needed a friend.

"I thought you might need a hand," he said as they began to walk up the hill.

"Thanks," she managed as she moved closer to the casket sitting above where the grave had been dug. "Don't let me do something dumb."

"I'm right here, Rea. I've got your back." He held her arm as she sat down in one of the chairs, then moved behind her.

As light spread over the land, people covered the hill. Pat Matheson, as she had promised, sat at her left, and other old men and women took the remaining chairs. Most were either Mathesons or McAllens. The three families had started together on this land, and they seemed to band together when they buried one of their own.

A preacher Reagan had never seen gave a simple service as the sun rose, warming the air a few degrees. She looked out over the cemetery. There were people everywhere. Some standing in family groups, some alone, all facing the hill. Jeremiah Truman, a man who lived alone and liked it that way, had a world of people he'd touched.

When the last prayer was finished, Reagan stood and waited as one by one the people passed to touch the casket, to say their good-bye to Jeremiah, to hug her.

Two aging veterans folded a flag that had been draped over the casket. They started to hand it to Reagan, but she indicated that it belonged to Pat Matheson. The old men agreed. Everyone in town knew that Pat Matheson and Jeremiah Truman might have been married if not for the war.

Reagan thought of what Noah had said about hugging and knew that the people passing needed to give a hug more than she needed to receive one. An hour passed before Big walked her back to the funeral home's family car.

"Mr. Wright, would it be all right if Big took me home? I don't want to put you out."

"It's no trouble," Tyler said.

Big nodded at the man. "I'd like to take her home if it's not breaking any rules."

"Of course," Tyler said, understanding.

Reagan climbed into Big's pickup and cuddled close to his big frame for warmth. The morning felt suddenly cold to her.

He started the truck and pulled slowly away.

She didn't look back at the grave. She couldn't yet. Someday, maybe in a few weeks or months, she'd bring flowers and sit beside it for a while, but not now, not today.

Big didn't turn out toward Lone Oak Road but drove onto the highway. For a long while they just drove. Reagan didn't really care where they were going. After the weeks in the hospital and months before that when she'd been afraid to leave the house for more than a few minutes, just driving felt great.

When he finally stopped for lunch at a truck stop that seemed miles from anywhere, Reagan realized how hungry she was. They ate huge hamburgers and malts while they made up stories about the other people in the place. When the manager announced that there was now a shower available for Ichy, Reagan laughed until she cried . . . and then simply kept crying.

Big didn't say a word. He paid the bill and began the long drive back to Harmony. It was late afternoon when he dropped her off at the farm.

"In the morning, I got to go over to Armstrong County and work with a crew there. It may be a week before the job's done and I make it home. Will you be all right till I get back?"

She opened the car door and noticed Jeremiah's old dog waiting for her on the porch. "I'll be fine. I've got lots to keep me busy." She leaned back in the cab and gave him a kiss on the cheek. "Thanks for the drive." She guessed he knew she was thanking him for a whole lot more than just a drive.

"You're welcome." He smiled that big goofy smile of his. "Only, thanks isn't enough, Rea. Not from you. I expect a whole pie when I get back. One of your chocolates would be nice, but I'll take whatever you make."

"You got a deal." She closed the door and walked to the porch. Then she waved good-bye with one hand while she patted the old dog on the head with the other.

Chapter 12

⸙

WRIGHT FUNERAL HOME

TYLER WRIGHT SAT DOWN AT HIS DESK WHEN HE RETURNED to his office after the graveside service and began to write the facts of an obituary, even though there was so much more he wanted to say.

After an hour, he shoved his efforts aside and took up other chores.

He spent the rest of the day working on never-ending paperwork, and now that the sun was almost setting he had one more duty before he could climb the stairs to his rooms above the funeral home. Tyler thought he might sit out on the tiny balcony off his living area and watch the sunset, like he'd seen Old Man Truman do, when he finished this last task.

He picked up his pen and thought about what to write. *Jeremiah Truman slipped into a coma on the first cold day of fall and, after the sun set, he departed this life, leaving a town to mourn his passing.*

That sounded good, Tyler thought, wishing he could add that when Truman's niece came to live with him, everyone began to see him through her eyes, and she loved him with a depth that surprised the entire town. Except the Wednesday paper took only the facts. They never allowed Tyler much room to add more.

Jeremiah Truman was a veteran of the Second World War, a man who never married and a farmer who loved his apple orchard. His only surviving relative is Reagan Truman.

"How are you coming on the obit?" Kate asked as she brought Tyler hot cocoa into the room she called "his mess" and not his office.

Tyler smiled at her. Another month and she'd be officially retired from the army and moving to Harmony permanently. Long weekends were never enough time with his Kate. "You know, Katherine, according to gossip, we're living in sin."

She laughed as she moved a few papers so she could sit close to him. "I know, and since I'm over forty, I can allow myself to say that I've quite enjoyed it. I doubt at our age anyone cares, but for your good name I feel like I should marry you. Mr. Wright, you're not a man to be gossiped about."

He kissed her hand. Neither had ever married, and he suspected that, like him, Kate thought she never would. Somehow they'd found one another, and with or without a piece of paper he knew they'd be together until death. "When, my Kate, will you do me the honor of becoming my bride?"

"When I settle in," she said. "Let me get used to not traveling. Living here will be a big change from my life in the army. I've had twenty-five years of drifting; settling may take some adjusting."

"When, Kate?" he asked gently again, knowing there would be little pushing the major if she didn't want to move.

She tried to look thoughtful. They'd played this game before. She always wanted to just run off and do it one night, no planning, no details to bother with. Just slip on the rings, say *I do*, and get on with their lives. But Tyler liked everything planned out. He wanted a wedding. "You know, Ty, it's usually the bride who wants all the trimmings and the groom who wants to run off. Somehow we've got it backward."

"I know," he shrugged. "You've got five people on your list and I have to invite the entire town or make someone mad. Running off to marry would be fun, but I want everyone to know I'm marrying the most wonderful woman in the world. I want my friends there. I want Hank Matheson to stand as my best man and his niece, Saralynn, to walk the aisle as flower girl. I want . . ."

"How about we book a room in Dallas when I finish this next assignment? We can start with the honeymoon." Kate interrupted his planning.

Tyler shook his head. "We can't keep having the honeymoon, Katherine. At some point we have to have the marriage."

"We can't?" She kissed his cheek. "But, Ty, you're such a loving man. Every day, and every night, I love you more."

When Kate whispered in his ear, he could never even think of saying no to her.

"Well, all right. One more time, and then you have to set a date and marry me." His Kate had done it again. She'd brightened his life on a very dark day.

She stood. "I'd better finish packing. My flight will leave without me."

"I wish I could drive you to Amarillo." He frowned. In the six months she'd been coming to spend every weekend she could with him, he'd grown to love the long drive. He'd think about her and all he'd tell her on the way to the airport, and on the way back he'd think of all they'd done and said.

They might be a little old to fall into love for the first time, but they seemed to make every minute count. He loved making love to her in the dark but still had a hard time imagining them married and walking about nude in front of each other. She must have felt the same way. They'd been sleeping together for six months and he still didn't know what his bride-to-be looked like without clothes, but he knew how she felt and that seemed more important because she felt perfect.

"I wish you could take me in too, but with the late flight it would be midnight before you got back," she said so much later that Tyler had forgotten what they were talking about. "Besides, with Autumn so close to delivery, I know you're needed here."

Kate rubbed her cheek against his as she continued, "And Reagan's all alone now and she'll need support to make it through this. I'm guessing you'll be the one to wrap up all the details tomorrow."

As they always did, he and Kate talked of the people of Harmony as if they were family. "She'll have Liz Leary helping her through the legal parts, though I don't know who will help Liz's husband with the twins. As for the Truman farm, this is their busy season and she's the only one who knows what to do. Reagan will have her hands full getting the crop in. I wouldn't put it past Jeremiah to have planned his death in the busy season just to keep her mind occupied."

"I wish I could be here to help her." She walked to the window, and he could almost see her organized mind putting all that had to be done in perfect order.

Tyler stood and put his arm around her shoulder. "You will be here to help soon. One more month and you'll be seeing me all day and night for the rest of our lives." His hand slid down and he patted her on her bottom, something he'd discovered always made her smile. He loved being able to touch her so. Even when she was asleep beside him, he often gave her a gentle little pat and felt quite wicked about it.

She smiled just as he knew she would. "I don't know about all day with you, Ty. I like my own time, but the all night sounds grand."

He patted her again, just because he knew she didn't mind. "I love you beyond all reason, my Kate."

"I know." She smiled as she shook her head. "That's what made you so irresistible." She kissed his cheek. "I have to be honest with you about something, dear."

She took a deep breath and straightened slightly like the soldier she was. "I've been on the phone for an hour and know about my mission. My last mission, I hope. I'll be moving in with a team to investigate a fire. I can't tell you where I'm going but it's a spot where Americans, much less soldiers, are not welcomed."

Tyler felt his heart speed up. He'd known that sometimes Kate's job was hard, identifying bodies, finding the causes of fires set to kill people, but he'd never thought that she might be in danger . . . in real danger.

Before he could tell her not to go, she added, "It's my job, Ty. I have to go. Most of the team is young and inexperienced. They need me to lead them. I'm not sure they'd make it back without me, and we wouldn't be going in if it weren't very important."

"I know," he managed to say.

He knew that ordering her to stay wouldn't work and he doubted begging would help, so he just held her tightly. "You'll be in my thoughts every minute until I know you are safe," he whispered, wishing he could go with her. If something happened and she didn't come back, he wasn't sure he wanted to be left to spend the rest of his life alone.

She pushed a few inches away. "I tell you what: I've never used a code before, but I've known men who did. When it's over and I'm safe back at a fort somewhere, but it may still be a few days before we're finished and can leave, I'll call and let the phone ring once, then call right back and do the same. I may not be able to tell you where I am or how many days until I'm home, but you'll know that I'm safe. You'll know to stop worrying."

"Two calls. One ring each. Make it to my private office line; I can forward it to my cell and no one will pick up but me." Tyler knew he'd be waiting for the two short calls before he would take a deep breath.

"It's my last assignment, Ty. I may be gone two or three weeks . . . a month at the most, but when I get back, I'm coming straight home to you."

He tried his best to smile. "You'd better."

A very pregnant housekeeper bumped her way into the study, took one look at them, and backed out.

"What is it, Autumn?" Tyler asked without moving away from Kate, though he did raise his hand to her waist.

A voice came from the other side of the door. "Nothing, Mr. Wright. It can wait."

He kissed Kate. "I'll walk you to your car when you're ready to leave, and I'm guessing Autumn made you a snack to eat on the plane. She's been baking like crazy these last few weeks. I think she fears we'll all starve when the baby comes."

Kate nodded. "She always bakes. I've noticed all your staff is looking well rounded these days. You'll watch over her while I'm gone, won't you? She only has a few more weeks before the baby. With a little luck I might be back."

Tyler nodded. "We practice drills around here every morning so we'll be prepared. The minute she says it's time, everyone on the staff has their assignments. If it is the weekend, Willie Davis and Brandon Biggs at the fire department want to be called. Willie says he can run the two blocks by the time we get her in the car, and Big will meet her at the hospital. Both the guys went through all the birthing classes with her. They consider themselves her guardian angels."

"I'm still worried about what if something happens when you're out at a funeral?"

Tyler grinned. "The minute I leave, either Willie or Big will be camped out at the kitchen table, probably eating until I get back. Ronny Logan says when she gets off work at the post office, starting tomorrow, she'll drop over and spend the night in Autumn's parlor downstairs. They've become such close friends I wouldn't be surprised if they talk half the night." He kissed Kate's nose. "During the day, one of the office staff will be on guard. Don't worry. She'll never be alone."

Kate brushed his shoulder as though she could dust worry away. "I know you'll all take good care of her, but I wish I could be here. You don't think she might consider going a few weeks over the due date just so I could be close? Ronny takes classes some nights, and Big is always working overtime at some construction site, and Willie might have a fire while all of you are busy with a funeral."

"I'll ask her about waiting, but I don't think she has much say in that," he promised. "And I'll call Stella and ask her to come in to stay here for every funeral we have until the baby comes."

After Kate kissed him at her car, Tyler stood in the parking lot and watched until she disappeared, then turned back to his work. Life goes round and round, he thought, ever changing. Jeremiah Truman had lived a long life doing what he loved, and maybe the best thing Tyler could say about him, or anyone, was simply that he'd be missed.

He finished the obit and e-mailed it in. Kate would be back in a month or less. Until then, he planned to worry about her. There were already enough folks worrying about Autumn.

He smiled, thinking about what his grandmother used to say about not wasting worry on things you could do nothing about. When Kate got back, she'd be safe with him and he'd have no use for worry again. They'd live out the rest of their lives in Harmony.

Two calls. One ring each. He'd worry till then.

Chapter 13

AN HOUR AFTER SUNSET, SHERIFF ALEXANDRA MATHESON left her office in a full run. She'd planned an evening of paperwork while her husband, Hank, held his monthly volunteer fire department meeting across the street at the fire station. But that was before a call came in that there had been a shooting at the trailer park just outside town.

Alex reasoned it was probably only a misfire or a neighbor shooting at a stray dog, but the dispatcher who notified her sounded near panic. He said a kid called in the shooting and was crying so badly, the dispatcher couldn't understand him.

Alex called for backup as she pulled out of the driveway and headed toward the trailer park. "Weekends," she mumbled to herself, "and a full moon to boot." If someone had frightened a child, they'd be real sorry by the time she got through with them.

The sleepy little trailer park beneath old cottonwoods hadn't recovered from a spring tornado. Piles of junk still gave the already slim streets an abandoned feeling. She'd heard that several families had moved out, leaving trailers as rentals for seasonal workers drifting in. As she navigated through the park, Alex thought of suggesting that this place become a cleanup project for city planners.

When she parked at the third mobile home from the end of the park, folks were standing around staring as if expecting a ball to drop from the TV antenna. A few of them pointed at the old Airstream almost enclosed in overgrown brush and hanging limbs from a cottonwood tree. As she got out of her car, she passed one of the deputies' cruisers already parked in front of the trailer.

"That's where it came from," one watcher shouted at Alex. "I heard it even over the TV." He was holding a kid in front of him.

"There's a sickly woman moved in there with her kid. Ain't heard a sound from them in two days except for the shot," someone else shouted.

"They're home," came another voice out of the darkness. "I've seen lights going on and off."

Alexandra Matheson asked them to move back as she walked toward the home, but they were more interested in watching. None seemed aware of the danger. They must have thought there was some kind of safety in numbers.

The mob shifted like warm Jell-O. As a few stepped back, others slid into their places as if the show were about to start and they had to have the best seat.

Her deputy, Phil Gentry, emerged from the doorway of the home and moved toward her. "We got a boy about four or five years old with a gun," he whispered as his greeting. "We need to get these people out of range. If he fires, it could go right through the wall of the trailer and hit someone."

Alex nodded. "You clear the area. I'd rather go in and face the kid with the gun."

Phil shook his head. "I already tried. He told me he'd fire if I got any closer."

"Have we got either of the kid's parents on scene?"

Phil shook his head. "Not that I know of. The neighbor said the mom leaves him home alone all the time. I don't think there's a father in the picture."

Alex took a deep breath. This was her job. This was what she was trained for. "Get the people back. I'm going in." She could almost hear her husband, Hank, telling her to be careful. Warning her not to take risks. "Have any idea what the kid's name is?"

"Jamie, I think. And he's got a mouth on him. Cussed me out for even saying hello."

Alex moved toward the door.

"Jamie?" she whispered. "Jamie, are you in here?"

"I'm here, but don't come in. My momma said anyone knocking on the door would be coming to take me away and I ain't going, damn it."

"Jamie, I'm Alex, and I swear I'm not here to take you away. I just want to talk to you."

"I don't want to talk to you," the boy whispered. "I don't want to talk to no one."

Alex had reached the end of the hallway and saw a ragged little boy sitting in the corner of the kitchen. The gun rested at his side.

"Jamie, were you playing with the gun?" she asked, keeping her voice as calm as she could.

"No. I had to use it. My momma told me not to, but I had to."

Alex took another step, calculating that she would have time to step back to safety if the boy reached for the gun. "Why?" she asked as the kid raised his eyes to her.

He seemed so tiny. "I had to 'cause he was eating the last of my food."

Alex glanced at the counter and saw a spilled box of cereal and a seven-inch dead rat lying beside it.

"You did what you had to do, Jamie," she whispered. "But your mother was right when she told you not to touch the gun. It's very dangerous."

One tear bubbled from brown eyes. "You going to arrest me for killing the rat?"

"No, Jamie. I thought I'd invite you to go out to eat with me, just till your mom comes back. I haven't had supper yet and was hoping someone would join me."

The boy wiped his eyes. He might be starving, but he didn't trust her. "I don't want to go to jail. My momma's here—she's sleeping and told me not to wake her or there'd be hell to pay."

"Where is she? She must have heard the shot." Dread settled in the pit of Alex's stomach.

"She's in the bedroom. The door is locked. I tried it when I ran out of milk yesterday."

Alex moved closer. "Do you have any relatives in town?"

The kid nodded. "We came here looking for my aunt. She lives here on a farm somewhere. My momma says I can ride horses when we find her. She says I'm going to stay there once we find the place, but Momma hadn't been feeling up to looking for it yet. She gets real sick if she don't get her medicine."

Alex knelt down a few feet away. "What's your aunt's name? I'll help you find her place. I know almost everyone around these parts."

"Aunt Lori Anne. I remember 'cause she has the same middle name as Momma and that's funny. My momma says she ain't seen her in years but she remembered her writing from Harmony and telling her to come visit anytime she wanted to. They got different mothers, but the same daddy, but Momma says he's dead."

Alex put her arm around the boy as she slid the gun away. "We'll find your aunt." She lifted the bony body and carried Jamie to a couch. "How about I wrap you up now that it's getting colder outside." She lifted the blanket he must have been using for covers at night.

Jamie's fear slipped away with the tears. "All right."

Alex hit her radio. "Phil, tell the neighbors to go home. The show's over. Grab a couple of candy bars from my car and come on in."

"Will do."

Alex sat beside Jamie. While the little boy cried, she looked around the room. The trailer didn't look lived in. It seemed more like an old used trailer rented by the week than a home. No pictures. No books or magazines. Several of the cabinets were open and empty. In the corner of the bar she saw a soda bottle with several branches of a honeysuckle vine growing out of it. Strange, the tiny flowers looked so out of place in the colorless room.

"How long has your mom been asleep?"

"I don't know. She told me I could watch TV and she'd be awake before the cereal and milk ran out, but I drank the milk too fast and it's been a long time since I've had any. Some men came to visit her last night, but they didn't see me. I disappeared into the boards beneath the table, just like she told me to if I heard them. But it's dark now and I don't like it in there."

"Have you seen her moving around today, or did she come out to go to the bathroom?"

Jamie shook his head, sending earth-brown hair flying.

Alex put her arm around Jamie and was silent for a few minutes. She didn't want to ask questions too rapidly and frighten the child.

Phil brought in a few candy bars, a bag of chips, and an orange drink. "I had these in my cruiser. I thought they might help."

"Thanks."

He offered the kid the drink, but Jamie didn't reach for it.

"It's okay," she said. "Officer Gentry is a good guy. He's got kids, so he knows what they like. I'll tell your mom that I said it was all right, and I'll ask her if you can have supper with me."

Gentry knelt in front of the kid. "I thought I'd get hungry tonight, but turns out I didn't have time. You're welcome to them if you'll tell me your full name."

"Jamie," the boy whispered as he reached for the drink. "Jamie Noble."

Phil opened the chips and passed them to him. "Noble. That's a fine name. I used to know a Lori Anne Noble. She married a farmer out on Timber Line Road about ten years ago. They were nothing more than two kids at the time."

"That must be his aunt," Alex smiled. "You see, Jamie, I told you she wouldn't be hard to find."

Phil shook his head. "I'm real sorry to tell you, boy, but if Lori Anne Noble was your aunt, she passed away three years ago." The deputy looked at Alex. "I guess her husband would be this boy's uncle. He's still out on the place."

Alex nodded at Phil. "You remember who he was?"

"Sure. It was probably while you were away at college, but Lori Anne Noble married Tinch Turner. They were the talk of the town for a few months. No one thought they were old enough to marry, but neither had any folks around to stop them."

"Jamie, we're going to go check on your mom. If she's still sick, we may have to take her to the hospital, but I'll talk to her and see if you could stay with your uncle until your mom is better. Would that be all right?"

"Does he have horses?"

Gentry smiled. "He sure does. I saw him riding a beauty the last time I passed his place. Prettiest paint I've ever seen, with a long mane flying in the wind."

Alex motioned for Gentry to stay with the boy as she backed down the hallway to the only closed door. After knocking lightly, she tried the knob.

It was locked.

Alex leaned her shoulder against the wall and shoved hard, popping the lock on the aluminum door. The smell that greeted her almost knocked her down.

A woman, her body across the bed, a needle still in her arm, lay dead. In the warm room the body had already started to decay.

Alex took it in all at once. The marks on her thin arms.

The dried blood on her mouth. The blank eyes staring up at nothing. A tiny bag of pills in the palm of her gray hand.

Looking away from the bed, Alex saw the contents of a purse spilled out across a cluttered dresser. She picked up the ID. Sadie Ann Noble, age twenty-four; address, Kansas City, Kansas. There was fifty dollars in the billfold and another ten scattered out in ones on the floor. A tattered white legal envelope was crumpled near the trash as if she'd been about to toss it aside along with flyers addressed to occupant. It had what looked like a hurried note scribbled in the corner. *Turner Farm. Timber Line Road.*

Alex tugged the seal free and pulled out what looked like an official document. The last will and testament of Sadie Ann Noble, sole parent of Jamie Noble.

She read down until she saw that Sadie must have come here to give custody of her son to her half sister. Maybe she knew she was dying, or maybe she couldn't stay off the drugs.

"Sheriff?" Phil called from the other end of the hallway. "Everything all right?"

Alex straightened as she moved so that she could see Phil. She kept her voice low as she pulled her phone from her belt. "I'm taking the boy for a meal. Can you wait here for the coroner and Tyler Wright? I'm calling them now."

Phil looked at her, knowing what she'd found in the bedroom. "I will. Once they're here, I'll find you."

"Fair enough." She walked out of the bedroom and closed the door. When she reached the living area, she smiled at the boy. "Jamie, I think it will be fine if you come with me to eat something. There's a diner downtown that serves real good hamburgers."

"Are you sure my momma won't mind?"

"I'm sure."

Alex took his hand. As they moved to the porch, she looked back at Gentry. "Call Turner and tell him we'll be delivering his nephew."

Alex lifted the boy, blanket and all, into her arms as she walked toward her car. He didn't say a word, but she had a feeling he knew something was wrong. His thin body was shaking beneath the covers, and she wondered if he offered no protest because wherever he was going couldn't be as bad as where he'd been.

An hour later the sheriff listened as her deputy gave her a full report. The coroner said Sadie's death looked like an accident, though it might have been a suicide. The body would have to be taken to Amarillo for an autopsy, so it would be a few days before the ruling was final. Dispatch had contacted the Kansas City police and found that Sadie Noble was a known drug addict with several arrests for everything from petty theft to prostitution. Her last address listed had been her mother's house four months ago. The car in front of the trailer was registered to her mother, who'd been dead for more than a year.

"What's the bad news?" Alex asked sarcastically.

"Tinch Turner doesn't have a phone," Phil answered. "If the boy is his late wife's nephew, we'll have to drive up and wake him up to find out."

Alex watched the bony little boy eating his second order of chili fries as she paced a few feet away from the table. "Can you meet me out there, Phil? I'd like you to wait with the boy until I talk to him. We don't want to make this any harder on Jamie than we have to."

"Will do. Meet you at the entrance of the Turner farm in fifteen."

Chapter 14

TURNER RANCH

TINCH SAT ON HIS PORCH SWING, HIS LONG LEGS CROSSED and propped on the railing as he watched the two police cars meet at the entrance to his farm. He'd been sitting there since before dark and hadn't gotten up to turn on a light, so he knew they couldn't see him.

When they turned onto his property, he wondered what he'd done wrong, but he couldn't think of anything lately. In fact, he had barely been off the property since he drove home from Buffalo's after dancing with the doc more than a week ago. Still, the urge to run from trouble tempted him, even though he'd learned a long time ago that was impossible.

Slowly, silently, he stood and watched them moving toward him. Until he noticed them, he'd been enjoying the night. He liked this time of year, the stillness of late summer just before it turns to fall. It had taken him a long time, but he'd finally taught himself not to think or worry about anything, but just be.

The sheriff stopped twenty feet from the house, and the deputy behind her climbed out of his car and into the front seat of hers. No one else seemed to be in either car, but still the deputy waited behind.

Alex Matheson moved toward him in the low glow of parking lights. She was a few years older than he was, but Tinch remembered her from school. Everyone always liked Alexandra McAllen, now Matheson. They said she had her mother's beauty and her father's bravery. Tinch had managed to stay out of her way most of the time, and the few times their paths had crossed it had been nothing but business between them.

He grinned, remembering something else he'd heard about the sheriff. Folks said she was Hank Matheson's girl years before either of them figured it out. Tinch had seen Hank drag her out of Buffalo's one night with her fighting and screaming, and not one person in the bar seemed to think anything was wrong with the picture.

If Tinch had decided to pick sides, he would have probably stood with Hank, since Hank was his second cousin on his mother's side, and family. He guessed that since she'd married Hank, the sheriff was family now too, but they'd never been more than nodding friends when they saw one another.

"Evening, Sheriff," he said as she neared the porch.

Alex looked up. "Got any lights, Mr. Turner?"

Tinch reached around the screen door and flipped on the light in his wide living room that ran the front of the house. A soft yellow glow flooded the porch. "Just drive out to check on the electricity, Sheriff?"

Alex almost smiled at him. "No. I'm afraid I'm here on business. Very sad business."

Tinch shrugged. Every person he cared much about was dead, so how bad could bad news be? He owned his land outright and the taxes were paid. The night was clear of clouds. Nothing was blowing in, and the last time he checked he had enough money in the bank to make it through the winter even if he didn't earn another dime. So whatever the business was, he doubted it would affect him one way or the other.

"Mind if I sit down?" She moved onto the porch and took one of the chairs.

He waited. This wasn't a social call. He didn't have to offer her a drink or make small talk. He'd just as soon hear whatever she had to say outright.

"Do you remember your wife having a sister?"

Tinch relaxed. If that was all this was all about, it wouldn't be anything that might knock him off his feet again. "Her dad had a second wife after he left Lori Anne's mother. Lori Anne only visited them a few times when she was growing up. I think they lived in Kansas City. As far as my wife knew, she only had one half sister, who was several years younger. Sadie, I think was her name. They traded Christmas cards for a few years after we married, but I don't know where Sadie is or if Lori Anne's stepmother is even still alive." He noticed the sheriff wasn't taking notes. "Is that of any help, Sheriff? That's about all I know. We lost touch maybe six or eight years ago."

"A great deal of help," Alex answered. "We found a woman in a trailer tonight who had overdosed on drugs. Right now we don't know if it was an accident or suicide, but according to her driver's license her name was Sadie Ann Noble. You know anyone who could ID her for sure?"

"No." Tinch shook his head. "I never met her, and even if Lori Anne was alive, I don't think she could. The last time my wife saw her, the girl couldn't have been more than ten or twelve." A sadness settled in his thoughts. Lori Anne had always thought of her sister as a chubby cherub. He remembered Lori Anne saying once that from the minute she saw Sadie, she wanted to hug her. "After my wife's dad died, she lost track of his second wife and kid. I tried to find them to let them know Lori Anne died three years ago, but I had no luck.

"If this woman was Sadie, she'd be about twenty-three

or four by now." He looked straight at the sheriff. "What makes you think it might be a suicide?"

"There was a last will and testament in her bag, all signed and notarized. It was addressed to Mr. and Mrs. Tinch Turner, General Delivery, Harmony, Texas. According to the will she didn't have much, but what she had Sadie Noble left to you and Lori Anne."

Tinch shook his head. "I didn't know her. Lori Anne hadn't heard from her in years. I don't want anything she may have left. Give it to some charity in town, would you, Sheriff?"

"I can't do that, Tinch." For the first time Sheriff Matheson didn't look too sure of herself. "At least until we get all this straightened out, I'd like you to keep him."

"Him?" Tinch groaned. The last thing he wanted was a pet left to him by his dead wife's half sister. He already had a barn full of horses no one wanted, and every stray that was dropped out on the road seemed to end up at his place.

"We don't have any paperwork on him. Don't even know how old he is for sure, but I think he'd be better off here with you for the time being." She waved toward the deputy. "Just for a few days."

Tinch was compiling reasons he didn't want to take in a pet when the back door of the cruiser opened and a little boy stepped out. He took one look around and darted out of the light's glow and into the total blackness of night.

Tinch raised his eyebrow. "A kid," he whispered, then turned to the sheriff. "I'm guessing you didn't bother asking him if he wanted to come stay with a total stranger before you tossed him in your car and drove him all the way out here. Hell, this place must look like the end of the world to a kid."

"I would have talked it over with him," Alex yelled as she tugged her flashlight off her belt. "Only he fell asleep as soon as I fed him. He knows about you. Told me his uncle Tinch had horses. I just didn't plan on the sight of you scaring him away."

The deputy swung his car around and pointed his bright

lights in the direction the boy had gone. Nothing. In a plowed field they'd be lucky to find a footprint before dawn.

Tinch shifted and flipped on the yard lights.

Nothing. The kid was faster than a jackrabbit.

He sat back in the swing and crossed his legs over the railing.

"Aren't you going to help us find him?" Alex snapped.

"No. There's a hundred places he could already be curled into by now. If he doesn't want to be found, you're not finding him tonight." Tinch stared at her, making it plain that he considered his logic sound. "Wherever he is, he can see my lights. If he wants to come in, or gets cold or hungry, I'll be waiting. If not, you'll have better luck finding him after dawn."

"You're really not going to help, are you?"

Tinch shook his head. "If he wants to stay with me, he can, but I'm not forcing him, and I'm guessing neither can you, no matter how hard you try, Sheriff."

"Officer Gentry," she yelled in her most professional tone. "Grab your light. We'll start circling, widening ten feet with every lap. No use calling in backup. They've got their hands full with the suicide."

She turned to Tinch. "When I find him, I'll call Child Protective Services and get him into the system."

Tinch didn't say a word, but he knew he'd never let the sheriff take the boy if he wanted to stay. The kid was Lori Anne's blood and he'd always have shelter here.

Chapter 15

TRUCK STOP

A LITTLE AFTER NINE, BEAU YATES DROVE OUT TO THE truck stop and picked up Willow. He smiled when he saw her waiting outside for him. Maybe she was as excited about their date as he was. They'd talked several times in the truck stop during her breaks, and once he'd waited two hours and driven her home, but until tonight they'd been just friends.

Tonight, they had a real date . . . well, almost a real date. With her working most nights and him playing weekends and trying to keep up with his classes at the community college in Clifton Creek, they had little time and no money to date. But tonight Big and Border's neighbor had invited them over to eat some new Italian dishes she was trying out. Beau knew there would be lots of food and laughs. With luck, he wouldn't have to talk much and could still have a date.

Willow climbed in his car. "I'm starving." She laughed. "And for once I don't have to eat the truck stop food."

Beau backed out of the drive. "T-that the reason you agreed to go out with me?"

"Of course." She laughed, and he hoped she was kidding.

"Tell me about this lady who cooks for the likes of you and Border Biggs. She crazy or just like to feed the wild things?"

"S-she's a nice woman. Maybe ten years older than us, but not old. Her friend, a guy in a wheelchair, lived next door to the Biggs brothers for a while. When he moved out, she moved in. I-I think she's waiting for him to come back, but Border's brother doesn't think he ever will."

Willow wiggled out of her uniform top and Beau tried to keep his eyes on the road. After a few deep breaths he remembered what he'd been talking about. "S-she w-works at the post office, h-has for years." *Concentrate*, he screamed inside his mind and tried to forget about the woman changing clothes beside him. "N-now she's learning to cook and w-we're the judges."

"Or the guinea pigs," Willow said as she leaned forward and pulled a blouse out of her huge purse. "I thought I'd dress up a little. It didn't seem right to come to a dinner party in my uniform."

Beau risked a glance at her. The bra she wore wasn't much of a cover. "I-I think you look just f-fine the way you are."

He didn't know if she blushed, but he felt his face warm. Preachers' kids don't even get to look at Victoria's Secret catalogs. He'd never seen a real girl wearing just a bra. Looking back at the road, he decided he must have some kind of fixation on breasts. If he wasn't careful, he'd catch himself just thinking about them for no reason at all.

Willow pulled on a knit blouse and began combing her hair back. "I've been looking forward to this all week, Beau. I don't get out of the late shift very often, and all my friends work, so they don't want to do anything in the mornings when I'm free. It'll be nice to talk to people near my own age."

"W-who do you usually talk to?" Now that he knew what was beneath her blouse, he felt like Superman. She was fully clothed, but he could still see what was underneath. It would take a hard hit to bounce that picture out of his mind, and he planned to hold on to it as long as possible.

"I usually sit around and listen to my mom and her buddies from her work. I only had two good friends in high school, and they left for college a month ago. Now I mostly hear about the loser boyfriends my mom and her friends find. They say by the time a man's forty, if he's not married, a girl needs to look long and hard at him before she even dates him."

"Your p-parents are divorced?"

"Yeah. Since I was two. I think my dad must have been her first loser boyfriend. She hardly ever talks about him. Maybe she doesn't remember him. He was so far back in the line of men she's bedded."

Beau pulled up in front of an old Mission-style duplex near downtown and turned off the car. Before she could move, he said, "Willow, I-I don't date much." He laughed. "T-that's an understatement. I-I don't date at all unless you count a few group dates in middle school, and one of my p-parents was usually driving us all."

She didn't interrupt, but he thought she looked like she was smiling.

"I-I don't know how this is going to go tonight, s-so do you think I could kiss you now?" He stared straight ahead and said each word slowly. "That way, if I-I do something dumb and you're sorry you came, at least I-I will have kissed you once before you decide never to speak to me again."

He waited, half expecting her to laugh. Asking for a kiss before an almost-date was probably dumb enough to scare her off already.

To his surprise, she leaned over and touched her lips to his.

When she didn't move away, Beau raised his hand to the back of her neck and continued the kiss. After a few long seconds, she placed her hand on his chest and straightened away from him. "Beau, this is already the best date I've ever had, and whatever happens next won't change anything."

"Really?"

"Sure." She laughed and climbed out of the car.

Halfway up the walk, he caught up with Willow and took her hand. Neither said a word as they walked up the stairs.

Beau spent the entire evening wondering when he could kiss her again. Willow, on the other hand, seemed to love the little dinner party. She asked all kinds of questions and offered to help Ronny with the dishes. When Beau wanted to call it a night, Border told everyone that they'd play a few songs as a thank-you for the meal.

Willow and Ronny pulled up chairs and Big leaned against the window as they began to play. As always, Beau lost himself in first one song and then another.

After a few songs, Border leaned back and listened as Beau played his guitar and sang a few pieces he'd been working on. One was about how loneliness slowly smothers a heart.

When he finally looked up, both Ronny and Willow had tears in their eyes. "Y-you didn't like the song? It'll be b-better when I work on it some more."

Ronny shook her head. "I loved the song."

Willow smiled. "So did I."

Beau was surprised by their reactions. He didn't know if the song would work at the bar. It really wasn't a 'dance to' beat. The one he called "Smothered Heart" was just one he liked to play when he was alone.

Everyone picked up and said good night. Border offered to go with Beau to take Willow home, but his big brother jerked him toward their half of the duplex.

Now that the date was almost over, Beau wasn't sure what to do. He thought of asking for another kiss, but he wasn't sure if that would sound right. They drove away in silence with him thinking that when he got her home and walked her to the door, he'd just lean over and kiss her. If she didn't want it, all she had to do was step back. If that happened, he'd probably just mumble good night and run for the car.

"Pull over there," Willow said as she pointed to the park a block off Main.

He turned into the parking lot between the closed swimming pool and a bunch of old elms that shaded the playground equipment in summer. Half the leaves were gone from the trees, but they hadn't lost their color. His lights flashed across a carpet of fall.

"Want to get out and walk?" she asked, already opening the door.

"Sure," he said, thinking that walking in the park after dark didn't seem like a real good idea, but this part of town was usually safe.

As they walked he liked the sound the leaves made beneath their feet, almost like the sound a drum makes when a brush whooshes across it.

The wind made a low howling whistle deeper into the park, and the chains on the swings clanked in time. Beau smiled. There was music in the air tonight. He thought if he listened closely he might capture it in his head.

They walked to where shadows crossed before she stopped and turned to face him. "You want to kiss me again?"

"Yes," he answered without hesitation.

Moving closer, she whispered, "I wouldn't mind if you did."

He lifted his hand and cupped her cheek and was surprised to find she was shaking. She was as nervous as he was. He leaned down and touched his mouth to hers. Her lips felt warm and so soft.

She made a little sound and then opened her mouth, and he learned a great deal about kissing real fast.

Finally, he looped his arm around her shoulder and they walked back to the car. He'd discovered that Willow didn't know much more than he did about dating, but he sure did enjoy kissing her. Maybe they should be talking, but the silence between them was good and he didn't stutter when he kissed.

When they were back in the car, he leaned over and kissed her again. This time he moved his hand up her side until he was almost touching her breast. She felt so good.

She didn't seem to mind as he moved his hand along her ribs.

"I-I like this between us," he whispered. "I like it a lot."

"So do I," she answered, and awkwardly planted a quick kiss on his cheek. "Does this mean we're dating?"

He brushed his hand along her throat and beneath her hair. Her skin was warm and he wondered what it would be like to kiss her there. "W-would you mind if w-we were?"

"No." She looked down. "But, Beau, the way you play and sing, you're gifted, really gifted. In no time girls will be throwing themselves at you. Pretty girls. Rich girls. Girls with a lot more going for them than I'll ever have."

"Y-you're pretty, Willow. Real pretty." He moved two fingers down the neck of her blouse, barely touching her skin. "I-I like the way you feel." His fingers moved up and brushed across her lips, still wet from their last kiss.

She shook her head. "I'm just saying that when fame happens for you, I won't hold you back. I'll let you go and I'll count myself lucky to have been your girl for a while."

"M-my girl?" Beau looked at her in the moonlight and thought he should have said she was beautiful, not just pretty.

He drove her home with his arm around her shoulder. When he walked her to the door, he whispered, "Thanks." He wasn't sure what he was thanking her for. For going out with him. For kissing him, really kissing him. For believing in him.

When he leaned down to kiss her one last time, she leaned into him and he almost couldn't let her go. She felt so good against him. She was the one who pulled away and said good night. He let her go and walked back to his car, the lyrics to a new song already playing in his head.

Chapter 16

SHORTLY AFTER TEN O'CLOCK ADDISON MADE IT HOME TO her little house in the country. Sometime in the past few weeks she'd been thinking of it as her hideout, as if she were an outlaw running from the law and not a doctor trying to disappear from her parents.

She walked across the darkened rooms of her rented place, stripping off clothes as she headed for a warm shower. The smell of blood and antiseptic always seemed to linger on her skin after she left the emergency room. She'd just finished an eight-day work week and planned to do nothing but sleep and eat for the next three days.

Her father had tried to call twice while she was working. Addison didn't pick up and, as always, he didn't leave a message. He knew she rarely answered her cell when she was working, and she guessed he suspected she often didn't return his calls even when she wasn't at the hospital. He was also a doctor who was rarely available to family. She'd learned her communication skills from him.

If she called him back, she'd hear the same lecture she'd heard since the day she'd piled two suitcases in her little car and headed for Texas. He had plans for her. At first, he wanted her to specialize in plastic surgery and join his practice. When that campaign failed, he moved to his second line of attack. He picked out the perfect man for her to marry. When she'd objected, he'd insisted that Dr. Glen Davidson was everything her first husband was not.

He'd told her simply, "You could do little better than a top-notch researcher on his way to being a legend in his field. If you ask me, Addison, you're lucky he's willing to take a look at you."

She'd felt like a shelter dog being paraded in front of the dog show judges as the bad example.

Addison was glad she hadn't called her father back. She'd had a lifetime of never quite measuring up, and she didn't need to be reminded of her failures after a long work week. When she'd been growing up, his lectures over her shortcomings had hurt far more than any belt. The carrot before her, just out of reach, had always been his love, but no matter what she did she never quite deserved it. She'd tried escaping once into an early marriage. She'd found a hell even lower than what she'd known at home. This time when she broke the ties to her father, she'd walk away strong enough to stand alone.

As was her habit every night, she stood under a warm shower until the water grew cool, then pulled on a clean pair of underwear and an old college T-shirt. She needed sleep. Everything could wait until morning, including her father's weekly lecture. Though he'd talk for fifteen minutes, the summary boiled down to *grow up—come home—get married to Glen.* Her life had all been planned and organized for her, and no one understood why she'd taken this one-year assignment in the middle of nowhere. No one but Addison.

The last time she'd run, she'd been eighteen and rushed to the first guy who'd paid any attention to her. The marriage lasted less than six months. Her father's constant reminder of her mistake hung in the air between her and her parents forever.

In her young husband, she'd thought she had a friend she could trust, but neither of them knew about love or loving. After a few awkward attempts at sex, he gave up and shifted his full attention to spending her savings. She'd known the marriage was a mistake after a week, but she'd hung on, hoping something would happen and she wouldn't have to go home. When the money was gone, so was her first husband.

She closed her eyes, remembering how he'd hit her several times as he'd packed. He'd even screamed at her, more out of frustration than hate. She'd made a mistake in marrying, and somehow he'd blamed her for all their problems. In a way, he was like her father; he blamed her for not being good enough. She'd had no choice but to go back to her parents, not only bruised but broken.

As Addison combed her wet hair, she thought about how that time in her life seemed more like a dream than real, or maybe a nightmare. She'd turned off all feelings that winter, and now not even regret haunted her. She'd welcomed her parents making all her decisions. When they'd sent her to New England to school, she'd let the cold weather seep into her heart as well.

Only this time when she'd run to Texas to work, she had no regrets except that soon she'd have to go back and make choices she wasn't ready to make. In a few months she'd have to face her father and tell him she planned to live her own life. There would be no engagement to Glen, and she'd never work with her father.

When she stepped out of the bathroom, the curtain blew in the night breeze along with the hint of fall in the air.

She took a long breath, thinking of how much she loved the stillness of this place. If she could bottle it, she'd take it always with her wherever she went.

The triangle of light from the bathroom spread across something in the middle of her bed as if spotlighting it on a darkened stage. Addison froze.

She thought it might be an animal. It could have crawled in, not knowing or caring that the house was occupied, or maybe the kittens were out of their box in the kitchen and old enough to explore. She'd left food for the mother cat in the garage, but she hadn't returned.

Addison took a step toward the bed.

The shadow moved slightly, and she saw that it was a small child. A little boy curled up next to one of the kittens Tinch had found in her barn. She could make out the boy's dirty face and sandy hair. His chest moved in the slow rhythm of someone deep in sleep.

Addison backed out of the room and grabbed her cell. She waited until she reached the porch, then dialed 911.

When the dispatcher picked up, she said calmly, "This is Dr. Spencer. I'd like to speak to the sheriff, please."

"She's on a call. How can I help you?" The dispatcher sounded bored.

Addison didn't feel like repeating her story to first him and then the sheriff. Her tone grew hard and impersonal. "This is Dr. Spencer. I need to talk to the sheriff."

"Yes, ma'am," the dispatcher answered. "I'll patch you directly to her cell."

Addison glanced back into the house. She could barely make out the boy, but he was still sleeping.

"Sheriff Matheson here."

Addison was used to talking to cops who only wanted facts. "This is Addison Spencer. I'm out on Timber Line Road and I've just found a child sleeping in my bed."

There was a pause, a few muffled words, and then the sheriff was back on the line. "I'm on my way."

The phone went dead. Addison looked at it for a moment, feeling like the sheriff must have left out a piece of the plan. Then she noticed the lights at Turner's place to the south. He looked like he was having a party. Every light in the house was burning bright. She watched what looked like a police car speed away from his house.

Addison reached for her lab coat as the car turned into

her long driveway a minute later. Something was definitely going on.

Tinch and the sheriff climbed out of the cruiser and ran to the porch. In a low voice Alex explained what had happened. She ended with, "We'll wake him up and take him back to Tinch's place if he'll go. If not, I don't know what I'm going to do with him this time of night. If I call in Child Protective Services, it will be a few hours before they get here."

Addison frowned. "Has anyone examined the boy?"

"Not yet. The night shift has its hands full dealing with his mother's suicide and the drugs we found scattered around her place. At last report she had no next of kin to notify."

Addison was all business. "I'll take a look at the boy. If he's been living in a trailer with rats, there's no telling what he's been through." She looked at Tinch as if just noticing the cowboy standing beside the sheriff.

She had no idea why he was involved in this mess, but he might as well help. "Why don't you make a few of those egg sandwiches you're famous for, and a pot of coffee? When I'm finished, I'd like to make sure he eats something before you take him back."

She disappeared into the house.

"Bossy, isn't she?" Addison heard Tinch comment. "Expects her orders to be followed, I'm guessing."

"She's right," the sheriff said. "I should have had him checked out at the hospital first. I was just thinking about how frightened he looked and how being with you might help. I was worried more about him having just lost his mother than what would be the usual procedures in a case like this."

"Bringing him to my place obviously didn't work." Tinch walked into the house and headed for the kitchen. "You want an egg sandwich, Sheriff? Four are no harder to make than two, and I plan to have one."

"Sure, but I need to call Phil Gentry and tell him he can

call it a night. He's been on overtime for five hours. There's no sense having him waiting at your place if we know the boy is here."

"Tell him to turn off the lights when he leaves, would you?"

Tinch walked to the bedroom door and saw Addison in the shadows. The only light was a yellow slice from the bathroom. She looked like a ghost in her white coat and pale skin and hair, but there was a kindness, a gentleness in the way she touched the boy.

"Jamie," she said as her hand brushed his shoulder. "Jamie, are you all right?"

The little boy moved and looked up at the doc. Tinch expected him to bolt, but he just stared at her with eyes almost too big for his thin face.

"You're an angel, aren't you?" he said. "My mommy said if she ever went away an angel would come take care of me. She'd watch over me and make sure no one would hurt me."

"Then I'm your angel, Jamie." Addison clicked on the nightstand light. "I'm here to help you, but first I have to make sure you're not hurt."

"The bad guys didn't hurt me when they came this time 'cause I hid real good, but I think they hurt my mommy. I heard her scream a few times, and then they came out and looked around. I don't think they knew I was there." The tiny boy moved into her arms, and for a few minutes Addison just held him. "She told me never to bother her when she was asleep with the door closed, so I didn't, even when I got hungry.

"I think the bad men were looking for something, but I don't think they found it. They didn't find me either. Mom showed me a place under the table to hide. In the day it's dark and hard to get to, but at night no one can see anything under there."

Tinch watched as she picked Jamie up and moved to the bathroom. As the doctor pulled off the boy's dirty clothes, he saw her examine him for bruises or broken bones. Then she helped him step into the shower. While he played with the warm stream of water, the doctor washed dirt off.

She glanced toward the door and saw Tinch. "Did you hear what he said?"

Tinch nodded. "It may not have been a suicide."

"Tell the sheriff. And tell her the boy is covered with bad bruises. I'm guessing they're about a week old. It looks like someone hit him across the back of the legs and over his back with something about the size of a broom handle. There are also bruises on his upper arms left by the grip of a big hand. He was either jerked around during the beating or held down while he was being hit."

Tinch's gut tightened.

Addison grabbed her medicine bag and went back into the bathroom. Tinch didn't trust words. He walked to the kitchen and forced himself to make eggs even though every cell in his body wanted to go after whoever had beaten Jamie.

When the sheriff walked back in, she took one look at Tinch and said, "What is it? What's wrong?"

Tinch filled her in on what the boy had revealed.

Alex lowered her head and took a deep breath. "If that's true, we may be dealing with a murder and not just a suicide or accidental overdose. She might have been running from them and they caught up with her. I've heard of it happening. It's almost a free crime to kill a druggie. All you have to do is give them too much and they're dead."

"Why would drug dealers kill a druggie? Wouldn't that be bad for business?"

"Maybe she worked for them. Maybe she wanted out. Maybe she threatened to turn on them and go to the cops." Alex shook her head. "But they'd have to have done something really bad to make her even threaten something like that. Even if she was using, she'd have to know that threatening a drug dealer could be a death sentence."

Tinch raised his head. "What if they did do something terrible, like beat her kid?"

Alex met his stare. "Did someone beat the boy?"

"Doc says he's covered in deep bruises."

Alex began to pace. "If Jamie saw the men come in and go into the bedroom, then he's a witness. The men may be murderers, and the only one who could ID them is that little boy. If word gets out that this is a possible murder, the men *will* come after him."

"You mean, they'd come to kill him."

Alex agreed. "I can't lock a kid up, but we have to keep him safe."

Tinch gripped the table with both hands. "Who knows you took him?"

"There were several people watching: the EMTs, my deputy, people around the trailer park."

"Who knows you brought him to my place?"

"Just Gentry and me. I didn't tell anyone else what we found. No one saw the will but Phil and me. The envelope was still sealed and scattered amid trash. The minute I saw your name, I knew what I had to do. All I could think about was getting the little boy out of there before they brought his mother's body through. I didn't want him to see her dead, so I didn't stop to talk to anyone."

"Good." Tinch forced himself to calm down. "Call Gentry back and tell him not to write up a report or tell anyone about the boy. The fewer people who know where he is, the safer he'll be."

"Right." She followed his logic. "Even if the bad guys were watching with the crowd, they won't be able to follow a paper trail if there isn't one. I'll issue a statement that Jamie has been turned over to Child Protective Services in Amarillo and that we are looking for relatives."

"Lori Anne didn't have any other kin after her mother died, and neither did her father. I'm thinking her little half sister may have been in the same boat. If she left her kid to Lori Anne, whom she hadn't spoken to in years, there must not be anyone else."

"Then," Alex smiled, "it should be real interesting who shows up to claim the boy."

"I'll keep him safe here." He faced her directly. "You were right to bring him to me, Sheriff."

"For the time being, I agree. If or when his blood relative shows up, then we'll handle it from there."

The doctor walked out of the bathroom carrying her little patient wrapped in a towel. "Agree to what?" she asked as she sat down still holding him.

Alex said they'd talk about it later.

Addison nodded and asked the sheriff if she could grab a shirt from the stack of clean laundry by the kitchen door.

As Alex moved to the dresser, Addison met Tinch's gaze, and she didn't miss that his anger matched her own. She also knew without asking that he'd protect the boy, whether he was a relative or not.

"I found a red Texas Tech shirt, will that do?" Alex said when she returned.

Addison looked down at the boy. "You want to wear a Tech shirt? It's like a football shirt."

He nodded and slipped off her lap. As he raised his arms for the shirt, the doctor let the towel fall. Tinch saw the bruises striped across the boy's back and legs. He thought for a moment that he might pass out. The cruelty of the act slammed against a heart Tinch would have sworn hadn't beaten in three years.

The shirt hung like a nightgown to the boy's knees.

Tinch moved closer and knelt to the kid's eye level. "Jamie," he said in the same kind of low voice he used with horses.

Jamie leaned against the doctor and watched Tinch. His fingers gripped her wrist.

"I'm your uncle, Jamie. Until a few hours ago I didn't even know you existed, or that your mother was looking for me. But now that I know, I'm here to help you. Your mother and my wife were sisters. That makes me your uncle."

He looked at Tinch for a minute, then said, "My momma says you have horses. Is that true?"

"It's true. I raise a few head and take care of others that have been hurt. I've got a barn full right now. If you'd like to stay with me for a while, I could really use your help to take care of them."

"Can my momma come too?" His eyes bubbled with tears.

Tinch fought to keep from touching the boy. He didn't want to frighten him, but he couldn't lie. "No, son, your momma is dead. The sheriff told me."

Tears waterfalled over the boy's eyes as if he'd just remembered. "I know. The sheriff told me too."

"Do you know what *dead* means, Jamie?"

"Sure. My grandma died last year and my grandpa has been dead since before I can remember. It means that my momma isn't coming back. Not ever."

Tinch stood while the doc talked to the kid softly. The boy seemed to know more about death than he did. It had been three years since Lori Anne died, and Tinch hadn't cleaned out her closet or pulled the things she used off her side of the sink. He'd been acting like one day she'd just walk back into his life . . . like he'd tripped and fallen into hell and any day now he'd climb out and all would be the same as it had been before cancer came to visit.

Not ever, Tinch thought. *Not ever coming back*. He slammed into the reality of his life, and the blow hurt too deep for tears. Somehow he thought if he just didn't think, didn't live, he'd get past the mourning, but in truth, he couldn't get over it.

He moved to the kitchen, away from the others. As he cooked, three words kept rolling over and over in his mind. *Never coming back*.

By the time he got the egg sandwiches ready, the boy was playing with the kitten. He watched the kid eat and the cat clean up every piece he dropped. Somehow the kid's laughter let Tinch remember to breathe.

"You want me to take you and the boy back to your place when he finishes?" Alex whispered.

"It's a nice night. I could carry him across the field."

"I wouldn't mind driving you," Addison added in a whisper. "If you don't want to ride in a police car. Maybe it brings back bad memories."

The doc was looking at him again as if trying to figure out what felony he'd committed lately.

Tinch glared at her. "It doesn't."

"I can hear you all talking," the boy said. "I don't want to go anywhere. I want to stay with my angel doctor."

Alex smiled. "Don't you want to be with your uncle? He's a good cook."

"I want him to stay here too," Jamie said without looking up.

Tinch raised his eyebrow and looked at the doc.

"You two can have my bed and I'll sleep on the couch for tonight." She sat down and helped herself to half of Tinch's sandwich.

"Not bad," she added after her second bite. "If you're spending the night, you're cooking breakfast."

Tinch smiled. "Thanks for the invitation and the compliment on my cooking, but I don't want to put you out."

"No trouble. If you left, I probably wouldn't sleep anyway. The boy will feel safer with you around, and I'll feel better being able to see that he's safe, at least for tonight."

"I agree." For a moment she studied him, noticing he didn't blink or look away. "We can do this," he added with a slight nod.

"We can," she nodded back, sealing a pact between them.

Addison stayed with the boy as Tinch walked the sheriff out. The cowboy no longer frightened her, Addison realized. When she'd taken the time to look in his eyes, she'd seen an honesty that surprised her. She almost laughed aloud at her own fears. If he'd planned to rape and kill her, he could have crossed the land between their houses anytime the past few weeks. She'd even slept with her Mace next to her bed a few nights, just in case.

Now, somewhere out there was a real threat. No matter how much Addison wanted her peaceful little house to herself, the boy's well-being was more important. Tinch might be the fighter, but she was the healer. Right now, Jamie wanted them both.

An hour later, she awoke to the boy's crying. She slipped off the couch and tiptoed to her bedroom.

Tinch lay on his side with the boy in the middle of the bed. "I can't get him to stop crying, no matter what I say," he whispered.

Addison curled up around the boy on the other side of the bed. "Jamie," she whispered. "Jamie, do you want to hold my hand?"

The boy wiped his eyes. "Yes." He rolled to his stomach and held her hand. Then slowly, breath by breath, he went to sleep.

In the bathroom light's glow Tinch could see the doc's blue-gray eyes watching the boy. She looked so pale beside him with her light hair and long bare legs—like a porcelain statue, he thought.

She looked over the boy and saw Tinch watching her. "Go to sleep," she ordered in a whisper.

"Any chance you'll hold my hand till I do?"

Addison couldn't stop the smile. "Not one chance in a million."

When the boy was sound asleep, Tinch reached with his free hand to the blanket he'd tossed on the floor beside the bed. With one swing, he floated it over all three of them.

"Thanks," the doctor whispered.

"You're welcome." He grinned.

Chapter 17

AN HOUR BEFORE DAWN, REAGAN WALKED AMONG THE apple trees on her land and cried silently.

The autumn wind whirled around her, whispering of change in the dampness before sunrise. The past week had been day after day of settling, of moving from one life to another. She had details of her uncle's will to work out and plans to make for what he wanted done. He wanted money deposited for a new fire truck anonymously, and he wanted Foster and Cindy Garrison to have a house he owned in town that his sister had once lived in. Only he'd left a list of repairs he wanted done before they moved in, as if he thought the gift had to be perfect when it was given. Because the former home nurse and his wife had moved into a hotel after Jeremiah went to the hospital, Reagan wanted the repairs completed as fast as possible.

The Garrisons loved her uncle, and he'd known they'd lost their home a year before they'd come to help him. Jeremiah wanted them to have a home back, and as always, he wanted it done right.

Once she'd taken care of those details, he'd told her to get busy with the fall work in the orchard. She could see through his plan. He wanted her busy so she wouldn't spend her time grieving for him.

She knew what she had to do, but she felt so hollow inside she wasn't sure her whole body wouldn't implode. Every day for a week, details and work had kept her running. Still, when her head hit the pillow, she couldn't sleep. In the back of her mind one fact kept circling. Noah, her closest friend in the world, hadn't bothered to come, or even call. What if he was hurt somewhere? What if he'd had a car accident? What if a bull had finally killed him? What if he no longer cared or remembered her?

Forcing herself to walk back to the house, Reagan didn't even bother to push the tears off her cheeks. She just ignored them, feeling like the only way she could survive another day was to become hard as rock and feel nothing, like she had years ago when she'd been running the streets alone.

The memory of all those years when no one cared about her, when no one loved her, came back like an avalanche of ice washing over her, freezing her to the bone. She remembered waiting in a hallway of a big building when she'd been four or five. People passed her for what seemed like hours and no one stopped. No one even looked at her. She'd been told to wait and not move. So she sat, her things in a bag on one side of her and a bottle of water someone had given her on the other. When a woman came to get her, Reagan was scolded for spilling the water. No one noticed she'd also wet her pants. They just moved her to another chair, another bench, another house, and so on.

Everywhere she moved was always temporary. It was never home. Never right. Until, finally, on a rundown farm on Lone Oak Road, she'd found her home, and no matter what happened she'd never leave. She'd become a Truman as truly as if she'd been born on a branch of the family tree. She knew all the old stories and the names of all the relatives who had passed on. She knew every inch of the land.

As she walked out of the trees, she saw Brandon "Big" Biggs standing beside his truck waiting for her. In his work coat and the beard he'd started growing, he looked like a bear dressed up in a man's clothes. He'd called her every night from his job. He'd even called Saturday morning to tell her he wouldn't be in until Monday. From the looks of him, Big had left the job and driven through the night to reach her.

With a sob, she ran toward him, needing someone to hold her before she shattered completely.

He caught her in a welcome hug and lifted her off the ground. He didn't ask her why she was walking in the cold. Big never questioned her. He was first and always her friend. Maybe because his parents hadn't wanted him either, he always seemed to know when she needed him to stand close.

He shifted, lifting her legs and carrying her into the house. "Have you slept, little one?"

She shook her head, not remembering the last time she'd even tried. For the past two, maybe three days she'd sat on the porch watching the night and wondering if there had been anything she could have done to keep her uncle alive for just a few more months, a few more years. Then maybe she'd have been ready to let him go.

"He's gone," Reagan whispered.

"I know. That fact's not going to change, Rea."

Big carried her up the stairs and into her bedroom. He pulled the covers back with one hand, dropped her on the bed, then tugged off her boots and wet jacket. Without a word he tossed his own coat on the floor and crawled into bed with her.

He cuddled her close against him and kissed her forehead. "When you stop shivering, I'll go turn up the heater."

Bundling the covers around her, he fussed over her.

"Just stay with me," she whispered. "I don't want to be alone."

He sat up and leaned away from her.

She stared at his back, wishing she could take the words back. He was a good friend, but no one should see her so broken.

Then she realized he was removing his sweatshirt.

A moment later, he was back, scooping her up against him. "Go to sleep, Reagan. I'm staying with you till you run me off. In the meantime, maybe we'll both get some needed sleep."

Reagan closed her eyes and let out a breath, warm against this bear of a man. "Thanks," she whispered as she relaxed into sleep.

Four hours later when she heard a pounding on the door, Reagan cuddled deeper against Big. The last thing in the world she wanted to do was wake up and face the world.

"Honey," he whispered as his hand cupped the back of her head and tugged. "You got to wake up. Someone's pounding on the door like all hell's broke loose."

Reagan tried to think of swear words to put together to let him know how little she cared, but he was pushing her out of bed.

"It might be important," he said.

She stumbled out of the bedroom and was halfway down the stairs when the front door came flying into the foyer, knocking over the line of framed pictures of all the old Truman relatives.

"Rea!" Noah yelled. He stepped over the lumber and glass as he looked around. "Rea, are you here?"

The shock of seeing Noah after months of missing him made her light-headed, and she sat down on the step. As always he was dressed western in jeans, a wool shirt tucked into his slim waist and boots, but this time he looked thinner, older, harder than when he'd left six months ago. Same beautiful almost-black hair, same brown eyes, same handsome face but no easy smile.

It took him a few seconds, but he finally looked up. He didn't look like he'd shaved in days. He shoved his Stetson back and smiled just like he always did as if playing to a crowd. "Hi, Rea. I came as soon as I heard."

"Noah?" She hadn't called him last night. For once, she hadn't even sent him a text.

"Yep, it's me." He started up the stairs. "Dear God, I've missed you, Rea." A smile dimpled his cheek. "I've even missed that wild hair of yours. Don't tell me you always wake up with it looking like that . . . a red ball of fuzzy fire."

Reagan brushed the side of her hair, knowing that it was hopeless. It had gotten damp during her walk and had probably curled into the tumbleweed style she faced every morning.

Before he reached her, Reagan heard heavy footsteps behind her.

Noah looked up and frowned. "What are you doing here, Biggs?"

"Sleeping," Big answered simply.

Reagan saw in Noah's face what he thought and knew she'd better act fast or both men would be tumbling down the stairs fighting.

"Uncle Jeremiah's dead," she said, half crying and half screaming.

Both men started patting her, trying to comfort her. Noah never could stand to see her cry, and Big was more worried about her than Noah. If a fight broke out, Noah would go all out, and Big, for her sake, would probably try not to hurt the bull rider. Of course, if Noah got a good punch in, Big would probably fall on the cowboy and crush him. She figured as long as she was crying, they wouldn't think to start swinging.

Amid all the comforting and crying, the doorbell rang. For a moment, Reagan couldn't figure out what it was. Everyone who came to the place always went to the back door, or knew they'd be welcome to come on in so they didn't bother with the bell.

She looked down and around Noah to see Sheriff Alexandra Matheson standing as if waiting for someone to open the door, which was lying in several pieces on the floor.

"Is something wrong here?" Alex had her hand on the butt of her gun and she was staring at her brother Noah as if she didn't recognize him. "Was there a break-in?"

Noah straightened. "No, it was me, Sis. I thought something must have happened to Reagan, and when I noticed the door was locked, I knew something was wrong and I was right. The house has been invaded by Biggs here. You need to do your duty as sheriff and arrest him."

Big looked confused, then angry. "I didn't invade. I walked in carrying Reagan after I found her outside cold and crying." He glared at Noah. "And I locked the door. You're the one who broke it down, not me."

The sheriff looked like she'd already had a long morning. "Reagan, you got any coffee? I could use a cup before I arrest both of these guys. Brother or no brother, Noah, knocking down the door just doesn't seem right."

Reagan led the sheriff to the kitchen while Big and Noah continued to yell at each other as they picked up the pieces of the door and tried to put it back together.

Once in the kitchen, Alex removed her hat and watched Reagan make coffee, "You okay, Reagan? I'm real sorry about your uncle."

"I will be. He lived a long life. I guess I should be thankful for that and not so selfish to wish him here. His sister, Beverly, said to me once that to wish for someone not to die is to wish them one less day in heaven."

"I remember your grandmother," Alex said. "She was a nice lady, as friendly as Jeremiah was cold."

Reagan concentrated on the coffee, not wanting to let Alex see her eyes and guess the truth. Beverly had just been an old lady at a nursing home Reagan became friends with as she cleaned her room. She'd told Reagan about Harmony, Texas, and when Reagan decided to run, she took Miss Beverly's last name. That was how she ended up at the Truman place five years ago.

Alex continued, "He and Beverly never got along, you know." Alex glanced back toward the front door. "I know how he felt. I love my little brother Noah, but most of the time he's home I'm frustrated with him."

"I guess brothers and sisters don't always become best friends. Uncle Jeremiah never talked about Beverly, but I found a box of birthday cards she'd sent him all her life. The fact that he kept the cards says something. They might have not been close, but they were still family."

"Nobody got along with your uncle Jeremiah, but he will be missed. I've been sheriff for almost eight years, and he still treated me like I was a kid trying to steal his apples. I think he was a good man who loved his privacy, and," she added, "he loved you."

Reagan smiled. "I know. I'm not sure why. Maybe because he saw that I just needed someone to care about me, but I never doubted his love."

The two men in the foyer finally smelled the coffee and wandered into the kitchen. Whatever they'd said to one another, or threatened, they didn't seem willing to share.

Alex fell into her big-sister mode. "I don't care why you broke that door, Noah, you're not leaving here until it's fixed."

She looked at Biggs. "You were right to lock the door, Big. I can't go into details, but for the next few days everyone should be on alert."

"What happened?" Noah asked. "You can trust us."

"If I tell you three, at least one of you will tell someone else, that you trust of course, and they'll tell someone and by nightfall it will be the main topic of discussion from the diner to the bar."

"You're right, Sheriff, Noah's got loose lips," Biggs said. "It goes with his shifty eyes."

"Me!"

Alex held her hand up. "Don't start or I swear I'll take you both in, brother or not, and put you in the same cell until you fight it out once and for all." She waited until they both looked calm. "Just be aware that there is a possible danger in town. A real danger."

Noah nodded as if he'd been talking to himself. "Then it's final, I'll stay out here with Reagan to keep her safe."

"You? What makes you think you'd be any help?" Big shouted. "Being able to stay on a bull for eight seconds doesn't make you a guard. Hell, you're the one who knocked down her door. And I can't help noticing that this danger hanging around town seems to have come in about the same time you did."

"I'm staying to protect her," Noah said.

"Fine. I'm staying to protect her from you."

"Me?" Noah looked hurt. "You're the one who was sleeping with her when I got here." He glanced at Reagan. "Which, by the way, I want to talk to you about as soon as we're alone."

"You're not going to be alone." Big grinned. "Because I'm going to be right next to her day and *night* until this trouble leaves."

Noah took the challenge. "Then there will be three of us in the bed."

Alex looked at Reagan. "You sure you don't want me to lock them up?"

"No, they're just like pit bull puppies. They're just playing around." She handed them each a cup of coffee and a cinnamon roll, loving their arguing, knowing that they both loved her and were hoping they'd keep her mind off all she had to live through today.

Her life was starting to sound like a soap opera with the volume turned up too loud. She could almost hear Uncle Jeremiah laughing all the way from heaven. He liked both "the boys," as he called them. He'd complain that Noah probably had brain damage from falling off too many bulls, and Biggs was so big he'd eat them out of house and home.

"Pick one," he used to say, "and I'll run the other one off with the shotgun."

"I can't," she'd always answer. "I love them both in different ways."

He'd always walk off down the hall, mumbling that he maybe should shoot himself so he wouldn't have to listen to them boys fight over his niece.

Chapter 18

When Addison awoke, the little boy, Jamie, was cuddled against her warm and still sound asleep. The cowboy uncle was nowhere in sight, which worried her full awake.

Carefully, she slipped from the bed and pulled on a clean pair of scrubs. Tying her hair back, she walked toward the kitchen.

"Morning, beautiful," Tinch said from where he sat making notes on what looked like a corner of a paper towel. The kitchen table was small and paint chipped, but the picture window beside it faced the sunrise, making the area shine golden.

"Coffee," she whispered, following the smell.

He grinned as he watched her. "It was nice sleeping with you last night, Doc. I'll never forget it."

Addison frowned at him. "I bet you say that to every girl you sleep with."

"I can't lie. I probably have."

"Hundreds of them, I'm guessing." She straightened her back as she spooned sugar into her cup. "Men like you are all alike." She'd heard her friends talk about them in college. Good-looking, wild cowboy types who hang out in bars like fishermen looking for their next catch, and if they didn't get in a fight by last call, a different girl got reeled in every night.

"Men like me?" he said, leaning forward to lower the front two legs of his chair to the linoleum floor as he stuffed the paper towel scrap in his pocket.

She poured her coffee. "Men like you, reckless and free. Wild with no strings." The night's stubble on his chin and his wrinkled unbuttoned shirt did nothing to take away from his solid good looks.

"So, let me get this straight, Doc. You think I'm wild?"

She couldn't believe he managed to pull off a surprised look even though she caught the hint of a grin.

"I met you while I was patching you up, remember. Must have been a slow night, cowboy. You didn't go home with a bar butterfly."

"They're called barflies, not butterflies, and if I remember that night, I went home with you."

"You were too drunk to drive." She swallowed her first coffee of the day and frowned at how strong he'd made it. "Just a regular Saturday night for a man like you, I'm guessing."

"Oh, right." He raised his eyebrow. "Not to mention bleeding and passing out from loss of blood."

"Must have been a real hit to your ego that I didn't stay to tuck you in."

Tinch frowned. "Wait a minute, Doc. How did we get off on the wrong foot this morning? Do you always wake up in rattlesnake mood? If so, I swear I'm never speaking to you again until after noon."

"Forget it," she snapped, more angry at herself than at him. As she passed him, she patted his arm, wishing she could erase away her words. She had no business running down his lifestyle. He hadn't broken any rules last night.

"We've got more important things to worry about than your conquests and fights at the bar."

She stared out the window, refusing to look at him three feet away. After a long silence, she whispered, "I'm not a morning person, I guess." He was right; all he'd said was good morning and she'd jumped on him. She barely knew the man. He had a right to live his life any way he wanted. It was nothing to her if nightly orgies went on at the farm next door. "I've had a long week." It wasn't an apology, just a statement.

"And you didn't sleep worrying about the boy," Tinch said as he stood and moved just behind her.

"How do you know?" She crossed her arms over her breasts, suddenly feeling the cold as she leaned against the window frame.

"Because," he whispered, now even closer. "I was awake watching you try to sleep. Every time you relaxed and almost drifted off, you'd jerk awake as if some internal alarm went off."

"I wanted to make sure the boy was safe." She didn't add that she knew, with all the excitement, if she'd allowed herself to sleep, she'd be letting her guard down.

"I was right there. You were both safe." He stood so near she could feel his words against her ear.

Closing her eyes, she leaned back into his warmth. Just for a moment she wanted to believe she could lean on a man without him trying to take control.

He wrapped his arms around her and pulled her back against his warm chest. For a while he just rocked her gently in his solid arms.

"We'll figure it out, Doc. We'll protect the boy until the sheriff knows no one is looking for him. You don't have to do it alone. I don't have to do it alone."

"Can we protect him?" She wasn't sure, and the boy's life might depend on her. "My almost-fiancé back home said I didn't have a mothering bone in my body, so children wouldn't be part of our bargain. He . . ."

Tinch whispered in her ear. "He was an idiot."

"What makes you say that?" She tugged a few inches away and faced him. Everyone she'd ever known had always bragged about what a wonderful man Glen Davidson was. Top of his class. The best in his field. Destined for greatness in research. No one had ever called him an idiot.

"Because," Tinch whispered. "He let you go."

"No," Addison shook her head. "He's waiting for me to answer his proposal."

"You don't love him." Tinch brushed a strand of loose hair back behind her ear.

"What makes you say that?" Logic told her she should put more distance between them, but she didn't step back.

"Because, Doc, if you loved the guy, you'd answer him and he wouldn't be an *almost-fiancé*."

Then, as if he'd done it many times, he raised his hand and moved his fingers into her hair. When she didn't protest, he closed the distance between them and kissed her lightly on the mouth. The shock of it rattled her all the way to her toes.

She'd wondered once if she stood on a train track and saw a train barreling toward her, would she jump or freeze? This morning, Addison learned the answer. She'd be flatter than a pancake on the tracks.

Addison just stood there as his hand gently curled into her hair. He tugged her to him and kissed her again with the same tenderness of a first kiss. When she swayed toward him, his arm moved around her and held her solid against him.

Closing her eyes, she went with the perfection of the kiss. She drifted in pure pleasure as his heartbeat pounded against hers. Never had a kiss affected her so. She'd been kissed with purpose, with passion, as foreplay and as routine, but never like this. Tinch kissed her as if there were no world other than right here, right now. He wasn't saying hello or good-bye. He wasn't starting something or ending something. He was simply and completely kissing her as no one from her first kiss in fourth grade to Glen's good-bye ever had.

Tinch pulled away so suddenly, she almost fell. Before

she could get her bearings on what had happened, he was half a room away.

"I'm sorry." He grabbed his hat. "You're right. I am wild. Not even housebroke, apparently. You'd be wise to stay as far away from me as possible, Doc."

Like a man on fire, he shot out of the house, yelling that he'd be back in an hour with clothes for the boy.

Addison walked to the porch and watched his pickup flying down the dirt road. Apparently Tinch Turner hadn't planned on kissing her and was more upset about it than she was.

Until this assignment, she'd followed every detail of a life her parents organized for her after she'd come home from her train wreck of a marriage at nineteen. She'd sworn she'd listen to her father from then on. The right schools, the safe vacations, the sensible friends. One heartbreaking six months was enough pain to last her a lifetime she'd convinced herself.

When she'd signed on for Harmony, Texas, for a year and packed her bags, she'd known this would be her last escape before forever settling for what was expected of her.

She was eating breakfast with Jamie and the kittens a little over an hour later when Tinch's pickup flew back up the drive.

He hauled in two huge bags. He smiled at Jamie but didn't even look at Addison.

"I got you some clothes, buddy," he said as if the kid were alone at the table. "If you're going to help me with the horses, you got to be dressed for it."

"Aren't you afraid someone in Harmony will notice you suddenly buying little-boy clothes?" Addison had worried about that last night. Harmony was too small; anyone buying clothes might be noticed, and that would somehow spread to the wrong people.

"They probably would have, only I drove over to Bailee. The guy who checked me out at the Walmart was still half asleep. He wouldn't have noticed if I'd bought a tank and a dozen grenades." Tinch still didn't meet her eyes as he set the one bag in the center of the living room and the other on the kitchen counter.

"You don't have to keep replacing the food you eat," she said, guessing what was in the kitchen bag.

He didn't answer as he pulled clothes out of the second bag. "Underwear, socks, jeans. I got two sizes, hoping one will fit, and a belt if neither does."

Jamie looked at the new clothes carefully, as if he'd rarely seen anything with a tag still on.

"This stuff is for me?" he asked.

"If you want it," Tinch said. "I'm new at this uncle thing, but I think uncles are supposed to buy clothes. I read that rule somewhere."

"Oh." Jamie nodded slowly.

"I bought several shirts. You pick the one you want to wear today." He spread them out on the coffee table. "I forgot pajamas. Men don't sleep in them, but I thought boys might."

Jamie shook his head. "I can sleep in my football shirt."

"That sounds good." Tinch propped a baseball cap on the boy's head, then took it off to adjust it.

He took his time letting the boy pick out what he wanted to wear, then handed him a new toothbrush and comb. "Can you take care of this?"

Jamie nodded. "I'm four years old."

"I thought so."

When the boy left the room to brush his teeth, Addison asked Tinch, "How'd you guess his shoe size?"

"I measured it against my hand while he was asleep." Tinch didn't look at her. "They didn't have boots, but I'll get him a pair as soon as we know it's safe for him to go to town."

Addison moved into his line of vision. "Look, Tinch, about what happened before you left. It was just a kiss. I'm sure you've kissed a hundred women. It just happened, that's all. I'm not mad about it as long as you understand I have no interest in a repeat performance. I know we've kind of been tossed together, but there's no reason we—"

"You think I've kissed a hundred girls?"

Addison almost laughed. "No man kisses like you do

without a great deal of practice. I've never—" She broke off, not wanting to tell this man any of her private life.

"It won't happen again," he said quickly. "You're right. It never should have happened in the first place."

"Good," she managed as she began helping him pick up the clothes. Wanting to get back to the polite strangers they'd been developing, she added, "You did a good job of picking out the kid's clothes."

He seemed to understand what she was trying to do. "I don't have any kids, but on my mother's side I'm kin to all the Mathesons in town. Which means I get invited to at least one or two birthday parties a month. Lori Anne always used to want to take clothes as gifts. . . . Of course, since she's been gone I just send a gift certificate."

"Lori Anne was your wife?" Somewhere in the back of her mind Addison remembered one of the nurses saying that Tinch Turner's wife had died of cancer.

"Yeah," he said, looking away from her. "I bought a phone." He changed the subject abruptly. "It's nothing fancy, but it's a way for the sheriff or you to get hold of me if you need me." He looked at it as if he had no idea how to use the thing. "I'll try to remember to keep it with me."

Addison took the small phone from his hand. "If you'll see how Jamie is doing, I'll program the sheriff's number in along with my cell phone. There's a house phone here still working, but I'm not even sure of the number. All you have to do is push two for me, three for her, and hit the green button."

While he helped Jamie lace up his new shoes, Addison used her phone to text the sheriff Tinch's number and add him to her list.

"If ever you need me, just push the button and send."

"I won't call unless it's an emergency."

"I understand. I'll be on my way when I pick up."

Tinch looked at the phone, then at her. She expected him to say something funny, like he now had a doctor on call, but he didn't.

"Thanks." He met her gaze for the first time since the kiss. "I'll do my best to keep up with this."

Tinch knelt down to the boy's level. "We're going next door to my place to work for a while. No matter what's going on, the horses need to be fed."

Jamie shook his head. "I don't want to leave my angel. Can she come too?"

Tinch looked up at Addison without smiling. "She can if she wants to, and so can the kittens, but I'm sure the doc's got lots to do."

"I usually go in and work on paperwork on my day off." She had no idea if she was helping or hurting his plans. "But I might come back from town around lunchtime and bring you two a box of tacos."

Tinch frowned, and she guessed she'd said the wrong thing. He'd probably hoped for a day without her.

Jamie slipped his hand into hers and smiled. "I don't like onions, or lettuce, or tomatoes on mine."

"Got it." She turned to Tinch. "How do you like yours?"

One look told her he wasn't thinking about lunch. He took a deep breath and said in a low voice, "Any way at all is fine."

Chapter 19

~~~

REAGAN SPENT THE MORNING MOVING FOSTER AND HIS wife into their new home. She could have thought of no better use for the little house her uncle owned in town than to give it to the two people who'd stood beside her all during his illness. Foster was a good nurse and he'd find other work, but for now, at least, he and his wife wouldn't have to worry about a roof over their heads.

Midafternoon, she drove back to Jeremiah's little farm on Lone Oak Road. Only it wasn't his anymore. It was hers. It had been for a long time, but as long as her uncle was alive she always thought of it being his even if he had put her name on the deed. Jeremiah had slowed down last year, but he never stopped working in the orchards. He had one old stand of trees near the border to the Matheson place and another a few hundred yards behind the house. The second one he'd started for her, and it would bear fruit next fall. He'd also overseen the building of a new barn to hold the equipment Reagan wanted to help in the packing and shipping of apples. Their apples were perfect for making jam and pies. She planned to sell their crop to small-time canning houses within a few hundred miles, until someday she'd be shipping across the states.

As she drove home, she thought of her uncle and how everything he'd done since the day she stumbled onto his place had been to ready her to be able to take over.

Even the business degree she was working on, he'd suggested so she could read and understand legal papers. "Never let anyone handle your books," he'd said. "Always write your own checks."

When she reached the house, she noticed Noah's truck was back, but Big was probably still at work. She'd put them down the hall from her, since they'd both decided to keep her company for a while. To her surprise they'd gone to bed without a fight. Knowing they both were near helped her sleep, though she couldn't imagine enduring Noah's suggestion that they all three sleep in the same bed.

After checking on the work going on in the new barn, she walked through a stand of elm toward the house and found Noah asleep in the hammock. For a man who rode lightning for a living, he sure needed his sleep. When she touched his boot, he raised his hat. "Afternoon," he said, as if they were just passing strangers. "Did you get everything taken care of, Rea?"

"I think so. The funeral home was my last stop. I just wanted to thank Mr. Wright, but he'd given his house-keeper a ride to her doctor's visit. The bookkeeper at the funeral home told me their little housekeeper is going to pop any day now."

"Where's the father of the baby-to-be?" Noah didn't sound very interested. "I know he was some bum of a guy who tried to kill Biggs during the last tornado that blew through here, but where is the bum now?"

"You're not keeping up." She slapped his boot. "The guy is doing twenty in Huntsville. Seems the law doesn't like a man breaking into a funeral home to kidnap his ex-girlfriend and shooting a fireman, even a volunteer one, along the way."

"Tell me, Rea, does Big have a scar across his chest from that bullet he took?"

"I don't know," Reagan answered, just as she figured out why Noah would ask. She'd never seen Big without a T-shirt.

"That's good news, at least," he answered with a smile.

She thought she smelled whiskey on his breath but didn't want to think about the possibility that he might have spent the afternoon drinking with one of his cousins.

"How about you swing with me, Rea? Come here." He tugged her onto the hammock.

Reagan pushed away, fighting him as she tried to get her balance.

Noah lifted his hands. "Okay, okay, I won't touch you. Just lie next to me and enjoy the silence. It's beautiful leaning back and looking at autumn drift down. I promise I won't touch you till you figure out you like me again."

She settled. "You can't just disappear and come back and expect everything to pick up like it was the day you left. Half the time, when you don't call after a ride, I think you're somewhere dead in the dirt. Caring about you wears me out, and you don't even know about it. I can't even watch you on TV. I think, what if you fell and got hurt. I wouldn't be close enough to help."

"I know." He pushed with one foot and made the hammock swing. When it did, their shoulders bumped. "I guess I just think nothing ever changes around here. The way I feel about you doesn't change either." He was silent for a while, then said, "I am really sorry about your uncle. Sadness stays raw for a while, but it'll ease eventually."

"It was his time." She didn't want to think about the pain; she was struggling to keep from falling apart. The entire world seemed off balance without her uncle. She knew it was time to start trying to pull herself back together, but she wasn't sure where to stand to make it happen.

"What you going to do with the place?" Noah broke the silence.

Reagan turned to look at him, surprised he'd even ask. "I'm going to live here. We've got the harvest in full production, and as soon as it's finished, I'll need to get the trees ready for winter." Her mind began to plan her days in order of what had to be done. "I'll have to hire more help, but I can manage."

He didn't comment for a long time, then said, "I'm glad you're going to stay. Your roots run deep here."

"Don't yours?" she asked. He was a real McAllen. She was only a make-believe Truman. His great-grandfather had started it all. The town, the ranch, the family.

Noah shook his head. "I don't know anymore. This town, even my place that Dad deeded to me, feels like a part of my past. Like it belongs to a me I used to be. The longer I'm away, the less of a part of my life it becomes. I got to stay out on tour to keep my ranking, so even if I did get homesick, I couldn't come back often."

He was frightening Reagan. He'd always had this dream to make it big in rodeo, but she thought he'd eventually give it up and come home. Noah had been her best friend. He was the first boy she really kissed. He was the only one she thought about spending the rest of her life with.

Only right now, she wasn't sure she knew the man he had become. She wasn't sure she even liked the man he was now. This Noah was in some kind of grand parade, and all he seemed to be seeing was the gutter below. She knew he was pulling in big winnings from the rides but wondered how much of that money, if any, he'd put away.

She put her hand in his. Somewhere, the old Noah was still there. She had to believe that.

Big's huge pickup turned down the driveway, and Noah helped Reagan out of the hammock. They met him at his truck.

The construction worker climbed out and nodded toward Noah. "Have a good day doing nothing, cowboy?"

"Great." Noah smiled. "It's hard work figuring out how to work doing nothing into a schedule."

"Don't suppose you cooked dinner?"

"Nope. I was hoping you would bring bags of food home, since Reagan's been working in town all day. One of us should have been thoughtful and picked up takeout on his way home."

It was Big's turn to smile. "I got a better idea; if Reagan wants to, we could go down to Buffalo's. There won't be anyone much there. My brother and Beau are practicing a few new songs. We could listen to them while we eat."

"I could warm up some leftovers." Reagan frowned at her own suggestion. "You wouldn't believe all the food that was delivered last week after the funeral."

Both men turned toward the truck.

Reagan gave in. She didn't want leftovers either.

Thirty minutes later they were at a corner table at Buffalo's. Or rather Big and Reagan were; Noah was at the bar talking, as every man who walked in the place insisted on buying him a drink.

"He's a hero," Reagan said as she lifted her glass to Noah's back.

"I guess, though it don't seem so heroic just to ride a bull." Big didn't look in Noah's direction. "Think they may have bravery mixed up with stupidity."

She took a bite of her fries. "You may be right. I think he's been working on pickling what sense he has left all day. I noticed several empty beer cans scattered around the house, and a whiskey bottle was on the counter in the kitchen."

They ate and listened to Beau play songs he'd written that were deep and moving. For the first time in more than a week, Reagan forgot her troubles and just listened. She noticed that several people came in to do the same. They sat close to the dance floor and watched the kid on a little stage behind chicken wire play song after song.

A half dozen nursing students, who must have just finished a shift, and several men who looked like they worked

with Big on construction crews also wandered in. Big might
have talked them into coming in, but they stayed to listen.

When Noah didn't circle back to the table, Big ate the
cowboy's basket of wings and fries.

"He won't be happy when he sees the empty basket."
Reagan giggled.

"He'll be too drunk to notice. I've been watching him.
I'm surprised he's still standing."

After a few more songs, Reagan was ready to go, but she
didn't want to hurry Big. He was so proud of his little
brother.

Then she noticed he was watching the crowd and not the
band. Correction, she thought, not the crowd, Big was concentrating on one table of nurses.

People were starting to dance to the slow, beautiful
music. All except one of the nurses had moved to the dance
floor. The one stood out from the others. She had to be
more than six feet tall, and though built in proportion, she
seemed huge among the smaller women. Not fat, really,
just big. Reagan thought she was pretty enough to be one of
those plus-size models, but the uniform wasn't very flattering on her.

"She's pretty," Reagan whispered to Big, knowing he'd
already noticed.

"I guess so. I've been watching, and no one asks her to
dance. Probably because she's a head taller than any of
these jerks." Big didn't take his gaze off the nurse. "I don't
like that she's getting her feelings hurt. Every time another
girl leaves the table she looks down like she was wishing
she could vanish."

Reagan didn't like seeing the nurse forgotten either.
"Why don't you ask her?"

"I don't know how to dance."

"She won't care. Just move slowly from one foot to the
other. The important thing is that someone asks her to
dance. Are you more worried about embarrassing yourself
or about her feelings?"

Big swore. "I don't give a damn about what anyone thinks of me."

"I know." Reagan laughed. "That's what makes you so darn lovable. Now go over there and help the poor woman out."

He nodded and slid out of the booth, then walked right over to the table that was empty except for one very pretty nurse, and offered his hand.

Reagan wasn't sure he said a word, but the girl took his hand and stood. They moved to the dance floor, and Big hadn't lied. He didn't know the first thing about dancing, but the nurse didn't seem to care. She smiled up at him and moved back and forth.

A few minutes later, when Noah sat down beside Reagan, he was well on his way to being blind drunk. He didn't seem to notice that he hadn't been the one to eat his dinner. He just swigged a longneck and watched the dance floor. "Is that Big dancing?" He squinted. "I'll be damned."

Anger sparked in Reagan. "At least he's sober. Which is more than I can say for you." She'd always hated it when Noah drank. He said things he didn't mean, then passed it off on the whiskey, like some alien took over his body after so many drinks and everyone should forgive him, or better yet feel sorry for him.

Noah looked at her with one raised eyebrow. "Did I sit down at the wrong table? What did you do with my friend Rea?"

"Shut up," she said. "Nothing's wrong with me. It's you, Noah. You're not the same. I want my Noah back. I want the Noah I love. The boy full of dreams. The guy who cared about this town and everyone in it."

He looked like she'd slapped him. "The boy grew up. He didn't stay around here like some people and refuse to change."

"I want the Noah I knew and trusted." She glared at him as if somewhere behind the bloodshot eyes her Noah were still there.

"I'm right here waiting, Rea. Waiting, as always, for you

to grow up. How long you think it'll be? You need to live another twenty years before we can act like two adults, or are you planning on being a virgin all your life?"

"I'm not the one wandering all over the country drinking and sleeping with every girl in every town I pass."

"No." Noah lowered his voice to a deadly level. "You're the woman who won't let anyone, even someone who loves her, touch her. Every time I look at you, I hate the fact that you let something that happened when you were a kid come between us. You always have, and I can only wait so long for you to get over whatever it was. You're the farmer, what is it they say about fruit left on the vine?"

She slapped him so hard everyone in the bar turned.

Big whispered something to his dance partner and stormed toward them. As far as he was concerned, whatever happened was entirely the cowboy's fault.

Reagan stepped into his path before he could beat the hell out of Noah. "Take me home," she said. Tears bubbled down her cheeks. "Please."

He gave Noah a kill-you-later look and walked out with her.

They didn't say a word when they got back to the farm. Big had never asked questions. He was her friend, without needing reasons.

She went straight to her room and paced to keep from crying. She felt like she'd cried a lifetime's limit of tears. The house was quiet except for Big moving around his room down the hall. She knew Noah wouldn't be coming back tonight. Maybe not for a long time. Reagan wasn't even sure how the fight started. She wasn't in a good mood. He was drunk. Who knew. Who cared.

She stripped and climbed into her old flannel pajamas and fuzzy red socks. It wasn't that cold outside, but she felt like her insides were freezing.

Even though she turned on every light in the room, the whole world seemed to be growing darker and the air thinning. Maybe she was having a nervous breakdown, or a heart attack. The possibility that Noah might have been right about her not growing up wasn't something she could accept. She was the mature one. She was the sober one. Just because she didn't want to jump into bed with him didn't mean she didn't love him. She liked kissing him. Someday she'd like making love to him too. But she didn't know how to start over every time he came home. She didn't know how to jump into the loving part.

Reagan whirled and stormed down the hall.

She banged on Big's door so loud it shook the second floor.

"Come on in, Reagan," he yelled. "We're the only two in the house; it's not like I don't know who is knocking."

She darted into his room. He stood a few feet away wearing only pajama bottoms. The sight of all that muscle and hair shocked her speechless. In all the time they'd been friends she'd never seen him without a shirt on. Noah must have known that when he'd asked about the scar. If there was one on Big's chest, the overgrowth of hair had completely hidden it.

"What do you want, Rea?" he asked as he set down the book he must have just pulled from the shelf behind him. "It's getting really late and I have to be at work at seven."

"Can I sleep with you?"

"Sure, honey." He stepped to the bed, pulled the covers up, and motioned her in, as if she were stepping into a car and not his bed.

Reagan climbed in before she changed her mind.

When he lay down, he didn't touch her. Big simply stacked his pillows, crossed his arms over his chest, and waited as if he'd seen the lightning and was holding his breath for the thunder.

"Aren't you going to touch me, make love to me, you know, sleep with me?"

He looked at her for a long minute, then said, "In that outfit, it's real tempting, but I don't think that's what you came in here for. If I believed you wanted me that way, I'd be a lucky man, but you don't."

She burst into tears, and he opened his arms to hold her.

Between sobs she mumbled how much she hated Noah and how she was a woman, not a girl.

Finally, when the tears stopped and most of the tissues in the box beside his bed were wadded on the floor, she sat up and brushed her hand across his chest. "How'd you get so much hair? You must have started growing it in grade school."

He grinned. "Don't you have hair on your chest? Let me see."

She slapped his chest laughing. "Not on your life, and no, I don't have hair. When people say you're a bear of a man, I didn't think to take it literally."

Big laughed, "My little brother is getting it too, big-time. I keep telling Border that he's wasting his time getting tattooed. By the time he's twenty no one will see them unless he shaves his whole body."

She laid her cheek on his chest. "Maybe you need all this hair to protect such a big heart."

"Well, don't go telling folks about my hair, or my heart. I might have to split a few heads open if they thought I was getting soft."

She smiled and cuddled beneath his arm. After a while, she said, "Noah called me a virgin."

"That's not a bad thing," Big said slowly, as if he felt he had to choose his words carefully.

"I know. But I'm not." The need to tell the truth had weighed too long on her mind. "I was raped when I was fourteen."

Big tightened his arm around her slim shoulders and pulled her close enough to kiss the top of her head. "I figured it was something like that. You want to tell me about it?"

"No. It was a long time ago." She waited awhile, knowing that some sorrows have to come out before a wound can heal. In a low voice, as if reading from a script, she began. "A group of girls and guys went out. One of the boys was old enough to drive and we all piled in, not really planning anything, just driving around, you know. The guys took me home last because I didn't have anyone waiting up for me.

Only we didn't go straight to my house. The kid driving turned off in the driveway of an old house that looked abandoned. They each took their time hurting me while the others stood outside the car holding the doors so I couldn't get out. When they were all finished, the driver dragged me out of the car and kicked me for scratching him, then left me to walk home. It was almost sunup when I made it in. I took a shower and told myself to forget it, but I couldn't."

"I'm sorry, Rea," he said simply, and she knew he meant it.

"Now that I've told someone, it doesn't weigh as heavy." She patted his fur. "How do I get over it?"

Somehow she knew this one man would know. When he was a kid, he'd been the biggest bully in town, and she'd always known he was trying to pay back an ounce of the hurt he'd had done to him.

"Maybe you don't get over it. Maybe you just get through it and spend the rest of your life moving one day further away from what happened."

She smiled up at him. "I love you, Big. I really do."

"I know. I love you, too. Now go to sleep before I start wondering what's under all that flannel and fuzz."

She laughed, pulled up the cover, and turned onto her side of the bed.

He reached and turned off the light. "Oh, by the way. Thanks for making me dance with that nurse."

"You're welcome. So, it wasn't so bad."

"It was good," he said. "So good we plan to do it again next week. Same time, same place."

She laughed. "Don't tell her you're sleeping with me."

"She wouldn't believe it anyway. I'm not even sure I do."

Chapter 20

TURNER RANCH

TINCH WORKED MOST OF THE MORNING WITH THE HORSES.
He liked having Jamie around. He helped out any way he
could, and on the gentler horses Tinch let the boy ride as he
walked the animals.

About one o'clock Addison showed up with a bag of
Mexican food, fast-food style. Tinch and Jamie stopped to
have lunch. The morning was cool, but without wind it
seemed perfect jacket weather. Tinch disappeared in the
house and grabbed a gallon of milk, glasses, and a cookie
jar before meeting them at a picnic table under a hundred-
year-old live oak his great-grandmother had planted out
back.

"How'd it go?" Addison whispered as she passed out
tacos and burritos.

"Fine. No problem. The kid never runs out of questions." What were the horses' names? Why would someone

hurt them? Why did Tinch have so many canned goods? How come he could cook?

"You any good at answering questions?" She smiled as he handed her a glass of milk.

"You should try me sometime, Doc," he said as he clicked his glass to hers in salute.

Jamie drank his milk and started on his second taco. Between bites he asked Addison questions.

His third question drew Tinch's attention.

"How come you're not married?" the boy asked.

Addison finished chewing and said simply, "I was once. It didn't work out."

"What happened?"

"We were too young. It turned out I wanted different things than he did. I think of it like a marriage that lasted a week, but breaking it took almost six months."

The boy didn't seem all that interested, but Tinch listened, waiting, until Jamie asked, "What kind of different things did you want?"

Addison shrugged. "I wanted to go to school and he wanted to travel. I wanted to settle somewhere and he wanted to live out of a van. I wanted to save my money, he wanted to spend it."

"That doesn't sound good."

"We should have talked about it before we got married. My parents told me it was all wrong from the first. When they told me to stop seeing him, I thought I'd show them, so we ran off."

"Did you love him?" Tinch asked.

She shook her head. "I was in love with the idea of love. I thought it would be romantic to be Gypsies, but after six months all I wanted was to go home. I wanted out of the marriage, and he must have felt the same way because he beat me to the door."

Tinch could think of a few more questions, but Jamie seemed more interested in his food. "You want some more milk?" Tinch asked, more to break the silence stretching than from any need to push the milk.

The boy looked surprised. "I can have more milk?"

"Sure." Tinch gulped down the lump in his throat. "You can have as much as you want." By the time he poured the kid another glass, Jamie had finished his second taco. Tinch reached for the cookie jar. "Since you've got milk left, you might as well wash down a few cookies."

The boy ate a half dozen cookies while Tinch finished his meal. The back view of his place spread out before him. The grass was still green, but the aspens along the creek half a mile away were beginning to turn yellow and brown. This was his favorite time of year. Lori Anne had loved the spring and got all excited every year when the earth began to bloom. Every March she'd start planting flowers too early, and the last frost would catch them, but she didn't care. She loved working in the dirt. She loved making things grow.

He fought down sadness, thinking about how she would have loved meeting Jamie.

Tinch stilled, his cup halfway to his mouth as he realized that he hadn't thought of Lori Anne all morning, until now. For three years she'd always been in the back of his mind if he was awake, but this morning she wasn't there. He had the feeling she'd somehow moved on, leaving a new hollow spot inside him.

Glancing over at Jamie, Tinch grinned. The kid was sound asleep, his head on an arm that rested on the table, a half-eaten cookie still in his hand.

He stood, lifted the boy slowly, and headed for the house.

He walked across the yard and up a few stairs to his study door at the side of the house. There he laid the kid on a long leather couch and covered him with a throw.

Jamie wiggled a little as Tinch tugged off his muddy tennis shoes, but he didn't wake. The kid had been at a run all morning, wanting to do everything, understand every detail.

Tinch stared down at him. He was a good kid with more than his full share of problems. He hadn't missed how dearly the boy loved animals. All morning he'd helped whenever he could.

Without turning on any lights, Tinch moved across the shadowy room to his desk and computers. He might not own a phone, but he had a computer system better than most banks. He followed the markets, ordered supplies, and communicated with everyone who needed his help with horses. The past few years, when he couldn't sleep at night, he'd started a blog about caring for horses that had thousands of readers.

He made sure the volume was off on the speakers and hoped the low sound of the printer wouldn't wake Jamie. As he walked out of the room, he left the door wide open so he could hear the boy if he yelled out.

Addison was right where they left her when Tinch made it back outside.

"He's asleep. I took him through the house twice this morning to go to the bathroom, so he knows his way around well enough to find us when he wakes." Tinch sat down across from Addison, not trusting himself to be closer. "Any news from town?"

Addison nodded. "I touched base with the sheriff. No one has asked about the boy yet, but one man called to see when Jamie's mother's funeral was. When the sheriff said they were waiting on next of kin, the caller hung up."

Tinch shrugged. "It could have been someone from the trailer park."

"Alex asked if I could stay with Jamie a few hours this afternoon while you go in and talk to Tyler Wright. She says if there's no family back in Kansas, the county will pay for the burial, but you might want to have some say in the service."

"I'll pay for the service. It's my responsibility." He looked at the doc. "Do you feel safe alone here with the boy?"

She nodded but didn't look too sure. "You'll be back before dark?"

"I'll be back before dark." He stood and began collecting the trash.

"I'll do the dishes," she said as she helped him.

He led the way into the kitchen and began stuffing the remains of their meal into a trash bin under the sink. When he looked up, Addison was still standing in the doorway.

"What is it?" he asked.

"Nothing." She finally moved. "I just didn't expect your house to look like this."

"Like what? Clean? I have a woman who comes in once a week."

"No, not just clean, but decorated and everything in order." She gave him a quick smile. "It's just that every time I see you, you look like you just stepped away from rolling in the dirt. I kind of thought you'd live in a cave." Her grin gave away her attempt at teasing.

Tinch frowned as if offended. "So you figured I'd live in a pigsty?" He walked across the room to a beautiful pine staircase. "Lady, every time you see me, I've been in a fight." He popped the buttons on his shirt. "The work I do with the horses is hard and dirty, so if you'll excuse me, I think I'll go clean up before I head to town."

He heard her laughter as he took the stairs two at a time in a hurry to hit the shower. Tinch wasn't sure if he wanted her to see that he could clean up, or if he just hated the thought that she was in his house. No one except the housekeeper had ever set foot in his place, not since Lori Anne died.

He walked across the wide bedroom and into his bathroom. As he stripped, he noticed Lori Anne's things lined up on one side of the sink, exactly as they had been the day she died.

The memory of his words to Jamie drifted into his mind. "Do you know what *dead* means, Jamie?" he'd asked, and the boy said simply that it meant someone's never coming back, not ever.

"Not ever." Tinch picked up the laundry basket beneath the sink and raked all her things into it.

He did the same to her drawer of makeup and the medicine cabinet on her side. After setting the basket in her closet, he stepped into the shower. He hadn't been saving them for her; all her things had been there for him. His Lori Anne was gone, and it was time he stopped pretending. He couldn't expect Jamie to understand death if he wouldn't face it himself.

An hour later he walked into Tyler Wright's office at the funeral home. One of his Matheson cousins, a lawyer who'd married Gabe Leary, joined him.

"Thanks for coming, Liz," he said as he gave her a light hug.

The petite blonde smiled. "Glad to help if I can." She laughed like a woman who laughs often. "I love leaving the girls with Gabe. He always gets that panic look in his eyes for a moment before he starts calling people to come over to help. Last week I spent a day at the office on an old case and he had my mother, my sister, my two great-aunts, and my niece as backup."

Tinch hadn't seen the Matheson clan in months, but he wasn't surprise when Liz dropped whatever she was doing to come when he called. Mathesons were like that. "I don't know what I'm getting into here, Liz. I don't even know if I have a right to make any decisions for Lori Anne's half sister."

Liz pulled a file from her bag. "Alex dropped by our place and filled me in on what happened. I'll check everything out once the autopsy is done. If Sadie Noble had no kin but the boy and she wanted you to have him, I'm guessing what you're doing is right with the law."

Tyler Wright walked in looking a little flustered. "I'm sorry to keep you waiting," he said, "but I just returned with my housekeeper from her checkup and it took forever. I guess I thought women who got pregnant simply waddled around until one day it popped out. I never dreamed it was so complicated." He laughed. "I must have made Autumn nervous because she made me let her out downtown, saying she needed to walk the last block alone. I would have followed her in the car, but she gave me that look that told me I'd better not even try. I wish my Kate were back. She'd know what to do."

Tinch almost felt sorry for the man. Tyler Wright seemed a man of order. He'd never seen him when his shirt wasn't pressed or his tie not perfectly tied. The funeral director always seemed a model for the perfect gentleman.

"How is Kate?" Liz asked, as if they were just in the funeral home director's office to visit. "I hear she's retiring from the army soon."

"She's off working somewhere right now, so I'm not sure how she is at the moment." Worry wrinkled his forehead. "Top secret stuff, you know. But she promised me she'd be home in a month. I'm counting the days, I can tell you."

Tinch had no idea what the man was so worried about. Tyler was one of those people who seemed to care about everyone. He wasn't surprised the man worried about his housekeeper, but she wasn't likely to get too lost in Harmony, and his future wife didn't look like the type who would be sent on a dangerous mission just before retirement.

Sitting down behind his desk, Tyler opened his book as if signaling that it was time to get down to business. Then he turned to them with his caring gaze and asked, "How may I help?"

Tinch waited a few heartbeats, hoping Liz would explain, but when that didn't happen, he began. "My wife's sister died, and I think my wife would like it if she could be buried close to her."

The funeral director nodded. "I've already checked with the cemetery, and there is a pair of plots just east of where your Lori Anne rests."

Tinch thought of screaming that his wife wasn't resting, but he knew the funeral director was just trying to be kind.

Tyler began to write. "The sheriff told me her name was Sadie Noble; do you know her birthday?"

"No."

"Was she ever married?"

"I don't think so." Tinch realized how little he knew.

"Her license listed her birth date as June 3, 1987, and she renewed it a few years ago still using the name Noble," Liz offered. "I've talked with the records office in Kansas City, and they have no record of her ever filing for a marriage license."

Tinch looked at Liz. He'd always thought of her as an airheaded cheerleader type who'd never grown up, but suddenly he realized he was wrong.

Tyler wrote down the information. "So, do you want just her dates of birth and death on her small stone?"

"No," Tinch decided. "Add '*Loving mother of Jamie*.'" He wanted the boy to know that no matter what happened with the results of the autopsy, his mother loved him. "And Jamie told me his mother's middle name was Ann. I'd like that added also."

Tyler smiled. "That sounds nice. Now, moving on."

Tinch lifted his hand. "Mr. Wright," he said. "I'd like everything else set up just like my Lori Anne had. Same casket, same flowers. Everything. When the body is returned and the paperwork is done, schedule a service in the chapel."

As always, the funeral director seemed to understand. "I'll take care of the details and let you know."

As Tyler stood to walk them out, Liz leaned forward in her chair. "Mr. Wright, would it be all right if I talked with my cousin for a few minutes longer? We'd like to use your office."

"Of course, dear." He hurried out, probably to go check on his housekeeper.

Tinch stared at Liz, trying to guess what she knew that couldn't wait. "What did you find out about Sadie Noble?" he asked directly.

She shook her head. "Nothing, but if you want, I could hire someone to tell us what the police report won't."

"I'd like that. If the boy is going to stay with me, I'll need to know as much about his life before as possible. If there is a direct relative claiming him, I want to know he'll be safe there."

"The boy got to you." Liz grinned.

Tinch thought of arguing, but he couldn't lie. "I just want to know he'll be taken care of. I don't think I'd be any good at it, but I want to make sure no one ever hurts him again." He smiled. "The kid's something, Liz. He likes to tickle horses under the chin, and then *he* laughs. Near as I can tell, he's had shit for a life, being moved around by a mother on drugs who didn't even make sure he had food all the time, but he still finds such wonder. He's four years old and he already knows what death is."

Liz put her hand on Tinch's arm. "I'll do everything I can; in the meantime, you've got to keep him safe and I have an idea that might help. My husband and his friend who bought Gabe's old place were specially trained to install security. It might be worth our time to install something that will let you know if anyone uninvited comes on your property."

They spent a few more minutes talking, and then Tinch followed her out on Lone Oak Road to Denver Sims's place. Denver and Liz's husband, Gabe, had been in the army together. They knew security. Within an hour they'd given him a list of everything he could do and packed Tinch's pickup with tools.

The two men followed Tinch home, and by dark they had a gate put up on the entrance to his property. One step onto his land was wired with sensors that set off a chime that sounded in every room of his house and the barn. If anyone drove onto his land, he'd know it.

When he finally waved them good-bye and walked back into the house, Tinch felt as tired and dirty as if he'd been working all afternoon with the horses.

Addison sat at the dining table working on her laptop, and Jamie played in the living area twenty feet away, with two boxes of dominoes he'd found.

"Thanks for staying with him," he said as he sat down.

"I didn't mind. Jamie's nice company." She stretched her long legs across one of the other chairs. "We walked around your place and then went through your drawers looking for something for him to play with."

"Good. Find out all my secrets?"

She raised her pen and tapped her cheek. "Of course. Apparently, I was wrong about you. Completely wrong. You read books about horses, nothing R-rated. Play stock market games all day on your computer and have no tobacco or junk food in your house. Which, by the way, is carrying being good way too far, in my opinion."

He shrugged. "Sorry to disappoint you. I grew up an only child who lived in order. I used to think it gave me control, but I gave up on believing that a few years ago."

"If you're wild, Tinch Turner, one would never know it from your life here."

He didn't like talking about himself. "Any chance you found anything for supper, Doc?"

"Jamie didn't want to eat until you came in. We made sandwiches. I told him we could eat and watch an old John Wayne movie we found under your TV."

Tinch smiled. "I've been looking for that movie. I'll clear the dominoes off the coffee table if you'll bring the food in. We'll have a wild night."

Halfway across the wide living area, Jamie looked up and noticed Tinch coming from the kitchen. The boy jumped up, spilling dominoes everywhere as he ran to hug his uncle. They both held on tight for a moment. The world might be shifting constantly around them, but they had each other.

When he let go, Tinch said, "You want to help the doc bring in those sandwiches or help me pick up the mess you just made?"

"I'll help her," Jamie whispered. "She needs a lot of help in the kitchen."

Tinch laughed. "Good idea. I'll meet you in front of the TV."

Halfway through the movie, Jamie was sound asleep, his head on Addison's leg and his feet in Tinch's lap.

"How'd he do this afternoon?" Tinch asked as he muted the TV.

"He cried a few times. Told me not to tell you because you'd think he was a baby." She stroked the little boy's hair.

"He asked about you every half hour. I think he was afraid you'd go away for good like everyone else in his life."

"I'm not going anywhere." He lifted Jamie over his shoulder and took him upstairs. If he stayed here, Tinch decided he'd fix up one of the bedrooms down the hall from his room, but for now, if the boy woke up, he wanted to be close. From the few things Addison had said while they ate, he knew she felt the same way.

When he came back down, Addison was curled up on the couch sound asleep. He thought of telling her he could handle this tonight, and she could go on home. Neither of them had slept more than a few hours last night. But Tinch didn't want to say good-bye to her and he was too tired to think about why.

He took her hand and pulled her slowly to her feet. "Come on, darlin'," he said. "It's time to call it a night."

She mumbled something as he guided her up the stairs. "I laid a shirt out for you to sleep in if you want to get out of those scrubs," he said, as if having a woman in his bedroom were a normal night. "The bathroom is that way."

When she came out of the bath, Tinch lay on one side of the king-size bed. Jamie was curled up in the middle. He watched through slits as she slowly lifted the covers and slipped into the other side.

He planned to stay awake and listen to her breathing, but he fell asleep within seconds, too tired to even think about how good the doc looked wearing nothing but an old flannel western shirt with the sleeves rolled up and the first few snaps left undone.

Chapter 21

BEAU BEGAN SKIPPING HIS CLASSES TO WRITE SONGS DURING the day, and then he'd meet Willow, no matter how late, after she got off work. They didn't talk as much as he figured most couples did. They just drove out to some isolated spot and made out. They went about as far as a couple can go and not have sex. Willow was willing, but all those sermons his father had pounded into him for years kept Beau from going all the way.

That, and the fear that she might get pregnant and he'd be tied to someone forever. He liked Willow, but they'd pretty much run out of anything to talk about by the third date, and he couldn't see not talking to someone sleeping next to him for the rest of his life. Once he asked Willow what she thought would happen if she did get pregnant, and she said it wouldn't matter. Beau didn't know much, but he knew it would matter.

Some nights he thought he'd lose his mind. He was so close to losing control. He wrote a song about standing on the edge, wanting to fall. Border thought it was about suicide and started watching Beau like a warden. Willow was the only one who knew what the song was about, but she told him she didn't like the idea of him writing something about their personal lives. She said her mother said it sounded a lot like bragging to everyone about what they'd done.

That night they didn't park out in the dark or talk. He just drove her home.

Beau spent the next two days working on a song about the deafening sound of silence and how sometimes a man feels alone even when he's holding someone's hand. When he picked her up on her day off, they drove to the duplex and he played both songs, then tried not to act disappointed that she didn't want to hear them again.

They kissed awhile on the couch at the Biggs brothers' duplex and got about as naked as a couple can get and still be ready to look dressed by the time someone unlocked the door. When he drove her home, she wanted to continue the heavy breathing session, but for once Beau needed to talk.

After he asked a few times, Willow finally said she didn't like either of the new songs. She suggested he write about something else, like the weather, or prison, or train rides. He told her he couldn't.

The next night when he drove out to pick her up, she'd already left.

Beau felt like they'd broken up and somehow he'd missed the fight. He sat in the truck stop parking lot and wrote words on scraps of paper about being too dumb to date and how it was hard to break a never-was.

The next Wednesday night he went along with the Biggs boys to the old bed-and-breakfast where their grandmother worked. She always cooked for them on Wednesdays when there were no guests staying at the Winter's Inn. Beau went along for the meal and because Border thought it might cheer him up.

He loved Mrs. Biggs's cooking, but like everyone he just tolerated the old lady who owned the place. Martha Q Patterson was one of those people who seemed to have lived several lifetimes in her almost sixty years. No matter what anyone talked about, she had an experience to tell. She also had the habit of one-upping every story. If someone said he broke his leg, Martha Q had had her leg fall off. If someone said she'd fallen in love with a guy from France, Martha Q would relate how she once had an affair with twins from France who didn't speak a word of English. She thought of herself as the star in this life and all others were simply bit players.

So when Beau found himself sitting alone with her in the parlor, he decided to ask for advice. Why not? He couldn't feel much more depressed about breaking up with Willow or missing the fight they should have had to end it. Plus, he figured, listening to Martha Q ramble along about what all he did wrong would somehow serve as penance. He figured it had to be some kind of sin to touch a girl like he touched Willow, even if she was doing her share of the touching.

He sat on the edge of his chair, waiting for her to build her nest with pillows. The room was a mixture of cowboy western and Victorian. If Queen Victoria married John Wayne, they'd probably hire Martha Q to decorate.

"So." Martha Q folded her hands over her middle roll of fat. "I heard you broke up with this girl you finally got to go out with you."

"Looks that way, but we didn't say any words or yell at each other. She wasn't there when I went to pick her up, and the next night when I dropped by on break she said she didn't have time to visit because they were shorthanded."

Martha Q raised one eyebrow. "Was the place busy?"

"No." He didn't want to admit that he'd sat out front and counted all eight people in the truck stop even though only three were sitting in the café.

"Then she was saying good-bye to you," Martha Q said matter-of-factly. "Might have been that hair of yours. Double too long, if you ask me."

"But shouldn't she have at least said something like 'I don't want to see you again' or 'Drop dead, loser'?" He pushed his hair out of his face. "And I don't think it was the hair, Miss Q."

She'd told him a dozen times not to call her Miss Q. First, she'd been married seven times, so she didn't qualify to be "miss," and Q was not her last name or middle initial. It just followed along after Martha.

Martha Q frowned and ignored his last comment. "It's been my experience that in this life you don't always get a good-bye kiss, and some folks don't want to stay around for the autopsy for who killed the relationship. Others, unfortunately, want to beat any feelings between the two of you to death so that you can't remember the good times without feeling the pain of the breakup. I've tended to get involved with the second type myself, and I can tell you I'd prefer your girl's choice."

"So you're saying I got off easy."

"That's about it."

"But I don't even know what I did wrong."

"Maybe you didn't do anything wrong, Beau. Sometimes it's more a matter of not doing anything right. Tell me, what did you like about this girl?"

Beau smiled. "I liked the way she kissed." He thought of adding how he loved the way she felt and smelled. He liked the way she kind of giggled when he touched her breasts. She had nice breasts, not big, but nice. They sure had felt good in his hands.

"What was her favorite color?" Martha Q interrupted his R-rated thoughts.

He shrugged. He'd never thought to ask.

"Her favorite TV show?" Martha Q shot questions. "Her favorite movie? What class did she hate in high school? When she was little, what doll did she collect? What would she be if she could be anything? Where would she live if she had the world to pick from?" When he didn't answer, she added, "What kind of underwear did she wear?"

When he opened his mouth to answer, Martha Q held up her hand. "I've figured it out. Boy, you didn't love this girl or probably wouldn't even like her, I suspect, if you spent a few hours talking to her. But you do love women, and I fear you'll break many hearts because there are a great many women out there who can't tell the difference between a man loving them and a man who just loves women. I suspect you'll write your share of sad songs too."

Beau put his head in his hands. The old bag was right. He liked Willow but probably for the wrong reason. Maybe she liked him for the wrong reason as well. She seemed to just want a boyfriend, and he happened to be the one who came along.

"What do I do?" he asked.

"About what?" Martha Q snorted. "About being a man and looking at women just because they're women? Well, I'm not a doctor, but I'd say your illness is terminal."

"Thanks a lot."

She laughed. "All right, I'll tell you what you got to do, but you have to promise to do it. I don't like giving advice that's not used."

He wasn't sure if she really had the answer or if she just saw her chance to get even with the entire male population by picking on him.

"Next time you meet a girl, look at her eyes. Don't walk away without knowing her eye color, and don't look down once you start talking to her."

"All right."

"Second, if you get lucky enough to have another female come up to you, you've got to spend at least five hours talking to her and listening to her before you touch her. That means no hand holding or kissing, or anything else. Five solid hours of talking to any girl. If she says one thing that bugs you in that time, walk away. No, run. If she does anything that bothers you, run. I've got enough experience to know that it's those little things people overlook the first hundred times that will drive you crazy when you marry someone."

Beau remembered the hiccupping girl and decided old Martha Q might have something. He hadn't been with them thirty minutes, and both of those girls would have led him to murder within a few hours. When he'd climbed into the backseat of their car after he finished playing, the one now hiccupping grabbed him and started kissing him. If the truck stop had been a few more miles away, she would have had his clothes off before they had time to order breakfast. At that moment he thought she was pretty near perfect. Ten minutes later in the café, he couldn't wait to get out of there.

"Thanks," he said, and meant it.

She leaned closer. "If you really want to make it as a singer, boy, you got to concentrate on that goal. Women can get you mixed up and lost faster than you think it's possible. I know, I've been the mixer for many a goal-seeking man."

He smiled. "You sound like my dad."

Martha Q laughed. "Well hell, I ain't never been compared to a preacher."

She stood and walked to a cabinet. Pulling a pair of scissors out, she cut one long strand of rawhide on a pillow that said *Happy Trails*. "Tie that hair back, boy, and buy you a black hat. There's got to be more to you than the music."

Beau tied his hair back and smiled as Border called for them to come in to dinner. He didn't talk to Martha Q any more that night, but he thought about what she said. Five hours of talk seemed like a long time when girls anywhere near his age made him nervous. Half the time he couldn't stop the stuttering when he first met them, so he'd better look for one who really loved to talk if he planned to ever get kissed again.

Martha Q had been the first female in a long time who hadn't made him fall over his words. Maybe he should just date old bags. The thought made him shake his head to rattle that idea out.

Saturday night he stepped into the cage with his hair

pulled back and wearing a black Stetson that he'd found at the secondhand store. Halfway through the second set, Border took a break and Beau picked up his old Gibson and began to play one of the sad songs he'd written. Everyone was already moving off the dance floor, planning to grab a drink between sets. Without the speakers, his song would be little more than background music, but Beau needed to play even if no one listened.

As the song ended, he looked up. No one was dancing. No one was even talking at the tables. Everyone in the place, including Harley behind the bar, was staring at him.

For a moment, Beau thought he must have broken some huge rule of what to play in bars, and then a roar went up. Folks were clapping and yelling and laughing.

"What's wrong?" Beau looked at his friend just behind him.

Border smiled. "I'm not sure, partner, but I think they just witnessed the birth of a star."

Beau grinned and touched two fingers to his hat in thanks. "Maybe Martha Q was right about the hat," he whispered.

Chapter 22

TYLER WRIGHT SAID GOOD NIGHT TO AUTUMN AND CLIMBED the stairs to his quarters above the funeral home. He could hear the wind whipping around the buildings downtown like an angry teenager stirring up trouble. Tomorrow there would be leaves and trash to clean up as well as branches, but tonight all he wanted to do was be alone. His Kate had been gone two weeks and he hadn't heard a word from her.

He told himself he'd be happy, he could make it this one last time, if he could just hear from her. He just wanted to know she was all right. He needed to tell her he loved her one more time, and then he'd be fine with waiting until she got back. Major Katherine Cummings wasn't just an arson expert for the army, she was his one forever love, and Tyler needed to know she was fine.

He didn't even have a number to call. Officially, he

wasn't family yet. She never talked much about her work, and he couldn't remember her ever calling anyone she worked with by name. There was one she called *the kid*. Tyler remembered she'd said she was worried about him holding it together. One was another woman—much younger, Tyler thought he remembered her saying. Once she'd said something about a captain who was all army.

Tyler stepped out on the little balcony off his living quarters and let the wind pound at him. Why hadn't he listened closer when she talked? Why couldn't he remember at least one name? Tyler knew the answer. When Kate talked about her work, he was more interested in watching how she felt. Was she going to miss it? Would she give up all the excitement of travel and knowing that what she was doing was important for a life with him?

All his life he'd known his place in the world. He could never remember not knowing that he'd grow up to run the family business. Tyler had always taken pride in his work, in his reputation. He'd never really looked at it from the outside, except through Kate's eyes. Maybe the reason she kept saying *someday* when they talked of marriage was that she still wasn't sure.

He watched the stormy clouds rising black across the sky, and he knew all the way to his bones that his Kate was in trouble. Whether she wanted to live in Harmony, or marry him, didn't matter as much as her coming back safely.

Wherever she was. Whatever she was doing halfway across the world right now, he could feel her and her mood, her emotions, just as he always did.

Major Katherine Cummings, his slightly plump, forty-five-year-old future bride was in trouble, maybe fighting for her life, and he could do nothing.

He straightened, trying to be a fraction of the soldier she'd been for more than twenty years.

Chapter 23

ADDISON'S THREE DAYS OFF HAD MELTED AWAY WITH THE time spent at the ranch, and she had to go back to the hospital. Tinch told himself he didn't mind; she was mostly in the way. She couldn't cook, didn't know how to play any board games, and asked almost as many questions as Jamie about ranching.

He was surprised that no matter how late she worked, Addison continued to come over to his place at night. He'd grown used to sleeping with her on the other side of the big bed. When Jamie cried in his sleep, she always pulled him close and hummed a little tune to him. About dawn he'd hear her cell phone alarm chime. He'd wait until she climbed out and hit the shower, and then he'd pull on his jeans and go downstairs. Some mornings, with no more than a nod, she'd greet him as he handed her a cup of coffee before she ran for her car.

Other times they'd talk out on the porch over coffee. Neither knew much about the other's work, so both were full of questions. In a way, what they did was more alike than different. They both tried to ease pain. Tinch was surprised how much he enjoyed their early-morning talks. She'd fire up quick when she disagreed, but she'd settle down more often than not with a smile.

Sometime during their week together, he figured out she had a good heart inside that ice princess body of hers. He was even getting used to her long bare legs that she didn't seem to see any need to cover. He'd asked her one morning, when she was sitting at the bar eating breakfast in just his shirt, if she ever let the sun see those legs, and she'd answered simply, "Why?" like he was the odd one for even making the suggestion.

After waving her good-bye a little after dawn, he worked with the horses, very aware of where Jamie was at all times. The morning was cold, so Tinch wrapped the kid and the kittens in a blanket and set them out of harm's way for a few hours. By lunchtime it had warmed up enough for Jamie to play in the yard with the two pups one of his cousins had brought over, promising they would help with security.

Not to his surprise, Liz had told her mother, who'd told her sister, who told her daughter, who told whoever.

Apparently every Matheson in town knew what was going on. Which translated to almost half the town knowing he was hiding the boy from the drug dealers who might have killed his mother. The upside to every Matheson relative knowing was that they'd be watching for strangers. The downside was that they were in his business.

He remembered his dad complaining once that marrying into the Matheson clan was like having fleas. There are too many to count, and if you don't watch they're always moving around in your life. Tinch saw that firsthand now.

One second cousin brought by a box of toys and games. Another brought a box of clothes containing a pair of boots that fit Jamie as if they'd been made for him. Two of his third cousins brought by casseroles and a pie that lasted two days.

One mentioned that she sure liked the doctor. She'd

even made Tinch laugh when she said, "You get some sun on that girl and she'd be a real beauty."

Tinch didn't dare make a comment. He didn't think they knew about the doc spending the night, and he wasn't about to tell or one of his cousins would start planning a wedding reception. He thought about mentioning that any drug dealer in town would simply have to follow the parade to his place, but much as he hated the interruptions, he appreciated the caring.

He'd turned them all away after Lori Anne died, but cold as he'd been, they seemed more than willing to give him another shot.

After lunch, Jamie crawled up on the long couch in Tinch's study. The boy always seemed to want to be within sight of him. Tinch flipped on the computer, after he'd tossed the boy a pillow and blanket and told him and the cat to rest. Both were asleep before Tinch's programs uploaded.

Fifteen minutes later he heard the chimes sounding for the fourth time since Addison left at dawn. Tinch walked to the door and watched his lawyer cousin drive up. Liz had gained a little weight with the recent pregnancy, and he thought she looked almost too pretty to be real.

"Afternoon," he said, trying not to let the worry over possible bad news show in his face.

"Afternoon." She climbed from the car. "How you holding up at being an uncle?"

"I'm surviving." He smiled. "It's not so bad."

She pulled her briefcase and a plastic cake box from the backseat. "You got time to visit for a few minutes?"

"I got time. Jamie's asleep."

Liz handed him the plastic cake box. "Cookies from Aunt Pat. She said growing kids need them."

Tinch thanked her and set them inside the screen door.

They moved to the chairs on the porch. While she spread out notes, he grabbed a couple of root beers and Moon Pies from the kitchen. When they'd been kids and gone to the family reunions at the lake at Twisted Creek, they'd always come back from swimming and sneaked into the big kitchen off the main hall where all the old relatives played dominoes. Tinch and a dozen cousins would hide beneath the long tables and down the creamy pies and root beers until they made themselves sick.

When he held them out to her, Liz laughed and took the snack and the memories. Tinch spent a few minutes asking about family and talking of nothing important, as if laying down the framework that would hold steady no matter what problems needed discussing today. Finally, he relaxed back in the old rocker and waited for the reason she'd driven out from town.

She'd dug up some facts that didn't surprise him. Sadie Noble had dropped out of high school. She had several nothing jobs, none of which she kept more than six months. She'd been arrested for a half dozen small crimes; none ended with jail time. She'd listed the father of her child as unknown on the birth certificate and still kept her mother's house as her only known address. The trailer she'd died in had been rented for a month and all of her belongings, including the food found there, wouldn't fill the trunk of a car.

Liz guessed that Sadie must have already been into drugs when her mother died because the mother's house was left to Jamie. Sadie could live in it if she paid the taxes. If the taxes went unpaid for a year, the house was to be sold, with the money put in trust for Jamie. No other relatives were named in the will.

"I talked to the lawyer charged with setting up the trust, and he said he'd get it done as soon as the house sells. Jamie will have the money waiting for him when he turns twenty-one. It won't be much, but it'll give him a start."

"Are you sure there are no other relatives?"

"The lawyer didn't think so."

"He'll stay with me." Tinch realized he'd worried that someone would come to take Jamie away.

Liz finally closed the file. "We can tell the investigator to continue digging, but it will be expensive and I doubt we'll learn much more. He said it appears Sadie had only one half sister, Lori Anne Turner of Harmony, Texas. She may have been on drugs and probably running from something, but she took the time to draw up a will, which shows her love for the boy."

Tinch nodded. "So I shouldn't hate her for being so messed up that she left her kid in a dirty place with nothing but cereal that he had to shoot a rat to protect."

Liz stared out over Tinch's place. "Maybe she was doing the best she could. I'd like to think she was trying to get the kid to you and her sister. Otherwise, why would she have been in Harmony?"

"Maybe she just figured hiding here was as good a place as any. Maybe she wanted to hit Lori Anne and me up for some money. Who knows, maybe Sadie was opening a new drug business in the area." Tinch realized that the more he'd grown to care about the boy, the madder he'd gotten at Sadie for not taking care of the kid.

Liz was right, he didn't know what Sadie Noble had been through. Maybe he should cut her a little slack. Jamie was a good kid.

"I don't think it will be much more than paperwork to get you legal custody of the boy, but, Tinch, you got to ask yourself if you really want this kind of responsibility."

He smiled at her. "You mean I'll have to give up my wild ways and settle down."

"To be honest, you'll have to pretty much give up your life. You'll have to be there for him twenty-four hours a day. He'll be sick and get hurt. He'll outgrow clothes as fast as you buy them. He'll take all your time and then some. Tinch, I love kids. I wanted kids, but you had him dumped on you. Make very sure you're up for it before you sign on for the job."

"What if I say no?"

"He'll become a ward of the state. Who knows, he might get adopted by a great family."

"And he might not," Tinch said, making up his mind.

Liz waited, giving him time.

"I don't think I had a life before he dropped in." The

realization of just how true his words were shook his insides. "You know what he told me last night? He said I was his only uncle and that made me his forever uncle. Then he hugged my neck so tightly I couldn't breathe and said he'd been trying to get to me ever since his mom told him about me. He said he ran that first night when the sheriff brought him out because he was so afraid I wouldn't want him."

Tinch glanced through the window to where Jamie slept, looking so small curled on the couch in his study. "I guess I've been waiting around for him too, only I didn't have anyone to tell me he was coming. When I saw him that first night, his back all striped with bruises, I took on the job of making sure that would never happen again, whether I was his legal guardian or not."

"You're sure, then?"

He nodded.

Liz finished up the paperwork and left. Tinch walked inside and stared down at Jamie for a long time before he moved to his computer and began work. Ready or not, it was time to make some changes, and he might as well start with buying the Rogers place next door. The Rogerses' daughter had told him she'd give him a good deal and let him pay it off over a few years. It would mean a lot of hard work, but that didn't matter. He'd been sitting around for three years alternating between trying to drink himself to death and dying from grief. He might as well try working himself to death.

In a few years the Rogers place would start paying for itself, and by the time Jamie was grown, they'd have double the land.

While he waited for the Rogers daughter to answer, Tinch moved a few of the stocks he owned into safer investments and accepted a few more horses people wanted him to turn into gentle riding mounts. That didn't pay much, but it would cover the cost of keeping Jamie in boots for a few years.

Finally, he wrote a note to the lady who cleaned his house. Lori Anne's closet needed cleaning out. She'd always be with him in his heart whether the clothes were there or not. Maybe someone down on her luck like Sadie could make use of them.

Tinch felt solid for the first time in three years. He was looking ahead and not back. He cared about someone. Jamie was going to need him, and Tinch planned to be there for the boy. There would be no more bar fights. No more late nights drinking. No more time for wishing he were dead. Tinch had a boy to raise, and he planned to make Lori Anne proud.

Jamie woke and they moved upstairs. There were two smaller bedrooms Lori Anne had called the someday rooms. She'd always said maybe someday they'd have kids or someday she'd start quilting. Only the somedays never came.

Tinch opened the first room, half full of scattered boxes and books. After glancing at the wall of books from his childhood, he moved across the hall and noticed that the second room had extra furniture that needed to be moved to the attic. Lori Anne never wanted to get rid of anything. He used to kid her and say that she must believe furniture had feelings. She'd always look at him and say, "You don't?" like it was strange that he didn't know old rockers hold generations of memories and little school desks trap the laughter of children.

Jamie walked from one room to the other as if looking for hidden treasure among the dust.

"Which one do you want?" Tinch asked, trying to push the memories away.

"It doesn't matter." Jamie hiccupped a cry as he backed toward the hallway. "Put me in either one and I'll stay. I promise. You don't have to lock the door."

There it went again, Tinch thought; that heart he'd given up using was pounding so hard it might break his ribs from the inside. Shoving his grief aside, he knelt down so he could see the boy's face. "I thought you'd like a room of your own."

Jamie shook his head and began to cry.

Tinch lifted him up and walked back downstairs. They were on the porch before he sat the boy down and knelt to

Jamie's level. "We'll talk about it later, but you need to know one thing, boy. There is never going to be a door in this house that locks you in or out." Jamie held on tightly to Tinch's sleeve as Tinch added, "And no one is ever going to hit you. If they even think about it, they'll be answering to me. No matter what you do or don't do, I'll never raise my hand to you."

They moved to a rocker on the porch and Tinch sat down with the boy in his arms. Reason told him this would probably be one of the few times he got to hold Jamie like this. Too fast boys grow too big for this kind of holding, but right now he knew the kid needed to believe someone cared about him.

Jamie stopped crying, but he didn't let go for a long while. Finally, he asked in a low voice, "You going to die too, Uncle Tinch?"

"No. Not anytime soon."

Jamie didn't make a sound, and Tinch knew the boy didn't believe him. "You know that book I was reading you last night about the Knights of the Round Table?"

Jamie nodded.

"Well, I'll tell you a secret. I'm like one of those knights sent to protect King Arthur. You don't know it, Jamie, but you're like a prince, and my job from now on is to watch over you until you're grown. We're going to have time to read that entire wall of books, Jamie. Me and you."

"Promise?"

When Jamie finally pulled away and wiped his nose on his sleeve, Tinch said, "We'd better get our coats on and go check on the horses. I didn't like the way Stormy was favoring her front right leg."

The kid reached for his coat. "I didn't either. Got to watch things like that."

Tinch smiled as they headed off the porch with the two worthless pups following. He wasn't sure he wanted to know what had happened in the boy's life to make him act so afraid of being locked in, but Tinch planned to make sure it never happened again. If Jamie didn't like locks, he'd take every one off, and if the boy needed to believe that someone in his life would stay around and not die, Tinch would do his best to make sure that happened.

"How about, when we're finished, we ride over to the Rogers place and I show you where I used to catch tadpoles?"

"Sure," Jamie said. "What's a tadpole?"

HOURS LATER TINCH STOOD ALONE ON THE PORCH LIStening to the wind storm in with cold air from the north. Fall was slowly shifting into winter. It had almost been too cold to ride over to the pond, but Jamie hadn't complained. They'd sat on the bank and made plans for the summer when the water was warm enough to swim in. Memories of his childhood filled Tinch with a peace he hadn't felt in a long time.

As darkness moved in, Tinch turned his collar up against the wind and relived his day. He watched Addison's car turn into his drive. She'd called and checked on Jamie twice, and he'd promised to have supper ready. But she hadn't been able to leave the hospital, so he'd fed the boy and let him watch another western because he didn't want to go to sleep before his angel the doctor came home.

She climbed out of her little car and made a run for the house. The scrubs that seemed to make up her entire wardrobe except for the thin T-shirts she wore as PJs did little to keep the wind away. She was shivering by the time she hit the porch.

He held the door, then watched her dancing around acting as if it were below freezing even in the house.

Without much thought, he pulled off his heavy work coat and put it around her shoulders.

"Thanks," she said, already moving to the boy.

By the time Tinch warmed her soup, she was back in the kitchen.

"Jamie's already asleep." She was still wrapped in his coat.

"I'm not surprised. He only has two speeds: full out and stop. I'll take him up to bed while you drink your soup."

By the time he came back downstairs, she was curled up on the couch where the boy had been sleeping and watching the same western. "Better be careful." He handed her a beer. "That movie tends to put people to sleep."

She crossed her legs and tugged his coat around her to use as a blanket. He sat down about a foot away and tried to act interested in the western. He'd been thinking of things he wanted to tell her all day, and now that they were alone he didn't know where to start.

"How was work?" he finally asked.

She started, as if she'd forgotten he was there, then said, "Fine. The emergency room was so busy I stayed to help out for a few hours. Dr. Wilson could have handled it, but most were kids with colds and I hate to see the families waiting too long. I know they just want to get medicine and get them back home."

He waited, watching her straighten the coat, then fold and unfold her legs, then straighten the coat again, then lift her beer, almost drink it, and then set it down again.

Tinch decided sitting close to her was kind of like cuddling up to a live wire. Any minute she might spark and burn them both.

Finally, she looked in his direction for a few seconds and then went back to fiddling with the coat.

"What is it, Addison? What's wrong?" he said slowly. "Did you hear something or did something happen at work that's upset you?"

"No." She waved her hands between them as if washing the air. "Nothing like that. Everything is fine." She folded her legs. Then she unfolded them.

He figured she was an intelligent woman and eventually she'd find a way to tell him whatever was on her mind. All week they'd talked, sometimes for only a few minutes and mostly about Jamie, but they had developed a habit of visiting before they went to bed. Or rather, she went to bed and he stayed up pretending to work until he knew she'd be asleep. Only tonight, she didn't look as exhausted as usual.

He watched as she got up and took her cup of soup to the kitchen.

He waited. Whatever was bothering her probably had nothing to do with him because she never seemed to have any trouble telling him off when she was mad at something he'd said or done. So the longer she paced and fretted, the more comfortable he felt.

Maybe she was thinking about going back to her place at night. Neither of them had brought that subject up, and as far as he was concerned he'd just as soon *not* talk about her leaving. After three years alone, he liked the company.

Five minutes later he tried not to jerk when she circled the couch and stood right in front of him, blocking his view of the movie.

"This has nothing to do with you, Tinch, but I need to ask a favor." Her words came out so fast he wished he'd had a rewind button.

"All right," he said calmly, hoping to settle her down.

She frowned. "I'd like to kiss you again, just as an experiment."

He raised one eyebrow.

"I was married once when I was still in my teens. It didn't last, and after that I was afraid to get involved. The few times I did"—she hesitated, waving her hands like he should fill in the words—"you know, try dating while I was in med school, well, every time I went out, I regretted it. Either I had a terrible time, or worse, the guy hung around forever thinking we had a thing."

Plopping down beside him, she added, "A few months before I came here, my father talked me into dating a fine doctor who just happens to be fifteen years older than me. We went out a dozen times, and he's never even held my hand, which was fine because I really enjoyed learning about his research. Or I *did* like talking to him. That was before he decided to talk to my dad. They'd been friends for years. Without saying anything to me, they decided we, me and him, should get married. When I confronted Glen, he simply said I'd get used to the idea, like I had no say. He didn't hit me, but I felt a blow. It was like I was back married at nineteen and having no control over my own life."

"Breathe, Addison," Tinch ordered.

She took a quick breath and added, "I didn't argue with Glen or Dad. I ran, which is probably a habit I've developed over time, but that's not important here. I'm just saying that my year is almost over and I still haven't come up with a strong plan of what I want to do with my life. If I don't take Davidson's offer, my father is going to be furious with me, and believe me you don't want him furious. I don't remember vacations or family dinner or bedtime stories. All I remember from my childhood are lectures on how to correct my shortcomings."

Tinch wondered if she'd let him take notes. She was moving way too fast. "What does that have to do with me kissing you again?" About the time he'd decided they'd just be friends and help Jamie, she wanted to play spin the bottle.

She moved closer. "Don't you see? Until you kissed me I always thought it was me. Something was wrong with me. I was the one broken. I'm like brain dead in the relationships department. But after you kissed me, I began to consider the possibility that it was them. From the wild boy I ran away to marry to one of L.A.'s top plastic surgeons, not one made me feel like you did with that kiss. When I go back and Glen finally does kiss me and I feel nothing here"—she pointed to her middle—"then I'll know for sure. It's him and not me. All I have to find out right now is, did I really feel like I think I did when I kissed you."

Before he could answer, she added, "I'm not asking for anything but another kiss. We both know we have little in common, and neither of us is looking for any kind of a relationship. Just consider it as one friend doing a favor for another friend. Nothing more."

Tinch fought down a grin. "I don't know, Doc. I'm starting to feel like a lab rat."

She swore as she fell back against the cushions, then bounced back like a jack-in-the-box. "I'm not going to beg some hick cowboy hermit from the sticks to kiss me. Forget the whole thing. It was a dumb idea."

The ice princess was back. She shook her sunlight-blond hair back and added, "I'm not getting enough sleep. That's it. I'm losing my mind. What kind of nitwit goes around asking some guy she met after a bar fight to kiss her? There should be some kind of Z-pak for what I've got. I could just shoot myself full of antibiotics, take a sleeping pill, and sleep this off."

When Tinch finally got a word in, he said, "Would you be willing to bargain?"

He'd surprised her. For a moment she just looked at him, and then she said, "What bargain?"

"One kiss, a real kiss that doesn't end when one of us runs, traded for a date. I haven't been out on a date in years, and I'm tired of everyone looking at me like they feel sorry for me. After this is all over, we go out and paint the town. Me and you. A real date." He grinned. "I'll even pay."

She looked like she was weighing the pros and cons.

He stood his ground. She was the one who'd started this, but he planned to be the one who finished.

"All right. It's a deal." She sat next to him, shoved a few strands of hair out of her face, closed her eyes, and waited.

After a few minutes she opened one eye. "Aren't you going to do it?"

"Not yet," he answered. "The movie's not over."

She made a little yelp and fell back against the couch.

Tinch swore if the woman hung around long, she'd wear out his furniture. "Relax," he said. "Watch the movie. We're getting to the good part."

He pulled a comforter over her legs and she scooted away from him a few feet. As they settled into watching the movie, she kicked off her shoes and pulled her feet up. Tinch put his hand over them.

"Trying to guess my shoe size?" she asked.

"You're so cold. I can feel icy toes even through the

socks." He didn't remove his hand, and after a few minutes, when she didn't pull away, he began gently rubbing her feet.

They talked over the movie, neither very interested in the plot. She told him of her day, and he told her how Jamie had reacted when he'd asked which room the boy wanted to be in.

When the movie finally ended, he clicked off the TV and studied her in the dim light. She'd calmed some and warmed up finally, but she still didn't act like a woman wanting to be kissed. There was something untouchable about her. Maybe it was the way she moved, holding herself always in check, that turned him—and most men, he guessed—away. But she'd asked to kiss him, and he had no intention of backing down, if for no other reason than she needed and wanted to be kissed.

He was trying to decide if he should stand up to kiss her or just lean over to her on the couch, when she moved closer. She folded her legs beneath her and faced him as if about to give a lecture.

"Well?" she said. "I think it's about time."

"So do I," he whispered as he slid his hand along the back of her neck and pulled her to him. He smiled as his free arm circled her shoulders and drew her down against him. Her mouth was open to protest when his lips closed over hers.

For a moment she went perfectly still and he thought she might bolt even though she had been the one to ask for the kiss. Then warmth seemed to run into her blood.

"Relax," he whispered against her lips. "I got you, darlin'. Just relax."

He didn't give her time to answer before he began lightly kissing the corners of her mouth. Then he tugged on her bottom lip and she opened to his kiss.

Tinch shifted, without breaking the kiss, until her body rested under him. As the kiss deepened he let her feel the weight of him above her. He liked the way she molded to him. Her breasts flattened against his chest as he felt the length of her. Kissing her deeply, he moved with the feel of her breathing.

She took her time, but slowly she reacted to his every move. She was a woman awakening and from what he could tell, she was waking up hungry for more.

After a while, he shifted slightly to his side so he could move his hand along her long body, feeling her beneath the one layer of material.

It had been so long since he'd kissed a woman and he felt like he was near starved, but he took his time, slowly turning the kiss from tender, to playful, to passionate. Her arms circled around his shoulders, molding him closer, and he smiled, knowing this time she had no intention of pulling away.

Her lean body reminded him of a fine racehorse, and he had no doubt she loved the feel of his hand moving over her.

She made little sounds of pleasure and arched her back when he spread his hand out over her middle. She was feeling the passion all the way to her core, and he spread his fingers out, loving how she was reacting to him.

He was lost, beyond thought. He moved his hand to the waist of her scrubs and pushed them down so that he could spread his fingers over her stomach. Her skin was warm and alive to his touch as he stroked her. The pleasure he saw in her eyes made him smile as he lowered his mouth to her throat before returning to her mouth.

As the kiss deepened, he moved up until her breast filled the palm of his hand. She jerked slightly and broke the kiss.

"Relax," he whispered. "I got you." Staring into her gray eyes, he kept moving his hand over her breasts until he felt her calm beneath his touch, and then, pressing his thumb on her chin, he opened her mouth and continued the kiss.

He felt her, more than heard her, laugh with delight as his fingers tightened over her tender flesh. Now her sounds of pleasure echoed in his mouth as she moved to his touch.

The kiss turned wild and hungry, taking them both into the madness of passion. He shoved his hand down until her scrubs were almost off, then up, molding her breasts with bold strokes. She moved, greedy for his nearness, kissing him as deeply as he kissed her.

When she wrapped her long legs around his waist, he rocked with the feel of her surrounding him.

"Relax," she whispered as she laughed. "I got you." Her long legs tightened around him once more.

Tinch was so lost in the feel and taste of her, he almost didn't hear the chime sound. It took him two heartbeats to figure out what had intruded on the silence.

Then an instinct born as long ago as passion took over. He stood, pulling her with him. "Go upstairs," he whispered as he held her close one more moment. "Make sure Jamie is safe. Someone just drove onto the property."

She ran for the stairs as he reached above the six-foot console and grabbed his rifle hidden there. Anyone coming this time of night better have something important to say.

Tinch was on the porch when the sheriff's cruiser pulled up. "Is Addison here?" she yelled as she ran around the car.

"Yes," Tinch answered as he lowered his rifle.

"Good. I need to talk to you both." The sheriff didn't wait to be invited into the house. "I've got news from Dallas and it's not good."

Addison moved down the stairs. "What's happened?"

If Sheriff Alex Matheson noticed anything unusual about the two people standing before her, she didn't comment. She simply began her report. "The coroner is ruling Sadie Noble's death a murder. She was a drug user, but there were bruise marks where she'd been beaten and held down within hours of her death. The final needle that went in her arm went in the right arm. It was the first and only needle mark on her right side."

Addison was following every word. "She was right-handed? When I interned in L.A., I saw druggies who were so right-handed that they couldn't handle the needle in the other hand."

Alex nodded. "There was also a hairline fracture on her jaw. I'm guessing the men who came that night got tired of trying to hold her down and finally knocked her unconscious. The autopsy also found evidence that two of her fingers had been broken weeks ago and never treated, along with several scars and old injuries. Either she was very clumsy, or she'd been knocked around several times before."

Tinch fought down bile in his throat. He was glad Lori Anne wasn't there to hear how her little sister had died. It would have broken her heart. He only hoped that the two sisters had finally found each other in heaven.

Addison asked a few questions, but he'd heard all he wanted to hear. Sadie was dead, and now it was his responsibility to take care of Jamie. If that meant protecting the boy with his life, Tinch knew he would.

The sheriff sat down in one of the dining room chairs and folded her arms. "Except for a few relatives, no one knows that either of you are connected to Jamie. We're not dealing with professional killers here. There's a good chance these guys think they've gotten away with the murder, and I'd like to keep it that way until I catch up to them. We don't have much to go on right now. A few people around the trailer park saw a man parked outside Sadie's place a few days ago, but I couldn't get a description worth putting out on either the man or the car."

"So they've been back to the scene of the crime?" Tinch asked.

Alex shrugged. "The company that rents out a few of the trailers in the park said someone called and wanted to rent that exact trailer. When the receptionist said it needed to be cleaned, the caller claimed that wasn't necessary."

"They're looking for something," Tinch added.

"That would be my guess." Alex stared at him. "Something besides the boy. If they don't find it in the trailer, they might think Jamie has it—or knows where it is. The next step could be to find him."

"He didn't come with anything but the ragged clothes on his back." Tinch said what all three of them already knew. There was no way Jamie had anything the men wanted, but that might not stop them from coming after him. They might think he knew something.

"So, what is the plan?" Addison sat down beside Tinch, brushing his leg as if she'd done so many times.

The sheriff leaned forward. "I'm thinking, maybe they're stupid or desperate enough to show up at Sadie's funeral. We could put it off a few more days. I could get the paper to run a story about how this woman died alone without any relatives. If the drug guys read it, they just might think they could get a good look at Jamie and find out where he's staying." She looked at Tinch. "I don't want you or Jamie or Addison there. I'll have men watching. It shouldn't be too hard to spot these guys if they show up."

"If that fails, I've got a team in Dallas digging up who Sadie worked for. Maybe we can track it that way. I'd really like to find out who did this, but my first priority has to be keeping the boy safe."

"Both chances of catching them are long shots." Tinch frowned. "I've never lived looking over my shoulder, but it's a habit I plan to pick up. Between the doorbell at the gate and the dogs, no one will get on my property without my knowing it. Tomorrow I'll call Denver Sims and see if he won't come by and help me make the Rogers place more secure."

"Won't you have to check with the owner?" Alex asked.

Tinch shook his head. "I bought the land today. All that's left to do is the paperwork. The way I see it, there are only two ways to get to Jamie. One, across open fields from the Rogers place, but I'm guessing these guys are lazy. A locked gate will probably keep them out. Two, they come through my front gate. If they do, no matter what time it is, I'll know they're coming."

Alex asked Tinch to walk her out while Addison went up to check on Jamie. They were at her car when she said, "The autopsy showed signs that Sadie Noble was raped postmortem. We have DNA, but even if they're in the system, it will take time."

Tinch nodded. "I don't want the boy to ever know that."

She agreed.

"And." He lowered his voice. "I'm dealing with the funeral home in cash, so there will be no paper trail to me if they check. Tyler said he'd write it down as a county burial, if it's okay with you."

"Fine. Is the doc staying here with you?"

"She is until I get security at her place. You got a problem with that, Sheriff?"

He caught her smile in the porch light.

"No problem at all. In fact, that's the only good news
I've heard today." Alex straightened her tall, slender frame.
"I'm only thinking of her safety, of course."

"That and the boy are the only reasons she's here," he
said, more roughly than he'd intended. He wasn't any better at lying than the sheriff was.

When he walked back inside, he found Addison upstairs,
curled up next to Jamie. Tinch had no way of knowing if
the boy had cried out or if the doctor thought this might be
the best place to hide.

He pulled off his boots and slipped in on the other side
of Jamie.

Addison's arm circled above the kid.

Tinch turned out the light and reached for her hand. He
didn't say a word as he gripped her fingers in his. She didn't
pull away, and Tinch fell asleep wondering why he hadn't
settled for a nice sweet kiss when she'd asked him. The way
she'd kissed him would flavor his dreams for a long while.

The answer as to why, he refused to acknowledge, but it
kept circling in his mind. He hadn't settled for less because
he wanted more. Much more.

Chapter 24

ADDISON WOKE UP LATER THAN USUAL. JAMIE WAS STILL asleep beside her, but Tinch was already gone.

She showered and put her clothes back on, knowing she could get a clean pair of scrubs when she got to the hospital.

Then she rushed downstairs, planning to dart to her car and hopefully not see Tinch at all this morning. After the fool she'd made of herself last night, she needed time to think about what to say to him. First she'd asked for the kiss, then she'd attacked him. She'd wrapped her legs around him so tightly he couldn't have gotten away if he'd wanted to.

Apparently, he hadn't wanted to, since he'd kissed her like he was a dying man and she was his last breath.

She made it to the porch before she saw him walking

across the yard, a bridle over one shoulder and his hat low against the morning sun. For a few moments, Addison was unable to look away. There was something so beautiful in the rough strength of this man. This man, she remembered, who handled a rifle last night as easily as he'd handled her.

"Morning," he said when he noticed her.

"I have to go," Addison said. She didn't move. If she headed toward her car, she'd have to pass him, and she wasn't sure she wanted to be that close to him. Not yet. Her nerves were still too raw. Just thinking about how she'd acted made her blush.

"About last night," he started as he faced her straight on.

"Forget about last night." She couldn't, wouldn't talk about how she'd acted. "It never should have happened. I owe you an apology. I was wrong about saying you were wild. Apparently, I'm the wild one. It was bold of me to ask for a kiss and then attack you. My behavior was appalling."

Tinch pushed his hat back and stared at her as if he were trying to converse with an alien. "I was thinking about holding your hand while we slept. It was nice."

"Oh." She felt as if she'd just been sunburned from the inside out. "I forgot about that."

A slow smile dimpled one of Tinch's cheeks. "And about the other. You didn't attack me, Addison. I was there and I remember every detail that happened. If anything, it was me who got out of line, not you."

"Thanks for that." She'd expected him to deny what had happened or brag about it. Maybe even tell her that she was some kind of nut job. That seemed to be the usual plan of action with men she'd had dealings with, but then she'd never met anyone like this cowboy before her.

"It was nice." He moved a step closer. "I'm sorry if I frightened you."

"You didn't frighten me." She could feel herself shifting from foot to foot and moving her arms. Her father's voice echoed from childhood, demanding she stop fidgeting. "Can we talk about this later? I have to go to work."

He stepped away from the porch, giving her plenty of room. "We don't have to talk about it at all, Doc." He raised his hat a few inches and then settled it back low on his head. "You have a good day."

She almost ran to her car. Part of her wanted to say she wouldn't be back tonight. She didn't know what she was doing here anyway. Jamie had settled in and Tinch could take good care of him. She should just go home and call to check on the boy. But Addison couldn't stay away. She cared about Jamie and wanted to help him, but she knew down deep inside that she was coming back to see Tinch, not the boy.

As she drove the ten miles to the hospital she couldn't stop thinking about the way he'd held her. To her surprise, she realized the man had been giving, not taking. He'd been pleasing her, something that no one had ever done before.

She had a slow day, with time to catch up on paperwork and even take a nap in the break room. Georgia Veasey told Addison she looked tired and asked if she was feeling all right.

Addison couldn't tell the nurse, her good friend, anything. Even if she'd wanted to and it had been safe, she had no idea how to explain what was happening between her and the neighbor just down the road.

How did she explain that for the first time she wanted someone for no other reason than she needed him?

About five the emergency room was empty. Addison called Tinch to tell him she'd bring supper, and then she changed into jeans and a sweater and left the hospital.

Thirty minutes later, when she walked into Tinch's house, Jamie ran toward her. "Food," he shouted. "I'm starving. Uncle Tinch let me ride a horse by myself today and we rode for miles and miles."

Addison smiled, realizing she'd been waiting all day to get back to this place. "How about we eat and then you can teach me to play Chinese checkers?"

Tinch pulled a soda from the refrigerator. "I'm glad you're here. I've got a few hours' work to do with a horse I got in today, if you don't mind staying with Jamie. I'd rather he not be around this mare just yet."

"She's mean," Jamie said between stuffing French fries in his mouth.

"No," Tinch corrected. "She's hurt. The vet stitched her up, but I need to change the bandage and she's not too happy about having anyone close."

"Of course I'll stay with Jamie." Until that moment, she hadn't thought about how hard it must be on him to get his work done and watch over a four-year-old.

"Thanks," he said, then leaned over and kissed her cheek.

Before she could react, he was out the door and Jamie started asking her questions about which food was his.

As they ate, Jamie told her about his day. "We cleaned out a closet today and boxed up a bunch of clothes." As he tried to feed the kitten lettuce, he added, "We also picked which room is going to be mine. Tinch says I can put my things in there, but I don't have to sleep in it until I'm ready. He says its okay to sleep with you and him."

"You know, Jamie, my house is down the road. At some point, I need to go back home."

"I know"—Jamie looked like he might cry—"but not tonight."

"Not tonight, but soon."

Jamie nodded. "Tinch says one of the pups can sleep in my room when I decide it's time for me to bunk in there. He says when they're grown they'll be the best guard dogs around. No one will step foot in our house without them barking."

"You and Tinch talk a lot today?"

"Sure, we talk all the time, and you know what?"

"What?"

"He never tells me to stop talking or be quiet like my mom always did. He lets me ask as many questions as

I want to, but he says for me to remember the answers 'cause there ain't enough time in this world to answer them twice."

Addison laughed. She could almost hear Tinch saying those exact words.

"I told him my momma always called me a bother. You know what Tinch said?"

Addison couldn't wait. "What?"

"He says it don't matter what folks call you, it's what you answer to that's important." Jamie frowned. "I don't got no idea what he means, but it made me feel better."

At nine Addison put Jamie to bed and stayed with him until he fell asleep. When she heard Tinch banging around downstairs, she climbed from the bed, slipped on his old shirt that she used as a robe, and tiptoed down to join him.

He was sitting at the bar downing a cold sandwich and a glass of milk. For a moment she thought he looked exhausted and wondered if all the worry over Jamie had taken its toll.

He must have heard her coming, for he straightened and looked toward the stairs. His hat was propped far back on his head, as if he hadn't quite realized he was finally inside, and his shirt and jeans were so dirty he must have wrestled the horse.

"Mind if I join you?" she asked.

"Only if you promise not to ask any questions."

"Deal."

She climbed onto the stool across from him and propped her elbows on the bar. "I could warm that up for you." She pointed to the steak sandwich that had once been hot. "Though it's still not much worth eating."

"No thanks." He tossed his cold supper back on his plate. "I wasn't that hungry anyway. It's been a long day. A vet over in Clifton Creek brought over a half-wild Appaloosa mare who got into a roll of old barbed wire. She was cut all the way to the belly."

"I could look at her." Addison couldn't believe she was offering to treat a horse.

He shook his head. "It's too dangerous. The cuts have been sewn and treated. If they don't get infected, they'll heal." He stood and reached for a beer. "I'm in for the night."

"You want to talk about what happened between us last night?"

His blue eyes met hers. "Not really. Not if you're going to tell me it never should have happened again."

"It probably shouldn't have," she admitted, "but I'm not sorry it did. I just want you to know that what happened wasn't me. Not the real me. I'm not like that." She stared down at her hands. "I've never been like that before with anyone."

"Like what?"

"You know, wild, reckless, passionate, demanding." She glanced up at him and was surprised to see him smiling. "It's not funny, Tinch. I'm not sure, even if you'd tried, I would have let you go." She closed her eyes, remembering the way she'd wrapped not only her arms but her legs around him.

"Are you trying to say that you took advantage of *me*?" A laugh rattled from his tired body.

"I've had all day to think about it, and I've decided that's about it. But I want you to know I've never acted so wild, and I promise it won't happen again. I still respect you."

He spewed beer across the floor as he fought down another laugh. "You're something, Doc. Really something. I can't believe you think I've been worried all day about the way *you* took advantage of me last night. If the alarm hadn't chimed, there's no telling what *you* would have made me do."

Addison stared at him. She couldn't tell if he was serious or if he was teasing her. "That's why I think it best if we just be friends and try to get through this like reasonable adults."

"I agree," he said. "I wouldn't want you losing control again. Who knows what you'd do to me?"

"Exactly." She jumped off the stool. "Well, now that that's settled, I suggest we go to bed."

"Darlin', I thought you'd never ask."

He followed her up the stairs. "I'd better take a shower and change into some fresh clothes; otherwise you'll be smelling dirt all night."

"You don't have to sleep in your clothes. Now that we've reached an agreement, there is no reason we can't be comfortable with each other. Why don't you sleep in whatever you usually do?"

"I usually don't sleep in anything," he answered. "But how about we compromise. Since you're sleeping in my shirt, I'll settle for a pair of old jeans."

Fifteen minutes later when he came to bed, Addison tried to act like she didn't notice all he had on was a pair of tight jeans. There was so much about him she didn't understand. He was so gentle with Jamie and the horses, and her, but she'd met him the night he'd taken on five men in a fight. He lived all alone in a house big enough to hold a family. He made her feel like a woman.

When he rolled over, she could tell he was watching her even in the pale moonlight.

"What?" she whispered as she noticed his frown.

"I want to touch you," he said simply. "I'm not going to, but that doesn't stop the need I have. I just want you to know. We can play this game of being friends for as long as you like, but that doesn't change the ache I have in me to pull you near and run my hand over you."

She said the first thing that crossed her mind. "You've just been without a woman for a while. Having Jamie here must slow your dating life down."

"I don't have a dating life," he corrected. "And I'm not wanting *any* woman, Doc, I want to hold *you*."

No man had ever been so direct. Tinch wasn't flirting or playing mind games. He was simply being honest, and that frightened her.

"It's not happening," she whispered. "We're not happening."

She rolled over, turning her back to him. Part of her knew that he was just being honest. She also knew he wouldn't cross the line she'd drawn without being invited. The problem was, Addison felt like she was going slowly insane, and she had little faith that she wouldn't jump over every line the next time they were alone.

Chapter 25

BEAU WATCHED THE BAR FILL UP FOR THE SECOND TIME on a practice night. Even the half dozen nurses were back.

"Now, try to be cool tonight, partner," Border told him. "My brother said he talked Harley into unlocking the cage and letting us go say hello between sets. It's a pretty big deal. Harley's going to announce the bar is closed while we greet our fans."

"What fans?" Beau had noticed them listening, but he doubted the drunks wanted to talk to him. "I wouldn't mind seeing a few of the nurses up close, but I don't think anyone else will want to meet me."

Border kicked his chair. "Okay, go out and meet the nurses. But, remember, when we do, be nice. My brother says the tall one is kind of a friend of his."

"What's her name?"

"Big didn't know. He forgot to ask her. I guess that's where the 'kind of' comes in."

Beau didn't want to know more. He decided he should probably stay in the cage at break time. He'd get nervous and just stutter anyway, or worse, look at their breasts. Martha Q had made it plain if he didn't stop thinking about breasts he'd be moved to the pervert line pretty soon.

Beau thought about writing a song about how it felt to touch a woman's breasts, but he figured only half of the crowd would like it. As he played through the next set, he tried to apply logic. Women liked showing their breasts off. They were always pushing them out there or leaning over so a guy could get a good look. Men liked the feel of them, so it made sense people should just give up shaking hands and start touching breasts as a greeting. It would make the world a lot friendlier place.

Almost choking, Beau thought about what his father would say if he suggested such a thing. To his knowledge his dad had never even said the word *breast*.

When the break came, Harley announced the bar was closed for ten minutes and opened the cage. To Beau's surprise, people rushed forward to shake his hand. He didn't have to say a word as one after the other they all said how much they liked his music.

Border was at his side and thanked each one.

After a few minutes the crowd died down and Beau came face-to-face with one of the nurses. He'd noticed her before when she danced.

"Hi," she said. "The other band member told me to bring you this. He said you were always dying of thirst after a few songs."

She shoved a soft drink in his hand. "I like listening to you play. Some of your songs made me want to cry. I think we all feel that kind of lonely sometimes. You've got a way of saying things that touches me."

Beau didn't trust himself to say a word. She was being

nice to him, thinking he was something. He didn't want to start stuttering and have her realize he was nothing special.

"I also like to dance to your music."

He forced his eyes wide open as he stared at her forehead. He didn't even trust himself to blink for fear he'd start staring at her breasts. She had short blond hair and a nice smooth forehead.

"The girls and I decided we'd come over every week when you play. You're the best entertainment going in this town. Even Harley knows it."

Beau nodded, then gulped down half the drink.

"You got songs I've never heard before. Songs that make people want to cuddle up close and sway with the music. Do you make them up?"

He managed another nod.

"Maybe some night after you're finished, if you want to, we could . . ."

Beau handed her back the empty glass and shot toward the cage door Harley was holding open. He felt like some kind of caged monkey who'd been given a moment of freedom and couldn't wait to get back into captivity. Another minute with that girl and he'd be staring where he shouldn't or stuttering so hard he'd sounded like a stuck record.

He could hear Border behind him talking to the girl about how they had to get back to work, but Beau didn't look up. He concentrated on setting up his equipment and organizing his notes.

When Border climbed into the cage and bumped his way to the back, he mumbled, "What did you say to that cute little nurse?"

"Nothing," Beau whispered.

"That explains it." Border picked up his bass guitar. "She asked me what was wrong with you."

"What'd you tell her?"

"Don't worry, partner, I covered for you. I told her you were an idiot savant. A regular Rain Man, only you work with music and not numbers. I thought that would frighten her off, but she wants to talk to you again."

"Great." Beau could see himself becoming one of the world's leading forehead experts.

"Any time. I've heard the only way to get over one girl is to find another."

"Who told you that? Some girl on a nine hundred number?"

"No." Border strapped on his guitar. "My big brother got the bill for a few of those calls and told me he'd break my fingers if I ever dialed them again."

Beau smiled at his friend. "Might improve your playing."

Border turned on the amplifier. "So you're not mad about me trying to fix you up with that pretty nurse?"

"No, but don't do it again. I'm on a two-step recovery plan after my last two run-ins with the opposite sex."

"What's that?"

"One, stay away from all females. Two, repeat step one."

They began the first song, a fast one to warm up the small crowd.

When Beau looked up halfway through the song, he saw people all around the room lift their glasses to him. Even the little nurse was smiling at him.

Beau smiled back, noticing she was wearing a sweater. Winter might be the answer to his problem, he thought. Only date girls who were cold natured. The more clothes, the better.

Chapter 26

TYLER WRIGHT CARRIED HIS CELL PHONE WITH HIM EVEN to the bathroom. No one ever called him on his cell, so he knew if the phone rang it would be either Autumn telling him to pack the car because they were on their way to deliver a baby, or Kate calling to tell him she was heading home safe and sound.

He tried not to dwell on the code she'd mentioned. He didn't want to think of the possibility that she might be somewhere in danger where she couldn't talk. Over the months they'd been engaged, she'd told of having to be escorted into places to investigate a fire. Places that weren't safe. Places where snipers might be waiting or bombs might go off.

Her expertise was in developing a profile of the arsonist from the signature he or she left at the scene. There were a thousand reasons Tyler loved his Kate. What he'd never understood was why she loved him.

Major Katherine Cummings was a wonder in complexity. She'd traveled the world and made it safer for thousands. She was educated, intelligent, and—to him—beautiful. He, on the other hand, lived a simple life doing what his father and grandfather had done. He had a good fifty pounds he should lose, seldom read a book, and usually found even the Monday crossword in the *Times* too hard to complete.

As Tyler prepared for the chapel service for Sadie Noble, he let his mind walk through his and Kate's story as if it were a great love affair played out on the screen in his brain. They'd met one icy night at Quartz Mountain Lodge in Oklahoma. Neither one had planned to stop, but the road conditions made it impossible to travel. By chance they'd ended up at the same table and talked the evening away over red wine, and then they began to e-mail. As the months passed, Kate became part of his life.

No. He rewound the movie in his head. She became the only thing that seemed real in his life. Once, when he'd thought he'd lost her, he could do nothing but wait for her to contact him, checking the computer screen endlessly until one night she finally responded to his note. For the last six months she'd spent every weekend she could in Harmony . . . no, edit. She'd spent every weekend with him. They'd taken long walks through the night streets and laughed. They'd talked of everything that was important to them and held each other until dawn.

"We need to marry," Tyler mumbled to himself as he set up extra chairs in the chapel just in case they were needed. "When she comes home, I'll put my foot down."

He knew he wouldn't, but it sounded solid to say so. His Kate had a mind of her own. She'd never be a woman to be controlled, and he wouldn't have it any other way. All he wanted for her to be was loved, and that was one job he felt up to. He'd been saving up love to give for most of his life.

"Come home, Kate," he whispered as he worked. "Come home safe and sound to me."

"Mr. Wright?" Calvin called from the front of the chapel.

"You figure anyone will come to this poor girl's funeral? I don't think she knew a soul in Harmony."

Tyler glanced over at the bare steps, at the front, where Calvin always placed flowers people sent to the service. No one had even sent a potted plant. Usually the number of flowers paralleled the number of people. "Calvin, bring some of the silk sprays in from the viewing rooms. Whether anyone comes or not, I'd like to make the place look nice. Dust off those white ones too and put them in the back."

"The angel wings?" Calvin asked.

"Yes," Tyler smiled. "The ones that look like angel wings."

An hour later Tyler was so glad he'd filled the front of the chapel with flowers. From near the back, he watched Tinch Turner walk up to the casket with a thin little boy by his side. Only a few lights were on because the funeral wasn't for another two hours, but everything had been prepared. The small chapel, which hadn't been changed since his grandfather built it, looked grand. Rich polished wood, carpet on the floor to buffer any sounds, and chandeliers that made lace on the ceiling with shadow and light.

Tyler saw the boy touch the casket, and then the cowboy picked him up and let him cry on his shoulder. Tyler had no doubt the boy was the son of Sadie Noble, but he was surprised to see him still with the rancher. If Tinch had the kid, there must be no other relatives.

They walked up the aisle and out the front of the church. When he passed Tyler, Tinch said simply, "Thanks."

Tyler straightened with pride. If no one else showed up at the funeral, it didn't matter. He'd done his best for the little boy and that was enough. He would always remember the fine polished box and the flowers and angel wings surrounding his mother. His last memory of her would be peaceful.

He held the door as they passed, with Tinch still carrying the boy on his arm.

"We weren't here, if anyone asks," Tinch whispered.

"I understand." Tyler didn't need to know the details.

Somehow the boy's safety was at stake, and that was all he needed to know.

Two hours later a dozen people from the trailer park came to the funeral, more out of curiosity than mourning. Tyler stood in the back greeting them as formally as if they were dressed in suits and not shorts. He had to ask two women to leave their drinks on the steps, and one man frowned when Tyler insisted he not smoke.

He heard one teenager complain that the casket was closed. Another woman blew her nose loudly and dropped the tissue between the pews as if she thought she was at a ball game.

Just before Tyler closed the doors, several people dressed in black climbed out of a gray van. They reminded him of the cast from a horror movie: all thin, red eyed, and in need of washing. One was trembling as if it were cold in the chapel, and another had a drippy nose but he didn't seem to have noticed. Druggies, he thought, and wondered if Sadie had been one of them.

The driver of the van, a small man who looked like he'd been frowning at the world since the day he was born, entered the chapel last. He seemed to be the only one totally aware of where he was. He herded the others along like they were ducks. Tyler decided the driver had a hard look about him, prison hard, that not even the suit he wore could hide.

Fighting down a grin, Tyler could almost hear his Kate asking him how he knew what *prison hard* was.

Alex and Hank Matheson followed the horror group in but took their place on the last row of the chapel. The sheriff wasn't in her uniform, but Tyler had the feeling she was still on the job. Hank seemed more relaxed. He smiled and whispered to Tyler while Alex signed the book. "Interesting group you got here, Ty. Let me guess, it's BYOB for the wake."

Tyler glanced at the people in the chapel and tried not to laugh. Two huge thugs in black must have entered through the side door. They didn't sit with the van people or the

trailer park folks. They wore bulky jackets that could easily conceal a few weapons. Both were scarred and tattooed,
but it was their permanent frowns that probably kept folks
at a distance. One glared at the van people but nodded at
the driver as if he knew the little man.

Miss Dewly, who played the ancient organ, came in and
took her place. So did her two friends. They always tagged
along if Miss Dewly had a morning funeral so all three
could go to lunch afterward.

It occurred to Tyler that Alex might have shown up
because she thought whoever killed Sadie Noble might come
to the funeral. Tyler knew he wasn't supposed to know the
death was a murder, but the coroner in Dallas liked to talk.

Tyler looked around. Except for Miss Dewly's buddies
and the Mathesons it would be hard to pick the most likely
murder suspect from this crowd. Half the people at the
funeral looked like they'd kill someone for pocket change.

He thought of the little boy who'd cried for his mother
and was glad Tinch hadn't brought him to the funeral. He
was better off with the rancher than with any of these people posing as friends.

As Tyler closed the door he noticed a deputy writing
down the license plates of every car on the lot, even Miss
Dewly's.

The preacher came out and announced they'd be singing
song number 172. No one picked up a songbook but Miss
Dewly's lunch buddies. The preacher and the three old
women sang "Amazing Grace" while everyone else watched.

The service was short. One song, two prayers, and a
five-minute sermon about the beauty of life as God's gift.
No one looked like they believed a word the preacher said.
Two of the druggies from the van group had been put to
sleep by the song.

Tyler made an executive decision not to announce that
there would be coffee and cookies in the parlor after the
service when he noticed that the woman who'd blown her
nose so loudly was busy stuffing the complimentary tissue
boxes into her mammoth purse during the prayer.

As everyone filed out, Tyler thought he saw the deputy taking pictures from the evergreens across the lawn.

Finally, the man who'd driven the van and the two huge thugs were the only ones left in the church. Alex and Hank were in the foyer watching with Tyler through the tall slats that separated the chapel from the entryway.

To the funeral director's shock, one of the thugs opened the casket.

Tyler would have moved to stop them, but Alex put her hand on his arm.

The three men stood in front of the open coffin. In the silent church their voices traveled easily to the back.

"You didn't think she'd have it with her, did you, Sullivan?"

"Naw, I guess I thought we might just get lucky. Don't know where else it'd be."

"She never was real pretty, but she looks terrible dead," the biggest one of the three said.

"Most folks do," the van driver snapped as he pulled on his gloves. "She got what she deserved lying to us about where she left the stash."

"Yeah," the big one agreed as he dropped the lid of the casket. "That's one druggie who won't cross us again."

Tyler felt Alex tug him toward the door, and by the time the three men walked out she was busy telling him how nice the service was while Hank blocked most of the view of Alex and Tyler from the men.

Once they'd driven off, Tyler dropped the small talk. "You think those were the men who killed her?"

Alex raised an eyebrow. "How'd you know it was . . . oh, never mind. Yes, they could be. If you see them around here again, let me know."

Hank stood guard even as their cars disappeared. "Why didn't you arrest them?" he said to his wife.

"They don't know we know it was a murder. As far as they're concerned, all we believe is what we read in the paper: accidental overdose. By the time they even suspect, I want an airtight case to take to the DA."

"Well, you may get your chance to ask them a few questions." Hank stared at the cars heading downtown. "Looks like the car with the two thugs turned toward the police station."

Alex took off toward the deputy's car.

Hank just stood beside Tyler and yelled, "See you at dinner, honey."

Tyler looked up at his best friend. "How do you do that?"

"Do what?"

"Let her go into danger like that? Those two may have been the men who killed Sadie Noble. She's going to meet them, maybe even confront them."

"I know." Hank frowned as his hand slowly uncurled from fists. "But when you love somebody like I love Alexandra, you have to let them do what they love. She's good at her job. I've got to trust that. I guess if you love someone, you got to love them all. People don't come in parts you can divide out and pick what you like."

Tyler watched Hank walk away to his truck. He knew the fire chief was right, but what if Kate came back from her mission and told him she wasn't retiring? After all, the army had been her life for more than twenty years. She was good at her job, and she'd said once that all her friends were people she worked with. Could he stand and watch her go on mission after mission, knowing that it might be dangerous?

He walked back into the chapel and began folding up chairs that hadn't been needed. Halfway through, in the silence of the empty chapel, he called himself a coward. He knew he couldn't let Kate go away again. His heart couldn't take it. When she got home, if she got home, he'd have to tell her that it was the army or him. For more than two weeks he hadn't slept. He'd panicked every time he didn't know exactly where he'd put his cell phone. Everyone around him was excited and waiting for Autumn's baby to be born. He couldn't tell them that Kate was on her last mission and she might be in danger. He'd had to keep it locked inside with his fear.

Stay with me or choose the career, he'd say.

She was his only love for this lifetime. She'd understand, he reasoned.

Or, she'd leave . . .

Chapter 27

REAGAN WASN'T SURPRISED WHEN DAYS PASSED WITHOUT Noah coming back. He had a dozen other places he could sleep in town, or he could always go home to the rundown old homestead that his dad had deeded over to him a few years ago.

A few mornings after the fight in the bar, she drove past his parents' old place and noticed his pickup parked in the drive. She felt as if the friendship that had lasted for years was dying. *Maybe people struggle too hard to hang on to friends*, she thought. Maybe sometimes they should just let them slip through their fingers like the ashes of what once had been.

She wished she could use the excuse he always used. If nothing he said mattered when he was drunk, maybe nothing he heard should either. Maybe they could just wipe away all the conversation they'd had in the bar and start over. She wouldn't complain about him being drunk, and he wouldn't call her a virgin again.

She thought of showing up at his door, but wasn't sure he'd be alone. Half the single girls in town would love to get a chance to go out with the great Noah McAllen. Reagan told herself she was strong, but she didn't know if she could remain standing and take the blow if Noah was with another woman.

Time drifted by in Reagan's world. Big moved to the fire station at night and focused on being one of the guardian angels over Tyler Wright's housekeeper. Autumn Smith had shown up in town more than six months ago, pregnant and on the run from her boyfriend. Tyler had found her parked at the cemetery, and after he confronted her one snowy night, they'd both slipped on the ice and ended up at the hospital.

When the funeral director found out she was pregnant, he'd taken her in, and now Autumn was part of the family. Big and his friend Willie Davis took turns watching over her in the evenings and making sure Autumn got to all her classes at the community center. Now that the time was near, they planned to be ready for what they were sure would be a midnight run to the hospital.

Reagan missed Big. He was one of those rare people who would just go along with her in life. If she said she wanted only pudding for supper, he'd reach for the spoons. He knew her secrets and liked her anyway. She hadn't crawled in bed with him since that one night, but she knew his door would always be open and he'd never push like Noah sometimes did.

That was Noah's problem, Reagan decided. He pushed. He always wanted something bigger, better, as if the world as it was just wasn't good enough for him.

When he didn't show up to listen to Beau Yates practice the following Monday, Reagan knew that this time they weren't going to patch it up. She sat listening to the beautiful songs Beau played and watching a very tall nurse trying to teach Big to dance. He didn't do very well at the fast dances, but the slow ones left them both smiling.

Big sat out one dance while the nurse visited with her friends. Reagan knew Big was simply keeping her company and trying to cheer her up.

"I heard Noah's riding again. Someone says he's making money."

When Reagan didn't ask any questions, Big changed the subject to all he'd learned about babies. "With my luck, I'll probably never get married, but kids are sure interesting little things. Not real bright. Think about it, a bird is born and a few days later it can fly out of a nest and make its own way. But a human, they are totally helpless for months. It's a wonder we survived. You'd think the world would just be full of birds."

Reagan enjoyed his efforts, but she decided to call it a night. When he offered to drive her home, Reagan shook her head and left alone.

She needed time to think . . . to heal . . . to grow. Big had been right; humans must not be very bright. She was twenty-one and still trying to figure it all out. Maybe she should turn her energy to work.

Concentrating on the harvest during the day and redecorating the upstairs of the house kept her busy for a while. Late at night she worked on her online classes and tried not to think about Noah. She'd seen the girls line up on TV after he rode and made the best time. They all wanted a kiss, or a date, or more from him, and they all had perfect hair, perfect bodies. The guys called them *midnight rides*.

Reagan didn't just think she'd never be able to compete with the women he met, she didn't want to. The Noah she wanted lived here. The other Noah belonged to the rodeo, not her.

Then, as if nothing had happened between them, one windy evening Reagan walked out of the barn and saw the cowboy standing on her doorstep.

He had his hat low, like most bull riders prefer wearing them, and his jeans a few inches too long and snug along his slim frame. As she walked closer, she noticed the spurs on his boots and the gloves tucked into his back pocket. For once he looked like a working cowboy and not one dressed for show.

Glancing around, she realized his pickup was missing. Noah had ridden over, but she wasn't sure from where.

He didn't say a word as he watched her near.

When she was close enough to see his eyes, a sober brown gaze met hers. She stood a few feet away from him, having no idea what to say. She hadn't started the fight they'd had at the bar that night, but she'd ended it with one slap.

"I've missed you," he finally said, so low she barely heard him.

"I've missed you too," she answered.

"I'm sober. Have been since you slapped me."

She grinned. "Don't tell me I knocked some sense into you."

"You woke me up, Rea. Climbing on a hundred bulls takes less courage than coming out here to say I'm sorry. I was wrong. I was way out of line."

Her emotions were too raw to face trouble. All her life she'd had to fight to survive, and if surviving meant letting go of Noah, she'd do it. "What do you want, Noah?" She wasn't sure she could even handle being friends right now. She needed solid ground.

"I'm leaving tomorrow. I've got to make the rodeo in Houston."

He didn't smile his easy smile at her. The hardness she'd seen in him that first night, when he'd broken the door down, was back. Just as time had changed her, it had changed him, and they both knew they could never go back to being the kids they'd been when they first met.

"You came to say good-bye?"

"No," he said. "I came to ask you to have dinner with me tonight. Call it for old times' sake."

She looked down at her dusty jeans and shirt. It was almost sunset. By the time she cleaned up and put on something else, every restaurant in town would already be closed. "I'm tired," she whispered, knowing this was a one-time offer. There would be no tomorrow. "I don't want to go out tonight, but thank you for the invitation." She wasn't sure, but this might be as close to a date as he'd ever offered.

"We're not going out," Noah said. "I packed a meal and thought we'd eat in the orchard. I just want to talk to you. If we went into town, we'd be interrupted by every other person who passed."

Reagan was shocked. She thought he loved the attention. "I don't know. It's windy."

"It won't be in the trees."

Reagan didn't want to fight with him. Maybe this would be a kind ending to what had almost been between them. They could eat, talk about years past, and she'd be able to wish him well. She figured a part of her would always love him.

"All right," she said. "I'll get a blanket."

Noah stepped off the porch and offered his hand. "I got everything. It's waiting over by the trees."

Glancing toward the orchard, she saw his horse tied to one of the apple trees. In the fading light she made out a picnic basket, a lantern, and blankets. Hesitantly, she took his hand and they walked up the path.

He moved among the trees until he found a clearing big enough to spread the blanket, and then he lit the kerosene lantern, which looked to be a hundred years old. "I found this out in my barn. When I was little, my dad used to take me on campouts and he'd always bring this along."

Reagan pulled the food out of the basket. Peanut butter, jelly, and a loaf of bread. "You went all out."

That easy smile came to him then. "I brought cookies, too." He dug out a bag of Oreos. "Remember that time you went with me to a little rodeo in Oklahoma and said you'd only go if we drove back that night. I had bruises all along my backside, but I got you back by midnight."

She grinned. "We didn't have time to stop to eat. All we had between us and starvation was two canned Cokes and a bag of Oreos."

Then, as simple as that, they were talking again. He'd picked the one place in the world where they could just be themselves . . . where they could be best friends again.

When the wind died down and the moon came out above the bare branches, they lay on their backs and finished off the cookies while they talked.

When they were finally silent for a while, Noah said simply, "Rea, don't sleep with Big anymore."

"I don't . . ."

"I know," he interrupted. "But I don't want you even sleeping next to him. I always like the idea that you only did that with me."

"You've no right to ask, Noah. You fade into and out of my life."

"I know I don't have any claim on you, but we're more than friends and you know it."

She closed her eyes, remembering the kisses they'd shared and the rare times she'd felt so close to Noah that she'd almost believed in something silly like soul mates.

"Knowing you, Rea, just having you curl up next to me means more to me than a full-blown wild affair. I didn't mean what I said about you not growing up. Believe me, I see folks all the time who are acting like rabbits in permanent heat who haven't shown any sign of being an adult."

"What are you asking from me, Noah?"

He was so quiet she wasn't sure he planned to answer, and then he began. "I want our friendship. It's strong, like none I've ever known before or ever will again. And if that's all you want to give, I'll count myself lucky, but I want that from you for as long as we live. I have to believe that nothing, not me being a jackass or getting drunk or even you sleeping with Big, will break it."

She wanted that too, and she knew he was right. She had several people she called *friend*, but none like Noah. He'd been there when she'd come out of the darkness that had been her life for years. He'd been her friend when no one else would speak to her. She owed him friendship. "All right, but that doesn't mean I can't get mad at you."

"Fair enough. Only no matter how mad at me, you'll take my calls."

Raising her head, she added, "You don't take mine."

"I lost my cell."

She hit him hard. "You used that excuse the last time you disappeared for a month."

He acted like he was in pain. "I suppose it would be too much to ask for you to take hitting me off the table, Rea."

"Definitely." She laughed. "It's one of my great pleasures in life."

He matched her laugh. "I must be some kind of masochist because if that's the only way you'll touch me, I'll take the hits." He rolled easily to his feet before she took another swing at him.

She took his hand without hesitation as he walked her back to her house.

"You planning on riding that horse all the way back to town?" she asked as she stepped onto the porch.

"No. I borrowed him from Hank Matheson next door. I've been helping him out for a few days before I have to leave. We've been moving stock. He says he's finally got his place paying the bills."

Reagan smiled. In this part of the country folks talked poor. Paying the bills meant they were doing good.

"I've got a few details to finish up, so I'll be in the saddle from dawn to noon, then hopefully I'll have time to clean up before I catch a flight." He took a few steps before he added, "You wouldn't want to drive me over to Amarillo, would you? We'd need to leave about four."

"I could. I've got a few things to pick up in town." They were at the porch, but Reagan didn't invite him in. "Thanks for supper."

"You're welcome." He leaned down and kissed her on the cheek, then stepped away into the shadows.

She listened, hearing him swing into the saddle and ride away. Part of her felt like she was walking on paper and might fall through any moment. She had no idea what Noah was up to. Did he really just want to go back to being friends?

Chapter 28

TINCH DIDN'T WANT TO TAKE JAMIE BACK HOME AFTER they'd visited the chapel and said good-bye to his mother, so they drove over to Bailee and had an early lunch. The vet in town mentioned in his e-mail that he'd had a busy week delivering three foals. Tinch thought Jamie would enjoy seeing them.

He'd been right. Jamie couldn't wait to get out of the pickup the minute he saw the little horses. Newborn foals always made Tinch smile with their funny bushy tails and the mane sticking straight up on the back of their necks.

He let Jamie climb on the fence and watch them while he talked to the vet about his latest problem mare.

"The boy reminds me of you, Tinch, when you were about that age. Your dad would bring you over and, if I didn't watch, you'd be in the stalls with the newborns. You had something, even then, a way with horses that even the horses could smell. I've seen devil bucking horses who hate the whole world eating out of your hand in no time."

Tinch didn't want to talk about himself. He'd never been comfortable when people described him as being gifted; he considered his talent more one of understanding when it came to any animal. Only, the more he denied it, the more people bragged to others about how they'd seen him work magic with a horse. A publisher of mostly animal nonfiction had even been asking him to try writing a book for people who bought horses, then had no idea how to handle them.

He reached over and straightened Jamie's cap, wanting to change the subject. "He's my nephew. His mom died last week, so it looks like he'll be living with me."

The old vet grinned. "It's a lot of work raising kids. I got four of my own. Kind of takes over your life before you know it, until one day you realize they are your life."

Tinch didn't want to tell the vet that he wasn't doing anything with his time anyway, but he decided to stay on the safer topic of horses.

While they talked, Tinch noticed Noah McAllen's truck pull up with a trailer attached. The professional cowboy had one of those fancy trucks he'd seen only in ads. It even had his initials on the door.

Noah bounced out and headed his direction. "Afternoon, Tinch. Glad I caught you. Hank asked me to deliver a few bags of feed to your place. While I was picking them up, the guy who helped me load them said he thought he saw your pickup turn off here at the vet's."

Tinch groaned. He figured he'd go pretty much unnoticed forty miles from Harmony, but evidently not. Suddenly, getting home as fast as he could seemed like a good idea. "We could shift the feed to the bed of my truck and I'll take it back with me. Save you a trip."

Noah shook his head. "We also loaded up that cutting horse for you to take a look at. He's been acting like he's half-broke for a week. Getting so bad the men at Hank's place are refusing to ride him."

The bull rider glanced back at the trailer and looked frustrated.

Tinch smiled. "I don't know what's wrong with the horse, but how can I help you, 'cause something's got you worried?"

Noah explained that he had a plane to catch and was running out of time. Even with Reagan Truman driving over the speed limit, they'd barely make it now with having to deliver a horse and feed to Tinch's place first. "It's my fault." Noah swore. "I left in plenty of time, but half the people in the feed store wanted to talk to me and I lost track of time."

"It must be tough being famous." Tinch laughed. "Maybe I can help, with the horse anyway. How about we trade trucks? I'll drive yours home with the feed and the horse, settle him in, and then drive over to the Truman place. It's not all that far on the back roads, and I've got Jamie riding shotgun. You go catch your ride, but leave my keys in the truck. Before Reagan gets back from taking you, I'll have your truck parked at her farm and mine back at my place." He studied Noah. "If that's where you want to leave it?"

The bull rider grinned. "That's where I want to leave it. I'll be back by next Tuesday."

Tinch offered him the keys to his old Ford, and Noah tossed his keys as he thanked him.

While Tinch visited with the doctor a few more minutes, he noticed that Noah took the time to talk to Jamie. Someday, Tinch decided, he and the boy would make it to a rodeo and maybe get to watch Noah McAllen ride.

It occurred to Tinch that Noah wasn't telling his stories of the rodeo to build himself up, but to entertain others. He was taking the time to talk because folks liked to say they knew him, understood him, cared about him. Tinch had always admired McAllen's skill; now he admired Noah's kindness. Noah might even forget he talked to the boy, but Jamie would always remember meeting the champion.

Fifteen minutes later, they climbed into Noah's truck and he and the boy headed back to the ranch.

Jamie didn't ask as many questions as usual. For a while he was fascinated that a pickup had a GPS and he could track them going down the back roads toward home. Finally, he asked, "You ever cuss, Uncle Tinch? You know, like Noah McAllen did when he thought he might miss his flight."

Tinch swore he could see the boy growing up.

"I do sometimes, but I try to save it for something worth cussing about, and I try never to do it around a lady. I've always had the idea that using the same few words over and over kind of wears out the need for them, so cussing isn't something I'd want as a habit."

Jamie nodded. "I agree. Is Doc a lady?"

"That she is."

"But she's not kin to me, is she?"

"No."

"Then, I could marry her when I grow up, right?"

"Right." Tinch fought down a grin. "Got any idea where you'd live once you've tied the knot?"

"Yeah." Jamie looked very serious. "I'm thinking she could have the extra bedroom upstairs. We could tell her that if she could sleep by herself, she could have the other pup to keep her company. I think that sounds fair, don't you?"

Tinch almost choked on the last of his malt. "Sounds like a plan," he finally managed. "But, you know, she could sleep with me as long as she needs to."

"I told her that last night," Jamie agreed.

"What'd she say?"

"She said, 'That would be interesting.' "

Tinch fought not to agree. He flipped on the radio, trying not to think about Doc moving into the extra bedroom, but once the image was planted in his mind it was hard to erase.

The afternoon turned cold and threatened rain by the time they'd unloaded and swapped the trucks. Reagan Truman's place was deserted except for Tinch's old pickup parked in front of the house. The old dog on the porch didn't even bother to raise his head as they traded trucks and drove away.

Once they were home, Jamie played with the puppies until he finally collapsed in front of the TV with his favorite food . . . cereal with bananas mixed in.

Tinch had tried a dozen meals and snacks, but the boy always turned to cereal when he felt hungry. He'd pick at other foods, but Tinch figured the boy ate as much oats as a horse.

Now wasn't the time to try to improve his eating habits, so Tinch stocked bananas and boxes of cereal within easy reach of Jamie. He also kept the milk on a low shelf so the boy could help himself.

While the TV played, Tinch cooked a late supper. He'd always been comfortable in the kitchen. His mother used to sit him on the counter and teach him when he wasn't even in school. Once Lori Anne got sick, cooking became his job. He used to make up foods like fried carrots and chocolate-covered celery sticks just in the hope that she'd eat a bite.

He made a hearty goulash with a salad and bread on the side. Just before sunset, he heard the familiar chime and moved to the door to see Addison flying up the driveway as always. He smiled, thinking he might ask her if she wound her little toy car up too tight this time, but the doc didn't take teasing well.

Climbing out of her car, she smiled, as if liking the idea that he'd been waiting for her. They ate at the kitchen table with her telling them all about her day. When Jamie asked to go back to the show he was watching, she began questioning Tinch on how the boy had acted at the chapel.

"He's fine," Tinch whispered as he reached across the table and covered her hand with his. All day he'd been wanting to touch her, just touch her.

She pulled away and explained that she'd talked to her father on the way home, and that always put her in a bad mood.

Tinch didn't push it. The feelings he had for her were too new . . . too unsure.

When Jamie went to bed, Addison said she wanted to take a long bath. Tinch cleaned up the kitchen and then went out on the porch to sit in an old rocker. The night air was thick with the smell of rain, and no wind moved through the trees. He could hear the horses settling down, and the last of the summer bugs had disappeared. The silence was almost haunting.

"He's asleep," Addison whispered as she stepped bare-foot onto the porch. She wore one of his mother's quilts around her shoulders like a shawl.

Tinch stretched his hand out, and this time she put her hand in his. He tugged her gently until she lowered onto his lap. The need to have her close enough to smell her skin had been a hunger growing in him all day, but he guessed that wouldn't be a very flattering thing to say to a woman.

"Did you need to talk to me about something?" She sat all prim and proper, almost as if she'd rather be somewhere else. Another planet, maybe.

"No," he said as he moved his fingers over her leg, still warm from her bath. "In fact, I don't want to talk at all." If she was going to bolt, he might as well know it now.

Tinch pulled her to him slowly, but firmly. He wanted to give her time to run, and he planned to make it plain what he was going to do.

She didn't protest or speak. She just stared at him with those beautiful stormy-day eyes, and he realized something odd. Addison was more afraid of herself than she'd ever be of him.

Her mouth was velvet against his as a long gentle kiss passed between them. She wasn't kissing him back so much as letting him take his time kissing her.

Then he broke the kiss and settled back, waiting for her to react. Knowing the doc, he wouldn't have to wait long.

"I thought we decided to go back to being friends?" She straightened as if she didn't notice she was sitting on his lap.

"This is me being friends," he whispered against her ear. He liked the nearness of her. The way he could feel a fire building in her. The way she gave nothing away, but made him earn every touch.

When she didn't answer, he added, "You have any problem with it, Doc?"

"No," she whispered as he moved his hand along her

back. She remained still as he opened the quilt and slid his fingers over her long legs.

If she knew how dearly he needed to touch her, she'd probably be frightened. His hand moved over the worn flannel shirt boldly. "Any problem now?" he asked as he kissed her throat and his palm rested over her breast.

"No," she answered, and leaned her head back. "No problem at all unless you stop."

Tinch smiled and tasted her throat. She was melting.

Slowly, she leaned against him, resting her head on his shoulder as he rocked her in his arms. She felt so good against him. He breathed deep and slow for the first time in a long while.

"I just want to hold you," he said, pulling the quilt over them both.

She opened her mouth, waiting for another kiss.

When he didn't act, she straightened, put her hands on his face, and pulled him into the kiss.

Tinch laughed when he finally broke free. "All right, baby, I'll kiss you as well as touch you."

She settled against him as if waiting for him to honor his promise, and he did.

After a while, she whispered with almost a cry, "I'm leaving in three months."

He didn't let go. "I know."

"I can't stay here. Everything is waiting for me back in L.A."

"I know." He moved his face into her damp hair, loving the smell of it. Tinch wasn't a man who ever kidded himself. He knew he had little to offer compared to a career in L.A.

"I . . ." she whispered, as if about to say something he didn't want to hear.

He kissed her again. Suddenly hard and demanding, as if he knew they were no longer at the beginning of something, but at the ending.

She pressed against him, forcing her heart to beat

against his. When he lifted her to face him, she straddled him, her knees on either side of his hips as she wrapped her arms around him and gave herself into one kiss with her entire body.

Molding her to him, Tinch let passion set fire to them both. In the corner of his mind, he knew if he didn't stop, there would be no stopping between them. He'd never kissed a woman like this . . . like it was more important than breathing . . . like they might both die if they mated and neither one would care.

Almost violently, he broke the kiss and just held her while she calmed. She didn't seem to want to talk any more either. He pulled the quilt over her shoulders and moved his hands down her body gently. When he reached her hand, he threaded his fingers through hers, taking back the touch she'd pulled away from earlier.

He nudged her head back against his arm and began tasting her neck, loving the little sounds of pleasure she made. Once she warmed, she was a wonder. But right now, he wanted her warm, loving, willing, not so hot with passion he wasn't sure he could handle her. He wanted to know all about her, mind and body, so when they made love it would take all night.

"It's not fair," she said as he tugged the quilt around her.

"What's not fair?" He moved his hand inside the open V of the shirt she wore, loving the feel of her warm skin between her breasts.

"It's not fair that you're not the one waiting for me in L.A."

Tinch stilled, trying to force at least a few brain cells to function. "So, the doctor you talked about is still waiting for you?"

She seemed to sober too. "Glen Davidson. He thinks we should collaborate on the research he's doing. It's actually a great honor. My father says it would be a great marriage for me, both personally and professionally. My father says that just the fact that he's waited a year for me should make me feel flattered. Today he yelled and told me it's time I came home and stopped playing around. They want to schedule the wedding as soon as I get back."

His hands felt wooden as they slid around her waist and lifted her off him.

"What's wrong?"

"You didn't tell me you had someone waiting for you. Evidently, a fiancé. I thought he was just some guy your parents were trying to match you with, not someone you were considering."

"Well . . ." She shrugged, as if she'd never thought about it that way. Glen was more than just some guy, but he wasn't her fiancé. He was more a career option that just happened to come with a marriage offer, but she couldn't say that to Tinch. He'd think her cold, maybe even heartless.

Tinch stood and moved a few feet away from her. "I thought you were talking about a situation you were running from, not a future husband. If you didn't want the guy, you should have told him, not left him hanging for a year. Sounds to me like you're still thinking of marrying him for the job."

"No. Not really. Not yet."

Tinch opened the door for her to walk ahead of him inside. When they were in the warm light coming from the kitchen, he said slowly, almost too calmly. "What am I, Addison, the fling you hope to work in before you go back home and settle down? I never thought I'd be the one to keep you here, but I hoped I was more than a fling. So tell me, what is it between us, Doc?"

She hesitated too long. She could probably see the hurt in his eyes, and they both knew he'd guessed the answer.

"If Jamie hadn't come along, this never would have happened. It's not something I planned between us. Would a fling be so terrible?"

"Don't blame the boy. He had nothing to do with what's started between us, and we both know it." Tinch felt like someone had just stripped the wiring in his entire body.

Every cell seemed to be jerking in pain, but he'd learned a long time ago that pain didn't kill him.

"Tinch, don't make it sound like I planned this. I didn't. There's just this thing between us. I think I felt it from the first. It's like this pure attraction neither one of us can ignore."

"I think you should go back home, Addison. We don't need you anymore." He didn't understand what was between them either, but he'd thought it was more than some animal attraction. He'd hoped it could be the beginning of caring, but what did he know about relationships? He was over thirty, and he'd had only one other. He'd never been one of those guys who played around. He didn't know how to keep something like loving light and meaningless.

Addison pressed on her eyes with the palms of her hands. "I don't want to fight with you. Can we just go to bed and talk about this in the morning?"

"Fine." He didn't want to talk either. He felt like a fool for thinking for one moment that they might be building something. Even now, mad at her for leaving some guy in L.A. hanging while she kissed him like the world was coming to an end any moment, Tinch fought the urge to touch her.

She was halfway up the stairs before she noticed. "You coming?" she called.

"No. I've got some work to finish," he answered just as coldly as she'd asked. "I'll be up later."

He grabbed the quilt she'd dropped and went to his study without bothering to turn on a light. He knew he wouldn't climb the stairs tonight. He couldn't. As he spread out the quilt, he mumbled to himself, "I thought I was becoming her lover, only to find out I'm just her lab rat. Someone she planned to experiment with before she went back to her real life."

He tried to fall asleep, thinking of Lori Anne and all the gentle nights of loving they'd shared. They'd been best friends, *forever friends* she used to say. He could read her thoughts, and she knew him so well sometimes he swore they could go weeks without talking. They breathed together, always knowing how the other would act.

He never regretted the years of taking care of her. To him it was just another way of showing his love, and he knew if he'd been the one who had cancer, she would have taken care of him. They were two halves of a whole. They always had been. When she died, he felt like someone had cut him in half and then left him to stumble around.

Only, tonight, when he closed his eyes all he could feel was Addison in his arms. She was totally different. Not only didn't she know what he thought, but Tinch had a strong feeling that most of the time she didn't care. Making love to her would never be calm and comfortable. It would be a battle, half surrender, half conquest.

He woke a little after dawn with Jamie standing over him.

"You all right?" Jamie frowned.

Tinch scrubbed his face. "I just need coffee."

A cup appeared from behind him. He took it with both hands, but when he turned, Addison was already heading back toward the kitchen. He couldn't tell if she was still mad at him or just in a hurry.

Tinch downed the weak coffee and tried to clear the river of cobwebs floating like scum in his head.

"What time is it?" he asked no one in particular.

"I don't know. I can't tell time." Jamie sat down next to Tinch as if he thought he needed to be watched carefully.

"It's after seven," Addison announced. "Your cell phone was upstairs and woke us both up."

"I answered it," Jamie volunteered. "The sheriff says she's on her way out to talk to you."

Tinch glanced at Addison, but she just shrugged. By the time he changed into clean clothes and remade the coffee, Alexandra Matheson was knocking on his door. He waved her in and reached for another cup.

The sheriff might not have any kids, but she must have learned a few tricks. She walked straight to Jamie and handed him a gift.

The kid was so excited he could barely open it.

"I thought you might not have seen *Treasure Island*. If your uncle doesn't mind, you could watch it while I have a cup of coffee with him."

Jamie glanced at Tinch.

"Sure," he said, knowing the sheriff's plan. "I'll bring you a bowl of cereal to eat while you watch. We have little enough time to watch TV with all the work around here, might as well catch a little while you eat."

Jamie ran toward the TV in the study. "Thanks," he yelled back.

Tinch delivered the cereal, made sure the volume was high enough to block any conversation from the kitchen area, and poured himself another cup before he joined the two women at the table.

"Good coffee," the sheriff said as she held up her cup.

Tinch didn't miss Addison's frown. The doc seemed to think coffee should be about the same color as tea. She'd been doing her best to ignore him, and he hadn't had enough sleep to figure out why he'd been so mad at her last night, but their problems, or rather her problem, would have to wait until the sheriff left.

"Any luck at the funeral?" Tinch asked, his voice low.

"Not much. We have no idea who the creepy people in the van were, or the two guys who looked like hired guns, but we did get a positive ID on the driver of the van. He's a small-time dealer named Memphis Stone trying to work his way up. He was one of several dealers mentioned from Dallas who might have been Sadie's supplier."

"Anything else?

The sheriff nodded, glanced toward the study, and added, "An undercover cop in Dallas got a tip that Sadie stole a great deal of money before she left. The dealer, our van driver to the funeral, is looking for information about her kid. Since he didn't find Jamie or the money at the trailer, my guess is he thinks wherever Sadie left the kid, she left the money. My source said all he knows is the guy goes by the name of Memphis and word on the street is that he's not a man to cross. He's not tall and from what the cop said, he loves to pick on anyone weaker. He heard Memphis broke a woman's fingers once just to see how many it would take before she passed out from the pain."

"And you think he's coming here?"

Alex nodded once. "I got a half million reasons that he's coming. In fact, I'm guessing the guy is already here. He didn't find out what he wanted to at the funeral, so he's settling in waiting for his chance and that means he'll be pulling into your gate soon."

Tinch got the picture. "If he's coming after the kid, I'll be waiting. It may take him a while, but eventually he'll find out Sadie had a sister and when he does, he'll find me."

Straightening, as if she had to say something, Alex added, "Tinch, he's not coming after you or the kid. He's coming after the money, and I think he'll do whatever he has to do to get it."

"I get the picture, but Jamie had nothing with him and he's never mentioned any money."

Alex nodded. "I'd suggest you and the boy disappear, but I'm not sure. If they can track you here, they might be able to follow you if you decided to run with Jamie. I can think of a few lowlifes in town who might be watching your every move right now just for the promise of drug money."

"I'm staying. I've got a barn full of horses who need care and a small herd over on the north pasture who will need to be moved after the first freeze. My life, my work is here. If we have to make a stand, we make it here. I'll leave the gate unlocked so if they come, they'll come in that way. I'll hear the chime and be ready for them."

"But the boy," Addison objected. "He'll be in danger if he stays."

Tinch faced the doctor. "He'll be in danger wherever he goes. I'll take care of him. Make sure he knows what to do if trouble comes. We'll manage."

The sheriff looked like she was debating which side to be on.

Tinch knew he was right about being able to make a

stand here. No one could get close without him knowing it, and he was already well armed. If they moved the boy, there was always the chance the drug dealers could find him, and if they did, he'd be less protected. No foster home or group house could watch him like Tinch could.

"All right, Jamie stays with you. I'll have a deputy drive by every hour, and you keep that cell within reach. If we get a call from you, we'll be on our way." She looked at Addison. "But you, Dr. Spencer, need to leave."

Agreeing, he let out a long breath. "She wouldn't even be safe next door. Right now the easiest way to get to my house is to cross the field between her house and mine. If she were gone, I could bolt the gate to her place. If trouble comes, I want it heading in straight on, not sneaking in the back."

The sheriff didn't give Addison time to object. "You're right, Tinch. Right now no one knows the doctor is involved. She'll be safe enough in town."

Tinch saw something in Addison's pale eyes. Not fear or anger, but determination. She felt the same way about Jamie as he did. It didn't matter what they'd fought about last night. Right now they had to keep Jamie safe.

He could see the logical side of her reasoning out what would be best for the boy.

Alex poured herself another cup of coffee. "I think I'll catch a little of *Treasure Island* with Jamie while you two talk. I think the boy might know something he's not talking about. Maybe his mother told him never to tell and he thinks he's staying true to her."

"I doubt it. The kids talks all the time. Seems like if he were holding a secret, it would have dribbled out already." Tinch watched the sheriff walk into the study and Addison climb the stairs. He followed the doc, having no idea what to say to her.

When he reached the bedroom, she was standing next to what he now thought of as her side. She held his flannel shirt in one hand.

"I'm taking this with me. You gave it to me." She said the words as if she held something of value.

"I loaned it to you," he said, fighting down a smile. Surely the doc wasn't going to argue over a ten-year-old shirt. "But you can have it. It looks better on you anyway."

She began rolling it up. "I'll go over and clean my stuff out of the Rogers house before I head to work."

"Where will you stay tonight?"

"It doesn't matter. I could probably sleep at the hospital till I find a place. Maybe book a room at the bed-and-breakfast. It's close to the hospital and at least I'd get one meal a day."

Tinch had so much he needed to say to her, but now didn't seem the time. "Thanks for your help with Jamie," he finally managed.

"You're welcome." She picked up her purse and cell phone.

"When this is over . . ." He didn't dare move one step closer to her. "When Jamie is safe, I'm coming after you. You owe me a date."

"I may already be gone." She bolted from the room before he could say more.

By the time he followed, she already stood at the door. As she stuffed his shirt in her big purse, she called to Jamie, "See you later, kid. Try to keep your uncle out of trouble."

Jamie waved. "See you later, Doc."

"See you later," Addison said as she ran for her car.

Tinch walked to the door and watched her go. *When this is over, I'm coming after you. Only problem is I have no idea what I'll do when I catch up to you.*

Chapter 29

TYLER WRIGHT TOOK THE ASHES OF A MAN WHO'D LIVED to be ninety-three to Tulsa so he could be placed with the remains of his wife in a garden mausoleum. As always, he talked to his passenger in the box beside him.

"You know, Benny, you've been away from Juanita for twelve years. You two will have lots to talk about." Tyler laughed. He'd known Benny and Juanita since he was a kid. They'd always been old. Near as he could tell, Juanita never stopped talking and Benny never started. That might explain why she died first; she just wore out faster with the volume turned up.

People would probably think he was crazy if they ever knew he sometimes talked to his customers. He didn't do it often, and mostly just to pass the time, but he knew he'd better stop forever when his Kate got home. She wasn't the type to put up with nonsense.

Tyler smiled. She put up with him. He loved her for a hundred reasons, but most of all he loved her for loving him.

He'd always worried that he might be one of those people who'd make it all the way through life without finding someone to love him. He knew the town respected him, cared about him, thought of him as a friend, but no one thought of him as special except his Kate. She'd told him more than once that he was the most adorable man she'd ever met.

He frowned. She'd been gone eighteen days. She'd said she'd be back in two or three weeks, a month at the most. He'd counted, not only the days, but the hours each day. He told himself he could make the three weeks, but he wasn't sure he could make a month.

Touching his cell, he remembered what she'd said about when she was safe she'd call and let the phone ring once, hang up, and let it ring once more. Tyler knew when he got that call, he'd be able to take a deep breath. He might not know where she was, but he'd know that she was safe.

After he delivered Benny, Tyler headed back home. It was a long drive, and he hated the boredom of the highway between Tulsa and Oklahoma City. If Autumn weren't already due to deliver her baby, he would have pulled off the main road and wandered through the back towns, but today he needed to get home as fast as possible.

It was a little after dark when he made it in. Autumn had his dinner warming. In her last month of pregnancy she'd been cooking up meals and freezing them as if Tyler might starve the few days while she was in the hospital. In truth, he was looking forward to eating out. Between Autumn and Kate, fast food was almost impossible to sneak in. Once in a while when he met Hank Matheson for breakfast at the diner, Tyler ordered a hamburger and fries from their Round the Clock menu.

Two volunteer firemen were also in his kitchen when he made it home. They'd come so often, Tyler had begun to consider them the world's largest salt and pepper shakers at his counter.

They were good men. Brandon "Big" Biggs and Willie Davis both stood guard waiting for the stork.

Tyler nodded at them as he passed. If the stork did

happen to come, either one of the two would probably frighten him off.

"How are you feeling tonight, Autumn?" Tyler asked.

She gave him that don't-ask-me-again look. She was ready to deliver. "I'm fine, Mr. Wright, and before you ask, no one has called all afternoon."

He patted her hand. They were both circling the airport waiting to land, her with a baby and him with Kate.

Tyler ate his soup in his office, then went up to bed, thinking that as soon as he went to sleep, he could wake up and be one day closer to Kate being home. For a moment, in the darkness of his room with only his dog, Little Lady, beside him, he let himself think about what would happen if she didn't come home.

He'd survive, he decided. He'd go on, but he knew he'd never feel truly alive again.

Chapter 30

SATURDAY
OCTOBER 8

ADDISON SPENT ONE NIGHT AT THE HOSPITAL AND DECIDED she'd be wise to check in at the Winter's Inn Bed-and-Breakfast before she died of exhaustion. She'd been awakened to assist in emergencies that any one of several nurses could have handled. The staff was used to waking doctors who sometimes worked twelve-hour shifts and were cat-napping when times were quiet.

After a day trying to work without enough sleep, she checked into the B and B with only one bag. She'd never really thought about how few clothes she had until she'd packed at the Rogers house. Homeless people with their shopping carts had more stuff than she did.

Martha Q, the owner of Winter's Inn, asked how long she planned to stay, then raised an eyebrow when Addison said three months.

Addison had her choice of rooms, so she picked the small one at the back. It had a great shower and a small bed. She didn't even bother to open her suitcase. She just took a shower, put on Tinch's old shirt, and crawled into bed. The little bed seemed just one more reminder that she wasn't where she needed to be, but the silence of the old place rocked her to sleep within minutes.

After a good night's sleep and a huge breakfast, Addison felt like she could face the world again.

There was really no need to go back to the ranch house, even if the law did manage to put Memphis Stone and his gang in jail. Tinch owned her little rented house now, and it would be awkward. Addison couldn't stand the thought of a hotel or of trying to find another place to rent. The B and B just seemed the best option for the time she had left, and Mrs. Biggs, the cook, put heaven on a plate for breakfast.

The second night she laid out her pajamas but ended up sleeping in the flannel shirt again. Every night she called Jamie to say good night. He'd tell her all about his day and she'd lie and tell him she was too busy to make it out to the ranch tonight. He seemed disappointed, but he didn't cry.

When the kid passed the phone back to Tinch, he never had much to say to her. All was fine. Nothing had happened. No news from the sheriff. Addison knew the time waiting was hard on Tinch. She also knew he'd never complain.

On the third day, Addison called Alex and asked if they could meet for lunch. The sheriff and the doctor drew a few looks when they sat down together at the Blue Moon Diner near the old downtown square.

"I'm worried about Jamie," Addison said, seeing no need for small talk.

"He's fine. We're building a strong case against Memphis, and we're doing the best we can to find him. It shouldn't be long. Harmony isn't a town where hiding out is easy. If I have to do door to door, I plan to know if he's still close. Keeping Jamie safe is on all our minds."

When Addison didn't smile, the sheriff added, "You could probably go out and check on him."

Addison shook her head. "I'll be leaving in a few months. It wouldn't be fair to the boy for him to get attached to me and then have me be just one more person in his life who disappears."

The sheriff agreed with a nod and switched topics. "How's Autumn and the baby watch coming along at the funeral home?"

Addison laughed. "She's overdue. I offered to induce but she insists that she wants to go all natural as far as she can. If she doesn't go into labor soon, I'll have to induce or give Prozac to everyone at the Wright Funeral Home. Tyler came in with her yesterday, and I swear the man didn't look like he'd slept in a week."

Both women laughed, drawing the attention of several diners.

As their food arrived, the sheriff asked as casually as if she were just making conversation, "You going to see Tinch again, Doc?"

Addison looked up, surprised by the directness. "I don't think so," she answered, just as directly, and the subject was dropped.

Only that night, when Addison was alone in her room at the B and B, she couldn't stop thinking about him, and she knew she'd have to see him again. If she didn't, there would always be a sense of unfinished business in a corner of her life.

Chapter 31

BEAU AND BORDER SET UP THEIR EQUIPMENT AND WATCHED
the building crowd filling the tables around the dance floor
at the Buffalo Bar and Grill. Harley told them he was paying
them each a hundred even on the practice nights. He might
not get as big of a drinking crowd, but folks were packing in,
eating supper and listening.

"Look at all of them out there." Border peeked through
the chicken wire. "I don't think even my brother knows this
many people he can bully into coming."

"Maybe they're here for the wings?" Beau tied his hair
back with the leather strap Martha Q had given him.

"I don't think so. Harley's served the same wings for
years. I think they're here to see us practice."

Beau shook his head. It had taken him an hour a few
months ago to talk Harley into letting them practice on

Monday night. The only reason he'd let them do it was because no one ever came in on Mondays but the hard drunks, and a cannon going off in the place wouldn't bother them. Only, each week the crowd seemed to double.

"Ronny Logan is here." Border pointed at his neighbor. "I'm always asking her to come, but she says she's too tired after working at the post office. Then, tonight, she just walks over and bangs on our door asking what time we start playing."

Beau glanced up from his notes. Ronny looked nice tonight. She'd combed her hair and had on a pretty sweater. The longer he knew her, the prettier she seemed to get. There was some kind of glow inside her, like she was just waiting for something wonderful to happen.

"She got a few boxes delivered UPS this morning. I didn't open them, but it looked like a complete setup for a computer, printer, and the works."

"Maybe her mother sent them for her birthday?"

Border shook his head. "Old Lady Logan hasn't spoke to Ronny since she moved in. Word is the old bag tells everyone Ronny's dead."

"Nice relative," Beau said. "She have a fairy godmother, maybe?"

"No. She don't have no kin that I know about, except a mother who Big says is so mean she wouldn't spit on a frog on fire." Border smiled at his own little joke. "I asked who it was from and Ronny said she didn't know, but from the way she was smiling I think she had an idea."

"The nurses are here," Border said, wiggling his eyebrows. "Too bad my brother can't make it tonight. He's on duty at the fire station. I think he's crazy about that tall one. He threatened to murder me if I saw her and didn't go over and talk to her when we're on break."

Beau glanced over at the six nursing students as they sat down. The tall one was there, but all he saw was the cute little blonde with the perfect forehead.

Border must have seen her too. "You going to talk to her tonight?"

The lights went down and the twinkle lights came on like stars above them as Beau answered, "I'm going to hope for fifteen minutes with her. If I can keep that rate up, by Christmas I might be able to ask her out."

They began to play the first song as folks took the last few seats, and Harley smiled from behind the bar.

With everyone watching the stage, no one except Beau saw the short man in a dark suit slip through the front door and take a seat in the back of the bar. He kept his head low and when he did look around, he never looked at the stage.

Beau watched him, wondering if the man came to listen or to hide out in a dark corner for a while. There was something about the guy that gave Beau the creeps. His dad used to preach about demons who walk among us. Beau decided the little man fit the bill for what he would have guessed the demons looked like.

Chapter 32

IN THE COOL OF THE MIDNIGHT BARN, TINCH WORKED with the new horse Noah had passed along from the Matheson Ranch. Tinch had mentioned his fear of trying to work with the animal with Jamie around to his cousin and lawyer, Liz Leary. Like all the family, she thought she had to get involved. The next thing he knew Liz's husband, Gabe, and his friend were e-mailing that they'd be over at ten to babysit Jamie so Tinch could work.

When Tinch wrote back that Jamie would be asleep, they added, "Great."

So two guys who'd served years in Special Forces were watching the house and the boy so Tinch could get a few hours' work in. Life made little sense these days, but he felt good being able to just work and not be on guard.

When Tinch had time to think, he bounced between worry over Jamie and frustration over Addison. She'd been gone four days and he couldn't remember what they'd argued about. He knew she was safer away. The last thing he wanted was her getting in the way when trouble found him, but his body didn't see the reasoning and still ached for her. Every morning he missed talking over breakfast with her, and every night he stared at her side of the bed wishing she were there. The bossy, opinionated, skittish woman had gotten under his skin. All he could think about was the way she treated Jamie and how she made him laugh, and how she felt when she melted in his arms.

But here and now was not the time. He had to think first of Jamie.

Tinch felt like he'd done all he could to be ready for any unwanted company. He'd placed a rifle, well out of Jamie's reach, in every room of his house and the barn. He and Jamie had made a game out of seeing how fast the boy could disappear if Tinch even whispered, "Red Alert." They'd cleaned out the space beneath the stairs. A small door opened out and disappeared when closed. Lori Anne had wanted it to hide the vacuum, but it made a perfect secret hiding spot in the center of the house.

The two of them had also built swinging boards, just big enough for a boy, on both sides of the barn. Jamie could be gone in seconds and, before anyone could follow he'd be far enough away in a hiding spot that no one would find him. They saw it as a great game. Tinch prayed they'd never have to put the escape plan into action.

To the boy, it was just an adventure. A *Treasure Island* escape. But to Tinch, it meant Jamie's survival.

Leaning against the barn to catch his breath, Tinch pulled out his phone that Addison had programmed for him. One number would bring the sheriff, she'd said. Another would bring the doc running.

He held his finger over the button that dialed her cell. What if he called? He needed her. Would she understand? Would she come?

Tinch shoved the phone back into his pocket. He had work to do. This wasn't the time to act like some lovesick fool. He couldn't allow her to mean anything to him. He obviously didn't mean anything more than a fling to her before she went back to the big city. He didn't plan on standing like a fool watching her leave with his heart broken.

He brushed the mare he'd been working with, careful not to touch the wound she had received when she'd fallen. An inexperienced rider had taken her too close to the edge of a canyon wall. The clay soil hadn't held, and it was a wonder both the horse and the rider hadn't been killed. She wasn't as unruly as the Matheson horse, but she still needed his attention.

As Tinch turned to toss the brush and pick up a hoof pick, he saw a slight movement out of the corner of his eyes. For a heartbeat he thought trouble had come to call, and then he recognized the tall slender form. Addison. He swore the woman was so pale she glowed in the dark.

She took a step into the circle of light. Her long legs were covered with jeans that showed off every curve, and she wore his old flannel shirt unbuttoned enough that he could see the lace of her bra. The jacket over her shoulders was midnight blue and unzipped. For a moment, he just stared, thinking if this was a vision he wanted to remember every detail before it disappeared.

She took another step toward him.

Tinch moved a few feet away from the mare. "How'd you get here?" His words were colder, harder than he'd meant them.

"I walked over from my . . . I mean the Rogers place. I told the sheriff I needed to pick up a few of my things, and she texted the huge guys you've got babysitting so they'd unlock my gate and turn off the alarm for an hour so the chime wouldn't wake Jamie and frighten him. Once I parked in front of my house, I walked across the field in the moonlight."

"It's not your gate anymore, or your house. You moved into town, remember." He hadn't had time to ride over and see if she'd left anything, but ghosts probably left more clutter than she did. He closed the stall gate and tossed a latch so Jamie couldn't accidentally open this one. "What did you forget?"

"This," Addison whispered as she closed the distance between them and wrapped her arms around his neck.

Surprised, he took a step backward and bumped into the gate. She came right with him.

This time it was Tinch who stood frozen as she pressed her lips to his and leaned her body against his.

When he didn't react, she pulled away. "This is me attacking you again and, if you don't want what I'm offering, you'd better start fighting, cowboy, 'cause I didn't come all this way and tell a half dozen lies not to at least get one last kiss."

Logic told him if he had any sense left he should push her away. She was a heartbreak gift wrapped in long legs and soft skin.

Only, Tinch knew he couldn't turn away. Not now. Not like this with her body already against him.

"Convince me, Doc," he said with a slight smile.

She took the challenge. She kissed him for a long while before whispering, "Hold me like you don't want to let me go. Hold me so I don't just fade from your life." A slight cry escaped as she added, "Hold me, Tinch, so you'll never fade from my memory."

His arms wrapped around her and lifted her off the ground as he kissed her. "No chance of that, lady," he whispered against her lips. He didn't set her down when he broke the kiss but moved to her ear and added, "I don't want to let you go. Not ever."

Holding her off the ground, he crossed into the shadows at the back of the barn. She moved her fingers through his hair, pulling his head down so she could rub her cheek against his, needing the feel of him as dearly as he needed her.

Kissing her softly, he reminded himself to tell her sometime how much he loved it when she attacked him. When she bit his neck, he knew the period for gentle kisses was over.

He sat her down on a workbench and broke the kiss long enough to whisper, "How long do we have?"

"Only a few minutes," she answered as he shoved the jacket off her shoulders. "Those two guys sitting in your living room will come out if I take too long."

Leaning into her, he opened her knees so he could be closer. With her sitting on the bench and him standing in front of her, they were the same height.

For a moment, his mouth demanded more and he could feel her rock against him, giving him just what she knew he wanted. His hand found the front of her shirt and pushed her away roughly. Then, without hesitation, he balled the front of the flannel shirt in his fist and freed the snaps to her waist. Before she could cry out in shock, he covered her mouth once more and ended any protest.

When she turned molten in his grip, he leaned her back against his arm as he moved down her throat with light kisses, loving the taste of her.

She moaned softly as his free hand roamed over her. When she silently begged for more, he leaned her back on her jacket and spread his hand wide just above her waist to keep her still. He was advancing fast and hard. He needed to know she was with him.

One look into her eyes told him all he wanted to know. His fingers dug into her hair, pulling her head back, exposing her throat to his touch, to his mouth.

She rocked back and forth, wanting more.

Straightening away from her, he studied her in the shadowy light. The thin lace of her bra did nothing to hide her body. "You're beautiful, Addison." When he put his hand over her breast and tightened his grip possessively, she arched toward him and closed her eyes. He opened his palm over her and pressed gently before he circled her breast once with his fingers and gripped her tender flesh with rough work-hardened hands. She moaned with pleasure, as he hoped she would. "You come so alive at my touch. I don't think I'll ever get enough of you."

He kissed her completely then and left her gulping for air as he unbuttoned the first few buttons of her jeans. He knew if he went any further, he'd be going all the way with

her, and he couldn't do that. He wanted Addison, but he
wanted her body and soul and he wanted hours, not minutes, to make love to her.

All he could do tonight was brand his touch on her skin
and leave her longing for more. His hand slid over her as
she opened her mouth, waiting for his next kiss. No matter
how far she traveled away, she'd always dream of this night,
of this kiss, of his touch, and she'd know she'd left something unfinished between them.

He bruised her lips with the passion of the next kiss as
he pulled her to him. She was warm, liquid passion in his
arms. He found himself being rough one moment, demanding more, then so gentle she cried out in need. She seemed
to ride the waves, loving every level.

He buried his fist in her hair and tugged her back so that
he could see her face. He wanted to remember her with
passion in her eyes and hunger on her lips.

"More?" he whispered.

"More," she answered, trying to move closer.

"Then say you want me."

She laughed. "You know I do."

"Say it."

"I want you."

He moved his thumb over her bottom lip. "Are you sure
you don't just want a man, any man?"

"No. I want you, Tinch. All I've been able to think about
since I left was how much I needed you to hold me."

He kissed her then and somewhere amid all the passion,
Addison crawled into his heart.

Maybe he could show her how he felt, even if he couldn't
talk about it. He was afraid if he did, he'd say far more than
she was ready to hear.

After several last kisses, Tinch saddled a horse and carried her back to her car, parked in front of the old Rogers
place. He wished he could move slower, but he knew their
time was up. All he could do was hold her tight as they rode.

When he slid her off the saddle, he didn't kiss her. He
knew if he did, even once, there would be no leaving.

"Don't come back until this is over." His word came out hard, but his touch was loving along her back. "Promise me, Addison. It's too dangerous."

"I promise. You're right. I probably shouldn't have come tonight."

"I'm glad you did." He swung back in the saddle and was gone before either could say another word.

In the darkness between their two places, Tinch slowed and took a deep breath, but the smell of her had gotten into his lungs just as the feel of her against him had left an impression so complete that now she was gone he felt something missing, something wrong.

They were from two different worlds. They didn't belong together. They didn't fit.

Tinch stared at the sky wanting to yell and cuss until half the county heard him. If Addison wasn't meant to stand beside him, to lie beside him, to stay beside him, how could she feel so right?

Chapter 33

TUESDAY
OCTOBER 11

NOAH MCALLEN FLEW INTO AMARILLO WITH A NEW SIL-
ver belt buckle to add to his collection and a check in his
pocket that would pay the taxes on his little ranch near
Harmony for five years. Only, he hardly noticed either. His
mind was on Reagan Truman. It had been nearly a week
since he'd left her.

After their dinner in the apple orchard, he'd told himself
if he moved at all, he'd move slowly with any changes in
their relationship. He'd almost lost her as a friend and he
didn't want that to happen again.

Only, when she'd kissed him good-bye at the airport,
she'd kissed him on the mouth. The kiss had been polite,
even proper for an airport kiss, but to his way of thinking
it was more than a friend's kiss. Maybe he should just give
up thinking about changing anything between them and let

her set the pace. He'd called her every night since he'd been gone, and the talk had always been as friends. By the end of the week he'd decided he'd misread the last kiss.

He swung his bull rope over his shoulder and walked through the sleepy terminal. No one ever seemed around to welcome the last flight. In other parts of the country someone taking a saddle or a bull rope as a carry-on might seem strange, but not here.

He'd cleared the checking station when he saw her walking toward him, her hair flying around her in fiery curls. He made it two more steps before he dropped the carry-on and rope. He caught her in midflight as she ran toward him.

It might have been only five days since he'd seen her, but he closed his arms around her and held on tightly as people circled around them.

"I missed you," he announced honestly.

She smiled. "I missed you too."

Then she kissed him again. That on-the-mouth friendly kind of kiss that he couldn't quite read.

His mind had trouble figuring out what the kiss meant as she asked questions about the flight and the rodeo and the weather in Houston. Noah wasn't even sure he answered the questions in order, but she didn't seem to notice as they picked up his gear and moved toward the parking lot, where she'd had a devil of a time trying to park his long pickup.

Without much discussion they stopped for a bite to eat at an all-night place near the airport. The food was barely edible, but neither noticed. After three cups of coffee he decided he was awake enough to drive through the rain toward home. They settled into the truck, listening to music as they talked of their days apart.

Halfway there she mentioned a feeling she'd had for days that someone was following her. She said she hadn't had time to think about it seriously, it was just a feeling rather than anything based on fact. She'd noticed a car parked on Lone Oak Road where no one would stop. Twice a car had come up on her right after she turned toward town.

Noah turned off the highway onto the service road and noticed car lights half a mile back doing the same. A few minutes later he pulled back on the main highway and thought he could make out the car repeating his turn. The rain made it impossible to be sure.

Twice more the car followed his turns.

Reagan told him it was probably coincidence. With the rain it was impossible to tell if the headlights were even from the same car.

Noah let the subject drop and concentrated on his driving. He would have liked it if Reagan had sat close to him, but she seemed miles away on the other side of the bench seat. He'd promised himself that his days of trying to talk or push her into anything were over. If she wanted to stay the virgin all her life, he'd sign on as the fool who stayed her best friend. He knew she'd hate it if he mentioned it, but in his mind she was his girlfriend. She always had been.

They talked of the weather and the harvest. He told her all about his win and, of course, made himself sound grand. She laughed.

By the time they reached the turnoff to Truman land it was after midnight and she was dozing on his shoulder. Noah thought he saw a car slow behind him just as he turned into the dirt road to her place. He hesitated at the farm gate, but the car didn't pass. When he looked back, the night was black once more, no headlights. The driver had either turned around or flipped off his lights so that Noah wouldn't notice anyone watching.

Glancing at Reagan, he knew it would be wise to get her home before he confronted whoever it was. It could be just a nosy neighbor who'd wondered why Noah McAllen's truck was turning off at Reagan Truman's place. The Trumans, Mathesons, and McAllens had been the town's longest-running soap opera since Harmony was founded. Old Jeremiah Truman was dead and folks still talked about why he never married Pat Matheson when he came back from the war. Noah's sister, Alex, and Hank Matheson kept the gossip going until they finally married and settled down. Now, Noah guessed it was his turn.

Reagan would probably laugh, but there was also the possibility that the car behind them was a fan of his. Since his rides had been on TV, more and more folks were coming up to him and asking for autographs. With this latest ride there was talk that he might be the world champion if he could stay uninjured for the rest of the season.

"I'm beat," he said as he pulled up in front of her place. "Thanks for picking me up so late. After I get about a dozen hours' sleep, how about I come help you pack the last of the apples?"

She looked at him as if he'd become deathly ill in the last thirty seconds. "You're offering to help with the work?"

"Sure." He tried to look insulted.

"All right." She bit her bottom lip as if silently debating with herself. "You want to come in for milk and a slice of pie?"

Noah smiled, wanting to tell her any other woman in the world would invite him in for a drink. "No, thanks. Right now all I need is sleep, and you look like you could use a little yourself."

She nodded and moved to open her door. "Well, good night."

On impulse, he swung his door open and was around the front of the truck before she stepped out on the running board.

"What are you doing?" She laughed, shoving wet hair back from her face as he lifted her down.

"I'm walking a lady to her door," he said as he grabbed her hand and they ran.

They were both laughing when they hit the porch. Noah shook like a wet dog and said, "Well, at least I can skip the shower when I get home. Look at all the time you're saving me."

"Where's home?" she asked.

"I forgot to tell you I cleaned up the old foreman's

quarters at my place, well, at least enough that I can bunk there. I'm too old to stay at my parents' house even with them gone."

"With the way it's raining, every field mouse, rabbit, and prairie dog will be rooming with you tonight."

Noah shrugged. "At least it'll be quiet. At the hotel in Houston my room was right off the pool, and I swear some people never slept." He leaned against the porch railing and watched the downpour. The thought crossed his mind that he could probably ask to stay with her, but she'd offered only pie. If he went inside, he'd end up wanting more and she'd end up slapping him again. He shoved his hands into his pockets, trying to keep warm with his clothes already dripping wet.

"Noah." She drew him back from his thoughts. "Good night."

He turned into her kiss, surprised at how close she was behind him. Without touching him, she moved closer and gave him a kiss that had nothing to do with being best friends. He went along with the kiss but didn't move otherwise. He wasn't holding her. All she had to do was step away when she wanted what she'd started to end.

When she pulled back, he couldn't help but ask, "What did that have to do with you and me just being friends?"

Reagan smiled. "I'm getting used to you."

He grinned. "Then I'm coming home between every event." He stepped into the rain, figuring he'd better run while he was ahead. "See you tomorrow."

"It's already tomorrow. I'll see you later today," she yelled.

He watched her go into the house, the old dog at her side, then turned toward the road looking for any sign of the car that had followed him all the way from the airport.

After driving down Lone Oak Road for an hour, he saw no other car. It was late and anyone with any sense would be home in bed. Only, Noah had never been known for having sense. He drove over to the sheriff's office and told

Deputy Phil Gentry about what he thought he saw and what Reagan said she'd been feeling for days.

Gentry took the tip seriously. He said they were already patrolling Tinch Turner's place. Now they'd add the Truman farm to their rounds.

"You think someone is hiding out in Harmony spying on Tinch Turner?"

"No, not exactly. We've checked everywhere in town someone would rent, so no one suspicious is staying in town, but still there is evidence Tinch is being watched." Gentry frowned as if he'd already said too much. "This is not to go beyond you and me, Noah, but since you're the sheriff's brother and have already noticed something strange, I guess it would be all right to tell you." He pulled out a list of makes and models of cars that had been spotted on the back roads the past several nights. "This is a list composed by both us and the highway patrol."

"A few are scratched out." Noah raised an eyebrow.

"Those are locals who live along one of the roads. The others seemed to have no reason to be on the road between midnight and dawn. We've tried following the cars in question but have to stay so far away, so as not to be detected, that we lose them. It's as if they vanish in the night. Sheriff thinks they've probably got a base somewhere close, maybe Bailee or Twisted Creek. The back roads crisscross out here like a maze."

Noah looked at the list of old cars. "If I were you, I'd look for a used-car lot. You must have a half dozen different cars on this list. Maybe the strangers are holed up in a car lot."

Phil smiled. "Not a bad idea. If it's the same people in different cars, that would explain it. But whoever it is has connections around here."

"What do you think they're doing?"

"Maybe just watching. Maybe waiting for something or someone to appear." Phil smiled. "Maybe just building up their courage to take action." Phil finished off his tenth Diet Coke of the day before adding, "I can't say much more, only whoever it is thinks Tinch Turner has something that belongs to them."

Noah shook his head. "I've been to Tinch's place. All he's got is half-wild horses."

"And a kid," Phil finished more to himself than Noah. "I can't say more, but if I were you I'd keep an eye on Reagan Truman. Someone might think her and Tinch are somehow connected."

"I've been watching her for years," Noah said as he thanked the deputy and walked out. He didn't like the idea that someone was staking out not only Turner's place but Reagan's as well. He drove out the ten miles to Tinch's ranch and then circled by the Truman farm. Tomorrow he'd ask for the list of cars the sheriff's office was keeping, but knowing that it was all quiet at both places would help him sleep tonight.

A watery moon tried to show through the rainclouds as Noah felt adrenaline pumping in his veins as it did just before a ride. It was late. He should get home, but something didn't feel right.

He turned his truck around and decided to make another pass of both farms, knowing he wouldn't sleep tonight anyway.

Chapter 34

TYLER WRIGHT JUMPED OUT OF BED AND GRABBED HIS phone before he realized someone was knocking at his door. No one ever knocked at his second-floor quarters at the funeral home. It just wasn't done.

He shoved his legs, pajamas and all, into his trousers, forgot a shirt as he grabbed his jacket and rushed for the door. "I'm coming!" he yelled as the pounding sounded again.

When he opened the door, Willie screamed, "Hurry! The baby's coming!"

Tyler zipped up his jacket, shoved his phone into the pocket, and followed Willie down the stairs. He was out of breath when they reached the kitchen, but this was not the time to slow down. "Where's Autumn?"

Willie rushed past him and opened the door leading to

a large garage. "Big's getting her into your Caddy. We decided it has more room if we have to deliver on the way to the hospital."

Tyler tried to object, but no one appeared to be listening. Autumn seemed the only calm one, and she was breathing funny while she refused to climb into the backseat until she'd checked her bag to make sure she hadn't forgotten something.

Big stood next to her, holding everything she pulled out like some kind of giant clothes tree.

Forgetting about the plan to take Autumn's car, Tyler took charge. "Willie, you drive. I'll call the hospital and tell them to have everything ready." He calmed his voice as he faced Autumn. "How far apart are the contractions?"

"Four or six minutes," she said. "Willie got so excited he lost count."

Tyler frowned at Willie Davis, who until this moment Tyler thought had some brains. Before he could ask for the keys back, Autumn added in a whisper, "I think my water just broke."

"Change of plans," Willie announced, as if they were playing basketball. "Big, you drive. Mr. Wright, you call. Autumn, get in the back and lie down. We may be closer to the baby coming than we think."

Everyone moved at once. Willie was the last to climb in. "I'm riding back here in case I have to deliver the baby. I watched the film five times. I think I can handle it." He rubbed his hands together and flipped on the dome light.

Big started the engine and shook his head. "We're four minutes away. She'll make it."

Willie, who'd always been the calm one, suddenly looked very pale. "Now, Autumn, you tell me if you need to push. I'll try to get your pants off."

Autumn had had enough. "I'm not taking my clothes off, Willie Davis. Not in front of you guys, and right now the only thing I feel like pushing is you out of this car."

Rain tapped on the roof as they pulled out of the garage.

"It's all right, honey. Mothers-to-be often get upset. I'm sure the storm tonight put you on edge." His words were calm to her, but a second later he turned his head to yell in Tyler's ear. "Tell them we're coming in hot. Have everything ready for landing."

Big, to his credit, drove the speed limit to the hospital. Tyler made the call, but he wasn't sure he made any sense. If the hospital had caller ID, they probably figured out what was happening.

When they pulled under the emergency room entrance, two nurses and Dr. Spencer were waiting for them. A minute later Autumn was in a wheelchair heading inside and the three men were standing by the car trying to breathe.

"I'm too old for this," Tyler said.

"I'm too young." Willie shook his head.

Big laughed like he saw a joke no one else did. "Well, I'm just right, so how about we go check on our Goldilocks."

Tyler didn't even try to understand what Big was talking about. He just followed the two volunteer firemen inside. At least with the rain they probably wouldn't be called out on an emergency.

By the time they found where the nurses had taken Autumn, she had changed clothes and looked to be resting comfortably.

Dr. Spencer let all three go in and say hello, then told them how proud she was of them for getting Autumn to the hospital. The firemen beamed with pride, but Tyler had the feeling the doctor used the same tone when talking to first graders.

Tyler wouldn't have been surprised if the doc had patted them each on the head.

When the next contraction started, Dr. Spencer asked them to step outside. "We'll take it from here, boys. Why don't you all go have a snack? It doesn't look like you'll have too long to wait."

Tyler wanted to just stand outside the labor room door, but Big thought they should take the doctor's advice. None of the three had ever been around a woman giving birth, and they had no idea how long the wait might be.

A half hour later Big called his next-door neighbor, Ronny Logan. She was Autumn's best friend, and he said she'd want to know. Only Tyler noticed Ronny came in with a picnic basket of goodies she must have already had packed and ready. He suspected Big needed food more than company. Between Big and Willie, they'd already eaten through half the snack cakes in the machines.

"Evening, Mr. Wright," Ronny said when she offered him a brownie. "Have you heard from Miss Kate?"

Tyler shook his head. He hadn't thought of his Kate since he'd woken. "It's been over three weeks. She should be home soon." He tried to ignore the nagging worries in his mind.

He closed his eyes and made a deal with fate. Let her come home safe and sound and he wouldn't pester her anymore about planning the wedding. He'd give her all the time she wanted if she'd just come home safe.

"You all right, Mr. Wright?" Ronny asked in her shy way.

He nodded. "I will be. I was just thinking Kate will be sorry she missed the birth."

Ronny agreed. "If she were here, she'd have us all in line and organized. She's a sweet lady, but there's a general in her."

"A major," he corrected, missing her more than he thought it possible to miss anyone.

As the others ate, Tyler stood and walked to the window. The rain had slowed to a drizzle and the town looked newborn, as if asleep, without even a car moving along the streets. He loved this town, but he wasn't sure Kate would feel the same. She'd lived all over the world. Harmony must look very small to her.

He passed the time thinking of Kate as an hour, then two crawled by. Big started counting the times Willie said, "How much longer is this going to take?" Ronny worked every crossword puzzle in every magazine in the waiting room. No one bothered to turn on the TV in the corner. It was almost as if they all thought their job was to wait and they had to concentrate on just that.

Everyone jumped when Dr. Spencer appeared in the doorway. She smiled a tired smile. "Ladies and gentlemen, we have a girl. Eight pounds four ounces."

They all started asking questions at once, and the doc did her best to answer them all in order. Everything was normal. Mother and daughter were doing great. As soon as they got her settled in they could see Autumn one at a time, but only for two minutes each.

Tyler let the others go first. He stepped out on the little smoking patio and stared up at the moon, wondering if Kate could see the same moon.

"Autumn's had her baby," he said, needing to tell her even if Kate couldn't hear. "I know you'll want to hold her as soon as you get home." He almost added, *If you come home*. With each day's passing he felt less sure. She'd told him once that after all her years of being single, she'd become an expert at stepping away from people.

Was his Kate stepping away from him?

The phone in his pocket sounded once.

Tyler didn't breathe. He waited and waited. Nothing. Only one ring.

Several heartbeats later the phone rang again. One short ring and then nothing.

He let out a long breath he felt he'd been holding for twenty-three days.

She'd used the code. Kate was safe and on her way home.

He smiled. Tonight he was the luckiest man alive.

Chapter 35

TURNER RANCH

TINCH HAD TAKEN TO DRINKING COFFEE BY THE POT. IN the days since he'd seen Addison, he'd given up sleep completely. He tried. He'd close his eyes and relax, but the image of her ivory body lying on her midnight blue coat in the barn would always be there waiting for him. The feel of her, the way she tasted, the look in her eyes when she was starving for his touch, all were collaborating to drive him completely mad.

She must have felt it too. She e-mailed him several times and called to check in. Always, she asked how he was. What was going on? Was Jamie happy? But Tinch knew what both were not saying. He wanted her and she wanted him, but neither knew how to start talking about it.

When he saw her again, he planned to let her know how he felt without talking at all.

Last night, he ended his last e-mail report to her with

simply, *Someday, I promise we'll have time to finish what we started in the barn.*

He wasn't sure she'd even know what he meant, but a moment later the screen blinked and she answered. *Someday, I'll be waiting.*

It wasn't exactly a love note. Just a promise that they would have their time together. If a one-night stand was all she wanted, then he'd take it. One night would have to last him a long time, but he'd at least have the memory, and he'd learned he could survive on memories.

The temperature dropped with the sun and by the time they'd finished supper, Jamie was piling up blankets and still shivering. Rain tapped against the window to a lonely beat.

Tinch took the boy up to bed and decided to read him another story. The kid loved adventure, and Tinch's mom had kept all his old tales from *Tarzan* to *The Lone Ranger.* An hour into the first book the boy fell asleep, his arm looped around Tinch's as if he had to hang on even in dreams.

Closing the book, Tinch thought he'd just rest a minute before taking his shower, but sleep found him. Deep, dreamless sleep. The wind howled outside and the old heater in the basement clanked every time it came on, but Tinch and the boy slept.

Deep into the night, Tinch finally moved, feeling the crick in his neck while sleeping half sitting up. The book on his chest slid to the floor with a thud. Without bothering to pick it up, he rolled over, pulling covers over them both as he settled back into sleep.

The chime downstairs barely registered in his mind for a moment, and then he came full awake. Someone was on his land. As he climbed out of bed, he glanced at the clock. Three fifteen. This was no visit from the sheriff. Trouble was blowing in.

With one hand, Tinch shook Jamie awake. "Red Alert, son, time to put into action what we practiced." With the other hand, Tinch reached for his phone.

Panic shot through his veins like adrenaline. He must have left it downstairs. Damn, he'd worried about the thing for more than two weeks and the first time he needed it, the cell phone was missing.

Jamie rubbed his eyes but didn't question the order. The boy pulled on his boots as Tinch reached for the rifle above an old wardrobe.

A moment later Jamie followed him down the stairs, dragging his blanket behind him. Tinch opened the small hiding place that had once held the vacuum cleaner. "Get in. You'll be safe."

"I don't want to go in there," Jamie whispered with a sob. "I don't want to. It's dark in there. Don't make me. Please don't make me."

Tinch wanted to push the boy in and order him to remain silent, but the pain he saw in Jamie's eyes was too raw. Someone had closed him up before, maybe for a long time. In the daylight the little closet hadn't looked so frightening, but tonight the kid would be in total blackness. He'd promised he wouldn't ever lock Jamie away, and he wouldn't break his word.

Grabbing his own jacket off the stair railing, Tinch helped the boy into it as he instructed, "Go out the back door and run to the barn. Hide there and don't come back until I call you. If any stranger steps into the barn, go through one of the swing slats in the wall and run. Run like hell, son, promise me. No matter what you hear, keep running until you reach someplace safe."

Jamie nodded and bolted toward the door off the kitchen.

Tinch glanced out the long row of front windows. He could barely make out a gray van heading toward him with the lights off. They were moving slow, probably thinking they could sneak up on the house. Not even the two pups sleeping on a rug by the door had heard them yet.

If he needed any proof that trouble was coming, the fact that the headlights were off told him all he needed to know. Without turning on a lamp, he crept across the living area, feeling for his cell on every counter and table he passed.

Tinch pulled an old double-barreled shotgun down from above the bookshelf. He was all that stood between Jamie and these men, and he'd stand alone.

The van was in the yard thirty feet from the house when Tinch reached the porch. He held the rifle against his leg and set the shotgun six inches away at the railing.

As the passenger door of the van opened, Tinch flipped on the yard lights, keeping himself in shadows, but the men in full light. "That's far enough," Tinch yelled.

A big man had slid the back door of the van halfway open, but he didn't make a move to get out. The front passenger, his twin in age and size, slowly rolled from the seat and stood still, his hands in the air.

Tinch couldn't see the driver very well, but it looked like he did the same thing. With his hands high, he circled the van until he was in full sight. The driver was smaller than his passengers, but no more welcome.

"Sorry to bother you," he shouted. "We mean you no harm, Mr. Turner. You see, we're lost and were hoping for . . ." The short driver didn't seem to take the warning seriously. He sauntered toward Tinch as if he hadn't noticed he might not be welcome.

Tinch raised his rifle. "Stop right there and try again." Anyone lost wouldn't have called him Mr. Turner. These three knew exactly where they were and they had no doubt they were on his land.

The pups were awake now and must have sensed Tinch's mood, for they were both off the porch and growling at the driver.

The little man seemed more afraid of the dogs than of Tinch. He backed up until he hit the side of the van. "Look, Mr. Turner, we're not here to hurt anyone or cause trouble. We just came to ask you a few questions. Then we'll go."

"That why you came in with your lights off?"

The guy straightened as if stepping out of the sheep's clothing he'd been trying to wear. "All right." He held his hand up and pointed to the passenger. "It was Henry's idea to catch you by surprise. He thought you'd give us straighter answers, but we're not here to hurt you or anyone you got here. We just want to talk to Sadie's brat. You can ask the kid. He knows me. Just tell him Memphis is here and all I want to do is talk to him."

"What boy?" Tinch's words came cold.

"Don't try to pretend you don't have the kid here. We looked it up and Sadie Noble only had one living relative, your wife. It just makes sense they'd try to dump the kid off on you."

"No one dumped a kid on me. Why don't you just get back in that van and head out the way you came. Turn your lights on this time. I don't want you hitting my gate on your way out."

Memphis inched a step closer to the porch, his shoulders rounded as if in defeat. "Look, Turner, we just want to talk. You know, a friendly visit. There's a thousand dollars in it if you'll give us five minutes with him. He ain't nothing but trouble anyway. I should know. I've been the only discipline in his life for a year. His mom was always too strung out to care what he did."

Tinch remembered the bruises on Jamie's back and had to fight to keep from pulling the trigger.

Memphis took another step toward the corner of the porch. "How about five thousand for five minutes with the kid, then we leave. A small place like this, you could probably use the money and we won't hurt him much. If he claimed we hurt him, he's lying. If we didn't have some fun with him now and then, no one would ever pay attention to him."

"Get off my land." Tinch forced the words out as he pointed the barrel of the rifle. "One step on my porch and you're a dead man."

Memphis shrugged as if he'd given up. "Too bad," he said. "You could have made this easy."

Hearing the squeak of a door, Tinch glanced back at the van. The big guy in the front seat was still standing where he'd stepped out, but his hands were no longer in the air.

Tinch raised his rifle a moment before he noticed the thug in the back was missing. Both Memphis and the guy he'd called Henry were moving slowly toward different ends of the porch.

Tinch had never shot a man, and he hesitated a second before taking aim on Memphis. His father's word from a hunting trip flashed through his mind. *If you take aim, son, take aim to kill. Never leave an animal wounded.* As far as he'd seen and heard, calling Memphis an animal would be giving him an upgrade.

Memphis jerked, reaching for something in his coat as Tinch squeezed the trigger slowly and sighted on the center of the man's chest.

A shot blasted through the air like a cannon, knocking Tinch back and sending the bullet he'd fired wild into the night.

The whole world blinked suddenly as if lightning and thunder had hit at once. Tinch spun. He saw the man at the back of the van with a rifle aimed, ready to fire again. Memphis and Henry were running toward him, both with weapons pointed at him. Henry ripped the rifle away from Tinch's hand. Then, all within the same heartbeat, a fiery pain spread from Tinch's side, rippling and burning in waves through his entire body.

He touched his ribs, now covered in warm blood, a moment before the butt of the rifle slammed against the side of his head.

He crumbled, his eyes closed, into hell. A thought rolled around between the pain. He was dying. He'd be with Lori Anne soon. He'd finally get the one thing he'd hoped for since the day his wife died. He could simply rest and let the world slip away.

Then, like a hollow ache deep inside, he realized he no longer wanted to die. He couldn't. He had Jamie to raise. He'd made a promise to Addison. He couldn't leave. Lori Anne would have to wait awhile longer.

Tinch forced the pain aside and concentrated on what was going on around him.

"He's dead, Sullivan," Memphis shouted, his voice wheezy with excitement. "Don't waste another bullet on him."

The shadow of one of the thugs moved over Tinch, but he forced his body still. Let them think he was dead. It might be his only chance of living.

"If he ain't dead, he will be soon," one mumbled. "His blood is painting the porch."

The dogs were circling around the porch barking.

Memphis swore, then ordered, "Kill the dogs, Henry, I'm tired of hearing them yapping. Then we'll find the boy and get the hell out of here."

"Make Sullivan kill them. I hate killing dogs."

"You won't hate it so bad when one of them bites you."

Tinch heard a shot and a dog yelp in pain. Henry must be following orders.

Memphis laughed. "You just winged him, you idiot. Look at them run." His laughter ran high and loud before he added, "Just as well. No use wasting time looking for a black dog in the night. We came after the boy. Let's get this over with."

Tinch opened one eye just enough to see the little man moving into the house. He couldn't have been five feet four, but he carried his shoulders high, as if that stretched him a bit.

"Maybe we should burn the barn," the thug called Sullivan asked. "With it burning and his uncle dead, little Jamie will tell us anything we want to know, and we won't have to lay a hand on him."

Panic ignited where worry had been in Tinch's mind. He didn't know where Jamie had hidden. The barn? One of a dozen hiding places in the fields? The Rogers place?

"Someone will see the fire, you idiot." Memphis's voice sounded older, slower than before. He was either tired of the two thugs, or tired of the hunt. He wasn't a man who wore patience well, Tinch guessed.

"We'll be long gone before anyone would see a fire." Henry added his opinion from inside the house. "It's not like folks have a neighborhood watch this far out of town."

Sullivan must have stalled as if to discuss the choices, because Memphis swore, snapping insults like he might a whip to get the two men moving. "Forget the barn," he said, ending any plans the other two had. "I know how to make the boy talk. So help Henry find the brat. He's around here somewhere, probably whimpering like a little rabbit just waiting to be caught."

Tinch fought to keep from passing out. He could hear the men tearing through his home, breaking things as they searched. The damage didn't matter. Nothing mattered but Jamie.

Tinch stared out into the night, fighting to stay alive. As long as he could keep breathing and feel his heart pumping, he still had a chance.

One set of lone car lights moved down the road almost a mile away from his front porch. Tinch had no idea who it would be this time of night, but whoever it was might be the chance he'd been waiting for.

He reached for the shotgun, propped the barrel against the railing, pointed in the general direction of the van, and pulled both triggers. The thunder of a double blast rocked the sky and rolled across his land as the big gray van shook from the pelting.

Chapter 36

⁂

ADDISON WASHED HER HANDS IN THE PREP ROOM, THEN moved through the silent hospital hallways. She'd checked on Autumn and the baby. Both were sleeping, as was Tyler Wright in the waiting room. She'd told him to go home, all was fine, but he said he couldn't. He was too excited.

Grinning, Addison realized the usually reserved undertaker was beyond happy tonight, and she was glad. As she passed, she glanced in his direction.

He held his cell phone in his hand but, to her knowledge, he hadn't called a soul. The two volunteer firemen, who'd rolled in with Autumn between them, had left with a list of names Autumn gave them to call after sunup.

Ronny Logan, Autumn's friend, was sleeping in the recliner by the new mother's bed. The two young women seemed an odd pair to be friends. Autumn had suffered a rough life before she came to Harmony, and it still showed in her face. Ronny, on the other hand, looked like a woman who was just waking up to life.

Addison smiled. If she was thinking of odd couples, she and Tinch would win the prize. A month ago she would have sworn she'd never have anything in common with such a man, yet somehow he was always in the back of her thoughts. He wasn't a man who tried to make a good impression, but the longer she knew him the more she respected him. He was a man of his word, and in the world today that was rare. She'd never heard him brag about anything but his ability to two-step, or boast, or even defend his actions.

She decided to work a few more hours, then return to the B and B so exhausted she could sleep until she had to report for duty officially at noon. The hospital didn't need her any longer tonight. For once, the labor and delivery had more staff working than patients who needed care. Even the emergency room was empty except for the two nurses on duty and an orderly sleeping on one of the couches in the waiting room.

Stepping into her dark office, Addison relaxed, leaning against the door and letting the excitement of the birthing settle. There were days, sometimes months, when all she had time to be was a doctor; then there were moments like this where she just wanted to be herself. For as long as she could remember, her parents had wanted her to be a doctor. It was almost as if she were nothing until she completed med school and, now that she'd finished, they still wanted her to be more.

When she went home, her father would lecture until he got his way and her mother would simply frown at her as if she feared Addison and their real offspring must have been mixed up at birth.

Addison thought of one man who seemed to like her just the way she was. All she'd been able to think about since her few minutes in the barn with Tinch was the way he'd handled her. In the silence, those feelings floated back around her almost like a hug. He'd touched her as if he couldn't get enough of the feel of her. Like she was someone to be cherished. To be loved. She'd told herself it was just a physical attraction between them, but she knew it was more, far more. They seemed to both thrive on breathing the same air.

Tinch could have had sex with her in the barn. She was willing. But he hadn't. He wanted more. She saw it in his eyes. Felt it in the way he touched her.

Tinch wanted to make love to her, and she had no idea how many times it would take before either got enough. Maybe years. He didn't just want a woman, a body, a one-night stand. He wanted all of her, and that one fact frightened and excited her. With him there would be no polite affair, no casual one-night stand.

With him Addison felt she wouldn't just be good enough, she'd be all he'd ever want.

Flipping on her office light, she tried to pull her mind back to her work. She checked her messages and found a dozen from her father, all demanding she call him back immediately. As she erased them one by one, her cell phone rang.

"Dr. Spencer here," she snapped, expecting it to be the emergency room or an ambulance en route.

"Doc," a small voice whispered.

"Jamie." Addison heard panic in his high tone. "Are you all right? Did you have a bad dream?"

"I'm fine. I hid just like Tinch told me to when the mean guys came, but I keep hearing shots and I'm scared."

Addison started running toward the exit. "Where are you? Where's Tinch?"

There was a long pause, and then Jamie stumbled over words as he said, "I think he's dead. I couldn't see much, but it looked like he fell down. A guy at the van fired a gun. He shot at my puppy too. I ran as fast as I could toward your place, but you weren't there." He let out a cry. "Tinch gave me his coat and I found this phone in it. He told me to push two to get you, so I did."

"I'm on my way. Stay where you are until you know you're safe then run to my place."

Addison grabbed her medical bag and a field kit at the

emergency room's nurses' station, still asking questions. How much time had passed? Were the men still there? Had he turned on any lights that might draw attention?

No one answered. The phone was dead.

"What is it?" Georgia yelled from where she'd been reading a book behind the admissions desk.

"I think Tinch has been shot!" Addison shouted. "Call the sheriff and have someone meet me at his place."

Georgia grabbed her coat and caught up with Addison at the door. "I'm going with you. I'll call from the car. If he's hurt, you may need another set of hands. We only have one ambulance running tonight, and he's thirty minutes away with a heart attack victim who asked to be moved to the hospital in Clifton Creek."

"Why?" Addison asked as she shoved all the supplies behind the driver's seat and climbed in. She wanted to scream, *How could a town only have one ambulance?* but she already knew the answer.

Georgia talked as fast as she worked. "The woman he's transporting is ninety-three. She's been at the nursing home for ten years and never said a word. Then tonight she must have decided death might really come to get her and she wanted to die in the town she was born in."

Addison didn't have time to argue. While she raced out of the parking lot, Georgia placed a call to the sheriff's office.

As she shot through the night, Addison tried to think of what she might face. Having a fully equipped ambulance streaming behind her would help, but Harmony's backup ambulance standing on call was little more than a station wagon. A few nearby towns could have a unit in Harmony within thirty minutes, but with luck, she and Georgia would be back from the farm by then.

"Dispatch said they're sending two cruisers and calling the highway patrol for backup. He's also trying to reach the sheriff." Georgia's voice didn't sound as calm as usual. "Tell me what you think we're going into, Doc."

"I'm not sure. Jamie was out of the house and watching

from somewhere in the dark. He said Tinch got shot by some bad men." She couldn't bring herself to say that the boy thought Tinch was dead.

"How'd he call?"

Addison flipped her cell open and looked at the last call just to double-check. "He called from Tinch's phone."

Georgia was trying to reason. "So, somehow the boy had his phone. Even if Tinch is hurt, he wouldn't be able to call us."

"Right."

"Are the men still there?" Georgia asked. "The ones who shot Tinch?"

Addison nodded slowly, realizing the danger they were about to face for the first time.

The nurse looked at her watch in the dash lights. "At this speed we'll be there in seven minutes. If you go any faster on these wet roads, we may not get there in one piece."

Addison slowed slightly. Seven minutes might mean life or death if Tinch was hurt.

Chapter 37

TINCH FLOATED OUT OF THE PAINLESS BLACKNESS AND back into reality. Someone pulled him to a sitting position and tied one of his hands behind the porch pole. His side burned and one of his eyes felt swollen from the butt of the rifle colliding with his head.

"If he can fire a shotgun, he can damn well talk!" Memphis yelled as one of the heavyweights slapped Tinch hard.

"Where's the boy, Turner?" Memphis's tone rose with excitement. "You're going to die anyway. The only question is how much pain you can take before you do."

"Go to hell," Tinch said between clenched teeth as the thug split his lip with his fist.

The thug he thought he'd heard called Henry stomped out of the house with a handful of Jamie's clothes. "The kid's been here. My guess is he's been told to hide."

Memphis moved his face an inch from Tinch's nose. "Tell us or we burn the barn, still full of horses, and then the house."

Tinch spat blood in the little man's face.

He didn't hear any order, but the beating came in rapid-fire blows and kicks for several seconds before Memphis must have given the signal to stop.

"The brat ain't worth this, Turner," one of the men said. "Hand him over."

Tinch thought he heard Henry yell that a truck was coming up the road fast. Then all three men disappeared and Tinch slipped back into painless blackness.

Chapter 38

NOAH HAD BEEN DRIVING FAR TOO LONG, BUT WITH EACH round past Turner's place and then down Lone Oak Road he told himself just one more check and he'd call it a night. Reagan wasn't a woman to be jumpy for no reason. If she thought she was being followed, she probably was. He wished, for the hundredth time, that the rain earlier had let up enough on the drive back from Amarillo for him to see the car behind him. Noah felt like he was driving around blind, not even knowing what he was looking for.

When a gun blast rattled the night, Noah slowed. He thought he'd seen the flash from a rifle or shotgun firing a half mile ahead on his left. He scrubbed his face and tried to see into the night.

When he looked down the dirt road that led to Tinch's house, he noticed the yard lights shining bright. No one in the house could be asleep with all those lights on, and he would swear the place had been dark thirty minutes ago when he'd passed.

Then he saw the van. Tinch didn't own a gray van. Neither did anyone else Noah could think of. Turner had company. Unwanted company.

The sense that something was wrong, very wrong, crawled along Noah's spine like a dozen hairy spiders.

Noah swung onto Turner's property and reached for his cell phone. If nothing was wrong, all he was doing was wasting a few minutes of sleep. If something *was* wrong, he wanted backup.

The mud made the road slippery. Noah followed tracks that had to have been made since the rain stopped. Whoever drove the van had driven onto the ranch after midnight. The tracks were fresh.

Halfway between the gate and the house, he saw three men running for the van. Noah gunned his engine. One big guy slipped in the mud and had to run to jump in before the van shot away from the house and toward Noah.

Noah swerved into the grass, taking out a few fence posts as the van drove past him, slinging mud in waves on both sides.

He grabbed his cell and speed-dialed his sister.

She answered on the first ring. "Noah?" Though it had to be near four o'clock in the morning, his sister didn't sound asleep.

"Turner's place, fast," was all Noah had time to say before he pulled up in front of the farmhouse, dropped his phone, and took off in a dead run toward the body on the porch.

Chapter 39

THE NIGHT AIR AROUND HIM COOLED AS IF WINTER rushed in on snowy feet. Tinch could feel his heart slowing, taking a few last moments to remember what he'd never see, never feel, never smell again. Final snapshots to treasure but never share.

He relaxed, knowing he was leaving the only home he'd ever known. He'd learned to walk holding on to the railings of this porch, and now he'd die with his blood soaking into the tiny cracks between the wood.

It was time for him to see Lori Anne again.

Sweet Lori Anne, who'd made him smile every day they'd been together. He'd take her hand and they'd walk for a while with no direction in mind and no sense of time. He'd always loved the feel of her hand in his. Since they'd been kids she'd needed his strength. At one point in her dying days at the hospital, he'd thought if he held on tight enough she wouldn't pass. Best friends, first loves were supposed to live long lives together. Only, she'd left him. She'd died.

When she passed, he knew that all the reason, all the joy had dropped out of his life as well. She'd gone to heaven and he'd been left behind in hell.

But now, he was almost with her. He could almost feel her hand in his.

He'd tell her about Jamie. She'd like hearing everything the boy said. He'd tell her how the kid packed his pockets with Cheerios because the horses liked oats, and how the boy got all excited to hear that they'd swim with tadpoles in the spring.

The image of watching Jamie sleep passed through his thoughts. He could see Addison on the other side of the bed. A guardian angel in his flannel shirt. She thought she was so strong, so sure of herself, yet at almost thirty she still hadn't stood up to her father.

She needed him too, and a part of him needed her more than he'd ever needed anyone. Like steel sharpens against stone, he needed her to challenge him, to argue with him, to never accept anything from him but his best.

The chill of raw pain shook through Tinch's body along with a bottomless sadness. He couldn't leave the boy. He couldn't. Lori Anne was at peace, he felt it, but Jamie needed him and Tinch needed Addison because she'd take all the love he had left to give.

Tinch took another bolt of pain, reminding him he was still alive. Moving his hand a few inches, he grabbed the railing of the porch and gripped so hard he was surprised the wood didn't splinter in his hand.

"Hold on," he whispered. "I have to hold on. I'm not going anywhere. I can't."

Chapter 40

TURNER RANCH

HIS BRIGHT HEADLIGHTS FLASHED ACROSS THE FRONT porch. For a moment all Noah saw was blood, and then he made out what looked like a body tied to one of the poles.

Noah was out of the truck and running.

He'd grown up on a ranch, knocked around at rodeos for enough years to see cowboys twisted and bloody, but nothing prepared him for what he saw on the porch. Tinch Turner had been beaten so badly, Noah almost didn't recognize him. Blood was dripping from his mouth and head, but it seemed to be pouring in a steady stream from his side.

Noah pulled a knife from his pocket and cut the rope, then had to hold Tinch to keep him from falling. Slowly and as carefully as he could, he lowered the man to the boards of the porch.

"Tinch!" Noah turned the rancher's face toward him. "Turner, answer me!"

He shoved some of the blood away, trying to see any sign of life, and pressed his fingers along the cut on the side of Tinch's head.

Tinch jerked an inch away, and Noah almost laughed with relief.

Noah stood and ran into the house. If he didn't slow the bleeding, Tinch wouldn't be alive long.

The place looked like a tornado had hit. Broken dishes, slit leather furniture. Noah grabbed a blanket at the bottom of the stairs and another from the couch. He gathered all the kitchen towels he saw and headed back to the porch.

Sliding to his knees on the blood, Noah began to work. All he'd had in the way of emergency training was a course one summer when he'd volunteered with the fire department, but he put everything he'd learned to use.

Tinch was breathing and still bleeding. All Noah had to do was keep the first one going and try to stop the second.

It seemed like hours, but it must have been only a few minutes when first a police car, then a little sports car both came flying through the gate toward him. The deputy shouted for backup as he ran from his cruiser, but Dr. Spencer and a nurse rushed toward the porch, their arms loaded down with supplies.

Noah stood and stepped back as the two women moved in. For a moment, he just stared at his hands covered in blood.

"He's still alive," the doctor announced. "Let's get him stable enough to transport."

Noah stared as the two women worked. The doctor might be young, but she seemed to know exactly what to do.

"Since I don't see an exit wound," she added, "the bullet must still be in him." She worked quickly, like a fighter determined to win the round.

The deputy circled the yard, answering questions on his cell phone, or rather trying to answer questions. Finally, he looked at Noah. "Did you see who did this?"

"Three guys, I think," Noah answered, without taking his eyes off Tinch. "Two were big men dressed in dark shirts and pants. The third was smaller." All he'd seen was a flash of the men running for the van. "They're driving a gray van."

"Make and model?" the deputy shouted.

"I don't know."

"License plate?"

Noah shook his head. He'd walked into a crime and hadn't noticed the basics.

The doctor glanced up from her work to Noah and seemed to sense his panic. "You saved his life. If you hadn't gotten here first, he would have already been dead by the time we arrived."

Noah couldn't speak. He just nodded and moved out of the way. Two more cars pulled up, his sister's jeep and a highway patrolman's cruiser.

Thirty seconds later his sister stepped onto the porch, with the deputy filling her in with details as if he considered himself a newscaster. While she let the deputy finish, she put her arm around Noah's waist. She might be the county sheriff, but she was his big sister first. "You all right?" she finally whispered when the report was over.

Noah nodded.

"I need to ask you a few questions. What did you see? Who did you see? Remember every detail you can."

Noah pulled himself together, knowing exactly what he had to do. "I was just out driving. When I passed his place, I heard a shot. No, more like a blast. I turned around and decided to head in. When I was almost to the house, a gray van ran me off the road. Then I was here trying to help Tinch." Noah had a feeling he'd be asked the same questions again and again, but he doubted he'd remember more.

She smiled at him, but her smile didn't reach her eyes. "Did you see the boy?"

Noah shook his head, remembering the kid Tinch had with him at the vet's place in Bailee.

The doctor broke into their conversation. "The boy's

safe. He called me from Tinch's cell and told me there had
been shots. I told him to stay where he was until he knew it
was safe." She pointed with her head toward the Rogers
farm. "The phone went dead, but I'm thinking he's probably at my place."

"I'll check on him," Alex offered.

An ounce of worry faded from the doctor's eyes. "Right
now we've got to get Tinch to the hospital. We'll have him
ready to go in three minutes. He'll need to lie flat and we
don't have time to wait for an ambulance. Noah, can you
drive him in the back of your pickup? It'll be open to the
air, but probably less painful on him than trying to fold
him into a car."

Noah nodded, suddenly relieved to have something to
do. "I'll grab a mattress and more blankets."

By the time they loaded Tinch, another highway patrol
arrived and the place was starting to look like what it was,
a crime scene. One of the men noticed glass and chips of
paint in the yard where the van must have parked. Alex
lowered her phone as she looked at a broken taillight in the
dirt. Then she put the phone to her ear and announced,
"The men left here in a gray van that was sprayed with a
shotgun. Taillights and windows may be out."

"And it's leaking fuel," the deputy said, touching a
small pool of dark liquid in the dirt. "These guys aren't
going far tonight."

Alex followed Noah to the driver's side of his truck as
one of the patrolmen helped Addison and Georgia in on
either side of Tinch. "Get him there fast," Alex shouted.
"I'm going after the boy—make sure he's safe."

Noah nodded and opened his door. He was in, with the
engine started, when he noticed Jamie hiding in the floorboard of the passenger seat. Before Noah could call back
his sister, he felt a small hand tug on his pant leg.

"I'm going too," the boy whispered. "Don't tell or they'll
try to stop me. I got to go with Tinch, or the men will come
back and kill me."

Noah had no idea what was going on, but he threw the

truck in gear without a word. If someone was after the boy, he'd probably be safer right where he was than anywhere, and he could waste no time in making a decision. Tinch's life depended on it. He'd call his sister as soon as he could. Right now he had to drive.

One of the deputies led the way toward town as Noah pulled a Colt from the glove compartment. With both Tinch and the kid traveling with him, if anyone stopped Noah, they'd be facing a gun.

They were out on the main road with Dr. Spencer and Nurse Veasey riding in the back with Tinch before Noah glanced down at the kid again.

Big eyes stared up at him. "Is my uncle still alive?"

"He's alive and we're doing all we can to keep it that way. Dr. Spencer will pull him through this. She's a good doctor."

The tiny boy didn't look like he had shoulders big enough to take all the weight that seemed to be resting on them. "If he dies, it's all my fault."

"No . . ."

"Yes it is." Jamie gulped down tears. "I know where my mother hid what those men are looking for. It's a black bag just like the pirates hid money in on Treasure Island. I saw it deep down between the boards when I squeezed into the space to hide. I'm the reason they came to the ranch. My momma showed me how to pull a board off this place under the table at our trailer. She said I could hide there if anyone came asking questions. When I heard the men banging on the door, I wiggled down so low in that space they wouldn't have seen me even if they'd pulled the board loose."

"What's in the bag?"

"I don't know, but she said it might be our way out."

"Out of what?" Noah asked.

Little shoulders shrugged. "I don't know. For as long as I can remember, my momma said when she was real sick that she wanted out. She told me never, never to tell anyone about the bag so she'd have her way out when she needed it."

Noah watched the road as he asked calmly, "Where's the bag now, Jamie?"

"I left it when the sheriff took me. She told me my momma was dead, so I didn't think she'd need the way out anymore."

"You did right," Noah said, hoping to make the boy feel better. "The men hurt your uncle because they are bad men, not because of anything you did. I want you to know that, and I think your uncle would want you to understand that too."

Jamie hugged his knees to his chin. "All right," he said, but Noah sensed the kid didn't believe him.

Trying to think, Noah stared straight ahead. After a long minute of silence, he said, "Why don't you climb up beside me, Jamie, and watch for the hospital. I don't want to miss it this time of night."

"No," Jamie answered. "If those bad men see me, they'll kill you too."

Noah didn't argue. The boy might be right.

When they pulled up to the emergency entrance to the hospital, the staff was waiting for them. Noah just watched as the team moved in and, within seconds, transported Tinch inside.

Noah swung the pickup toward the back of the hospital and into the parking lot marked for employees. "You want to go in with your uncle?"

Jamie looked up from the floorboard. "You think they will let me in?"

"No, but I know the back way. Spent some time here once."

Jamie crawled up. "He's in there all alone? It's scary being alone. I want to be with him. Could you take me to him? My uncle says you got guts. He says you don't fear nothing."

"I don't know about that. If I were looking for a hero, your uncle would be first on my list." Noah had pieced together what must have happened at the Turner place. Tinch had stood alone and sent the boy to safety.

Jamie nodded. "He's a knight sent to protect me, I think. Only right now, I got to protect him."

"Sounds like a plan," Noah answered. "I'll help."

Noah smiled, thinking maybe someday he might be lucky enough to have a son who cared a fraction as much about him. "Climb on my back, kid, and I'll sneak you in."

Once the boy was hanging on tightly, Noah moved through the darkness to the back door of the hospital. No one came in that way except employees and the funeral home guys. The door should have been locked, but he wasn't surprised to find it cracked open an inch. The smell of smoke lingered around the entrance, a ghost of break times recently spent.

Noah moved silently through the hallways and stairwells to the waiting area for the operating rooms.

As he let the boy down on one of the chairs, he whispered, "They'll bring him out those doors after they get the bullet out. All we have to do is follow to see what room they take him to."

"You won't leave me, will you?"

"No way, buddy, but if you don't mind I'll call my sister and tell her you're safe. She's a sheriff, you know. It's her job to worry about folks, and right now I'm guessing she's about to go nuts worrying about you."

Jamie agreed.

Noah made the call, then bought the kid a soda and crackers from the vending machines. From the shadows of the waiting room they watched nurses come and go. "You know, Jamie, you could go home with me. We could stay at my folks' house. It's not far from here."

"No." Jamie curled up into a ball. "I'm gonna sleep here."

Noah had a feeling if he tried to change the boy's mind, he'd have a fight on his hands. He laid his arm over Jamie's shoulders and stretched out his long legs clad in jeans so covered in dried blood they could have stood on their own. He couldn't worry about how he looked now, so he might as well get some sleep too. They wouldn't be getting any news on Tinch Turner for a few hours.

Before Noah could get to sleep, Alex appeared in the doorway.

She motioned him to the hallway where they could talk and not wake Jamie. "You shouldn't have brought him here."

He could see the anger in her eyes and figured she was right, but she hadn't seen Jamie curled up on the floorboard of his pickup. She hadn't seen the fear or the determination in the kid's eyes. The kid had been shoved around all his life, and now the one person he cared about was dying. All he wanted was to be close to Tinch.

"Sue me," Noah whispered, refusing to defend himself.

Alex frowned at him like she'd done all his life. No matter how old he got or what he accomplished, he'd always be her dumb little brother.

"You know, they'll probably come here to look for the kid. Those guys don't seem to operate according to any form of common sense. I wouldn't put it past them to show up at such a public place."

"So stay around, Sheriff, and do your job. Catch them."

"I plan to." She looked at the bulky windbreaker he wore. "You armed, Noah? Because if you are, I should tell you it's illegal to have a weapon in here."

Noah met his sister's gaze. "You want me to admit to a crime or lie?"

Alex straightened and reached in her pocket. "Raise your right hand." She pulled out a badge. "I'm deputizing you. If you're going to be the boy's guardian, you might as well be legal."

"How do you know I won't do something stupid?" Noah took the badge and slipped it into his shirt pocket.

"I don't know. You've been doing stupid things all your life. Maybe I'm just playing the odds that it's got to be about time you did something right." She glanced in at Jamie curled on the chair sound asleep. "I'll put a guard downstairs where he can see both the elevator and the front door, but no matter what happens, don't leave the boy anywhere."

"I wasn't planning on it."

For once she looked like she believed him. "Want to tell me why you were driving down the back roads at four in the morning?"

"Reagan said she thought she was being followed. When she picked me up earlier, I had the same feeling, but it was raining so hard I couldn't make out what or who was following me. When Gentry told me you guys were circling Tinch's house, I thought somehow the two might be related."

Alex frowned. "Tinch Turner and Reagan Truman have little in common. I'm surprised they even know each other. I can't think of any reason the drug dealers might put the two together."

Noah closed his eyes and swore. When he faced his sister, he had to force the words out. "Their connection could be me. Tinch and I swapped trucks the day I left last week."

Alex pulled out her cell. "We need to check this out. If Memphis followed Tinch to the Truman farm when he returned your truck, Reagan could be in danger."

Noah didn't care what time it was, he needed to talk to Reagan.

Her cell rang once, twice, three times. No answer. He hung up and tried the house phone.

Deep down he knew where she was. He'd seen her moving among the shadows of the orchard a dozen times as if a piece of her soul lay hidden there among the low branches and exposed roots.

Noah looked at Jamie. Part of him wanted to believe the boy was safe here. A half dozen people could keep an eye on him. Drug dealers weren't likely to storm a hospital. Alex had told him she would place a guard downstairs.

He gripped the phone in his hand, wishing Reagan would pick up on the other end. All she had to do was tell him she was fine. She'd be careful. She'd be on guard.

No one answered. He thought of all the times she'd called him and he hadn't taken the time to answer.

Noah had to do something. He had to act, but he couldn't leave Jamie.

He stared at Jamie as he disconnected her number and dialed another.

A half dozen rings later, Big answered the phone. "This better be important or you're a dead man, Noah McAllen." He sounded half asleep and furious. Which in Noah's observation was pretty much normal for Big.

"Rea may be in trouble. How fast can you get over there?"

Big didn't hesitate. "I'm on my way. Hang on."

Noah heard banging around and, a minute later, the sound of Big's pickup being fired up.

"Did you sleep in your clothes?" Noah shouted. "Or are you driving over there naked?"

"None of your damn business, McAllen." Big was wide awake now and, from the sound of it, moving fast. "Fill me in. I'll be there in three minutes."

Noah told Big all he knew, then hung up. He knew the phone wouldn't leave his hand until Big called back that all was safe.

While he waited, he told Alex all that Jamie had said about his mother's "way out" bag. They agreed it had to be drugs or cash, but there was nothing anyone could do about it now. Every lawman in the county was busy tracking the men who'd shot Tinch. If Memphis and his thugs hadn't found it hidden between the boards and the deputies hadn't discovered it, the bag was probably safe for a few more hours.

Noah sat down, staring at the phone, wishing it would ring. If anything, anything, happened to Reagan he'd blame himself. A dozen *should haves* came to mind, but finally all he knew was that he couldn't make it if she wasn't all right.

Chapter 41

TRUMAN FARM

REAGAN TURNED HER COLLAR UP AGAINST THE WIND and moved silently among the trees. In a few weeks the last of the leaves would be gone and they'd be no more than the skeletal remains of an orchard until spring. Her uncle had always frowned at the land in winter, but in many ways it was her favorite time.

There was an honesty about the orchard in dormant months. No pretense, no shadows over shadows until no one could tell where one tree ended and another began. She wished people were as easy to read in the goodness they carried as trees were. If a branch was rotten, it was easy to tell, but people could be decayed to the core and no one would know until it was too late.

When she'd been growing up, moving from one foster home to another, she'd been wrong more often than right about people. Some had sugar coating only a quarter of an inch deep, and others seemed gruff, but cared. She remembered liking Uncle Jeremiah, not because he was nice to her at first, but simply because he didn't hit her or call her names.

She felt close to him here, even closer than if she'd been at the cemetery. He'd put his sweat and blood into this farm. Maybe a part of him and all the Trumans who lived before were still here watching over her.

Standing on the edge of the orchard, Reagan waited for the sunrise. She liked seeing first light spread across her land. It warmed her as it warmed the earth.

Car lights moved slowly down the road and hesitated at the entrance to her place, where newly planted evergreens rose barely as high as the car hood.

She'd learned the sounds of both Noah's and Big's trucks. Jeremiah could close his eyes and name any visitor stopping by. If they'd driven onto his land once, he knew the sound of their engine.

Maybe she'd inherited his talent, she laughed.

Only, this car clanked and chugged like an old piece of junk that hadn't seen a tune-up or good gas in years. When it reached the end of the line of evergreens, Reagan saw the shape. A van, big and square, built like a tank.

A couple of carpenters were still installing some equipment in the barn, but they never came before nine.

An uneasiness settled around Reagan, and she moved backward into the trees as if they were silently pulling her into their folds.

The sky was still more black than gray when she heard a car door. It hadn't been slammed, but closed carefully so as not to make too much noise, but the sound carried the few hundred yards on the wind.

She made out the outlines of two men, both big and rounded. They walked to the porch and stood waiting while a third man, smaller in stature, joined them. All three looked up at her window and waited as if they expected her to appear or at least turn on a light.

When one pointed to the screen door, she realized she

hadn't closed the door or latched the front screen before she left. The house was wide open. Everything she owned was there for the taking, and it seemed obvious that these men were up to no good. Suddenly, the silent morning was shattered by Old Dog bolting out, knocking the screen door back with a pop. He barked once at the three men, then growled. All three men took a step backward.

Usually, Old Dog never barked. He knew everyone who came to visit. But he didn't know these men and he planned to protect the house. He jumped at the closest man with the energy of a pup.

She heard the man yelp in pain. The second big man shouted something while the little man ran for his open car door.

The instinct to survive, born on the streets, kicked in. Reagan turned and ran through the orchard. She tripped once, twice, but she scrambled to her feet and kept going toward the fence at the back of the trees.

In the distance she heard the van engine being gunned and guessed the short man had left both his friends behind to face Old Dog. Maybe he hated dogs, maybe he was just through with the thugs and figured he could disappear easier without them along.

She didn't think, she just ran. Evil had stepped onto her farm, and all she could do was escape.

Chapter 42

TINCH CAME AWAKE ONE PAIN AT A TIME. HE'D BEEN IN enough bar fights to recognize each injury. Cracked ribs, stitches on the side of his head, a lip that tasted of dried blood, and a half dozen more.

"Be still, Mr. Turner," someone close to him said. "I'm almost finished."

"Doc?" He knew it would hurt too much to open his eyes, so he just guessed. She had a kind of hurried sound to her voice when she was nervous or trying to act all professional.

"Yes, it's Dr. Spencer. I'm just checking your side. You've lost a great deal of blood, Mr. Turner."

Tinch shoved his pain aside and tried to clear his mind. Something was wrong. She hadn't talked like this to him since before their first kiss. Everything that had happened in the darkness washed back over him. Waking to tell Jamie to run. Meeting the men with rifles loaded. Being shot. Being beaten. Waking at the sound of Noah McAllen yelling at him.

"Jamie?" Tinch needed to know that the men who had beaten him hadn't found the boy.

"He's fine," Addison said as she touched his hand. "He's outside in the waiting room with Noah at his side."

Her touch had been light, her voice still formal, almost as if she didn't know him or the boy. Tinch remained still as she bandaged his side. He sensed more than heard others in the room.

His entire body felt heavy. If he could have, he would have pulled her against him and told her how much she meant to him.

The familiar sound of machines beeping and clicking reminded Tinch that he'd be out of this place as soon as he could walk. He hated hospitals. The sounds. The smells. If he could just wake up, he'd find a way to get out, but all he seemed to be able to do right now was listen.

"You did a good job, Addison," a man's voice sounded from several feet away. "This fellow will have very little scarring thanks to you. Your skills are meant for much more than sewing up cowboys who've been in gunfights."

The man with Addison sounded older, twice Addison's age. Tinch couldn't place the voice, but the accent definitely didn't belong in Texas.

He felt Addison's touch on his arm, a gentle pat as if to say she was close. "Mr. Turner wasn't in a gunfight. He was protecting a child from men who meant him harm."

"Whatever." The man's voice sounded bored. "Can we move on? I really don't have much time and I have to talk to you. I didn't fly halfway across the country to make rounds with you."

"No, you don't," Addison whispered as she tucked the sheet back over Tinch's arm. "We've nothing to say. You wasted a trip. I've told you that several times on the phone."

"Don't be ridiculous, dear. The sooner I get you out of this hick town the better. You've proved your point. Now it's time you come back where you belong."

Her hand was back, moving along his arm as if she needed to hold on to him even though he could offer her no support. "Tinch," she whispered.

He felt her brushing his hair off his forehead, and he moved slightly into the warmth of her fingers.

"Tinch, are you awake enough to hear me?"

He nodded.

"The sheriff wants to talk to you. Can you answer a few questions?"

"I'll try, Doc." His voice sounded broken and rusty.

"I'll go find her."

They moved away, Addison saying something to the man in the room, and Tinch could no longer make out the words.

An hour later, when he woke again, he wasn't sure he hadn't dreamed the strange conversation he'd had with the sheriff. She'd asked him questions, but the answers kept getting jumbled up in his mind.

Slowly he molded his hand into a fist. He was stronger now. Less groggy.

Blood seemed to be pumping in his veins again. The blinds were closed and machines created a dull buzz. He heard the door open and close almost silently, and then Tinch felt a small hand slip into his.

"Hello, Jamie," he whispered. "Glad you're here."

"You don't look so good, Uncle Tinch. Your lip is all puffed up and one of your eyes is funny colored."

"You should see how it looks from this side." Tinch laughed, then groaned in pain. He tried to open one eye. "You all right?"

Jamie nodded. "I didn't like what they did to you. I wanted to run and tell them to stop, but I remembered what you said about staying in the rabbit hole until I knew it was safe to come out."

"Rabbit hole?" Noah asked from somewhere behind Jamie.

"That's what we call this little spot halfway between our place and the doc's. It looks like flat land from our porch, but when you get to it, you see it's a little bump in the ground where the dirt piles up high enough to hide a person. I could look between the weeds and see the porch. If anyone came near, all I'd have to do was roll down in the hole a few inches and no one could find me."

"Pretty ingenious," Noah offered.

"Tinch says it's an old Apache trick."

"Jamie?" Tinch interrupted. "You stay with Noah until I get a little better. You understand? Go with no one but Noah or the sheriff or Doc."

"I understand."

Tinch wanted to ask where Addison was and when she'd be back in, but his brain felt like someone had poured pudding inside it. Thoughts could barely move forward enough to be voiced.

He knew there were details he needed to ask about, things he should know, but right now it seemed enough just to know that he was alive and Jamie was safe. The rest could wait.

Chapter 43

TRUMAN FARM

BY THE TIME REAGAN MADE IT TO THE PROPERTY LINE fence at the back of the orchard, she was covered in mud and her hand was bleeding. In the distance, she heard the sound of a siren, then a moment later, one, two, three shots in rapid fire from the house.

No one but the two guys left by the van driver was there. They wouldn't have any need to shoot a lock off anything, and no one was there to try to stop them.

So, why the shots?

Reagan fought down a cry as she realized why. They'd killed Old Dog.

Every ounce in her wanted to go back and fight, but reason told her she had to survive first. If the driver hadn't gone back for his partners, the men left behind would come looking for her after they searched the house. If they noticed her truck keys, they'd probably widen their search and head toward the orchard. From there, they might see her. She had no idea why they were here, but she knew they were trouble. Bad trouble.

As she moved along the fence line, she heard a car and looked down the road in time to see the sheriff pull into the farm entrance with sirens blaring. Two highway patrol cars were ten feet behind her.

Reagan smiled, almost wishing she could run back through the orchard in time to see the men's reaction. She didn't know why they'd decided to come to her place so early, but she had a feeling they'd be leaving in the back of one of the cars.

She watched the road. It bothered her that she hadn't seen where the van had gone. If he'd come toward Lone Oak Road, she would have heard him. From the front yard of the old house, he could have taken a half dozen turns. The orchard, the barn, one of Jeremiah's storage barns for the old tractors he collected. There was even a rough road that circled round the new orchard behind the house and ended up almost at the entrance to the farm.

Logic told her she wasn't out of danger yet. She'd learned a long time ago that trouble doesn't always need a reason to come calling. Her one and only plan right now was simply to stay out of their way.

Reagan climbed over the stile Jeremiah had installed just in case folks wanted to steal a few of his apples. Half the people in town admitted to the theft, including the sheriff. Reagan always thought her uncle was proud of that fact. He said once if he'd plant watermelons, his farm would be the stealing capital of Texas.

Trying to shake mud off her, Reagan walked toward town. She wanted to know what was going on at her place, but not enough to get between the cops and those guys. Trying to give them the benefit of a doubt, she thought they might just be lost. Only someone asking for directions usually didn't come before dawn or shoot the watchdog.

A diesel engine barreled down the road toward her. Reagan looked up to see Big heading straight for her.

"Rea!" he yelled as he jumped from his truck. "You all right?"

"I fell down." She felt like a child holding out her hand to show him the small cut. "What are you doing here?"

"Noah called me and told me you needed me."

"But . . ."

Big lifted her into the truck. "I don't know any answers. Noah just said when I found you to bring you straight to the hospital and, from the looks of that cut, I figure that's just where you need to be."

Chapter 44

TYLER WASHED UP AS BEST HE COULD IN THE WAITING room bathroom, then walked down the hall to the maternity ward.

It was far too early for visitors, and Tyler knew he had to get home and clean up properly before anyone saw him with his pajamas on beneath his coat. Only he couldn't leave without saying good-bye to the baby. He had to see her one more time. He'd wave. He didn't figure she'd wave back, but he wasn't sure.

He stood in the nursery window and watched Autumn's tiny baby sleeping with her little pink cap down over her ears. He'd be forty-six his next birthday—well on his way to fifty, he thought—and this was the first time he'd been part of a birthing. True, the two firemen, Willie Davis and Big Biggs, had done most of the work, but he had taken his turn at holding Autumn's hand tightly during a few contractions. Once they moved to the delivery stage, both boys had gone in with her to help, but Tyler took sole duty of pacing.

He must have walked ten miles before Big rushed out to tell him everything was going well. Near the end, both firemen joined him, and then finally the doctor came out with the news. Eight pounds four ounces. Tyler had no idea if that was big or small for a newborn, so he asked, "How much did you weigh when you were born, Big?"

Brandon "Big" Biggs sat down on one of the couches and took a deep breath. "I feel funny," he said, just before he rolled onto the floor, out cold.

Tyler watched in amazement as nurses, hearing the thud, rushed in to help. They managed to roll him over and prop the back of his head on the couch cushion. After two bottles of water and a cold towel, one very tall nurse announced that he'd simply fainted.

Everyone talked at once, saying things like they were glad he hadn't toppled in the delivery room, and one said she thought the big guy looked cute spread out like a bear rug in the waiting room.

When everyone left except the tall nurse, who was still patting Big's hand, Tyler finally got a word in. "All I did was ask him how much he weighed at birth."

The nurse had a kind smile. "I'm not due on until five. I just came up, when Big called, to see if I could be of help. It appears the best thing I can probably do now is take this one home."

Tyler agreed, though he doubted Big needed any help getting home. He lived only half a mile away and, though he looked a little pale, her constant patting seemed to have helped him recover.

The nurse helped Big to his feet. "Mr. Wright, will you tell Willie what happened?"

Tyler nodded, noticing Big had to lean on the pretty nurse.

"And Mr. Wright, you could go home too. Autumn worked hard tonight. She'll sleep for a few hours and so will the baby. You should get a few hours' sleep yourself and then come back in the morning."

He shook his head. "I'll wait until one of the girls from the office gets here. Just in case she needs me."

Tyler stood watching them go. He couldn't leave. Not yet. Not till it was morning. Then he'd go man the office while the others came. He couldn't leave and face his apartment alone.

Walking to the window, he stared out into the sleepy town. Today would be a great day. Autumn's baby was born and Kate was safe. All his worries over the baby being late or Kate not coming home washed out of his thoughts. He knew trying to get any sleep would be a waste. It was time to plan his day.

The women would come up straightaway after they were called. Then he'd clean up, transfer all calls to his cell, and go shopping. He and Kate had already decided they would be grandparents to Autumn's baby, and a grandparent should buy things.

Tyler was thinking a swing set for the square of grass off Autumn's apartment would make a nice gift. Maybe he could rip up ten feet of the driveway out back and make the yard bigger. And, of course, he'd need to plant a tree for shade. He thought he'd have a circle walkway poured so the little girl could ride her bike.

As he strolled back to his place in the waiting room, he thought maybe the walkway was something he could wait on.

Sitting down in the middle of a long empty row of plastic-covered chairs, he held his cell, wishing Kate would call back and give him a little advice. She might be in her forties also, but surely she'd been to baby showers over the years. Maybe she'd know what to buy.

As he planned, his eyes grew heavy and he closed them while he thought. The room was warm and still. Within a few minutes he was fast asleep, the smile still lingering on his face as the morning warmed into day.

Chapter 45

NOAH HAD BEEN PACING THE HALLWAY OUTSIDE TINCH'S room for ten minutes. Each time he passed the windows, he looked in on Jamie, sitting next to Turner's bedside. The kid looked so small as he held his uncle's hand. He was too young to be mixed up in such trouble.

Hell, Noah thought, *I'm twenty-one and* I'm *too young*.

A nurse from down the hall passed by, frowning at him, about every fifteen minutes. Each time she reminded him that Tinch was being carefully observed and didn't need visitors.

Noah ignored her comment. He wasn't a visitor and neither was Jamie. If she wanted them out, she'd have to bring more than a frown to the fight.

The elevator door rattled and Noah moved close to Tinch's door. He didn't care how many deputies were downstairs watching for the drug dealer, Noah planned to stand his guard until they caught the guy who did this to Tinch and Jamie was out of danger.

His sister had phoned in that the two thugs he'd seen running from Tinch's place were now in custody, but the little weasel leader had slipped past them somehow. She'd told Noah that Reagan hadn't been at the house when they made the arrest. He already knew that much. If she'd been home, she would have answered the phone and he wouldn't have had to call Big to go check on her.

Noah stared at the elevator, wanting it to be news of Reagan, but half wishing it would be the guy named Memphis. Noah wouldn't mind pounding on him for a while. Noah was a man who ate adrenaline for breakfast, and right now he was starving.

Big stepped off the elevator, and for a second Noah was furious that he hadn't protected Reagan, and then he saw her walking a step behind Big.

Noah felt the tug on his heart that he always did when he first saw her. He thought he fell in love with her that first day he saw her, the new kid in high school with no one to talk to and a chip on her shoulder so big she could barely carry it around. She wasn't tall and long legged like a beauty queen, but darn if she wasn't adorable.

As she ran toward him, he noticed her clothes were all muddy and she looked like she'd been crying. As always her wild red hair circled around Reagan like her very own cloud of fire.

Noah waited until she looked up when she was almost to him, and then he took one step and swept her into his arms. She was the one woman he'd ever known whom he couldn't get enough of. The one girl he couldn't hold tight enough.

"You all right, Rea?" he whispered against her ear.

"I look worse than I feel." She smiled.

"That's good." He smiled, thinking he'd seen men dragged around the arena by a horse who had less dirt and mud on them than Reagan Truman had.

She tried to explain what had happened, but there were too many pieces to the puzzle she didn't understand. "Big said he'd better bring me right here or you'd be fit to be tied."

Noah looked around to thank the huge man, but Big was nowhere in sight. "Where'd he go?" Noah had trouble believing three hundred pounds of muscle could disappear.

"He said as soon as I was with you, he'd go find someone to take a look at my hand. I told him not to bother. I've been hurt worse, but he just said he'd be back in a minute."

Noah hadn't noticed her hand until now. As he looked at the small cut running across her palm, he frowned. "Looks bad, Rea. I think we'll have to amputate."

"Shut up." She pouted. "It hurts."

Looking around, Noah saw his options as few. He couldn't leave Tinch and Jamie, and he didn't plan on Reagan stepping out of his sight. Somehow this one hospital room had become their bunker. "Come on." He opened Tinch's door. "You need to wash up before that hand gets infected. There's a sink in here and Tinch is too out of it to care."

They moved as silently as possible across the room and around machines until they reached the small sink.

While Reagan tenderly patted around the cut with a paper towel, Noah walked over and put his arm around Jamie. "How you doing, kid?" Noah whispered.

Jamie shrugged. "He's not going to die, is he?"

The man in the bed closed his fingers around the boy's hand. "I'm not going to die, son. I swear, so there's no need to worry or ask again."

Noah couldn't help but grin at the boy's smile. A Christmas morning smile in the middle of this was a welcome sight.

"Noah," Tinch added, his eyes still closed, "any chance you could get someone over to my place to feed and water the horses? I may be able to tomorrow, but I could use the help today." His voice was slowing. "Maybe leave some food out for the kittens and dogs. Look out for one that may be injured."

"I'll see that it's done." Noah knew it took a lot for a man like Tinch to ask for help. He also knew that somewhere down the line Tinch would return the favor. "Just got word that the sheriff's department has two of the trespassers who beat you in custody. She's taking them in now and will be over as soon as they're locked up."

Tinch seemed to relax, and a smile touched his swollen lip. "One more," he whispered before seeming to doze off.

Jamie moved up on the side of the bed, waiting for Tinch to say something else. "One more what?" the boy asked.

"One more man to catch," Noah finished the sentence.

"How about we let him sleep, Jamie," Noah whispered as he lifted the boy over to a recliner near the windows. "We'll be here when he wakes up, and you can talk to him more then." He covered Jamie with a blanket and added, "Why don't you sleep for a while. When the sheriff gets here, I'll go find us a couple of breakfast burritos; till then I'll watch over you, and I promise if Tinch wakes I'll give you a shake."

Jamie didn't argue. He was asleep before Noah finished tucking him in.

For a moment, Noah stood watching the sunrise over the roofs of Harmony. He hadn't been to bed in twenty-four hours, but he didn't care. He was home and needed. It felt good.

When he lived on the road from one rodeo to another, time passed in events and not days. After months, the memory of how it felt to be part of a town, a family, seemed to fade. An old man in a bar told him once that rodeo wasn't a way of life, it was a way of dying one piece at a time. He'd said that in the end a man can end up broken and alone if he's not careful.

Noah watched a very tall nurse walk through the door and head straight for Reagan. She had that all-business look about her. One brief glance at him made it plain that she didn't want to talk to him. If he wasn't the patient, he was near invisible to her.

When he noticed that Big followed her in, he asked, "You go get that one?"

"She's a friend of mine. She's on duty downstairs, but I talked her into taking a break to help Reagan." Big shrugged as he watched the nurse. "Or, at least she *would* be my friend if it weren't for you."

"Me? I don't even know the lady." Noah frowned at his almost-friend. "By the way, what is that you got on? You look like a side of beef wrapped in felt."

"It's a jogging suit." Big spread his arms. "I think it was supposed to be a birthday gift for Ester's brother, but she gave it to me an hour ago, so of course I had to wear it. Looks great, don't you think?"

Noah grinned. "Since when have you ever jogged?" Big probably burned a few thousand calories a day working. He wasn't the type to need more exercise.

"I'm thinking of taking it up." Big did his best to whisper, but he wasn't a man who practiced the habit. "Ever since a certain lady"—he pointed toward the tall nurse with his head—"gave this suit to me. She says it's just right for me to wear when we're cuddling."

Noah slapped himself on the forehead trying to get the picture of Big cuddling with anyone out of his head. "You and cuddling fit together about like a runway model and spurs."

He wore such a silly grin that Noah fought the urge to slap Big, but he had the feeling if he did, the construction worker would stomp all over him even if he was wearing a jogging suit made for cuddling.

The tall nurse ended their pointless conversation when she turned from the sink and held up Reagan's hand. "It's not really a cut, more like a scrape. She didn't need stitches, just some antiseptic cream and a Band-Aid." The nurse smiled at Reagan and added, "I think there are some at the nurses' station. I'll go pick up a few and be right back."

When she walked past Big, Noah didn't miss the way she brushed his shoulder like she couldn't keep her hands off his jogging suit. He doubted the gift would have had the same effect on her if the nurse had given it to her brother.

For some odd reason, the woman seemed to think Big was as cute as a toy bulldozer.

Reagan held up her hand as she joined them by the window. "All better," she said, then narrowed her eyes. "Were you two fighting?"

Noah and Big both tried to look innocent.

Reagan shook her head at them and went back to the sink to try to get some of the mud off her clothes.

Noah leaned closer to Big. "What do you mean, if it weren't for me that nurse would be your friend?"

"Nothing. Forget it."

"No, you started this. If you won't tell me, I'll go ask that pretty nurse. She looks like a sweetheart." Noah would have added something about even if she was a couple of inches taller than him and outweighed him by fifty pounds, but he figured if he said anything about her size he'd be lying next to Tinch in the hospital. Big had always been a little touchy about size. Noah had the feeling Big didn't think of himself as huge; rather, he saw himself as normal size, with the rest of the world too small.

"All right. I might as well tell you." Big groaned as if being forced to open up. "Ester will anyway when she gets back. She says it's something I need to deal with."

"Ester who?" Noah felt like he'd missed something.

Big looked angry. "Try to keep up, cowboy. I know you're brain dead from riding bulls, but keep it together enough to follow a conversation. Ester is the nurse who just helped Reagan. We kind of met and hit it off right away."

"What does that have to do with me?"

"You and Reagan are interfering with us. She's the first girl I've seen in a long time who might be interested in me and I can tell you from the moment I saw her, I was interested in getting to know her, but you and Rea haven't made it easy."

"What?" Noah needed sleep. He was lost again. He thought of mentioning that he needed air, but he wouldn't put it past Big to toss him out the third-story window.

Big tried to get him up to speed. "When we met, I had to leave our first dance because you and Reagan were fighting in the bar. Then I had to hang around to keep you both out of trouble. Now, this morning, when Ester took me home for breakfast, we'd just started getting nice and cuddly when you call again."

"But this time . . ."

Big shook his head. "Every time with you two is an emergency. There's no getting around it. If I'm ever going to have a full date anytime in this life, you two have got to break up. Swear never to see each other again and maybe, just maybe, I'll have a night off from babysitting you both."

"You've got to be kidding if you think you can break Rea and me up just so you can have a date. That's about the dumbest thing you ever said, and to my way of thinking, dumb things have been dribbling out of your mouth since birth."

"Why not break up? It shouldn't be all that hard. You guys have been together since high school, and near as I can tell you've spent more time *not* talking to each other than talking."

"I'm not buying any of this, Big."

"Then buy this: If you don't leave Reagan alone, I swear the next time you see me you'll wish you'd run headlong into a bull. I hate to have to do this, but I got to have a life and it doesn't seem to be a possibility with you two as friends."

"I can't deal with your insanity right now." Noah glanced at the boy. "I've already got a full plate."

"I understand," Big said. "But when this is over, I want you to say good-bye to Reagan once and for all."

Noah didn't have time to say more. Ester was back with Band-Aids.

After a few minutes, Reagan talked Big into going down to the cafeteria and getting them some breakfast.

Big didn't argue. He didn't bother to ask anyone what they wanted either. He just followed Ester out, frowning at Noah like he felt sorry for him.

"What was that all about?" Reagan whispered.

"Big thinks we should break up."

Reagan shrugged. "First of all, I didn't know we were a couple; I thought we were just friends. And second, why would he care?"

"He thinks we're ruining his love life, and by the way, we are a couple."

She backed into the space behind the door. "We are? Nice of you to mention it to me."

Noah followed. "Of course we are, Rea. We always have been, even though you won't admit it. Besides, no one kisses hello and good-bye like you do. I should have been having you take me to the airport every time I flew."

He leaned in and touched his mouth to hers. When she didn't object, he pressed her gently against the wall and kissed her the way he'd been wanting to since their first kiss at the airport hours ago.

She wrapped her arms around him and kissed him back. That wild, buckle-your-knees kind of kiss she'd given him far too few times.

He slid his hand along her body, loving the feel of her against him. She was small, but every inch of her was a woman and he loved pressing her to him. It was like their bodies had a memory of how to mold perfectly together. No one felt the same as Reagan in his arms. No one ever would.

A moment later, she pushed away and stepped around him. "I'm sorry," she whispered. "I can't do this here."

Noah tried to calm his breathing. He'd been playing this game with her for so long he wondered how she could still manage to surprise him. Anyone else would have walked away, he thought. But every time she pulled him close and then stepped away, he felt the kick of her gone in his gut like a fresh wound over old scars.

When he didn't say a word, she finally looked back at him.

He didn't turn away. For once he wanted her to see how she affected him, how she hurt him. She wasn't some woman in a bar who just walked up to him and kissed him. She was Reagan. His best friend. His only true love.

"What is it?" she asked.

"I'm standing on a ledge, Rea, halfway between heaven and hell, and right now I don't much care if I fall or if I fly. If you want me, then be with me. If you don't, then step away. I'll get over it in a few hundred years. We can be friends or we can be lovers, but I can't deal with being halfway in between."

She nodded as if she understood, but Noah had no idea which direction she was thinking about taking. If she said she only wanted to be friends, he'd take the blow and probably wait around for the next time she kissed him full out with no holds barred.

It occurred to him that maybe everyone was right. Maybe he *had* been kicked in the head one too many times by the bulls he rode. If she ever stopped fighting her feelings and him, he prayed he'd be man enough for her to love.

Chapter 46

DR. ADDISON SPENCER CLOSED THE DOOR TO HER OFFICE and leaned against it for strength.

Her father had already taken the seat behind her desk as if he belonged there. Though this was only a temporary office stocked with leftover furniture, he couldn't have looked more regal if he'd been in his huge oak-lined office in California.

He'd come sixteen hundred miles to have his say, and she knew he wouldn't leave until he did.

"I still don't understand why you signed on for this little town. Did you really think you could do something miraculous here, or were you just running away . . . as usual?" He cleared his throat, preparing to begin the lecture about how she'd never measured up. "It took me a while to locate you this time, but. . . ."

Addison held up one hand and took a long breath. She didn't intend to let him win this time. She might not know what direction she was headed in life, but it was her life.

They'd had this conversation over the phone a dozen times.

"Ten years ago, I left home because I thought I was in love when I was still more kid than woman. It was a mistake, not *usual* behavior. This time, I guess, I ran away, if you want to call it that, because I wasn't in love with my work or the man you seem to think is perfect for me. Part of me was afraid you'd be disappointed in me. Glen Davidson or your vision of what I should do for the rest of my life was all your idea, not mine. He's doing great research, Dad, but it's not what I want to do. I love working with people, not test tubes. I delivered a baby last night for a woman I'd treated seven months ago when she was hurt in a fall. I've been with her, fighting for that baby to be born."

She could tell her father wasn't listening, but she needed to say the words. "These people matter to me. I'm almost like family, there when they lose someone and there for the birthing. I know you don't see it, but the work I'm doing here is important. I'm not afraid of what you'll think anymore. For once I don't want to disappoint *me*."

Before he could correct her, she added, "People, Dad, not patients or subjects, but real people. That's what I want to work with." Until this moment she hadn't realized just how much she loved it. Delivering babies in the middle of the night, working overtime after a bar fight, sitting with the family when there was nothing else to do but wait for death. She loved it all.

"Glen won't wait forever." Her father hadn't heard a word she'd said. "If you ask me, he's been a patient man already."

"He doesn't want me. He wants an assistant." She could feel herself fading again, disappearing into the woodwork.

"I've already talked with your supervisors in Dallas. You're just one of a rotation line of doctors they move out to these small towns that need help keeping staff. They can find someone to take your place immediately."

Addison closed her eyes, remembering another time when she'd stood before her father, broken and alone. He hadn't listened then and he wasn't listening now. Before, she'd been willing to do whatever he suggested, whatever he demanded, because after one shattered marriage she'd lost all judgment.

But she wasn't nineteen this time. She wanted more than her father or Glen in L.A. could offer. She still wanted what she'd been searching for when she'd run away after high school graduation. Addison wanted love.

When she opened her eyes, all she saw was a cold man at her desk. Her entire life had never been about her. It had always been about what he wanted, what he expected, what he demanded.

She'd been wrong once. She'd probably be wrong again, but at least she wouldn't be invisible.

"I'm not going back with you." The image of Tinch standing alone on the porch before dawn flashed in her mind. "I have to do what is right for me."

"You're making a mistake. You're throwing away your future. If you'd just listen to me . . ."

"No, Dad, I'm finding it," she countered. "I don't want what you and Glen are offering. I want something else, something more." For the first time she realized her words were true. She wasn't hiding away settling for less; she was standing, demanding more.

"I'm not coming back to save you again, Addison."

"I won't be asking you to." At that moment she felt light enough to fly. "Good-bye, Dad."

She turned, opened the door, and stepped into the rest of her life.

Chapter 47

⁘

TYLER WRIGHT USED THE BACK ENTRANCE OF THE HOSPITAL. He might not be taking out a body this time, but he figured the way he looked someone might mistake him for a corpse. Few in town had ever seen him unshaven, much less with his trousers pulled over his pajamas. He'd been delighted when Stella McNabb showed up. He was also thankful the funeral home didn't have any services pending. They all needed time to simply enjoy the new life coming into their world.

Tyler was thinking about how he liked the name Autumn had picked. Brandy Lee Smith. It sounded like a country/western singer. She might be only hours old, but he could tell she was a bright little thing just by the look in her eyes.

A short, wiry man bumped into Tyler as he stepped onto the back parking lot. He seemed in a great hurry, not bothering to apologize as he hurried on. Tyler didn't recognize him. Over the years he might not have known names, but he was familiar with all the staff. This man in his wrinkled black suit and slicked-back hair didn't work at the hospital, Tyler was sure about that.

This guy didn't even look like he belonged in town, much less at a hospital.

Tyler's tired body pulled him toward his car, but reason stopped him. If his Kate thought something was amiss, she'd investigate, and so would he.

As he followed the man inside, keeping his distance, he noticed the odd way he moved, as if testing each step for a trap below the tile floor. He turned the corner and entered the stairwell, and after a moment, Tyler followed.

Tyler climbed the stairs as quietly as he could. He was almost to the second-floor door when he heard the man pull a door open on the third floor. Then not a sound.

Out of breath, Tyler reached the third-floor door and pulled the door open to an empty hallway. The stranger was gone. He could be in any room. The third floor stretched out in both directions from where he stood.

For a moment, Tyler thought of taking the elevator down and going to his car. The idea of stopping by for a dozen doughnuts on the way home sounded grand. He figured, with luck, he could have half of them eaten by the time he reached his own kitchen. Autumn or Kate wouldn't be there to stop him, so he'd finish the rest off with milk.

Then, he thought of Autumn and her baby in the maternity wing on his left. Their safety immediately overrode any thought of food. What if the stranger had come to steal the baby? Tyler had heard of it happening.

He had to check on them first. While he was at it, he'd check all unlocked doors and open rooms because he couldn't shake the feeling that the little stranger in the wrinkled suit was somehow walking, breathing trouble.

If Tyler didn't find him on the left wing, he'd search the right wing, then he'd move down to the second floor. He'd go all the way to the emergency room if he had to.

Chapter 48

ADDISON MADE HER ROUNDS HOPING HER FATHER WOULD get the hint and leave. By midmorning when she'd finished, she wouldn't even check to see if he was still waiting.

She knew he wouldn't be. She'd won a battle, but she had no illusions about the war being over. He'd be back to try again.

Before she checked out, she had one more patient to see. She couldn't leave, if only to sleep a few hours, without knowing how Tinch was doing. The image of how he must have stood alone and watched the three men come for Jamie kept flashing in her mind. He'd put his life on the line for a boy he'd known only a few weeks. There was a goodness, a strength in Tinch Turner that her father would never understand . . . but she saw it. Admired it.

When she walked into Tinch's room, Addison was shocked to see how many people were standing around. She thought of trying to order them all out, but she knew it would be a waste of time. Most of them she knew. Noah, the rodeo cowboy she'd patched up a few times. His friends, Big Biggs and Reagan Truman, she'd visited with often when Jeremiah Truman was dying. She also recognized Liz Leary and her husband, Gabe. One of the student nurses stood by the big construction worker.

Addison frowned at the nurse. "Don't you think you should ask a few of this gang to leave so your patient can rest?"

The student nurse shrugged. "I'm one of the gang."

Addison should have kept frowning, but she couldn't hide a smile. For a man who considered himself a loner, Tinch Turner sure had a wide assortment of friends.

"How's he doing?" she asked Noah, who stood at the end of Tinch's bed as if on guard.

"Check for yourself, Doc." Noah moved out of the way.

Addison was shocked to see Tinch propped up in bed. He had his arm around Jamie and appeared to be reading the boy a comic book.

She moved to his other side, needing to touch him. "You should still be flat on your back," she said as her hand moved lightly over his bandaged side until she felt the warm flesh at his ribs.

"I'm fine," he obviously lied. "That stuff you gave me is finally wearing off. I feel like hell, so it looks like I'll live." He winked at her, and Addison had a hard time maintaining a doctor/patient manner.

Jamie folded the comic and tried to push it into his back pocket. "We're about ready to go home, Doc. Can't you take care of him back at the house? He said if he had a day of doing nothing but watching movies he'd be back in the saddle for sure."

"It would probably be quieter at home." She faced the group. "Would all of you mind waiting outside the door while I check his wound?"

They looked at one another as if they were considering taking a vote, and then without a word they all shuffled out, leaving only Jamie.

"I'd mind," he whispered. "I'm not leaving."

Addison smiled, brushing his hair back out of his eyes. "I understand." She looked around the room for some place the boy could stand so he couldn't see her dress the wound. She spotted the wide windowsill, littered with papers and a dozen more comic books. "If I offered you a way to stay and still allow Tinch some privacy while I check where he was shot, would that be all right?"

"Sure."

"Then up you go into the window." After she lifted him up, she handed him a juice Tinch had left on his tray. "I'll close the blinds just enough so that you can still hear us."

Jamie seemed to think it was an adventure. He settled in behind the curtain with nothing but his boots sticking out.

Addison quickly moved back to Tinch. As she checked the stitches where she'd removed a bullet, she was fully aware of him watching her.

Her fingers taped the bandage back into place, but her hand didn't leave his ribs. "You're healing nicely." Her hand spread over the flat plane of his stomach as she met his stare. "But, you do look terrible. I doubt even the bar butterflies would pick you up tonight."

"Is that your professional opinion, Doc?"

She moved her hand to the center of his chest, letting her fingers rest there as she studied his blue eyes. Even beat up he was still the sexiest man she'd ever known. The memory of their few minutes in the barn warmed her insides.

"I'm not looking to get picked up, Addison. I think I've found what I want. If she's still interested in a man with a few added scars?"

"We'd never work," she whispered. "We'd fight all day."

He put his hand over hers. "How about we give it a try? After all, we've still got the nights free." When she started to pull away, he added, "How about we start with that date you promised me? Then we could just see where things go."

"All right. When you're well enough to give me another dance lesson, I'll go on that date with you." She brushed his hair away from his forehead, loving the way he watched her.

"You won't leave before then?"

"I promise."

Exhausted, he leaned back on his pillow. "Mind if I dream about you, Doc? It'll be R-rated."

She giggled. "I'm already dreaming the same thing and my eyes are wide open."

He closed his eyes as he smiled. "Maybe I should make that dream X-rated."

"Just rest," she whispered as she kissed his forehead and felt his hand relax over hers.

For a few minutes, Addison checked the chart and made sure all the instruments were correct. He still needed more blood and antibiotics and rest, but soon he'd be ready for that date.

As she turned to leave, the door slowly opened. Turning, she prepared to scold whoever came in uninvited, but before she could say a word, she saw the dirty hand that held the door.

A second later, a small man, barely over five feet tall, moved into the room. She saw a hint of madness in his red-rimmed eyes and a gun in his other hand aimed directly at her.

"Where's the boy?" he whispered as he moved toward the bed, as if making sure Tinch hadn't awakened. "Don't act like you don't know who I'm talking about. I know the kid was with Tinch. Has been since the sheriff took him out of the trailer."

Out of the corner of her eye, Addison saw the boy's small boots disappear behind the curtain. "He's not here. We don't allow children on this wing."

The man poked Tinch with the barrel of the gun, but Tinch didn't wake. "I figured that," he said, keeping his voice low. "But Tinch here will know where he is. All I want to do is talk to him, then I'll disappear. The boy has something that belongs to me and I want it back."

Addison studied the man before her. She'd seen the signs before. He was a druggie in need of another fix.

Slowly, Addison moved for the door. "I think you'd better leave," she said in her most formal voice.

As she opened the door, he moved behind her, pointing the barrel of the weapon against her back. "Why don't you come with me, Doctor. You live just down the road from Tinch—maybe you know where that boy is. I'll bet if we take a little walk out back you'll start remembering real fast."

Addison stepped into the hallway.

Noah was ten feet away talking to his sister. An empty gurney, used to move patients into surgery, stood just outside Tinch's door. Addison figured that gurney had something to do with how this man had maneuvered his way down the hallway without Noah noticing.

Alex saw Addison first and must have read the terror in her face. The sheriff put her hand on the butt of her holstered weapon. Noah stopped talking and turned, following her gaze down the hallway.

The little man made sure they saw the gun before shoving it hard against her back. "We're just taking a walk." He almost sounded conversational. "No cause for you folks to interrupt your conversation."

Addison saw the stairwell entrance a few feet away. Noah would never get close enough to jump the man, and Alex wouldn't pull her weapon for fear of what the man might do.

"Don't do this," Noah said as his lean body seemed to tighten, ready for a fight.

"Try anything and she'll be dead before you can reach me."

"You'll never get away with this, Memphis." Alex widened her stance. "You're wasting your time to even try. My deputies picked up the package you've been looking for about an hour ago." She took one step forward. "All this has been a waste of time. You'll never see the half million in cash you made selling drugs. You don't want to add kidnapping to your charges."

Memphis shoved Addison into the stairwell door. "Open it," he said as he pointed the gun at Noah. His hand shook as any plan he'd thought he had began to evaporate. "Don't even think about following us," he demanded.

Addison fumbled for the knob, and Memphis tried to hurry her with one hand over both of hers. She glanced back at Noah and Alex, wishing somehow they could help but praying they stayed out of the way and safe. If Memphis were pushed even an inch, he might snap and empty the gun.

In a fraction of a second, she met Noah's stare and saw him look back behind her.

Then with a sudden pop, the little man tumbled into her, knocking Addison to the floor. The gun in his hand went off, but Addison didn't feel any pain. She rolled and fought to get out from under the drug dealer as everyone rushed toward her.

It must have been Noah who pulled Memphis off her. She heard the little man scream as he hit the wall. For a few heartbeats, Addison kept fighting even though she knew she was no longer under attack. She kicked and pushed at the air, fighting the memory of her fear.

Then she saw the gun on the floor, forgotten. Memphis screamed about being mistreated as the sheriff handcuffed him. People flooded the hallway. Everyone else was trying to help her up and asking if she was hurt.

As she stood, Addison turned and faced the undertaker she sometimes saw moving through the hallways. He looked tired and frightened. He still had on the pajama top he'd worn to the hospital last night when he'd brought Autumn Smith in. She forgot her panic and thought of how she might help him.

Then she saw it. A crumpled pole that had once held an IV bag hung from his fist.

"I hope I didn't hurt him," Tyler said calmly. "I only knew I had to stop him."

Addison put her arms around Tyler Wright and hugged

him as tightly as she could. "You saved my life," she whispered. "I'll check him out if it worries you that you might have hurt him, but first I need to know you're all right."

Tyler nodded, and suddenly everyone was hugging except for Memphis, who was swearing that he'd been attacked and framed.

Chapter 49

❧

THAT NIGHT ADDISON TOOK JAMIE WITH HER TO THE BED-and-breakfast. Tinch talked him into sleeping with Addison so she'd feel safe, but the boy went along only when Addison promised they'd be back at the hospital right after breakfast.

For a four-year-old the old inn was a wonderland to be explored. "This place is old enough to be haunted," he whispered, "or owned by a witch."

Addison wasn't sure she could argue with his guess. "We're safe here. I promise."

"I know," he said. "Tinch and Noah both told me we would be."

Martha Q, the owner, reminded Addison that she was expecting another guest, and Addison quickly assured her that they planned to turn in early.

An hour later, right before he fell asleep, Jamie whispered, "You think Dad will be all right up there all alone?"

"Dad?"

"Tinch calls me son, so I figured I'd start calling him Dad. My mom always said I didn't have a dad, but I think if I ask him, Tinch might take on the job."

She smiled. "I think he already has."

The boy went to sleep, but Addison stared out into the shadows of the cluttered room she'd rented. She hadn't heard from her father. For all she knew he was still sitting in her office waiting for her to come to her senses. The thought made her smile. Her father wasn't the type who waited for anything.

And she had, Addison thought. She had no idea what would happen between her and Tinch, but she planned to stay around and find out. Tinch was a kind of man she'd never met before. He was maybe the first she'd ever met that she didn't dread getting to know better.

The next morning when they came down to breakfast, her father was sitting at the table eating pancakes.

"I'm not going back," she said as she sat down across from him. Somewhere amid all the chaos, the hold her father had on her had snapped. All her life she'd never measured up to what he wanted her to be, never done the right thing, never been good enough to be his daughter. Only now, for the first time, she saw that the fault was his, not hers, and that knowledge somehow set her free.

"So you've said," her father replied. He took a bite of pancake. "These are the best I've ever tasted."

Addison didn't trust his calm manner. "I've decided to call this morning and extend my assignment here."

"How long?" His words were as bland as a stranger's might have been. He'd always been an expert at timing his attacks. Only, this time it wouldn't matter.

"Indefinitely. I like it here and I'm staying."

"I realized that after I heard a gunshot in the hospital yesterday. I had to be told my daughter was all right by one of the staff." He cleared his throat and set down his fork. "You didn't come running back for help, like you usually do when you get yourself in trouble."

She poured herself a cup of coffee. He'd always managed

to make her feel that everything was her fault, but not this time. It had taken her more years than most, but she'd finally grown up. "I won't be back for help again."

She helped Jamie with his food, then took a bite of her pancake and smiled.

After a few minutes her father tried again. "You will come home to visit soon."

It was more a statement than a question. "We can talk more then about your plans."

"Of course I'll come visit, but not soon."

An hour later she left with Jamie for the hospital. Her father stood on the porch and watched without saying a word. Maybe he thought he was punishing her by his actions, but in truth he was freeing her.

He hadn't said good-bye or wished her well. He'd simply frowned at her with that look that said she'd be back asking for his help. She almost felt sorry for him and wondered how long it would be before he realized he was wrong.

A few minutes later, when she and Jamie walked into Tinch's room, Addison couldn't help but smile. Her blue-eyed cowboy was back. The bruises and bandages did nothing to take away from his good looks, and he was grinning at her like he'd been waiting for her to show up for years.

"Hello, handsome," she said.

"Strange way for a doctor to greet her patient."

Jamie rushed close and handed Tinch a muffin he'd carried all the way from Winter's Inn. "These are great," he said as he dropped the crumbles across the sheet.

Tinch laughed. "Got any milk to go with that, son?"

"I'll get it, Dad." Jamie ran for the door. "Noah showed me where the nurses hide it."

Both Tinch and Addison went still for a moment, almost afraid to allow the boy out of their sight. Then they breathed and smiled at one another. The danger was over.

He took her hand and pulled her to him. "Now that we don't have to guard him every minute, are you going to disappear on me? I kind of got used to you sleeping on the other side of my bed."

"You still owe me a date. I think I'll wait around until you pay up."

He touched his lip with his thumb, as though considering whether kissing her would be worth the pain.

She straightened. "Don't even think about it."

"You're asking the impossible, Addie."

"I'm your doctor and I plan to make sure you are completely recovered before . . ."

He grinned. "Before what?"

"Before I attack you again."

He studied her a minute before saying, "Draw up the papers, Doc, I'm checking out of this place. I think you just cured me."

Addison laughed. "Two, maybe three more days in here and then at least a week's rest before you can go dancing."

Chapter 50

TRUMAN FARM

NOAH NEVER LEFT WHEN HE TOOK REAGAN HOME FROM THE hospital. They were both exhausted, but there were things that needed to be done, and, Noah realized, things that needed to be said.

After they got back to her place, he made her a sandwich while she took a shower, and they ate out on the porch, watching the first winter storm come in from the north. Both had too much on their mind to notice the cold. They were both from the land, a part of the weather and the sun's passing and the storms.

For the first time in a long time, it felt good just to relax and breathe. He could think of nowhere else he'd rather be right now.

"One of the carpenters told me the sheriff had a neighbor bury Old Dog out by the orchard," Reagan said between bites. "Tell her thanks for me."

"I'm sorry about the dog," Noah said after they'd both been quiet for a while. There didn't seem any need to keep the conversation flowing.

"He'd seemed lost since Uncle Jeremiah died." Reagan leaned back and tried to prop her feet on the porch railing like Noah was doing, but her legs weren't quite long enough. "You think dogs go to heaven? I can't imagine Uncle Jeremiah being happy there if Old Dog isn't by his side."

"Sure, dogs go to heaven. Horses do, too, but I'm not so sure about bulls."

Reagan laughed. "What about ducks and chickens and alligators?"

Noah grinned. "Ducks, yes. Chickens are too dumb to go anywhere, and no alligators, not even the cute little ones."

They spent a while in senseless conversation. Noah liked making her laugh. He decided Reagan hadn't laughed enough in her life, and he knew she hadn't loved enough.

When it finally got too cold, they went inside. He said good night and took a shower before turning in. He hated the little room down the hall from Reagan, but this was as close as he was likely to get. The space must have been furnished for a kid, with a little nightstand, a little dresser, and a little desk. The bed was the only thing in the room big enough for him.

With the lights out, he bumped his way across the room and finally crawled into bed. A second later he almost jumped out of his skin when he bumped against another warm body.

Reagan was sound asleep in his bed.

It took Noah a few minutes to calm down and another ten to decide what to do. Maybe it was the thirty hours he'd gone without sleep. Maybe it was the flannel PJs she wore, but he decided to just sleep.

He pulled her close against him, took a deep breath capturing the clean smell of her hair in his lungs, and relaxed.

She'd come to him, he thought, and for right now that was more than he'd hoped for.

Just after dawn he felt her poke him in the shoulder again and again like she thought she was a morning woodpecker.

"What?" he grumbled.

"What do you have on?"

"Nothing," he answered. "Why?"

"I want to get out of bed, and I can't crawl over you if you don't have anything on."

"Why not? You've got enough layers on for both of us. Last night I felt your foot in my back and I thought a squirrel was in bed with us."

He pulled up the covers. "It's freezing in here. Didn't you turn on the heater last night?"

"Didn't you?" She punched her pillow and settled in. "Get out of bed. I won't look. Once you're decent, I'll climb out."

"I'm still asleep," he mumbled. "And, by the way, this is my bed. I have a right to sleep in or out of whatever I want." He fought to keep from laughing.

She kicked him with one of her squirrel socks, and he turned to face her. "Rea, if you didn't want to sleep with me, why'd you climb in my bed last night?" He raised one eyebrow. "Hey, wait a minute. You didn't touch me while I was asleep, because I'd hate to miss something like that."

"No, but I could have. You slept like a dead man. I don't think you rolled over except when I poked you to get you to stop snoring."

"You didn't answer my question. Why'd you get in my bed?"

He watched her bite her bottom lip and had about decided she didn't know the answer when she finally said, "I wanted to. I know you're not ready to settle down, and I don't think I want to either, but I want you in my life." She stared at him and slowly added, "I want you, Noah."

"As a friend?"

"No. I want more."

He brushed his hand over her wonderful, wild hair. "Are you sure?"

She nodded.

"I love you, Rea," Noah said, realizing how completely he meant it. He'd thought it every day for a long time, and finally it just slipped out. "I really love you. It didn't just happen, I've always felt like this." The words he was using weren't enough.

She cupped his cheek with her small hand. "I love you too."

"Like you love winter and blackberries and Big?"

"No." She kissed his nose. "Like I've never loved anyone. I crawled in your bed last night because I wanted to show you how much, but when you came to bed, I got scared."

"But you stayed. That's a start, Rea."

"I stayed. I'm not going anywhere. Big is right. I can't let something that happened to me as a kid rule my life."

Noah frowned. "Tell Big to get out of this bed."

She giggled. "He's not here. There's no room."

He pulled her close. "I'm so glad you're next to me, Rea, I can't even be mad at Big. But I don't want to hurry you, honey. A lot has happened, your uncle dying and all the mess at the hospital."

She covered his mouth with her fingertips. "None of that has anything to do with why I'm here. I feel like I've had a few endings in my life lately, but I think I'm ready to see what's just down the road. We've got years to love and fight. We might as well get started, because from the first moment I met you I had a feeling you'd always be there waiting for me."

"So you'll be my girl?"

She smiled.

"My woman. My one true love?"

"If no matter where you go, you always come home to me."

"You've got my word." He held her to him.

"Noah," she giggled. "You're naked."

"Get used to it, Rea." He kissed her neck.

"Well, I'm staying, but I plan to sleep in my pajamas." She sounded nervous, but not frightened.

"All right, honey, but those socks have got to go." He slid his hand down her leg and tugged off first one and then the other.

She giggled, promising he'd regret his action when cold feet touched his back.

Noah wanted to take his time loving Reagan. He never wanted anything he did to frighten her. "We got all day, Rea," he said as he began unbuttoning her PJs. "And I promise, I'll keep you warm."

She didn't try to stop him. He could feel her shaking, so he stopped and talked to her as his fingers moved slowly over first the flannel covering her body, then beneath to her skin.

When he finally pulled the material away, he couldn't help but smile. "You're beautiful, Rea, just as I always knew you would be. I'm going to love you until the day I die."

With the sun coming through the windows, he made love to her slowly and with great care. As he knew they would, they seemed to fit together perfectly.

Afterward, he lay back feeling more content than he ever had in his life. He might need the excitement of the rodeo, but he also needed the loving peace of Rea by his side. He just wanted to hold her next to his heart.

After a long while he felt her moving by his side. "How about we take a nap before we go down for breakfast?"

She wiggled in close. "I'm starving, but I can't get up because now I'm naked."

He laughed. "I can see there could be a problem. You know, at some point one of us is going to have to see the other one completely naked. That is, if you plan on sleeping with me again."

"I do," she whisper. "And the other part. The not sleeping. I thought that was wonderful."

"You did?"

"Sure. Maybe you wouldn't mind doing it again after we have breakfast."

Noah jumped out of bed, pulling one of the blankets with him as he went. "I'm starving. Maybe we'd better cook breakfast."

Rea reached for her top and pulled it on beneath the covers, then climbed out of bed.

A few minutes later, as he watched her cooking eggs and toast wearing a top that *almost* covered her bottom, Noah tried to think of food, but all his mind could do was remember the way she'd felt and all his eyes could do was stare at that inch where the top didn't quite cover her.

He forced down breakfast and carried her back upstairs in a run. This time when they made love she wasn't afraid. This time they laughed and teased and became true lovers.

A few hours later, Noah decided he'd be the first man in history to die from lack of sleep, but at least he'd die happy.

Chapter 51

TYLER PICKED KATE UP FROM THE AIRPORT THREE DAYS after Brandy Lee Smith was born. He couldn't wait to tell her all about what had happened that morning at the hospital and how he'd stopped a kidnapping. She'd be so proud of him.

When she walked toward him, Tyler couldn't stop smiling. As always, she was in her tailored gray suit with her high-necked blouse. She looked very much like what she was, a major with a very important job, but he knew her in a different light. He knew her curled up next to him as they watched movies and offering silent help when he worked a funeral. He knew her when she laughed at night as she knocked on his open door, knowing he'd welcome her into his bed.

He almost laughed, thinking he knew her best after they

made love and she always whispered *I love you* before falling asleep.

He caught himself before he yelled, *Marry me, Kate!* In the six months they'd been truly together, he'd tried every way he could think of to get her to set a date. He knew her retirement from the army was on her mind. She'd joined right out of college, and it was the only life she'd known. "Hello, darling," he managed as she neared. "Welcome home."

She gave him a quick hug and a peck on the cheek, then talked about Autumn's baby all the way back to Harmony. She wanted to know every detail of what had happened.

While he unloaded her luggage from the car, she rushed in to see newborn Brandy Lee. Ronny was staying with Autumn, helping out for a few days. She was a fair cook but didn't have Autumn's natural talent. The women had formed a circle by the time Tyler entered the kitchen. He swore there were times all three were talking at once.

The baby looked like a bald, little tiny old man wrapped in pink. As far as Tyler could tell, when she wasn't sleeping, she was either eating or pooping. The girls got all excited about putting clothes on her, only to watch her spit up on them. It seemed an endless cycle. After two days of watching, Tyler thought he'd figured out why his parents had only one kid. It wasn't near as much fun as he'd thought it would be.

What was fun, though, was watching how people acted. Normal rational adults would have hourlong conversations with a three-day-old and not manage to say one real word. Calvin, who worked in the basement, was the worst about jabbering on to the baby, but then he talked to all the bodies during the embalming too.

Half of one of Kate's suitcases was full of outfits. She must have shopped in every airport store on her way home.

After Kate fed the baby and changed her diaper, she finally said a proper hello to Tyler. While Autumn and the baby slept, he and Kate made sandwiches and took them upstairs. He thought about how young men dream of passion and adventure, but at his age, the true pleasures came with quiet times. With talks. With walks. With sharing.

They sat facing each other at a little table Kate had put by the windows. While they talked he told her of the panic he'd felt at the hospital and what he'd done to save the young doctor. She didn't seem to want to talk about where she'd been, but as always, she asked about everyone in town as if some great change might have happened in the month she was gone. Tyler liked telling her each event in order, realizing he'd kept a mental journal of all she'd missed.

Finally, when she reached for his hand, he said what he'd been waiting all afternoon to ask. "Are you really and finally back?" He needed to hear the words.

"I'm home, Ty. No more trips, no more army. I'm right where I want to be, with you. If you'll have me."

He was surprised she didn't sound sure of herself. "Of course, dear. There would be no me inside without you. I'd just be a walking shell of a man." He'd wanted to say those words to her all month. "I look forward to thousands of dinners right here talking and the movies we'll watch, and the walks we'll take."

"It's not going to be as quiet around here as it once was, not with the baby."

"That is true." Though he couldn't hear the baby when upstairs, he could hear her cry when in his office.

"Do you mind?" she asked.

"No, I love it. We'll make a great set of grandparents. Once Brandy Lee learns how to say something, that is. I've already decided I'll read to her every day no matter how busy we are. I think it would be nice to give Autumn a break. Now and then we could take her for a stroll or maybe keep her while Autumn has a date with Willie Davis, if he ever gets up the nerve to ask her."

"Autumn might want to get her own place one day."

"I've thought of that. Willie Davis was a great help to her during labor. I wouldn't be surprised if he doesn't keep coming around. But if Autumn moved out with him, she'd still come to work, and bring the baby, of course." He smiled. "And, if they marry, we might help them find their first house. Neither has any parents to depend on."

"You've got it all figured out, don't you, Ty?"

"I like to think I've thought of everything except maybe how to get you to marry me, but I've decided not to push, Kate. I'll give you all the time you want to settle in."

She looked down for a minute, then said, "You don't have to figure out a way to talk me into anything, Ty. I'd like to be married as soon as possible. We can do it fast. Tomorrow if you're not busy, or a month from now with a big church service."

Tyler couldn't form words. He'd been asking her for months, and now here she was saying yes, even pushing it.

"What's wrong?" He could see it in her eyes. Something had happened. She wasn't the same. "Did something happen on this last mission . . . something horrible . . . some illness?" She had gone into some other country. There could be a disease she'd caught. She could have been shot and her clothes were hiding a wound. "Please, Kate, don't tell me you're dying."

She smiled. "No. I had a complete physical three days ago as part of the mustering-out requirements. Everything is fine, but something did happen, Ty, and it happened right here before I left."

Tyler fought to remember the last few days they'd been together. He could think of nothing. They'd been happy. They'd been together. He could think of nothing he'd said or done. If anything the time had been extra sweet as they counted down the hours before she'd have to leave.

Kate took a deep breath and announced, "The doctor said I'm in great shape for a woman in her forties who's going through her first pregnancy."

"But how?"

She laughed. "I was told years ago I'd never have children, and for most of my life it wasn't an issue I had to worry about. Only the last few months with you, it seems I was exposed to the possibility quite often. I like to think it happened just before dawn that last morning we were together. That memory is very dear to me."

Tyler felt light-headed and sweaty. He could see dark spots before his eyes, and he thought he might throw up at any moment. He moved to the couch and lay down until the world stopped spinning.

When he finally rose to one elbow, he looked at Kate and smiled. "I'm sorry, dear, I thought you said you were pregnant."

"I am. We'll both be forty-six when we become parents. It'll be exciting."

He grinned at her, thinking she didn't look a day over forty. "It'll be exhausting. We'd better go to bed now, Kate. We're going to need all the rest we can get."

Chapter 52

FRIDAY NIGHT
OCTOBER 28

TINCH TOOK ADDISON'S HAND AND LED HER ONTO THE dance floor. They'd been on their date for two hours and all he could think of was getting her home.

He waved at Beau in the cage. The kid was getting better every week, and tonight he seemed at his best.

"Just relax, Doc, and let me lead," Tinch whispered in her ear. He'd heard once that some folks considered slow dancing to country music as foreplay, and he planned it to be just that tonight.

She'd been worrying about him and bossing him around for two weeks, and now it was his turn. Tonight he'd planned the entire evening. Dinner, dancing, a moonlight drive out in the canyons where they could hear coyotes howl, then home.

If he was lucky, she'd be moving out of the bed-and-breakfast and in with him by the weekend.

"Tinch," she whispered. "Should we check on Jamie?"

"He's fine. My cousin raised five boys; she can handle him for one night. The only danger he's in is from over-eating."

She relaxed a bit and he moved his hand lower on her hip.

"I love touching you," he whispered against her throat. "I missed out on a great deal of touching you since I was shot, and I plan to make up the time as soon as possible."

He could feel her melting in his arms, and he couldn't help remembering the first time they'd danced and she'd warned him not to get too close.

Later tonight he knew he'd hold her when she was wild and lost in passion, but right now he just wanted to feel her in his arms. He'd never known such an addiction as Addison, and he didn't plan on looking for the cure.

"Big and his date are here," she whispered. "And look, Reagan and Noah just walked in."

"I don't really care," he whispered as he smiled and waved at the couples. "Right now, Addison, all I see is you."

He watched her smile that deep kind of smile women have when they're totally happy. She'd been out at his place every day since he came home from the hospital. She'd even tried cooking a few meals.

"I've stopped fading," she whispered as she kissed him.

When he finally broke the kiss, he looked straight into her eyes. "This is no affair, Addie. No one-night stand. No fling before you go back to what you think is the real world."

"I know." She smiled. "I took the opening to be the new doctor on staff at the hospital."

He hugged her a little tighter. "I could get used to you being around."

He saw the fire in her stormy-day eyes. "I'm not sure I could ever get used to you, Tinch, but I'd like to try."

As he twirled her around the floor, he thought of how his heart had expanded and opened up to loving. When he saw Howard Smithers's wife, he'd have to thank her for starting the bar fight last month. If he hadn't jumped in, he never would have met Addison and learned there is always room for more loving.

Prologue

JANUARY 2006

A SLIVER OF A CRESCENT MOON ROSE OVER THE FARMHOUSE
Stella and Bob McNabb leased five miles outside Harmony,
Texas. Stella sat up in bed as if she'd heard a cannon.

Bob tugged off his headphones, flipped on the reading
light, and waited. He hadn't been asleep, but Stella always

insisted they go to bed together, so most nights he plugged in to a ball game on the radio and listened while she wiggled herself to sleep.

"I've had a vision," she announced. "A terrible vision, all black smoke and fire."

In the forty years they'd been married, she'd had a hundred visions and as far as he knew none of them had come true. "Now, Stella, just because you play the fortune-teller at the 4-H fair once a year doesn't make you psychic. The vision's probably tied to the three enchiladas you had for supper."

She glared at him, and he couldn't help but think she was one woman who definitely looked better with makeup on. Lots of makeup.

"But I saw it, Bob. Some strange kind of storm's coming. A big one. The kind of storm that shatters lives."

He patted her hand. "Don't you worry about a storm. We could use the rain."

She turned away from him and wiggled back down into the covers. "I got Gypsy blood in me on my mother's side and I know things. We better get ready, 'cause trouble's coming."

"All right, hon, I'll stay awake and worry. You go back to sleep." He put on his headphones and stared out the open window at the cloudless sky, knowing nothing much ever happened in Harmony, Texas. Odds were, nothing ever would.

Chapter 1

FEBRUARY 2006

AS THE OLD FORD PICKUP STOPPED AT THE FIRST STREETLIGHT past the city limit sign, Reagan jumped off the back. Harmony, Texas, population 14,003.

She doubted the driver even noticed her departure. At the truck stop in Oklahoma City he'd only looked at the pint of whiskey she offered him in exchange for the ride.

That was the way Reagan preferred it. In the sixteen years of her life, any time someone had bothered to watch her closely, trouble followed. No one could track her this time. By morning the farmer would have a hangover and little memory of her.

For once, no one would look for her—thanks to a runaway who'd taken her bed at the shelter. Even if the impostor was discovered, foster care wouldn't search too long or hard for her. In fact, if she guessed right, they'd mark Reagan Moore off their rolls by noon as if she were resting in

Resurrection Memorial Cemetery in northwest Oklahoma City. The druggie who'd climbed in to sleep in Reagan's bed had found a place to rest, and Reagan had found a way to disappear.

Flinging her backpack over one shoulder, Reagan slipped into the shadows. Harmony had been her goal for almost a year and, finally, she was here. It didn't matter if the place measured up to her dreams—nothing ever had—but at least she'd made it. She'd accomplished what she set out to do. She'd found the little town in the middle of nowhere. Reagan couldn't help but smile.

Six months ago she'd decided this place was her hometown, so she had to at least see the small farming community. No one would ever know this was her first time to set foot in town. For her, and for them, she was simply and finally coming home.

Walking in the shadows, she took in the place like an art student taking in the Louvre. Brick streets. Storefronts without bars that pull down at night. A movie theater at the far end of Main with lights blinking. Traffic moving as slow as if passing time and in no hurry to get anywhere. She felt like she'd stepped into an enchanted world.

This street was called Old Main, she remembered from an article she'd read. New Main was at the other end of town, where tire stores, a shopping mall of four one-story stores, and five small restaurants had been built. But here, on Old Main, was the way she always imagined the town to be.

The jukebox music from a diner, almost a half block away, drew her like a pied piper toward the center of town. A painting of a midnight sky and a full moon ran across the awning. Above the shade were the words BLUE MOON DINER. Reagan felt as if she'd stumbled blindly into a picture-book story. She'd heard the words but never seen the drawings, and now they were coming alive around her.

The place was ten years past needing a coat of paint, but the light glowed golden from windows in need of washing just as old Miss Beverly at the Shady Rest Home had said it would.

The old lady would always say, when she talked of the diner, "You ain't been to Harmony until you've eaten at the Blue Moon."

Reagan walked inside feeling like a preacher who'd studied heaven all his life and finally set foot in it. The diner even smelled like she thought it would. A mixture of grease, baked apples, and burned toast.

A year ago she'd been cleaning rooms in a nursing home in Oklahoma City for eight bucks a room when she'd found a newspaper, the *Harmony Herald*'s Centennial Edition. Reagan had read every article, what happened in the past, what was happening in the fall of 2005, what folks hoped would happen in the future. Somehow, the town filled a place inside her. A place that had always been empty.

Home.

"What can I get you?" The waitress startled her as Reagan stuffed her backpack under the table. "We ain't got much pie left, but if it's fries and drinks, we're still open."

Reagan looked at the menu written on the wall. "Fries," she said, "and a water."

"Chili or cheese?"

Reagan stared at the chubby middle-aged waitress who looked like she'd already had a long day. Her apron was spotted, her eyes tired, but her smile was real.

"You want chili or cheese on them fries? It doesn't cost extra after ten." The waitress tapped her pencil on her pad in rhythm to an Elvis tune.

"Both," Reagan answered, thinking the doughnut she'd had for breakfast had been far too many hours ago.

The woman winked. "You got it."

Reagan leaned back in the booth and took a deep breath. "Finally," she whispered as if she could wish it true. "I just know this time I'm home."

She'd cleaned that nursing home room for a week before she'd met Miss Beverly Truman and began to stay after work to read the old woman her mail. Beverly must have been pen pals with half the town.

After they'd read all the gossip, they'd talk about

Harmony. Miss Beverly might forget where she put her teeth, but she remembered every detail about the town where she'd lived most of her life.

Reagan closed her eyes as if filling in a blank on an invisible test: The night waitress at the Blue Moon Diner was named Edith. Miss Beverly always said she had a good heart and a husband who wasn't worth the iron in his blood.

She pulled her tattered manila folder from her pack and spread it out on the table. Someone had handed it to her years ago when she'd been moved from one foster home to another. It had a big label on the front with her name and nothing else. Like no address had ever belonged to her long enough to stick to paper.

She'd hidden the folder away while in transport and kept it. One envelope held all that was her. Birth certificate listing father as unknown, a copy of her mother's death certificate, a school picture from the fourth grade, and an award she'd won once in an art class. Tugging out a pencil, she scratched out her last name and wrote *Truman* in its place, then, with a bold hand added *Harmony, Texas* under her new name.

"I put the chili in a bowl so it wouldn't get your fries soggy." The waitress was back.

Reagan slid the envelope aside. "Thanks, Edith."

The woman seemed in no hurry to leave. "You from around here?"

"Yes." Reagan ate, chewing down the lies along with the fries. "But I've been gone a long time."

Edith studied her for a few minutes. "You must be one of the Randall kids that used to live north of here. Their youngest girl would be about your age."

"No," Reagan said just before she shoved another spoonful in her mouth. "This is great chili."

The waitress was on a quest and refused to be distracted by the compliment. "You Willa May Turner's granddaughter? I heard you might be coming to live with your grandparents."

Reagan shook her head. "As far as I know, I don't have a single living relative here now. Not one that would claim me, anyway."

The woman smiled. "You never know. Everybody's related in this town. We laugh and say if the gene pool gets any shallower in these parts we'll have to declare a drought."

Reagan swallowed down water and began her new life with another lie. "I'm Beverly Truman's granddaughter."

"I thought I saw Truman blood in you. Don't know where you got that red hair, but your nose is shaped just like every Truman I ever knew. Old Jeremiah Truman still lives on the homestead place a few miles out on Lone Oak Road. He's as mean as Beverly is nice; it's no wonder no woman in the county would marry him. We all miss Beverly, but we don't blame her for moving a state away just so she wouldn't have to live with him and clean around his collections."

Edith slid into the booth across from her. "How is your grandmother? We used to buy all our cream pies from her. Folks would come in here after the movies just for a slice of Miss Beverly's coconut pie. Cut our profits in half when she moved."

Reagan chose her words carefully, thinking of how Beverly would have answered. "I haven't heard lately; she may have passed on to be with the Lord." In the year she'd known the old woman, Reagan had never seen a visitor and, when she died, Reagan was the only one who cried. She guessed that made her more a relative than anyone else.

Edith leaned over and patted Reagan's hand. "We all have to make that journey, child, and you can bet your sweet grandmother made it on the express flight if she passed. Both her grown children and her husband going before her must have left her in a powerful hurry."

Before the waitress could start asking questions Reagan didn't have the answers to, the front door bumped open and the number of customers in the diner doubled when one man entered. He looked like he could have been a model for western wear except for the anger in his eyes. Tall, broad shouldered, and furious.

Reagan took one look and fought the urge to slide under the table.

The waitress just smiled at him as if he were cute as a newborn pit bull.

"Edith!" he yelled from the doorway. "Get a thermos of coffee ready. I'll be back for it." He plowed his hand through jet-black hair and shoved his hat down hard as if about to face a storm.

The Blue Moon Diner door slammed closed and he was gone.

"Who was that?" Reagan asked, figuring this would be the first name on her list of people to avoid.

Edith laughed. "That's Hank Matheson. He's headed across the street to Buffalo Bar and Grill to break up a fight." The waitress laughed. "It's Saturday night and Alex McAllen is either passed out drunk or starting a brawl. One of the bartenders calls Hank every time to come get her before she gets in too much trouble."

"Why don't they just call the police?"

Edith giggled. "You *have* been gone a long time. Alexandra McAllen has been the sheriff for three years. Barely had time to accept her master's in criminal justice down at Sam Houston State before she pinned on the badge."

Reagan smiled and quoted a line from the Harmony paper she kept. "Three families settled in to work at the Ely Trading Post in 1887: the Trumans, the Mathesons, and the McAllens. When old Harmon Ely died, he left a third of his land to each family and together they founded Harmony."

"Good." Edith smiled. "You do know your history. Most folks driving by think we was named Harmony after a mood, but in truth, folks just got tired of calling the town Harmon Ely and shortened it to one word. Kind of a private joke for locals, being the old man was as mean as a two-headed snake on a hot rock."

Edith stood and moved around a long counter to make the thermos. "If you know that much, you also know the three families have never gotten along."

"But Hank's helping Alex, and she's a McAllen."

Edith wobbled her head so far from side to side she almost tapped her shoulders. "Yeah, and she'll hate him for saving her in the morning. Once she got so mad he rescued her that she tried to get him fired as the town's volunteer fire chief. When that didn't work, because it's impossible to fire someone who's not paid in the first place, she blacked his eye with a wild punch."

"And he still goes into that bar on a Saturday night to save her?"

Edith screwed on the top of the thermos. "I guess he figures it's the best way to irritate her."

A scream and a string of swear words could be heard from outside.

"That'll be Alex." Edith rushed to the door.

Reagan watched through the window as the waitress hurried out with the thermos to give to Hank. He was shoving a woman, fighting and kicking, into the passenger side of a Dodge Ram.

He slammed the door and climbed in on the driver's side.

When he opened the window to accept the thermos from Edith, the wild woman he'd trapped managed to open the door and was halfway out before Hank jerked her back.

Edith didn't seem concerned. She just nodded at Hank and hurried back toward the diner.

Two feet inside, she ordered, "Truman, if you want a ride out to your great-uncle Jeremiah's place, Hank said hop in and he'll take you. He's headed that way anyway."

It took Reagan a moment to figure out who Edith was yelling at. Then she remembered. She was a Truman. She'd been one for at least ten minutes now.

"Great," she said, and pulled her pack out from under the table. She couldn't stay here; it would look strange.

Maybe she'd just hop out of the truck and find somewhere to sleep until morning. Down the road seemed as good as any place to go.

Edith walked her out and held her pack as she climbed into the bed of Hank's huge pickup truck. Reagan settled in between saddles and serious-looking riding gear.

She noticed that Alex, looking tall and blond, sat perfectly still in the passenger seat, but Hank was swearing that he'd handcuff the sheriff if she tried to get out again. Reagan wasn't sure either of them even noticed her hitching a ride.

She leaned toward Edith. "Doesn't anyone think they're a little strange?"

Edith frowned and looked at them, then shook her head. "He's the only one brave enough to stand up to her when she's had a few, and she's the best sheriff we've had in forty years. Besides—"

Hank threw the truck into drive and roared down the road before Edith finished.

Reagan leaned back on one of the saddles and tried to figure out the couple yelling at each other just beyond the back window. Somewhere in an old paper she remembered reading that a McAllen had died in the line of duty. A highway patrolman maybe, or a marshal. Or maybe, she guessed, the last sheriff of Harmony.

By the time Hank turned off on the farm-to-market road, he had to be going eighty. He hit the first pothole so hard Reagan almost bounced out of the truck bed. Three minutes later he was braking and she was rolling around in the back like the last pumpkin on the way to market.

He was out of the cab before she could settle enough to sit up.

"Sorry, kid," he said as he offered her a hand down. "Alex is threatening to throw up. I can't waste any time."

Reagan grabbed the strap of her pack and let him lift her down. He couldn't be much over thirty, but the worried tone in his voice made him seem older. When she put her hand on his shoulder climbing out, he felt solid as rock.

"It's all right. I understand. Thanks for the ride." She thanked her stars that Jeremiah's house wasn't farther from town.

"Will you be all right from here on?" Hank asked. "The old man's house is a hundred yards up that dirt road. I'd turn in there, but he's left holes wide enough to swallow the truck."

"I'll be fine." Reagan fought to keep her voice from shaking. The shady lane he pointed to looked like it could easily make it onto the "Top Ten Most Likely Places to Get Murdered" list.

Hank reached into a toolbox and pulled out a flashlight. "You can leave this at the diner or the fire station next time you're in town." He hesitated, then added, "Good luck with the old man."

Reagan took the flashlight. She didn't want to go on down the road, but she wasn't about to climb into the bed of Hank's truck again. One more mile and she would have had brain damage for sure.

They both heard someone vomiting.

Hank groaned and climbed back into the vehicle. He was gone before Reagan could figure out how to turn on the light.

4041

"Compelling and beautifully written."

—Debbie Macomber, *New York Times* bestselling author

FROM *NEW YORK TIMES* BESTSELLING AUTHOR

JODI THOMAS

THE COMFORTS OF HOME

A HARMONY NOVEL

Twenty-year-old Reagan Truman has found her place and family in Harmony, Texas. But with her uncle taken ill and her friend Noah lost and disheartened with his life, Reagan is afraid of ending up alone again—and she's not the only one. When a terrible storm threatens the town, the residents of Harmony are forced to think about what they truly want. Because making the connections they so desperately desire means putting their hearts at risk…

M1008T1011